Havana Heat

Lupe Solano Mysteries
by Carolina Garcia-Aguilera

Bloody Waters
Bloody Shame
Bloody Secrets
A Miracle in Paradise

Havana Heat

a Lupe Solano Mystery

Carolina García-Aguilera

William Morrow
An Imprint of HarperCollinsPublishers

WILLIAM MORROW
An Imprint of HarperCollins*Publishers*
10 East 53rd Street
New York, New York 10022-5299

FIRST EDITION

Designed by Kellan Peck

Printed on acid-free paper

Library of Congress Cataloging-in-Publication Data
Garcia-Aguilera, Carolina.
Havana heat : a Lupe Solano mystery / Carolina Garcia-Aguilera—1st ed.
p. cm.
ISBN: 0-380-97780-X (acid-free paper)
1. Solano, Lupe (Fictitious character)—Fiction. 2. Women private investigators—
Florida—Miami—Fiction. 3. Cuban Americans—Fiction. 4. Havana (Cuba)—
Fiction. 5. Miami (Fla.)—Fiction. I. Title.
PS3557.A71124 H38 2000
813'.54—dc21   00-031853

00 01 02 03 04 QW 10 9 8 7 6 5 4 3 2 1

To my three daughters,
Sarah, Antonia and Gabriella,
the loves and passions of my life.

And, as always, to my beloved Cuba,
an island in chains.
May they be broken soon so
she will be free again!

ACKNOWLEDGMENTS

I would like to thank my literary agent, Elizabeth Ziemska, for all she has accomplished on my behalf these past five years. Although, as a result of her having left New York to work in the film business in Los Angeles, she is no longer my agent, she still holds a special place in my life. Jennifer Sawyer Fisher, my editor at Avon/Morrow, deserves recognition for her support and encouragement, and, perhaps most important, enthusiasm for the Lupe Solano series. Quinton Skinner has my heartfelt gratitude for all the time and effort he has put forth to shape and mold this and the other previous manuscripts.

As I received much help while conducting research for this book, I would like to thank certain individuals who made it possible for me to tell such a tale. My brother, Carlos A. Garcia, being an expert sailor, explained the intricacies of boating without making any gratuitous comments about my ignorance. Sarah Jackson, of The Art Loss Register, deserves a special acknowledgment for her assistance in explaining the procedures her organization follows when tracing the ownership of works of art. Jorge Pedroso, an art dealer and childhood friend, was most generous in sharing information with me about Cuban painters. Dr. Max Castro was invaluable in sharing his expertise of Cuban affairs, especially in the field of politics and conditions on the island, and I thank him for his assistance and time spent with me.

My family, as always, is critical to my being able to write the books. My husband, Robert K. Hamshaw, has been supportive throughout the years, always encouraging me, assuring me that I can do whatever I set out to do. My mother, Lourdes Aguilera de Garcia, deserves my thanks for her unwavering pride in me, even though I know that at times she is perplexed by me. I am indebted to my sister, Sara G. O'Connell, my brother, Carlos A. Garcia, and my nephew, Richard O'Connell, for always being there for me, whether it be to offer advice, or simply to listen to me talk about the book.

How can I properly acknowledge my debt to my daughters, Sarita, Antonia, and Gabby? Thank you for accepting my limitations as a mother (and for not pointing out that other families don't have take-out restaurants' numbers programmed on their telephones). Instead, thank you for concentrating on the positive aspects of having a mother such as me, although at certain times it could not have been easy. Thank you for your unconditional love, support and pride in me, for, without that, I would certainly not be writing this now.

I know this is a bit unusual, but a special acknowledgment is long overdue. I want to thank my four dogs, Buddy, Alex, Matilda and Zeus, for their loyalty and devotion. Gracias for all the hours you lay patiently on the floor of my office, without complaining, keeping me company.

Gracias, Dios, por dejarme hacer lo que you amo hacer!

Havana Heat

I should have been born a man. I think like one, I act like one, I live my life like one. As a private investigator for the last eight years, I've worked in a field dominated by men. The men I've worked with, as well as the men I've been involved with, have always tried to ascertain who is the real Lupe Solano. Eventually they all discover that I have two sides: a gentle, feminine veneer that I display when I need to, and the ruthless heart and soul of a man underneath.

These idle thoughts flitted through my mind as I looked out the car window at the familiar scenery of Miami. Alvaro Mendoza, my current love interest, was driving, and we were heading north on Granada Boulevard toward the Biltmore Hotel to attend my niece Marianna's wedding reception.

Alvaro was actually more than just a passing liaison. He and I had been together for almost a year now, a record of sorts for me. And, another first, he was Cuban, the first Latino man I had ever been seriously involved with—Latino being the current fashionable word to refer to us Hispanics. One night I actually sat at the dinner table with my sister Fatima's twelve-year-old twins and concocted different possible terms that might be used in the future to refer to those of us who lived in the New World but had Spanish origins.

We came up with *peoplissimos, taninos, sípersonas,* and a few other ridiculous variations on the same theme.

I saw the lights of the Biltmore off in the distance and began to envision the scene at the party. Technically, Marianna wasn't my niece; she was my third cousin Mirta's daughter. Marianna was marrying into the famous Miranda cigar family. I had spoken with Tia Elena, the bride's grandmother, and learned that at last count the guest list was approaching one thousand. It was just your basic warm, cozy, intimate family wedding reception—Cuban style. The actual ceremony had taken place earlier that day, at the Church of the Little Flower, with only the immediate family in attendance—at the young couple's insistence and their families' displeasure.

I fidgeted in the front seat of the Mercedes, unable to find a position in which I wasn't being impaled by some article of clothing. Everything I was wearing seemed designed to divert my blood from where it needed to flow, from my emerald earrings with too-tight clasps to the Manolo Blahnick pointed shoes that I was certain had been designed by a conspiracy of podiatrists.

The drive from my home in Cocoplum to the hotel wasn't long—fifteen minutes the way Alvaro drove, seven if I had been behind the wheel. But it felt like an eternity. It had been a long time since I wore a long dress, and I was alternating between fits of pain and numbness. Ominously, I hadn't been tested by having to stand up for more than a couple of minutes at a time.

I tried to breathe slow and steady. My corset was rubbing against the girdle I'd been forced to wear in order to be poured into my form-displaying, not-one-inch-of-fabric-to-spare Helmut Lang dress. What the hell. All the pain and misery were going to be worth it. I looked gorgeous. The dress was black and backless, and it fit me like a second skin.

It was a triumph. The only problem was that the Austrian designer hadn't created the dress to be worn by a thirty-year-old Cuban woman who had a weakness for chocolate and a backslider's approach to exercise. Although I hated to admit it, perhaps I had relaxed a little during my time with Alvaro and put on a couple of pounds. Alvaro said he liked me sexy and voluptuous, and he was always trying to get me to eat seconds when we had dinner together. So far I hadn't resisted his entreaties.

Achieving my look that night hadn't been easy. Nighttime assaults on beachheads seldom are. Colin Powell spent less time getting ready for the Gulf War than I had preparing for this wedding. At society gatherings such as this I always wanted to look my best. It was a matter of self-esteem, not to mention my professional standing. I knew the Cuban women there would be scrutinizing me like a jeweler looking for imperfections in a stone, searching for evidence that I was letting myself go and that my sleazy profession was catching up with me. My complicated personal life had given them plenty to talk about over the years; I sure as hell didn't intend to add to the rumor mill by showing up looking less than stunning, or as though my chosen lifestyle had taken its toll on my appearance.

My ensemble that night had been the result of a team effort—and Aida, our housekeeper, deserved special commendation. Her great achievement had been to close up my dress without embedding any of my epidermis in the zipper's teeth, no small feat for an octogenarian. There had also been a valiant young saleslady at the Saks Fifth Avenue lingerie department, who hadn't lost heart when she heard me yelling, cursing, and grunting in the dressing room trying to fit into my corset. Instead, she leaped into the fray, helping me wedge my way in, then stuffing my ample breasts into the cups. The price I paid for beauty. I hated to be reined in, physically or otherwise.

Alvaro was quiet, concentrating on his driving. The winding streets of Coral Gables were notoriously badly lit. The residents apparently liked it that way, because every proposal to add more streetlights was inevitably voted down. The unspoken understanding was that no one wanted nonresidents to be able to find their way around.

We pulled up to the four-way stop at the intersection of Granada and Anastasia Avenue. The ochre-colored, dramatically lit Biltmore Hotel rose up in the distance like a castle in the middle of Coral Gables—it must have been a nightmare to build, considering the Byzantine code restrictions enforced by the town's building and zoning boards. The place had quite a history. The owners liked to showcase the Al Capone suite, as well as the fact that Esther Williams used to frolic in the swimming pool.

"*Querida*." Alvaro smiled. "I know why you aren't talking—because that dress is suffocating you. Why would you wear something that doesn't fit? Surely there are dresses in Miami that would allow you to enjoy yourself—or at least to breathe."

"I like this one, so I'm wearing it." As soon as the words were out of my mouth I could tell what Alvaro was thinking: that this statement amounted to the governing philosophy of my life. "You told me I looked beautiful in it," I added. "One has to suffer for beauty."

Alvaro leaned over and kissed my cheek. "Your natural beauty is enough," he said. "No dress is as beautiful as you." I might be a liberated woman who wears a gun as comfortably as a handbag, but I also appreciate a compliment.

Pretty proud of himself, Alvaro drove on. Taking the sharp turn up the hotel ramp, we both noticed immediately that there were only a few cars ahead of us in line for the main entrance. We looked at each other in mild alarm. We were either early or late; it was hard to determine which, given the idiosyncrasies of Cuban time.

The valet opened the door and I stepped out into the muggy evening. I saw Alvaro handing over the keys under the hotel lights, and enjoyed the smooth, confident ease with which he moved. He was tall and thin, his curly brown hair showing a few streaks of gray at the temples. His warm brown eyes shone out from behind professorial tortoiseshell glasses. He appeared at my side and held onto my elbow the way I liked, exerting gentle pressure as we went into the cavernous lobby. I took his hand and squeezed it.

I was a little apprehensive about how Alvaro was going to be received at this gathering, since his outspoken liberal political views clashed violently with the overwhelming majority of upper-class Cuban-exile guests who would be there. As we walked in we were both greeted warmly by the first few people we saw. So far so good. We hadn't gone to a formal occasion together, so this was our announcement to Cuban society that we were a couple. Our debut was made easier by the fact that Alvaro, like me, was from one of Cuba's most prominent families. He had received his own invitation, and wasn't there just as my date.

At the banquet room we gave our names to a young woman seated behind a huge table; she consulted her list and said we were assigned to Table 3, the bride's mother's party. She passed us our cream-colored place cards. Mine read "Miss Guadalupe Solano"—formal Cuban wedding receptions were not fertile ground for feminist statements. The card itself felt like it must have weighed a pound. I cringed at the thought of how many trees had been felled so that everyone there could pretend to remember each other's name.

I took a deep breath. My dress felt like a straitjacket, and in the back of my mind I was still worried that someone would confront Alvaro over his support of dialogue with the Cuban government. His position was considered wildly left-wing in Miami, where often the only acceptable political position was rabid support of the embargo against the country, if not a violent armed overthrow of Castro and his cronies.

The room was already full of people. Faces blended under golden light, voices merged into a loud rumble. Probably half the people there would be past or present clients of mine—although none of them would ever admit to needing a private investigator. Alvaro and I shuffled our way to the front of the line, where a pencil-thin Marianna—the new Mrs. Miranda—squealed with delight at each person who approached her. My cousin Mirta must have been having a stroke. The independent-minded Marianna had chosen to change into a fashionable black dress after the virginal white one she'd worn at her wedding. Probably as a concession to her mother, who would want to silence wicked Cuban gossips, Marianna had also chosen a dress that clung tight to her decidedly nonpregnant flat stomach.

Marianna's new husband, Jorge Miranda, looked like a nice young man. In spite of his extremely fancy social background, he seemed ill-at-ease and uncomfortable with his surroundings. He stood stiffly and smiled with the relaxed sincerity of a man who had a sharp object pressed against his back. It looked to me as though the heavy reality of being a married man was just sinking in for him.

The Mirandas had been in the cigar business in Cuba for centuries. One of Jorge's ancestors had sailed with Columbus on one of the first voyages to the Americas, settling a tobacco farm. The Miranda family sent tobacco leaf as a tribute to the Spanish kings for the next few hundred years, until Cuba gained independence. Then, when Castro came to power, all the Miranda farms and factories were nationalized. The family was forced to start over from scratch. They chose to establish themselves in the Canary Islands, where the soil and climate were much like Cuba's. Within a decade they had also started tobacco farming in the Dominican Republic.

Even then their troubles with Fidel weren't over. For years the family was involved in a very public legal battle with Castro over who owned the rights to the Miranda name in the cigar industry. Castro contended the name belonged to Cuba, where the cigars had been grown and manufactured for centuries. The Mirandas countered that they owned their own name and were respected throughout the world because of their unique, distinctive history. So far the two factions had succeeded only in thoroughly confusing the public, and spurring debate over whether the Miranda family cigars were better than the ones still being produced in Cuba. The Mirandas weren't the only family embroiled in legal disputes with Castro over who owned the rights to well-known and established family names associated with the manufacture of cigars and various other businesses. Battles were also being fought between Castro and rum and sugar producers. But the Mirandas were among the best-known, and probably the most visible.

Alvaro and I moved like trained experts down the receiving line, both of us air-kissing like crazy. Apparently, Tia Elena had imbibed a few too many *scotchecitos*, because she connected with Alvaro's cheek and left him with a bloodred lipstick mark that looked like a dueling scar.

"Oh, I am so sorry," she said, slurring slightly. I couldn't blame her. It wasn't every day one's family united with the Mirandas.

The ballroom was immense, and I started to feel the crush of people. My dress wasn't allowing me to get enough oxygen. All of a sudden it seemed impossible for me to walk normally, and I started to feel claustrophobic. I've always been very sensitive to smells, and now each breath I took seemed to fill my lungs with thick, expensive perfumes. Floral aromas mixed with the smell of cigar smoke. I began to feel nauseous. As I turned my head at the end of the receiving line, I smelled a rush of hair sprays, gels, and mousses: strong chemical odors that threatened to push me over the edge.

I felt Alvaro's hand at my elbow, rescuing me, steering me toward the balcony where there was a sweet promise of fresh air. My breath felt uneven, and he brushed through people to clear a path for me. He knew me well. I was moments away from a full-blown panic attack.

Outside, I breathed deeply. The warm night air felt like a cool breeze after the crush of the ballroom. Alvaro kissed me on the cheek.

"I'll go get you something to drink," he said. Before I could object, he held up his hand to silence me. "Don't argue. I know you planned not to eat or drink anything tonight, but you almost passed out in there. This is for medicinal purposes."

I took a long, deep breath. He knew I would never admit that it had been folly to wear the dress. *"Gracias,"* I said instead.

He moved a steel chair to the edge of the balcony. "Sit and wait for me," he said. Then he was gone through the glass doors.

I took a few steps, enjoyed the privacy and freedom. The night air was tinged with the slightest edge of salt.

The door opened behind me, letting out a burst of noise that was silenced a moment later. Before I had time to react, I felt the sharp pain of rapierlike fingernails digging through my corset.

"Lupe," a raspy voice said. "I've been looking for you everywhere. We must talk now. I cannot wait a moment longer."

2

"*H*ola, Lucia," I replied.

Damn. For a minute there, I had felt all right. Now I was engulfed in hot breath mixed with the heavy scent of Carolina Herrera perfume.

Lucia Miranda was the fifty-something aunt of the bridegroom. She pressed close to me on the otherwise vacant balcony. Her face was contorted into a frightening expression; she was trying an ingratiating smile, but her numerous face-lifts made it a complicated proposition. She could have been used as a living model for a facial-anatomy lesson at a plastic surgery school.

"Can we talk?" she asked, a Cuban Joan Rivers. It was more a demand than a question. I watched the forehead muscles around her hairline tighten as she raised her impossibly thin nose.

"Sure," I replied unenthusiastically. My new relative wasn't one of my favorite people. She was an awful gossip. Someone had once fantasized that she might get a tongue amputation during one of her trips to the surgeon.

I glanced through the glass doors and saw Alvaro's back. He was waiting in a long line at the nearest bar. I was stuck with Lucia for the time being. And part of me was naturally curious. My only contact with the Mirandas in the past had been superficial and fleeting.

A waiter poked his head out. Before he could say a word, Lucia waved him away like a queen dismissing her servant. I could have used a drink, but Lucia wasn't allowing it. Instead I sat down in the chair Alvaro had placed there for me.

"Guadalupe, first you have to swear that everything I say to you will be kept in total confidence. You must tell *no one!*"

She fixed her beady black eyes on mine. It was hard to compose the sober expression she obviously wanted from me because I was starting to feel mesmerized by her bad makeup job. Her black rings of eyeliner made her resemble a demented raccoon. Her hair was so black, her skin so pale, that she looked like Cuba's answer to Morticia. If she hadn't been so rich, she could have been laughed out of town or committed.

"Of course," I replied.

Lucia took a deep breath. "Guadalupe," she said slowly, as though reminding herself who I was. "Do you have contacts in Cuba?"

My antenna sprang up. I nodded slightly. Lucia might have looked like a caricature, but she was no fool. She obviously knew about my line of work.

"Are you aware of the unicorn tapestries that hang in the Cloisters museum in New York?" she asked, speaking fast.

"I know of them," I replied.

"So you know that there are seven of them," Lucia continued.

Now she had my attention. My mother had loved the early-sixteenth-century *Hunt of the Unicorn* tapestries, and I often went to see them whenever I was in New York. I pictured their lush colors, the mythical creature depicted in idyllic scenes. Mami owned practically every book that had ever been published about them, and had often put my sisters and me to bed with visions of their beauty. Mami used to show us pictures of the tapestries, tell us stories about the fantasy scenes they depicted. I knew those books were still on a shelf in our house. I hadn't opened them since Mami's death.

I tried to recall something on the fuzzy edge of my memory, some piece of information that connected the tapestries to the Miranda family. Lucia's surgically altered face was impossible for me to read. She paused a moment, examining my reaction. I felt as if we were two chess players locked in a game, each unwilling to reveal anything more than was absolutely necessary.

"I know that your mother was very well-educated in the history of art," Lucia said. "She was such a graceful, refined woman."

"I've seen the tapestries in person," I volunteered. I thought it was a cheap shot to bring Mami into the discussion. Though Mami had had a reputation as an astute and enthusiastic art collector in the exile community, I didn't like Lucia evoking her memory as an obvious ploy to get past my defenses.

"Beautiful, aren't they?" Lucia asked. Her expression seemed to soften somewhat.

The more I thought about it, I was certain that I'd heard a story about the tapestries and the Miranda family, probably something Mami had mentioned at some point. But the answer wasn't going to come, not after being overwhelmed by a noisy crowd, while wearing a dress that was cutting off the blood supply to my brain, and with Lucia seated inches away from me.

"You might have heard stories," Lucia said, now speaking so softly that I had to lean closer to hear. Her hawklike eyes noted my rapt attention to her every word. "There is one story in particular, about the existence of an eighth tapestry that has been unseen by the world."

I involuntarily gripped the arms of my chair hard. Of course. Now I remembered. I had heard of the lost tapestry—everyone who knew about the other seven had. For decades it had been rumored that the Mirandas either had it or knew where it was or where it had last been seen. The Mirandas were also rumored to be connected to the tapestries' secrets: who had created them, when and where they were made, and the reason for which they had been fashioned. I had heard the stories and quickly let them slip from my mind, dismissing them as idle gossiping about a well-known family.

I looked up. Alvaro was coming our way. I smiled and shook my head at him, nodding at Lucia. He looked confused for a moment, but when he saw who I was speaking with, he turned on his heels and disappeared. He probably thought I was saving him from social misery. Normally I would have been. But this was altogether different.

"You're saying—" I stopped myself, looked around to make sure we were really alone. "You're telling me your family has the eighth tapestry?"

"No, no!" Lucia snapped. "Guadalupe, you must control yourself. Watch what you say."

She looked up fearfully at the ballroom through the glass, as though someone in there might have read my lips.

"Lucia," I said when she had settled down. "Please tell me. Why are you telling me about this? What would you like me to do?"

I could smell a potential job. And this had the scent of a big one—maybe my biggest case ever, considering the Miranda fortune. My discomfort over being trapped with Lucia Miranda had turned into a child's excitement on Christmas morning.

Just then the balcony doors opened. Our tense silence was broken by a loud rush of female commotion.

"Lucia, Lucia, come on. The party's inside! Don't sit out there gossiping!"

"*Mierda*," Lucia whispered under her breath.

"Shit," I echoed bitterly. It was a social rescue squad, a group of older women including Tia Elena and Mirta, along with an assortment of Mirandas. They had obviously been dispatched to bring us back into the fold.

"We can't speak of this with people around," Lucia whispered into my ear. "Call me Monday morning, Guadalupe. It is urgent. And remember—not a word to *anyone*."

Her black eyes enveloped me, cold and determined. I nodded.

Tia Elena and Mirta came out onto the balcony. I could tell from their wobbly walk and loud voices that they had been celebrating the merger of the families quite strenuously. It was obvious that my curiosity would have to wait until Monday.

I struggled to my feet and tugged at my dress until it clung properly to my body. Fortunately, no one seemed to notice my difficulty. The women grouped around Lucia as if she was a long-lost relative and started to lead her inside. Lucia glanced over her shoulder and gave me a clipped, somber nod.

When they were gone, Alvaro stepped through the doorway with a puzzled expression on his face. He handed me a drink, a double scotch on ice. His eyes widened as I drained it in a single gulp.

"Let me guess," he said. "I'm not going to find out what you two were out here talking about, right?"

I gave him an apologetic smile. Alvaro had grown to know me very well. Eventually I would probably tell him everything, but not until the time was right and I knew what I was dealing with.

"You seem to be feeling much better." He brushed my

cheek with the back of his hand. "Maybe you'd like another drink?"

"Would you mind?"

"Of course not." He smiled and cocked his head a little to the side, as though seeing something in me that both perplexed and fascinated him. It was a very sexy look.

"You're too good for me," I said. "Much too good."

"Sit down again," he said. "I'll go fetch you another. Try not to get hijacked by any society ladies this time."

"I'll do my best," I said as he left.

I sat down, Lucia's perfume still in the air. The *Hunt of the Unicorn* tapestries were about the last thing I would have expected to discuss at the Miranda wedding. And it was strange how the mention of the tapestries brought back a forgotten memory of how fascinated Mami had been by them; I resolved to ask Papi and my sisters about their recollections as soon as I was home.

I let the balmy air wash over me. I didn't have to search my memory for information on the tapestries; recollections of time spent with Mami bubbled to the surface of my mind. She had said there was not much known about the early history. The tapestries had been woven in Brussels around the year 1500, probably in celebration of a royal marriage. They were designed as a set, although some historians felt the set was incomplete until an eighth tapestry was discovered, since typically such sets were manufactured in even numbers. Mami's face always filled with sadness when she looked at the *Hunt of the Unicorn* tapestries. Maybe the unicorn reminded her of her charmed life in Cuba before it was forever changed by the revolution. Maybe Mami compared the imprisoned animal to the fate of the people who lived under Castro's regime.

Or maybe I was reading too much into it. Maybe Mami simply thought the tapestries were beautiful.

Alvaro slid the door open and came out onto the balcony holding a pair of fluted glasses. I froze him in my mind for a second, like a camera's flash. He looked great in his black tie outfit, a far cry from his usual khakis, blue work shirt, and boat shoes without socks. During the day he was an outspoken political leftist, but for tonight he looked like the man Cuban society had tried to make of him—elegant, poised, the taste of a silver spoon still in his mouth. When tomorrow came, however, he would still be the Alvaro who received death threats by phone, fax, and e-mail. His client list read like a who's who of the pariahs of the Miami exile community. Still, I suspected that if any of the right-wing "Cuban patriots" found themselves in need of a top-flight lawyer, they might swallow their convictions and give Alvaro a call.

"Dom Pérignon," he said, handing me a glass. "I guess your cousin Mirta will be serving the good stuff from now on, since her daughter has just become a Miranda.

"When are they serving dinner?" Alvaro looked around. As usual, he was in fine tune with the demands of his stomach. All the men in my life seemed to have shared this trait. They could eat as much as they wanted and never gain an ounce.

"I think sometime after ten," I replied, although I knew that serving times at Cuban weddings were a combination of conjecture and wishful thinking. Knowledgeable guests usually ate something at home before leaving—it saved one from the indignity of ravenously grabbing food from every hors d'oeuvre tray in sight.

"It's almost ten already, and I don't see any signs of food." Alvaro looked at his watch, then into the ballroom. "If they're serving anything, it must be a stealth operation. Nothing's happening in there."

The needs of Alvaro's stomach weren't going to be denied.

He got up and motioned to a waiter inside. The young man came out to the balcony, and Alvaro reached into his jacket pocket and took out a money clip. He looked at the waiter's name tag.

"Jaime," Alvaro said. "I need for you to do me a favor."

Alvaro peeled off a twenty. His enemies might have accused him of being a socialist or a communist in his political views, but their opinion of him might have changed if they had seen this maneuver.

"I need you to bring us a tray of hors d'oeuvres—the ones with salmon and caviar, not that cream pastry stuff. You know what I mean?"

Jaime nodded soberly, trying to keep his eyes off the twenty dollar bill. Nothing more needed to be said. Money spoke for itself.

"And a bottle of champagne," Alvaro added. "Can you do that for us?"

Jaime disappeared so fast he might well have been an apparition. A minute later he appeared with both hands full— one with champagne in a silver bucket, the other with a silver tray full of hors d'oeuvres. He pulled up a short table, put the tray on it, popped the champagne cork, and discreetly left after pocketing Alvaro's money.

"That boy's going to go far in life," I said.

"*Salud.*" Alvaro handed me a bit of caviar piled on toast.

I finished a glass of champagne and ate several hors d'oeuvres. We sat quietly, listening to the increasing cacophony in the ballroom. A thousand Cubans in an enclosed space made a lot of noise, especially when they had spent the past couple of hours drinking Dom Pérignon.

In Cuban Miami, hosting a social event on this scale was nothing short of a logistical nightmare. It was almost impossible to arrange a seating plan without placing the wife and mistress of the same man at one table. A society matron had to be up-to-date on every romantic combination possible: who was and who had been married, who was currently and formerly sleeping together. There were also tricky business and legal situations: who was suing whom, who was under indictment, who was going into the witness protection program. It was a social minefield. Memories were long and precise, and severe social penalties would be exacted on those who failed.

"You think you can dance?" Alvaro looked at my dress and shoes with ill-concealed concern.

"I would love to." I winced as I stood up, teetering on my stiletto heels. I let Alvaro guide me back into the ballroom and onto the dance floor. I prayed for a slow song that would enable me to lean against him, not a merengue that would leave me on my own. I tried to block out the thought of the inevitable conga line that would form at night's end.

This was the first time we had danced together, a sobering milestone in terms of the seriousness of our relationship. As the music quickened into another song, I realized that we had passed the test. We looked for all the world like the happy couple I knew us to be. Now all I had to worry about was the zipper of my dress giving way.

3

Monday morning. I was driving down Main Highway headed for the office, sipping from a mug of *café con leche* and still feeling the effects of all the champagne I'd consumed at Marianna's wedding reception two nights before. I had a great time, but I was paying the price. I also hadn't had a good night's sleep in almost a week. Not the best of conditions for my meeting with Lucia Miranda. Whatever she wanted to talk about, it must have been important. She had called me at home on Sunday to firm up our Monday appointment.

I read a magazine article once that claimed sugar counteracted the aftereffects of alcohol, so I drank a couple extra glasses of orange juice before leaving the house. I was never one for moderation, so I also poured a couple spoonfuls of sugar into my first coffee, as well as the mug I was sipping from as I drove. The sugar and caffeine were speeding up my heartbeat, making my pulse thump so loud in my ears that I could barely hear the radio.

Ever since I first became involved with Alvaro, I'd started to listen to the local Cuban talk-radio stations. I had already begun following Cuban-exile politics more closely, after a case I worked the year before. Every so often a station would display a daring spirit of nonpartisanship and invite Alvaro to be a guest. I was used to the bitter accusations hurled against him, but I was still shocked by the hatred he evoked. He took it all in stride, even the death threats. This morning the talk was about baseball exhibition games in Cuba. It was a contentious subject—every topic was—but fortunately, Alvaro was no sports expert. I was too frail that morning to listen to someone insulting him on my car radio.

I drove through the tree-lined streets of Coconut Grove and replayed my conversation with Lucia Miranda at the wedding. Clearly, she had something to discuss with me that related to the *Hunt of the Unicorn* tapestries. It was interesting timing. I wondered if she knew that I had lately taken on two cases involving the recovery and return of artworks that belonged to Cuban collectors in exile. The works had been appropriated from their legal owners by the Cuban government—a hot-button issue that neither side involved wanted brought out into the open. As a result, I had tried to work the cases in secrecy.

Lucia Miranda, I had to remember, was no fool—her appearance notwithstanding. She'd come to me specifically, and I had to assume that she'd done her homework in advance. Exile Cuban society networked information at gigabyte speed, so I could also assume that she knew something about my recent cases, no matter how hard I'd tried to keep them secret.

I looked at the clock on my dashboard. Almost ten, two hours until my meeting with Lucia. I felt a pleasant tingle at the back of my neck at the prospect of starting a new case.

At that hour, school and work traffic had dwindled to almost nothing. I was able to reach the office in less than fifteen minutes. I finished the last of my *café con leche* just as I pulled into the driveway of the Solano Investigations cottage. I vowed not to touch any more caffeine, at least until that afternoon, as I set the car alarm and went inside.

The first thing that hit me when I walked through the front door was the smell of freshly brewed coffee. My senses went into overdrive and, as always happened with my best intentions, my vow of a few moments before went into the scrap heap.

"*Café con leche*, Lupe?" Leonardo called out from the kitchen. "I just made some. It's really, really strong!"

"*Sí. Gracias*," I said, shaking my head at my own weak character. I was a total slut for caffeine. I could never say no to it.

I dropped my purse in the reception area and picked up my message slips from Leonardo's desk. There seemed to be nothing that couldn't wait, at least until I saw the last one. It was from Angel Estrada, a dealer in Latin American art. I frowned and noted that he had called just a few minutes before. I had consulted with Angel on a case I worked recovering a Wilfredo Lam for the Riondo family. It seemed too much of a coincidence that he was calling me on the morning I was going to meet with Lucia Miranda. I had to wonder if there was some sort of connection, and whether there was something going on in the art world that tied Cubans together.

I went into the kitchen, almost holding my breath with the hope that Leonardo wasn't dressed too outrageously that morning. I knew I should have called him the night before and told him to dress as conservatively as he was capable of, since Lucia Miranda might freak out if she saw my assistant dressed in a lurid-pink unitard with matching terry-cloth headband. I let out a big sigh of relief when I saw he was dressed in black bicycle pants—to the knee, not the hot pants he sometimes wore—along with an oversized white cotton tuxedo shirt that came down to mid-thigh. He completed this ensemble with red Converse All-Star high-tops.

"I know, I know. I look like a pregnant penguin," Leonardo said, catching me inspecting him. "I stuffed myself with Cuban food three times this weekend and nothing in my closet fits! I felt so bloated I almost called in sick."

"You look fine, *primo*," I said, kissing him on the cheek. I held out my coffee mug and let him fill it.

Leonardo had been forced upon me by our family—his mother, Mercedes, was Mami's sister—in hopes that he would drop his acting aspirations and discover the world of regular employment and biweekly paychecks. I was only twenty-two when I started Solano Investigations, and Leonardo was just eighteen and right out of high school. It took a period of adjustment, but we worked through our differences. Now neither of us could imagine life without the other. Leonardo was my office manager, administrative assistant, chief financial officer, receptionist, nutritionist, channeler, and general helpmate.

There were still drawbacks. Leo was interested in anything spiritual, and ostensibly eschewed materialism. But he also considered it mandatory that we buy top-line exercise equipment for the spare room in the cottage that he'd converted into a gym—even if I had to work back-to-back cases following adulterous spouses to pay for it. He also didn't mind driving across Dade County in the middle of a workday to buy organic tomatoes at a farm in Homestead, paying for the purchase with our corporate platinum American Express card.

I still flinch when I remember the time he wanted to sublet our small extra storage room to a Santería priestess who claimed she could break Cubans' aversion to vegetables and legumes by making them drink a potion while hypnotized and performing a ritual dance. I had to refuse, even after Leo argued that we would be performing a public health service and that ceremonies would only take place on evenings of full moons.

I motioned for Leonardo to add an extra spoonful of sugar to my coffee, shrugging off his unspoken protestation. I took one sip of the scalding coffee and winced as I felt the roof of my mouth burning. As soon as I recovered enough, I held up a message slip.

"What did Angel Estrada want?" I asked.

My caffeine-charged voice sounded a little like a frog on speed. Leonardo pretended not to notice, bless him.

"I don't know," he replied. "He said to call back ASAP."

"By the way, I have a twelve o'clock appointment coming in. You'll never guess who it is." I paused for maximum drama. "All right. Don't guess. It's Lucia Miranda."

"Lucia Miranda?" Leonardo repeated, pronouncing the name slowly. "The one with all the lifts and tucks? I heard plastic surgeons in Miami think of her as their retirement plan."

I wagged my finger at him. "Behave. You know she'd be a good client. She can certainly pay her bill, and in cash. Plus we'd probably get some great cigars."

"I don't know," Leo said. "She's creepy."

"I seem to remember you have your eye on that combination cardio–weight resistance–massage machine," I said, going straight to what was dear to his heart. "Lucia Miranda might be the ticket to that flat ass you always wanted."

I left Leonardo in the kitchen, pondering the connection between our potential new client and the continued bane of his existence—his Cuban ass, which so far no machine or diet had been able to reduce. I went into my office and closed the door behind me.

The familiar squawks and complaints of the parrots living in the avocado tree outside my window filtered into the office. There were several generations living in harmony most of the time—although once or twice I'd been forced to go out there and wave a broom around and yell at them to settle a territorial dispute. My only grievance with them was that they wouldn't let anyone—human or otherwise—get too close to their turf. As a result, I couldn't pick any fresh avocados off the tree without being attacked. I watched them ripen and drop to the ground, where they were taken away by squirrels.

I tapped the message slip from Angel Estrada on the corner of my desk. Angel knew that I had just started to work in the field of art recovery, although I had known about the Cuban government's trafficking in stolen art for years. Everyone in the exile community heard stories, and my own family had firsthand experience.

My grandfather gave my grandmother an exquisite eight-panel black lacquered Coromandel screen for their twenty-fifth wedding anniversary. My family treasured it, and tears were shed when they had to leave it behind in their home in the Vedado district of Havana when they fled the country in 1961. They imagined it was gone forever, until my parents saw it in Florida almost twenty years later.

The screen was prominently displayed on the living-room wall of a Venezuelan couple's condo in Key Biscayne. My mother cried out and nearly fainted in shock at the sight, and in the commotion that followed, she told the couple that the screen was identical to the one her family had owned in Cuba. She looked closer, and found a small, barely visible scratch identical to the one our butler Osvaldo had made when he first installed it. Then Mami found the initials my sister Fatima had carved into the back of it when she was three years old—an act for which she had been severely punished, becoming part of our family mythology.

You had to feel sorry for the couple. One minute they were hosting a cocktail party in their newly decorated condo, the next a Cuban couple they barely knew were claiming that the centerpiece of their new decorating scheme had once belonged to them in Cuba. The couple refused to divulge where they bought it, but they turned out to be as honorable as they were wealthy. They insisted on giving the screen back to my mother, asking for nothing in return. Within a week it arrived at our house, where Mami installed it in a sitting room where she could gaze at it whenever she wished.

I was only about ten at the time, but my interest had been piqued. I listened intently whenever Mami was talking to grown-ups about the art world, and as I grew older I gradually learned about the basic workings of the art business. Since everything for me always comes back to Cuba, I started to avidly follow newspaper stories about exile families trying to recover appropriated works of art. The psychology of the families fascinated me, as well as the fact that the Cuban government had the audacity to continue to sell artworks while the rightful owners of the property were attempting to regain possession.

This plunder, as far as I could see, would continue as long as Castro was in power. He would go to any lengths to obtain cash, because his government was increasingly strapped and riddled with debt in the post–Cold War years. Public opinion mattered little—it was common knowledge that the Cuban government was selling pieces of the island to foreign investors without compensating the previous owners. Art was no different. Soon Cuba would revert to colonial status if the selling spree continued. But there really was no use crying to the world. Bad press might dry up the market for the possessions, effectively rendering them lost to their prior owners forever.

As an investigator, the scope of my involvement with this reality was still limited. Still, I had quickly discovered that the issues at stake were more than financial—there were deep emotions running through the core of the situation. It was more than a matter of being reunited with a valuable possession. It was an issue of being reconciled with painful loss, and the stark realities of a troubled past.

The first such case I worked was for my godmother, Alicia, Mami's best friend. She had approached me six months ago asking for my help in determining whether a painting she saw featured in a decorating magazine was the same one she'd last seen hanging in her grandmother's home in Havana. She'd almost fainted when she was flipping through the magazine in her dentist's office and saw her family's Amelia Pelaez painting featured in an unidentified Los Angeles couple's bedroom. I told my *madrina* that I didn't have much experience in that line of work but that I could try to find an investigator who specialized in stolen art. She insisted that she wanted me.

I wasn't eager to tell her the truth—that I didn't want to take the case because I was afraid I might not get the result she wanted. I was afraid our relationship would suffer, despite her protestations to the contrary. Fifteen minutes after I spoke with Alicia on the phone, Leonardo had buzzed me on the intercom to say she was in the reception area demanding to see me. She came into my office and opened the magazine on my desk, then produced a magnifying glass.

"See," she announced triumphantly. "Amelia Pelaez!"

I made a few calls and talked to someone at the magazine who told me who had photographed the spread. After a few more calls I tracked down the name and number of the couple in Los Angeles. I gave the information to Alicia, who asked me how she should approach them. She made it clear that her goal was to recover the painting.

I called Tommy McDonald, one of the top defense attorneys in Miami; he was also my friend and sometimes lover, although our relationship had cooled significantly now that Alvaro was in the picture. Tommy called the couple in Los

Angeles and explained the history of their painting. He went on to explain that, although they hadn't known it at the time, they had bought a piece of stolen property and might face legal liability. Within the month the painting was returned to my godmother for a relatively modest amount of money—on the condition that no questions were asked and the matter was kept quiet.

I explained the need for discretion to Alicia, and I'm sure she tried. But it wasn't in her nature to keep a secret, and she started to talk about how her beloved painting was returned to her. Soon I received a call from another Cuban exile, a friend of Papi's named Armando Rionda, who asked me to investigate a rumor he'd heard about a Wilfredo Lam that had once hung in the office of his house in Havana. This case led me to Angel Estrada, who facilitated a successful recovery and pocketed a considerable fee.

I punched in Angel's number from the message slip. He answered on the first ring. "Angel? *Buenos dias,*" I said sweetly, hoping I was disguising my dislike for him. "This is Lupe. How are you?"

"Lupe. Thanks for returning my call so quickly," Angel said.

Even his voice made me cringe. Angel hadn't been suitably named by his parents. Maybe they'd somehow known that he would turn out to be an untrustworthy scoundrel, and tried to counter fate with such a heavenly name. It hadn't worked. Angel was as devious and immoral as anyone I'd ever met. And that was saying a lot.

"No problem," I said. "What can I do for you?"

"I'd like to meet with you," Angel said. "It's a sensitive and confidential matter."

"Of course," I said. Everything was confidential to Angel. Most of what he did wouldn't stand up to scrutiny. I had heard from reliable sources that he fenced stolen paintings and, at one point, had been connected to a scheme to steal paintings in collusion with owners who would then claim the insurance money. But he was a necessary evil—his contacts were extensive throughout Latin America, and he had access to useful information an honest man would never come across. I wasn't interested in how he acquired his knowledge, just that he had it.

"Would you be free for lunch tomorrow?" he asked.

The very thought of being seen in public with Angel sent a shiver of dread through me.

"That would be fine," I said. We agreed to meet at Bice, the northern Italian restaurant located in the Grand Bay Hotel in Coconut Grove, then hung up. I had heard the anxiety in Angel's voice and knew that he had something big for me. But I would have to watch my back, or else I might eventually discover a sharp object protruding from it.

I had less than an hour before Lucia Miranda showed up. At the same time the next day I would be having lunch with Angel Miranda. My venture into the art world was throwing me into interesting company. I just hoped that my reputation would survive it.

4

Lucia Miranda was even more macabre-looking in the light of day than she had been on the hotel balcony a couple of nights before. My prospective client made her entrance dressed in an all-black, long-sleeved, high-necked, mid-calf-length raw silk dress. Her makeup left her face a smooth, chalky white that was relieved only by the crimson slash of her lipstick. She looked to me like a vampire who had gotten lost on her way back to her coffin.

I tried not to show any reaction as she slid slowly toward the client's chair in my office, placed strategically across the desk from my own seat. I could see Leonardo watching us from the reception area, his eyes wide, his mouth forming a shocked O. Leo never was good at hiding his feelings.

I willed myself to show Lucia a welcoming smile as I moved around the desk to greet her. What I had dreaded most happened—she tilted her cheek toward me for a kiss. I braced myself and gave her a light peck. Over Lucia's shoulder I saw Leo shiver with horror, shaking his head and moving out of sight. I knew he would be headed for the kitchen, where he would concoct a potion to counteract my contact with Lucia—some kind of New Age homemade anti-biotic. I moved back around to my side of the desk, trying not to think of what would be waiting for me once Lucia left—something powerful, no doubt, probably containing co-pious quantities of garlic.

"Guadalupe," Lucia croaked.

I tried not to flinch at the raspy, nails-on-blackboard sound of her voice. Leo appeared in the doorway again, looking down; he quietly closed the door, sealing me inside with Lucia.

"It's good to see you," I said, still trying to smile.

"Remember what I told you at the wedding," Lucia com-manded, done with any pretense of pleasantry. "Everything I am going to tell you is strictly confidential. No one—and I mean no one—is to know the details of our conversation." Lucia wagged her two-inch-long fingernail at me.

I nodded somberly. There was no way I was going to ex-pose myself to this woman's wrath—at least not without very carefully weighing the consequences. I may not have been a great beauty, but I liked the way I looked. A glance at Lucia's talons filled my mind with images of her leaping toward me, clawing at my face.

But in truth it was no problem for me to follow Lucia's wishes. I was a private investigator with eight years' experi-ence, and I was used to keeping my clients' confidences. It was more than a matter of obeying their wishes: Florida Stat-ute 493, which dealt with all licensed private investigators, demanded we keep our clients' information confidential. Our work, when retained by an attorney, as opposed to being hired by a regular client, is considered privileged, and is pro-tected by law. And most big cases involve a lawyer at some point.

I was about to explain all this to Lucia when she held up a finger to silence me. She glared at me, making sure I was sufficiently intimidated, then opened her oversized black leather bag and produced a manila envelope. She rested the envelope on her lap and began to caress it, her hand forming a delicate circular pattern much as a mother would stroke her child's head. I watched this unconscious display of tenderness. Perhaps Lucia had a heart, somewhere deep inside.

"I spoke to you at the wedding about the unicorn tapestries," she began. Her hand stopped moving. Her flinty black eyes locked onto mine. I shivered involuntarily.

"You mentioned the eighth tapestry," I replied, looking down at the envelope in her lap.

Lucia tightened her grip on the envelope, paused for a full ten seconds before handing it over, pushing it across the desk.

"You can open it," she said. "I am sure you will find its contents extremely interesting."

I flipped the envelope over, ran my index finger along its fold until it opened. I reached in and pulled out a few papers, which I arranged in a row on my desk. The first document was some sort of letter, only four lines long, written in spidery handwriting. My eyesight was good, but I had trouble making out what it said. I held it closer to my face. It was written in Spanish, I could tell, but the language was flowery and archaic.

Lucia watched me struggle, then gave me a slight smile. "You are looking at a copy of a letter from Cristobal Colon to my ancestor, Rogelio Miranda," she said. "It formally verifies Colon giving Rogelio a gift. The original letter is in a safety deposit box—it is too valuable and delicate for me to show to you."

I almost dropped the sheet of paper, blinking as I digested what Lucia had told me. I looked at the signature on the letter, just barely able to distinguish the name of Cristobal Colon—better known in the New World as Christopher Columbus. She watched patiently as I read through it.

I looked up at Lucia. Columbus had given Lucia's ancestor

a gift, if the letter was real. But what gift? And for what reason? The letter was maddeningly vague.

The second document looked like a certificate of authenticity. It certified that a tapestry depicting a unicorn—based on its dimensions, the tightness of its weave, and its quality and apparent age—was of the same vintage as the *Hunt of the Unicorn* series of tapestries. The letter was dated April 8, 1932, and signed by someone named Albert O. Manfredi. There was no title or position listed under the signature and name.

My heart was beating so fast and hard that I could have played the drums in a Sousa march without touching the instrument. I lay down the second document and picked up the third. It was a faded color photograph depicting a white unicorn leaping over a wooden enclosure. Even with the inferior quality of the photo, it was apparent that the tapestry was magnificent—and that it was not one of the seven tapestries hanging in the Cloisters in New York.

Well, one of my questions was answered. Now I knew the gift that Christopher Columbus had bestowed upon Lucia Miranda's ancestor. And what a breathtaking gift it was.

The eighth unicorn tapestry. I wished Mami were alive to see this. Just looking at the photograph filled me with longing for my mother. I was transfixed by it, staring into it as I remembered looking at the seven tapestries with Mami, speaking sometimes of the mythical eighth, lost tapestry. She had said she thought that one day it would be found. I could see her sweet smile as she was proved right yet again.

I looked up at Lucia, who was waiting patiently. "Beautiful," I said, putting down the picture. I didn't want her to see what a profound effect the contents of her envelope had had upon me. "So the rumors are true. The set at the Cloisters is not complete."

Lucia nodded in reply.

"Where is the tapestry now? I assume you have it."

Lucia took a deep breath. "Yes and no."

The reason for her coming to me suddenly became clear. "You own the tapestry, but it's not in your possession at the moment, right?"

Lucia looked stunned, so I knew I was right.

I pressed on. "And you want me to get it back for you," I said flatly.

"*Sí,*" Lucia said, her relief palpable, as though she had unburdened herself.

"You have to tell me the whole story," I insisted. "Beginning with how the tapestry ended up with your family."

I was in no mood to play twenty questions with Lucia Miranda, but I was definitely intrigued. She had my attention. And, bizarre appearance or not, I was certain Lucia had a hell of a story that she had been keeping to herself for a very long time.

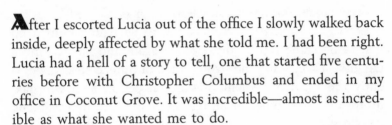

5

After I escorted Lucia out of the office I slowly walked back inside, deeply affected by what she told me. I had been right. Lucia had a hell of a story to tell, one that started five centuries before with Christopher Columbus and ended in my office in Coconut Grove. It was incredible—almost as incredible as what she wanted me to do.

"Is Morticia gone yet?" Leonardo called out from the kitchen, poking his head out the doorway. He paused for dramatic effect, looking around. I knew he'd heard the outside-door alarm signal that Lucia had left, so his question was his way of teasing me.

Not waiting for a reply, he came out with a can of Germs Away aerosol in each hand, spraying in every direction. It only took a few seconds for the reception area to smell like a hospital corridor. My eyes watered and I started swearing at him in Spanish, telling him to stop. A few squirts later he complied, but by then every surface glistened with germ-killing product.

"You can't be too careful, Lupe," Leonardo said, looking hurt by my reaction. "That woman looks like she lives in a cave and keeps bats as pets. She has bad energy, and her aura is even worse. We have to protect ourselves from that kind of negativity."

Leo capped both cans and moved back into the kitchen. He raised his shoulders in exaggerated disgust, making sure I noticed. He called out over his shoulder, "You know, I was just thinking. Maybe we should have a *lavado* just to make sure we clear the office completely of her presence."

I groaned at the mention of the *lavado*. Leo had been angling for a "cleansing" for months now. I had always said no, that there was no way I was going to allow Santería priests to come in and conduct a ceremony to get rid of evil spirits that were lurking around. Now, Lucia was strange, really strange, but she wasn't horrific or dirty.

Leonardo looked dejected, knowing he hadn't convinced me, as he came out of the kitchen again and handed me a tall glass. I winced at the strong smell of pureed garlic, apparently the main ingredient of the concoction he'd whipped up for me. The stench assaulted my senses, but he was being a good sport. I smiled and held it up to the light.

"Thanks, Leo," I said, retreating to my office. "I'll drink this right away."

I put the glass on top of my filing cabinet after I'd closed the door—the potion's temporary resting place until I could dispose of it without Leonardo's knowledge. I picked up the documents Lucia had left for me to study, then lay down on the sofa. I always did my best thinking stretched out.

My eyes closed, I remembered everything Lucia had told me. Her story challenged accepted, established historical facts. It was a tale that Rogelio Miranda's ancestors had passed down from generation to generation, and the crux of it was that Christopher Columbus had had a sort of affair, albeit platonic, with Queen Isabella of Spain in the late 1480s. She was wed to King Ferdinand, and could indulge in little more than what we today might consider light flirting with a man who was also married, but they had a sort of romantic link that made their relationship deep and dangerous. She was one-half of the Reyes Catolicos—the Catholic Sovereigns—and her feelings for Cristobal Colon had led her to finance his ventures into the New World.

I searched my mind for what I had learned in school about that period of history. I wished I'd paid more attention in Sister Mary Immaculata's tenth-grade European Civilization class, when we were supposed to be learning about the exploration of the New World. At the time, I had been more concerned with what I was doing that weekend. I hated to admit it, but Sister had been right when she said one day we'd regret not paying more attention to our studies.

I remembered that Queen Isabella had offered to sell her jewelry in order to finance Columbus's expeditions. It hadn't been necessary in the end, because the Spanish treasurer came through at the last minute to finance the exploration. Now that I thought about it, this story seemed to substantiate what Lucia had told me. No woman, not even a queen, would be willing to sell her jewelry—in this case, royal crown jewels—unless she was very serious about the man involved.

I was so intrigued by this scenario, centuries old, that I actually considered trying to reach Sister Mary Immaculata on the phone to ask her for information on late-fifteenth-century Spain. But I decided against it. After all, what was I going to say to her: Sister, do you think that the Catholic queen and Columbus wanted to get it on, and that was why she backed him on his trips to the New World? I couldn't see that conversation having a happy ending.

I held the evidence of the eighth tapestry's existence in my hand—if Lucia Miranda was telling me the truth. I had to stay objective, take nothing for granted until I had more proof. But then I considered the job for which she wanted to retain me—how and why would she be lying? It made no sense that she was telling anything but the truth.

I picked up my yellow legal pad of notes from the interview. My scribbled notes looked strange to me. They indicated information unknown to the world, and made me feel as though I was eavesdropping on the private life of two individuals—no matter that they had been dead almost five hundred years.

According to what Rogelio Miranda told his family, Columbus explained to him that Queen Isabella herself commissioned the eight tapestries. They were a gift to the French queen, Anne of Brittany, to memorialize her 1499 wedding to Louis XII. Isabella had given the newlyweds seven of the tapestries, but then, at the last moment, kept the eighth as a gift to Columbus, to symbolize their chaste love for one another. Only the weavers knew of the eighth tapestry, but they had no idea that the set had been broken up—even though they were honored artisans, they weren't invited to the French court.

I remembered one of the few occasions when I was actually paying attention in Sister Mary Immaculata's history class, when I tried to understand Columbus's motivation for seeking out the New World. It had been an incredibly risky undertaking into the unknown. I asked Sister whether the explorer came from a family of seamen—this might have explained it, if he had a heritage of sea adventure. Sister replied that no, his family had had little to do with the sea. In fact, Columbus's mother and father had both been wool weavers.

Had Isabella known this fact when she gave this tapestry to Columbus? Had this been part of the symbolism—a beautiful tapestry given to the son of weavers? If she had known this intimate information about his family, it strengthened the case for a deep closeness between them.

Not much was known about the fate of the seven tapestries until the beginning of the seventeenth century, when they emerged hanging on the walls of François VI de La

Rochefoucauld's Paris town house. They stayed in that family until the French Revolution, when French peasants took them to warm potatoes in their barns during the freezing cold winters. They remained in the barns for the next sixty years or so, when they were reclaimed by the La Rochefoucauld family. At that point only six of the tapestries were recovered. The seventh was in poor condition, and had been divided into two pieces that Count Gabriel de La Rochefoucauld kept for himself. The six tapestries were restored to their original condition and remained at the family's castle at Verteuil, south of Paris, until they were loaned for an exhibition in New York in 1922. John D. Rockefeller saw the six, fell under their spell, and bought them five minutes later. He loved them so much that he created a special room for them in his New York apartment.

In 1935, Rockefeller presented the six tapestries as a gift to the Cloisters Museum. Two years later the seventh tapestry was sold by the Count de La Rochefoucauld and added to the collection, where they have remained to this day.

The eighth tapestry has remained an elusive rumor. According to Lucia, Rogelio Miranda told his descendants that Christopher Columbus had sailed on the *Santa Maria* with the tapestry carefully packed away inside a trunk in his stateroom.

He was captain of the ship, and pretty certain that his belongings were safe from theft. Still, he realized that if it became known that he had such a valuable artwork on board—a gift from Queen Isabella, no less—it might be in danger for other reasons. The queen's enemies would have liked nothing more than to find such an artifact, which could be used to impugn her reputation and compromise her virtue. The tapestry, given in innocence to Columbus, could have been Isabella's undoing. So Columbus gave it to Rogelio Miranda, his faithful and loyal friend, for safekeeping until it was safe for Columbus to claim it again. Rogelio was no fool. He was a lowly ship's mate, and he knew that one day he might have been accused of stealing the tapestry. He told Columbus he would be honored to help, but on one condition—that Columbus sign a document verifying that the tapestry was a gift. It was a copy of this letter that Lucia had brought to me to prove her story.

Rogelio sailed on three of Columbus's exhibitions to the New World, the tapestry packed in his trunk and always available to his captain. On the fourth trip, after surviving a brush with a hurricane in 1502, Rogelio felt that he had tempted fate long enough. He disembarked in Cuba, intending to settle there for a few years, the tapestry still with his belongings. He promised Columbus that he would keep it safe until they were reunited. By then Columbus's relationship with the King and Queen of Spain was strained, and this seemed a prudent course of action.

This proved to be the last time the two men set eyes on each other. Columbus died four years later. Rogelio kept the tapestry, and it remained with the Miranda family for almost five hundred years.

Rogelio had left a detailed diary for his ancestors, describing how he came into possession of the tapestry. His ancestors added to it, and it became a sort of secret family history.

I had asked Lucia why the Mirandas kept the tapestry's existence a secret for so long. She paused, and in that second I understood. Rogelio's diary indicated that he had intended to keep the piece temporarily for Columbus; as such, Columbus or his heirs could be regarded as the rightful owners. Columbus had predeceased Rogelio, but that changed nothing in terms of his moral intentions to return the tapestry to his captain. Rogelio had intended to return to Spain with it, to return it to the Colon family, but died before he could carry out his plan.

Rogelio's heirs felt no such moral imperative; they ignored their ancestor's sense of obligation and made no attempt to return the tapestry. They were apprehensive, though, and uneasy enough about the issue of the tapestry's ownership to keep its existence a secret. They feared they might lose what had become the family's most treasured possession, and as a result adhered to a code of silence that had endured for centuries.

There had been rumors that connected the Mirandas to the tapestry, but nothing had come of them until 1934, when John D. Rockefeller was getting the other six tapestries ready for his donation to the Cloisters. He had heard the stories about the eighth tapestry and, through an intermediary, contacted the Mirandas to ask whether they had it or knew of its whereabouts. The Mirandas claimed they knew nothing, but they weren't sure whether Rockefeller bought it. Their fears were confirmed when a representative showed up at their house in Havana, a blank check in his hand from Rockefeller to buy the tapestry. The Mirandas turned down the offer, claiming ignorance of the tapestry's existence, but were shaken enough to call for a family conference to determine what to do.

The Mirandas knew Rockefeller's reputation, that he often got whatever he wanted. Rockefeller's money meant little to them; by then the Mirandas were very successful in the tobacco business, and no amount of cash could pry their hands from the tapestry, from their family legacy. They decided that Rockefeller was probably ruthless enough to try to steal the tapestry from them.

Until then the tapestry had been kept folded in Rogelio's old wooden sea chest, stored in the bedroom of each successive Miranda family patriarch. In the hundreds of years since the Mirandas brought it to the New World, it had been taken out only when it needed periodic restorations of oils—

ceremonious occasions that also served as family viewings. Now they realized it was time to move it to a safer location.

Lying back on the sofa, reading through these notes, I experienced anew the sense of wonder and amazement I'd felt when Lucia shared this secret family history with me. She recited her tale as one might tell a bedtime story to a child. Now, removed from the sound of her voice and my initial spellbound reaction, I still felt the story held up to scrutiny. The Mirandas had decided that their paramount goal was keeping the tapestry in the family. Their every action was consistent with this.

They had a long debate about where to hide the tapestry, where it would be safest and yet still accessible. Finally they decided to excavate a room under the patriarch's house, to create a sort of underground gallery kept under lock and key. An expert in the field of handling tapestries was hired, to make sure it was stored under optimal conditions.

The eighth tapestry was in an underground vault for the next sixty-five years, away from the prying eyes of the world. No documents or plans were left that might give away its location, nothing for the Communists to find after the Mirandas were driven into exile. As far as Lucia knew, it was still there today.

When Lucia had finished with her story, she looked at me silently for almost a full minute, as though taking my measure. Finally she began to speak again, slowly, her voice sharp and raspy.

"You know my mother, Doña Maria, is the head of the Miranda family," she said.

I nodded. I knew that Lucia's father had died several years ago from Alzheimer's. I also knew that, as the only unmarried child of the family, Lucia had been charged with caring for her ailing parents. She had a reputation as a fierce protector of her family's name and reputation—in part, I always suspected, because she had never made a life of her own.

"She has been diagnosed with brain cancer," Lucia said. Before I could offer my sympathies, Lucia waved them away. "It is an aggressive cancer, and it is spreading very quickly. The doctors say there is no treatment that will save her. She has accepted her fate with dignity and courage, but she has made one final request."

I said nothing. I could almost guess what was coming.

"My mother wishes to see the unicorn tapestry one last time," Lucia said, inching forward in her chair.

And I guessed this didn't mean taking Doña Maria to Havana.

Lucia reached into her black leather bag, took out a little pouch, tossed a key ring onto my desk. There were two keys on it.

"One is to the front door of the house in Havana," she said. "At least it was—forty years ago."

"And the other," I said slowly, "is to the room where the tapestry is located."

Lucia stared into my eyes. She said nothing. There was nothing left to say. She wanted me to go to Cuba, to bring out her family's greatest treasure for her mother to view one last time.

Dios mio.

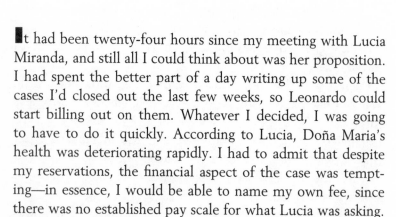

6

It had been twenty-four hours since my meeting with Lucia Miranda, and still all I could think about was her proposition. I had spent the better part of a day writing up some of the cases I'd closed out the last few weeks, so Leonardo could start billing out on them. Whatever I decided, I was going to have to do it quickly. According to Lucia, Doña Maria's health was deteriorating rapidly. I had to admit that despite my reservations, the financial aspect of the case was tempting—in essence, I would be able to name my own fee, since there was no established pay scale for what Lucia was asking.

I'd never worked a case in which my fee was basically limitless. I felt a little guilty about not telling Leonardo about the details of the case, but I knew he would bear down on me to take it. He would see visions of state-of-the-art, cutting-edge derriere-reducing contraptions occupying every square meter of our office. I didn't want the matter of Leonardo's ass clouding my judgment.

I glanced at the dashboard clock on my Mercedes as I drove to the Grand Bay Hotel on the way for my lunch date with Angel Estrada. Almost one o'clock; I was going to be on time. I didn't have far to go, since the hotel was just a few blocks from my office. In another city I might have walked, but no one walks in Miami. It's like issuing an open invitation to be mugged or arrested. A criminal seeing a pedestrian in Miami assumes he or she is a tourist, ripe for the picking. If a cop saw someone walking who wasn't wearing exercise clothes, they would likely stop the person for suspicious behavior.

I took my place in the line of cars inching up to the hotel entrance, thinking of the last time I saw Angel Estrada. It had been while tracking the Amelia Pelaez painting for Tia Alicia that I had heard of Angel as someone who dealt in Cuban art of dubious ownership. And when Armando Rionda came to me for help in connection with his Wilfredo Lam, I knew to contact Angel. I soon learned that, however physically distasteful Angel might have been, he lived up to his reputation for having his finger on the pulse of the market. No significant piece of Cuban art exchanged hands in the exile community without Angel knowing about it—and usually having a piece of the action. I suspected that Angel traded in the gray market for Cuban art—that is, he was involved in illegal transactions—but I hadn't heard anything definite to substantiate my hunch.

I waited patiently for the valet to take my car. Though curious about why Angel needed to see me so urgently, I was in no great hurry to see him. Angel would wait, because his seeing me meant he wanted something from me. When I had met with him on the Wilfredo Lam case, I often dreamt of a hot soapy shower to wash off the sense of sleaze that emanated from him. It wasn't a relationship that was ever going to flower into something beautiful. I knew, though, that he respected me as an investigator, and we had something in common: our occupations placed both of us on the fringes of respectability. We were both very accustomed to coming into contact with people who would never qualify for the Mother Teresa award for selflessness and honor.

I tucked away the ticket the valet handed me and stepped

out of the car. It was most curious, now that I thought about it, that two Cuban art cases—for, surely, this meeting with Angel represented the second, after Lucia's—had come my way in as many days. Call it coincidence, or fate, but it seemed that I was beginning to see a pattern of cases revolving around Cuban art.

I tried not to dwell on it. Leonardo entertained enough superstition and paranoia for the both of us. He excelled in divining meaning from the most mundane confluence of events, lately dragging in some obscure Santería god by way of explanation. I wouldn't mind, but then my cousin would typically go off on a tangent, warning me that disaster would befall us if we didn't follow a certain path. He thought he was plugged into the wishes of the gods and that we'd better start to pay heed. I had learned to keep my own superstitious impulses to myself.

As I entered the hotel I paused to take in the enormous floral arrangement in a Chinese vase, strategically located in the lobby entrance. I always enjoyed the Grand Bay Hotel: it created an air of Old World charm and gentility seldom found in Miami, a relatively new city composed mostly of exiles and immigrants in a hurry to survive and succeed. In such a city, refinement took a backseat to hustling.

Angel Estrada was waiting for me in the restaurant, where I knew he would be. He had already ordered champagne and was sipping from a fluted glass, a pensive look on his features. He hadn't seen me come into the room, so I observed him in an unguarded moment.

Then he sensed my presence, swiveling his head around until he saw me waiting in the doorway. He called out my name, smiled, and tipped his glass to me.

I didn't move. He had acknowledged my presence, and now I stood my ground until he acted in the proper manner of respect. His expression dropped a fraction; finally he realized what was expected of him, got up and started walking slowly toward me. Apparently he didn't want to grant me the satisfaction of having him hurry to greet me.

He kissed both my cheeks European-style. The problem was, we were both Cubans. I hated the affectation of the double kiss. Still, I had won the first mind-game of the meeting, so I tilted my face to the left then the right to receive his kisses. Thankfully his lips stopped a fraction of an inch away from actually touching skin.

Angel led the way to the table, then held out the chair next to his for me to sit. I cursed inside. I would much rather have sat across from him, where I could observe him better. But my manners won out, and I sat where he indicated. I figured the score was now equal at one apiece.

I accepted a glass of champagne and took a sip, the taste reminding me of the drinks I'd had at my niece Marianna's wedding. If I'd died of an accident that night, the medical examiner probably would have fainted from the alcoholic fumes coming from my body. He would likely have joined AA and never taken another drink as long as he lived.

Angel, as usual, was dressed exquisitely. He wore a perfectly cut light-gray pinstriped suit, a pale pink shirt, and a lavender Ferragamo tie. I let my eyes linger on the tie for a moment; it depicted two sharks fighting in the water, taking chunks out of each other. I had to admit, it was strangely beautiful. Angel seemed to be convinced—incorrectly—that dressing so nicely would distract from the fact that he was singularly unattractive.

To begin, Angel was very hairy. His eyebrows spanned his forehead in a bristly unibrow. I was almost tempted to suggest he try waxing, but there was no telling how he would react. His beady eyes were the color of dishwater, his nose was bulbous, with visible pores and blackheads. His wiry black hair was slicked back and shone. By contrast, his mouth was full and sensual—think a Cuban Mick Jagger—his only saving grace, but still not enough to counteract the rest.

"Shall we order now?" Angel asked, the perfect host.

"Whatever you like," I said, smiling.

"I'm not very hungry. I'm just going to order some pasta. But, please, you have whatever you like."

"Sounds good," I said.

"Please, have whatever you like," he said. He repeated himself, another unappealing trait.

"Pasta would be fine," I replied.

We ordered two manicotti alla toscana, the special of the day, and sipped champagne. I would have rather drunk a Barolo, though. The room was starting to fill up—not surprising, since Bice's had the most delicious lunch specials in Miami. I glanced around, hoping I wouldn't run into anyone I knew. Because of his appearance and reputation, Angel wasn't the best person with whom to be seen in public.

"Can I speak to you in confidence, Lupe?" Angel asked, breaking the momentary silence.

Here it comes, I thought. "*Sí*, of course, Angel."

"I have come across . . . well, some *special* pieces." Angel was starting to sweat already; I saw beads of moisture on his forehead. "It is a very delicate matter."

I waited for him to dab his forehead with his handkerchief and take a long, courage-inducing swallow of champagne.

"What kind of pieces?" I asked.

"You must promise me. You must give me your word of honor that you will not tell anyone what I am about to share with you. Please. Say it out loud."

"All right. I swear." I was baffled but definitely intrigued. I probably shouldn't have agreed to any sort of oath with Angel, but I knew I wasn't going to be able to walk away from the table without hearing what he had to say.

"I know the whereabouts of some very valuable artworks," he began. "Very valuable."

"So do I," I said, growing impatient. "The Hermitage, the Louvre, the Metropolitan—"

"Lupe," Angel said. "If you're going to—"

"Everything you deal in is valuable, Angel," I said. "I don't understand why this is any different."

Angel said nothing. He seemed to be waiting for something to click in my head.

Finally it did. "Stolen?" I asked.

Angel's expression dropped, as though he'd never before heard of such a concept. A flash of offense passed over his features, but then, an instant later, he simply shrugged.

"I do not like that word," he replied. "Let's just say that the owners of the works in question were never properly and fully compensated for their loss."

A nice choice of words. Very delicate.

"I don't deal in stolen property, Angel. You know that. I only get involved if it's been stolen by the Cuban government and sold. I work for the rightful owners."

Angel stared, a hint of condescension in his eyes. I reached down to the floor to pick up my purse. This lunch was over. I would have to find another source for Cuban art cases.

"Please, Lupe," Angel said. He reached out and touched my arm. That was another good reason to get out. Physical contact wasn't, and never would be, a part of our relationship.

"Please nothing," I said.

"You misunderstand me," Angel begged. "Please. Sit. I didn't mean to insult you in any way."

His voice rose in volume; people at nearby tables stopped their conversations and looked at us. The last thing I wanted was to make a scene at the Grand Bay. I reluctantly put down my purse.

"Five minutes," I said, tapping the face of my watch. "Explain what you have in mind. If I don't like what I hear, I'm going. If you don't talk fast enough, I'm going."

I meant every word. It would be very hard to replace Angel as a contact, now that I seemed to be developing a reputation as an investigator conversant in stolen Cuban art, but there were some compromises that I wasn't willing to make. Allowing my reputation to be dragged into illegal dealings was a prime example.

"It's just—" Angel stopped.

I tapped my watch again. This seemed to help him regain his focus.

"All right. What do you know about where Fidel Castro lives in Havana?" Angel almost spit out the words.

I shook my head and reached for my purse again. He was playing games, this was bullshit. I should have known better.

"Wait, this has to do with our business," Angel said. "Give me a chance."

I had, after all, promised him five minutes. "I don't know anything about Fidel Castro's house, and I don't care," I told him. "All I've heard is that he moves around a lot. He's scared of assassination attempts."

"That's right." Angel smiled, the pleased teacher facing an able pupil. "Remember, Lupe. You swore secrecy to me."

I was starting to get a different feeling about this conversation. Angel was obviously serious. I could tell something interesting was coming.

"There are luxurious residences in Havana, in districts such as the Vedado," Angel continued. "They are thirteen houses that Fidel has deemed comfortable enough to suit his needs."

"I didn't know that," I admitted. I wondered if Lucia Miranda's family's place was one of them. That would be quite a coincidence.

"Hey, the maximum leader has good taste," Angel said with a bitter chortle. "He doesn't exactly suffer along with the masses. And the rest of them—Raul, the ministers—they don't go without, either. They live better than the exiles they're always putting down. They're upper-class, living in luxurious homes, surrounded by fine furnishings and art. They've turned into their enemies."

I let Angel amuse himself with this diatribe on the corruption of the Cuban Communist government. He was the kind of man who liked to lecture—even if his audience knew everything he had to say and already agreed with him.

"Look, Angel," I interrupted. "I can see you find the situation amusing, but your five minutes are almost up."

Angel snapped back. "Sorry," he said.

Our waiter arrived with our lunch. We waited a moment until he was out of earshot.

"You're not counting the time the waiter was here, are you?" Angel asked. "I need more time to explain."

What a baby. I shook my head and took a bite of my pasta. I had decided that I would hear Angel out, no matter how long it took. I needed to know where this was heading. But there was no reason for me to tell him that.

"OK," Angel said. "You should know that I have a sister in Cuba."

I shrugged. I knew nothing about his personal life, and had never volunteered much about my own. Usually we communicated by phone and fax, which was just about enough for me. I was actually a little surprised, though, to think of Angel as having a family. From his smarmy demeanor I had him pegged as someone who lived outside the realm of human kindness and without close personal ties to anyone.

"All right," I said. "You have a sister in Cuba."

He swallowed hard, still having not touched his food. "Her name is Camila. She's a painter. Oils. She studied all her life and is a genius. If she lived outside of Cuba, she would be very famous by now."

"I see." Again I was surprised, this time by the obvious pride and affection in Angel's voice.

"Camila stayed in Cuba with my mother when my brother and I left during the Mariel," Angel explained. "Our mother was old, and she was scared of the idea of living in America. I guess she didn't realize that she wouldn't even have to speak English in Miami if she didn't want to. It's ironic. Anyway, we all thought we'd be reunited within a few months."

I wasn't surprised to hear about how Angel's family was split up; his story was nothing unusual. In 1980, Castro opened the port of Mariel to all Cubans who wanted to leave the country. Thousands of exiles set off from Key West to pick up relatives they hadn't seen in decades, and families had just a few hours to decide whether they wished to leave or stay behind in Cuba. It was total chaos—a mass exodus of 120,000 people in just a few days. Most had been law-abiding citizens, but Castro being Castro, some of the refugees were hard-core criminals set loose from some of Cuba's worst prisons—thus making them America's problem rather than Fidel's. Families were split up when people took to the seas on anything that might float, and many relatives hadn't seen each other in the twenty years that had passed since then.

"I'm sorry to hear that, Angel," I said. And I truly was. Angel nodded and paused for a moment as our espressos arrived.

"Camila doesn't earn a living as an artist," he continued. "No one in Cuba does. Unless they make those huge posters—you know, of the Castro brothers, Ché, all the others."

I knew what he was talking about. Huge portraits of Fidel

and Raul Castro and other "heroes" of the revolution were ubiquitous on the walls of Havana.

"She still paints," Angel said. "But in a different way—she's a house painter. Mostly interior details—floorboards, door frames, the skilled stuff. And she doesn't work in average homes. She works in government residences, houses where high Cuban officials live. She has access to all of them, even the ones where Fidel sleeps."

Angel's point eluded me. "I don't follow," I told him. "What does all of this have to do with me?"

Angel's face dropped, and I could tell I had slipped a few notches in his estimation. Well, I couldn't help it if I wasn't as shifty and devious as he was.

"You're an intelligent woman, Lupe. Think about it," Angel sighed. "Camila has been in the wealthiest homes in Havana. She's seen all the art there, and she has free access to it. Because of her educational background, she can identify which paintings are the most valuable. Come on. Think about what I'm telling you."

I was getting tired of this. I didn't appreciate Angel's games, and I really didn't care for his condescension.

"Get to the point," I said.

"Camila is very skilled." A trace of a smile played on Angel's lips. "One of her specialties is copying paintings. She's dedicated a lot of time and study to it, and she's capable of imitating the styles of nearly all the Cuban masters. She can copy a painting with such accuracy that no one can tell it from the original. She even fooled her old teachers at the institute."

I had to give Angel credit—he could drop a bombshell with aplomb. I looked around the room. The lunch crowd was starting to thin out. Before long we would be the only patrons there. Finally I was seeing what Angel had brought to me—and I was pretty sure I wanted no part of it.

"OK. Your sister is an artist," I said innocently. "I guess art appreciation runs in your family."

If looks could kill they would have been carrying me out of the place on a stretcher. Angel shook his head, realizing that he was going to have to spell everything out to me.

"Lupe, look. I think we can take advantage of this situation," he said. "We can make loads of money, and screw Fidel Castro at the same time."

"It's every Cuban's dream, when you put it that way," I said. "You know what buttons to push. But you have to give me more specifics. Don't tell me you haven't thought this one out in detail."

"This is how I see it." Angel leaned closer, apparently taking my interest for complicity. "My sister is going to give me a list of which paintings are hung in what home, and which ones she thinks she can reproduce. Your job is to hunt down the artworks' true owners—which I know you can do, and damned well. I saw you operate on the Wilfredo Lam matter. You know all the upper-class Cubans here, you move in those social circles. Those people trust you. They know your family."

"Sounds neat and tidy," I said.

If Angel picked up my sarcasm, he chose to ignore it.

"Then Camila can get to work," he added. "She'll replace the real paintings with fakes, and we'll smuggle the originals out of Cuba. The rightful owners will get their property back, and we'll turn a hell of a profit in the process."

Angel's eyes gleamed. I could almost see dollar signs floating there.

"The best part is that we'll be putting one over on those Communist bastards," he said. "They'll be looking at fake art, thinking it's real. It's so sweet, Lupe."

I had to admit it—at least to myself—that "sweet" was a fairly good word to describe this plan. It would be sweet revenge against Fidel and his cronies. But the plan also had more holes than a rickety raft on the Florida Straits—and was just as perilous.

"You've done your homework," I said. I wasn't shocked to hear how much he knew about my background—in fact, I admired his thoroughness. "But this is dangerous, especially for your sister. To begin with, how do you think you're going to be able to smuggle the paintings out of Cuba?"

"We have a small group dedicated to making this happen. I wouldn't be involved in something like this if it wasn't well-organized," Angel said, a little indignant. "Don't you think I considered all the contingencies before I approached you?"

"I'm sure you did," I admitted. "It's just that . . . you've hit me with a lot this morning. I have to digest it."

That was an understatement.

Angel's expression hardened; the sparkle disappeared from his eyes.

"I'm going," I said, picking up my purse. "I am going to think about everything you said, Angel, and then I'm going to get back to you. You have my word on that."

Angel frowned; he seemed to have thought that I was going to turn cartwheels right there in the Grand Bay over the prospect of entering into a partnership with him and possibly making millions. But I was a private investigator, not an art dealer. Angel's plan, in addition to being totally illegal, was too far out of left field for me to get a handle on it right away. I had to admit, however, that the prospect of screwing Fidel Castro had a certain appeal. Perhaps there was a way of implementing Angel's plan without breaking the law—something I would have to think through.

"I understand," he said, sounding like he didn't. "Remember your promise in the meantime. Keep this to yourself. I trust you, but I don't want anyone else trying to get a piece of the action.''

His words sounded more like a plea than a threat. I leaned over and kissed his cheek, this time actually making contact. In spite of my dislike for the man, I admired his audacity, and the fact that he had wanted to involve me in his plan. It took a creative—and very devious—mind to come up with it. I wondered what kind of person his sister was—obviously brave, if not desperate.

"I keep my promises, Angel,'' I said, turning to go. "You should know that by now.''

7

After lunch I decided not to return to the office and instead went home. I was suffering from information overload, and I really needed to get away from anything pertaining to the recovery of artworks from Cuba. As I left the Grove and headed south on Main Highway toward Cocoplum, I reviewed the strange sequence of events that had led to me receiving two serious offers in as many days.

Traffic was relatively light at that hour, and it was only a few minutes until I was being waved past by the guard at the security checkpoint on the road leading into Cocoplum, the development where my family home was located. I made the left turn onto Tahiti Beach, where the most exclusive—and expensive—homes were clustered.

I slowed in the driveway and admired Osvaldo's tropical landscaping, which he had carefully planted and to which he lovingly and devotedly tended. All of his hard work paid off. We had indisputably the most beautiful gardens in all of Cocoplum. I hoped that the beauty of the landscape—a public asset for everyone's eyes, after all—somewhat mitigated the effect of the enormous house Papi had built, one that overshadowed all the neighbors'. Which was quite a statement, since the concepts of restraint and understatement had never been uttered in the same breath as the word "Cocoplum."

My sisters and I had long ago gotten over our embarrassment from living in such a place. Our father was a building contractor, and when he planned the house, he obviously envisioned many branches of the family tree and multigenerations of children frolicking on the grounds and sleeping nights in all the bedrooms. I hoped he wasn't too disappointed; at the present, the only people living in the house other than Papi were my sisters Lourdes and Fatima, Fatima's twin twelve-year-old daughters, and Aida and Osvaldo, the octogenarian couple who had worked for my family for more than fifty years. Lourdes was a nun of the Order of the Holy Rosary, so it was unlikely she was going to have children—at least, she had better not—and Fatima had sworn off men entirely after her nightmare marriage. If Aida and Osvaldo were to conceive a child at their ages—eighty and eighty-three, respectively—they would have to move out because there would be a place waiting for them at the Smithsonian. Fatima's twins were, hopefully, still at least a decade away from procreating. As for me, I would be having children only if pharmaceuticals failed me. Poor Papi, destined to walk the corridors of his house without hearing the joyous voices of little children, at least for the foreseeable future.

While we were living in a far more modest home in the southern part of Coral Gables, Papi and Mami had owned the lot for years, not doing anything with it, just paying taxes and watching it increase in value. When Mami was diagnosed with ovarian cancer, Papi decided to finally build on the property. Soon the whole family was consumed by her illness. Each of us coped with it in our own way. Papi's was to design and build the house, his way of denying the reality of Mami's prospects for survival. None of us had the heart to tell him he was going overboard. Maybe we were all in denial, too, as we watched the house grow larger and more spectacular.

When I think back on that time, I realize we were all fantasizing about moving in as a family, and we spent countless hours with Mami talking about decorating plans. She knew about and approved every detail, and nothing major had been changed in the eight years since we moved in. The house was finished in the final weeks of her life, while she was in the hospital, so she never really lived in it. Her spirit, somehow, still permeated every inch of the place.

I parked the Mercedes in my usual spot, knowing I was inviting Osvaldo's wrath for parking too close to the impatiens. I got out of the car and sprinted up the stairs. I knew that Aida always looked at the TV monitor in the kitchen whenever anyone approached the place, so I waved at the security camera placed over the front door.

I dropped my purse on the glass console table in the hall, right next to a big photograph in a silver frame depicting me in my first-communion finery. I had never liked the picture, which showed me in a nimbus of white tulle and organza; I thought it made me look like a midget bride about to be sacrificed on an altar. White never has been, nor will it ever be, my color. I just don't look right in any shade associated with purity.

I walked straight out to the terrace, felt the gusts of salty air that rose up from Biscayne Bay. I leaned over the railing and peered down at the water. It was high tide, and I could see minnows congregating below me, anticipating their afternoon snack. I felt a little guilty for deceiving them—the fish that lived below the terrace were accustomed to the bits of food we threw down for them a few times a day. I stood there for a while, letting the air clear my mind, staring out at the bay in the distance. I was hoping to catch sight of one of the manatees that sometimes swam lazily up the canal adjacent to our house, but that day there weren't any. I contented myself watching the pelicans lazily swoop down and skim fish off the water's surface with their beaks.

I lay down on my favorite deck chair, closed my eyes, and drifted away. I felt the hot sun warming my body, listened to the waves crashing against the wooden pillars supporting the deck. I heard seagulls off in the distance, chattering to themselves. My mind felt pulled in different directions, but it returned to thoughts of my mother. Mami loved the sea fiercely, and she often took my sisters and me to the beach. I very much felt her presence with me there on the dock. Ever since Lucia Miranda told me about the tapestry, I had felt Mami occupying my feelings even more than usual.

It took all my powers of concentration to pull my thoughts back to business. The two situations that had been dropped in my lap—both involving reunifying Cuban paintings with their rightful owners—were a departure from the usual civil and criminal cases in which I specialized. And, because I relished and reveled in my Cuban heritage, I felt proud to be associated with any endeavor that contributed to it. I didn't know that much about Cuban art or artists, but I wouldn't hesitate for an instant to return a particular work to its rightful owner. It gave me a certain satisfaction to do so.

But now I had to wonder—would I derive the same sense of satisfaction and, dare I think it, righteousness, from the two proposals that had just been presented to me? Both affected me in a very personal way.

In the case of the eighth unicorn tapestry, let's say I agreed to take on its reclamation. How in the hell was I going to get it out of Havana, right from under the nose of the Cuban police state? If the Cuban authorities got wind of the fact that the tapestry was hidden in a secret basement in the Vedado district, they wouldn't hesitate to confiscate it and, probably, sell it off to the highest bidder to generate cash.

The government had been dismantling private art collections and selling them abroad for years. And the value of the eighth tapestry was incalculable. It probably wouldn't be offered to the Cloisters, since the museum would have no interest in stolen goods, but an individual collector could certainly be found to buy it, no questions asked, for his or her private enjoyment. I had to admit, I was tempted to be the one who returned it to the Mirandas, who at least had a long-standing claim to possessing it—a better claim, at least, than Fidel's government.

As far as Angel's plan was concerned, nothing would make me happier than to know I played a part in outfoxing the Cuban government. But the plan remained sketchy at best, and I could think of a thousand ways it might blow up in our faces. Yet I couldn't dismiss it outright. It was so bold that it appealed to my sense of adventure and rebellion. And even though I knew aspects of it could be viewed as thievery, I could justify it as stealing from parties who themselves had illegally appropriated the art in the first place.

No question about it. I had a lot to think about. I was mulling all of this over when Osvaldo emerged onto the terrace.

"Lupe," he said, smiling and shuffling toward me. He wagged his finger, trying to disguise his good humor long enough to scold me. "You parked too close to the impatiens, as usual. You know, one of these days you're going to kill the entire bush! When will you ever pay attention to what I tell you? *Dios mio*, I can't think of the last time you listened to me."

"*Ay*, Osvaldo," I said, trying not to laugh. "I'll never change, I guess."

He shook his head, his thin lips creased into a grin. "I know that. You are just like your sainted mother." He blessed himself; he loved Mami dearly, and a day never passed without him finding a way to mention her. "She never listened to me, either. She did whatever she wanted, ever since she was a little girl."

He looked at me intently. "You know, Lupe, your *mami* and you are alike in so many ways. She loved the water the same way you do. She was so interested in life, and so alive. Sometimes when I look at you, for a second I see her instead."

I nodded, feeling a bittersweet twinge. I knew I was Osvaldo's favorite, even though he would never say so to anyone. Of the three daughters, I most resembled my mother. I could never bring Mami back, but I could honor her memory the best way I knew how.

I watched Osvaldo walk slowly to the railing and peer down into the water. I knew what he was looking for.

"No manatees today," I said.

Osvaldo shrugged. "Maybe mas tarde." He looked at his watch. "Well, siesta time. You want anything?"

I thought for a moment, then decided I might as well get into full Cuban mode.

"*Un mojito, por favor,*" I said.

Osvaldo winked. "*Uno grande,* eh, Lupe?"

I loved the old man. He could always perfectly gauge my mood.

The *mojito* that Osvaldo prepared for me had made me quite sleepy, so when I was finished I went upstairs for a long nap. I awoke feeling completely refreshed and energized. I lay back in bed and relaxed by flipping through the dozens of magazines that had been accumulating on my night table. Nothing there interested me, so I picked up Hugh Thomas's book on the history of Cuba, which I had been slowly making my way through for months. It was thousands of pages long, and not exactly light reading; although it was full of interesting historical information, it took my full powers of concentration. Normally the book would captivate my attention after a page or two, but my mind couldn't escape the pair of opportunities that had been presented to me. After about half an hour of looking at the book, retaining almost nothing of what I read, I gave up and got out of bed.

I went downstairs to see which family members might be around, but Aida informed me that I was alone. I was getting restless, and it was still only late afternoon, so I decided to head back to the office for an hour or two. Being at home had given me time to regroup and assimilate my thoughts, but I knew I should try to make some headway on the mountain of paperwork Leonardo had been bugging me about— mostly on old cases that needed me to sign off before we could send out a bill. I had made a dent in them already, but not enough to satisfy my cousin. Leo loved to send out bills. Looking at a stack of envelopes stuffed with invoices, waiting for the mailman to come take them away, made him immeasurably happy. He would then sit and calculate how long it would take before the money started to roll in.

Leonardo was gone for the day by the time I reached Solano Investigations, so I switched on the lights and went back to my office. Out of habit, I walked over to the window to see what the parrots outside my window might be up to. They seemed agitated, squawking loudly and drinking some sort of green liquid from the shells of avocados that had fallen from the tree. I wondered if it were possible to get drunk from drinking fermented avocado pulp. It almost looked like the parrots were having their own aviary version of happy hour.

I sat down at my desk and started tackling the old files Leonardo had optimistically stacked on the corner of my desk; he thought that by keeping them in my sight, I would eventually get motivated to do something about them. Turns out he was right. It was really nothing but mindless busy work, but still I had trouble concentrating on it. My mind kept wandering, and concentrating on old cases was hopeless. I pushed the files aside, relegated back to their lonely corner of my desk, and took out my notebooks from the drawer.

I needed a reality check. It was one thing to fantasize about retrieving a lost art treasure out of Cuba to satisfy the last wish of a dying woman, it was another matter entirely to actually calibrate the risks of doing so. While I was at it, I also had to think about the hazards of Angel Miranda's plan.

I looked up at the clock. It was almost six. The parrots' party had entered the next phase, with shrieking and plumage flying as they bumped into each other and fell to the ground. No question about it. My feathered friends were getting hammered.

Watching them gave me an idea. I picked up the phone and dialed a number from memory. Alvaro and I might be an item, but I hadn't yet programmed his private office number into my speed dial. Sleeping together was one thing, but I wasn't ready to commit such a momentous and symbolic step. I knew I was on his speed dial, a discrepancy I tried not to dwell on.

"*Hola,*" I said, pleased that I had caught him still at work.

"Lupe!" The pleasure in his voice sent chills up my back.

"Are you busy tonight?" I asked. I hated to be so forward, but I wanted to do some preliminary background before I seriously thought about taking the Miranda case. I was tempted, but I didn't want to let my sentiment and excitement cloud my judgment. As for Angel, I decided that his place for the moment was on my professional back burner.

"Sort of," Alvaro said. "I've got that Alvarez trial coming up in a couple of weeks, but I can work on that later on. What did you have in mind?"

"How about dinner? On my expense account?" I tempted

him, although I knew it wouldn't take much to get him to accept my invitation. "I want to consult with you on a case."

"So, this is business, huh?" Alvaro asked. "Is it strictly business, or can I sexually harass you later on?"

"Maybe," I laughed. It was difficult to be restrained with Alvaro. He took such delight in our relationship. As did I, but I wasn't as open with my feelings.

"Good enough for me," he said. "When, where, and how? Or would you rather I pick you up at the house?"

"It depends," I replied. "Do you want to have dinner early or late?"

We sparred a little over the details; in the end we decided that Alvaro would pick me up at home. I always felt better if I had a chance to clean up and change before going out. Although I'd stopped by the house earlier, I was still wearing the same outfit I'd put on that morning. Alvaro might not yet have made it to my speed dial, but I wanted to be at my best for him.

It was a bit of a drive from Coral Gables to South Beach, but Alvaro and I decided to brave it in order to have dinner at the Tuscan Steak restaurant on Washington Avenue. We were both craving red meat, and we had a shared vision of the restaurant's house special steak that nearly left us both salivating. In these days of political correctness and uptight self-denial, it was a pleasure to be with someone who liked to eat, drink, have sex, and basically enjoy life without being plagued by guilt because some endangered beetle in Sri Lanka was edging one step closer to extinction.

In addition to the food, we both enjoyed the ambiance at Tuscan Steak—it was a treat to eat in a "grown-up"-style place, a rarity on South Beach. The decor was sophisticated, boasting a large open dining room with the tables set a perfect distance apart—a real luxury these days, when tables are often put so close together that diners feel as though they're eating elbow-to-elbow with dozens of strangers. I wanted to discuss the Miranda case with Alvaro, so I appreciated the privacy we were afforded by the banquette at which we were seated. I had imbibed two of Osvaldo's lethal *mojitos* before leaving the house, but I wasn't so mellow that I didn't stiffen inwardly at the memory of Lucia's bloodred fingernails in my face, warning me about spilling the information she had shared with me. I could trust Alvaro, but I didn't want eavesdroppers to be able to overhear any of Lucia's secrets.

Tuscan Steak billed itself as a restaurant that served "family style" meals; that meant their dishes were to be shared. Although Alvaro and I were alone at our table, we were brought enough food to feed a small army. Soon we started on a second bottle of Barolo wine. Fortunately, Alvaro was like me. He didn't let himself get caught up counting calories or glasses of wine.

We had just ordered dessert when I decided it was time to get to business. Alvaro could tell by my expression.

"All right," he said, smiling over his wineglass. "Chitchat time is over. What do you have to share with me?"

"Am I that transparent?" I asked.

"Only sometimes." He slid his hand over mine on the tabletop.

"First, you have to swear secrecy." He started to laugh. "I'm serious. Come on. Swear."

He lifted one hand solemnly. "I swear."

I told Alvaro all about my meeting with Lucia Miranda—although I omitted the details of what she wanted me to do. Naturally, he was fascinated to learn about the eighth tapestry, and even more captivated by the story of how the Miranda family had come to possess it. He didn't know as much about the tapestries as I did, but he had been to the Cloisters and seen them in person.

"So that was what she wanted when she cornered you at

your cousin's wedding," he said, trying to grasp everything I'd told him. "I had a feeling it was something big."

"Alvaro, I know you're very aware of what's going on in Havana," I began delicately. I had to be diplomatic when I brought up the subject of Cuba with him; although we were in agreement about many things concerning our homeland, especially the systematic human-rights violations occurring there, sometimes we were poles apart politically. We had learned to stop trying to convert each other, and tended to focus on the areas where our beliefs overlapped. At times Alvaro thought I was a typical knee-jerk, right-wing Cuban exile; in turn, I thought he excused many of the Cuban government's actions in the name of expediency and survival. We had had a great dinner, and I didn't want to start a disagreement. Still, I needed information from him—he was the only person I knew who dealt with Cubans on the island on a regular basis.

He seemed to sense something was up. "What do you want to know?" he asked in a no-bullshit tone.

"You know about the cases I've had recently, dealing with reuniting works of Cuban art with their exile owners?"

"Sure. The Pelaez and the Lam, right?" He took a sip of the Barolo, then carefully wiped his lips on the white linen napkin.

"Right. Now, the thing—"

"Let me take a guess," Alvaro interrupted. He paused, a frown playing at his features. "A wild guess. Lucia wants you to get that tapestry out of Cuba for her. She didn't meet with you to give you a history lesson. She wants to hire you to smuggle that thing off the island."

I knew that Alvaro was smart, so I expected him to connect the dots quickly; still, I was impressed he had done so after a couple of Osvaldo's *mojitos* and his share of two bottles of wine. I debated how to answer, though we both knew that he had fixed on the truth.

"You're right," I said. "That's what she came to see me about."

"OK," Alvaro said, glancing away from the table. "Now. What did you want to discuss with me?"

I picked at what was left of the chocolate decadence dessert on the table. "You're familiar with Cuban law," I said. "What is the punishment for someone who gets caught doing something like that?"

Alvaro's eyes opened wide behind the lenses of his glasses. His face tightened, as though he had expected such a question but had held out hope that it wouldn't come.

"You're not seriously considering her offer, are you?" He moved closer until his face was inches from mine. "Dear God, tell me you're not thinking about going into Cuba to smuggle out that tapestry. Please, Lupe, just tell me that."

I stayed quiet. I hadn't made my mind up yet, one way or the other. My intention had been to simply pick Alvaro's brain about my chances of success and what faced me if I failed.

I put my hand on his arm. "Don't worry," I said. "I'm not going to do anything stupid."

Alvaro looked totally unconvinced. We had been lovers for a short time, but we had grown up together. Alvaro had known me since we were both in diapers, so he knew my personality. Going to Cuba on such a mission was something I could seriously contemplate; in fact, the adventure of it was growing more and more appealing.

"Don't tell me any more, Lupe." Alvaro held up his hand. "I can't, I really won't hear another word about it!"

Alvaro was raising his voice to me, something that had never happened before. I didn't like it one bit. I never would have brought up the subject if I'd known I was going to get such a violent reaction.

"You'd be breaking both U.S. and Cuban laws," he hissed, shaking his head in total disbelief. "It's plain crazy. I understand that your mother loved the tapestries, I can see what that means to you—but really, Lupe, examine your reasons for doing something so dangerous. You know your mother would be the first one to try to talk you out of taking this case."

Alvaro's voice was carrying now; I looked around and saw that, mercifully, no one at the nearby tables seemed to be paying any attention. This was South Beach, after all, where all kinds of behavior were constantly on display and where people minded their own business. Still, I couldn't help but think of Lucia's talons.

"Have you thought about what it's like in a Cuban jail? Have you?" Alvaro continued. He stared into my eyes. I just sat there, frozen in my seat, waiting for his chastisement to end. I felt like a schoolgirl being lectured for talking out of turn. "And what about your family? What is it going to do to them, when you're rotting in a Cuban jail? And that's if you're lucky enough not to get executed!"

There was nothing to say in return. I wasn't going to utter denials that might have been lies. It was now obvious that I wasn't going to get any valuable impartial advice from Alvaro. I could see that he wanted to close the topic—forever.

Alvaro motioned to the waiter for the check. Dinner was apparently over, and it wouldn't make any difference that I had showered, changed, and perfumed myself before going out. The night wasn't going to end the way either of us had envisioned.

As I usually did whenever anyone was angry with me about my behavior, I stared straight ahead, unblinking. It used to drive Mami nuts. My nieces called it "zoning out."

Whatever it was, it was my way of not saying anything I might regret later on. I had a quick temper, and once it was unleashed I couldn't control it. It wasn't that I didn't deserve Alvaro's treatment of me—everything he was saying was correct—but I simply didn't want to hear it.

I looked away from him, to the wall opposite our table. I couldn't believe what I saw there. Hanging on the wall was a reproduction of the second tapestry from the *Hunt of the Unicorn* series, the one in which the unicorn was down on the ground purifying drinking water that had been poisoned by the Devil.

Very strange. I had eaten at Tuscan Steak at least a dozen times before, but I had never noticed the tapestry hanging on the wall. The power of this coincidence was too strong. But if it had a meaning, what was it?

I let my eyes take in the details. The unicorn was hunted, wounded. That was what would happen to me if the plan failed. I was so intent on reading the signs in the tapestry's appearance to me that I failed to notice Alvaro turning cold and silent. It was an ominous sign.

I turned and watched Alvaro whip out his American Express card to pay for dinner. He wasn't even going to accept my earlier invitation to put the tab on my expense account. There was no way he was going to be indebted to my client, who wanted to send me into the jaws of the enemy. And I hadn't even brought up the matter of Angel Estrada and his scheme for smuggling out paintings and replacing them with forgeries. I hated to think what his reaction would be to that.

Ay. Cuban men. Maybe I should have stuck to Americans. Everything would have been easier and less complicated. As it was, nothing between Cubans was ever simple. It was a fact that I should have remembered before opening my mouth to Alvaro.

We walked outside in silence and stood together for the

few minutes it took the valet to bring the car around. No sooner had we gotten in and begun driving away than Alvaro turned to me.

"You know, Lupe, you can't bring your mother back by going to Cuba to get that tapestry. That's not the way it works."

I recoiled and turned away. His heart might have been in the right place, but what Alvaro said sounded to me like a cheap shot. I wasn't going to use my mother's memory to justify questionable actions, and if that's what he thought I was doing, then he didn't know me at all.

"I'm sorry to be so blunt," he continued. "But you know how I feel on this matter."

I said nothing.

"Lupe?" he asked.

"Just take me home," I told him, still looking away out the window, unable to meet his eyes.

8

Leonardo was waiting for me the next morning when I arrived at the office. He was waving a copy of the *Miami Herald*.

"Read the paper yet, Lupe?"

"No." I frowned. "Should I have?"

"Didn't you meet with Angel Estrada yesterday?" he asked.

"Yes, I did," I answered slowly. I felt a creeping dread enter my body. "We went to lunch at the Grand Bay. Why?"

I clutched my purse to my chest as I sat down on the couch in the reception area. Leonardo pointed to the local-news section of the paper.

"Says here Angel was found dead in his condo last night," he said.

"Dead?" I repeated. "How dead?"

Leo held the paper closer to his face, seriously considering my question. "Doesn't say. Just that the police are investigating."

I took the paper from Leonardo and started reading. The article was brief, only two paragraphs long. It was just as my cousin had reported. Art dealer Angel Estrada had been found dead, fully dressed, on his bed in his Brickell Avenue condominium by a female who had come to visit late last night. Police were investigating the possibility of foul play.

A few minutes passed before I could move. I read the article over and over, as if I was going to find something new. It was almost impossible to imagine Angel dead, since I had seen him so recently. I went into private-eye mode. Sometimes it was possible to read between the lines in a newspaper article, but in this case there were too few lines for me to read between.

The *Herald* gave me no details to chew on. It could have been a heart attack. Angel certainly didn't look as though he visited a gym on a regular basis, or watched his food and alcohol intake. From the little I knew about him, I didn't think he was a moderation freak. Suicide was unlikely. He wouldn't have taken his own life, not with the plans he was hatching and the enthusiasm he showed for them. A break-in? I knew the building in which he lived. It was a fortress to get into. An overdose of drugs? Maybe. The article said that he was fully clothed in bed when he was found. That would seem to rule out asphyxiation during kinky sex games. What about this female visitor—what did she have to do with it?

I composed myself enough to get up off the couch and head into my office. I sat down at my desk, glancing out the window to check on my parrots. They were working on a new nest, babbling and flapping their wings. I watched them for a while, unsure what—if anything—I should do about Angel's death.

I ran through my options, and none of them seemed right. There was, of course, no real need for me to do much at all. Angel's death didn't have to have anything to do with me. All it meant was that there would be no further action on his plan involving his sister Camila. It was probably too soon for her to have heard about his death, although it wouldn't be long—news traveled between Havana and Miami with lightning speed. I quickly stopped myself from speculating on Camila's grief; there was nothing I could do, and dwelling on it was counterproductive.

I thought about calling one of my police contacts to see if I could get any information, but quickly decided against it. If foul play was involved, my call would alert the police to my professional interest in Angel's death. I had one contact at the *Herald*—Marisa Maldonado, a reporter on the crime beat—but she would also be curious about my interest and might start digging to see what she could find. There was nothing for me to hide, really, but Angel had been a good contact for me despite my negative feelings toward him. Professional pride and respect for him precluded me from exposing even a dead source.

There had to be another way of getting information, I just had to think of it. In the meanwhile, the matter of Lucia and the tapestry was still hanging over me. Lucia had made it clear that time was critical, and if I were to take the case, I would have to come up with a viable plan for handling it. I could still hear Alvaro's angry voice in my ears, lecturing me about the danger I was courting and saying that I was using my mother as justification.

The *Herald* article stared up at me from my desk. I tried not to let frustration creep into my mind. I kept rereading the sentence about the late-night female visitor, the one who found Angel. I knew Angel was unmarried, and that he had come to Miami with his brother. I assumed he had no close female relatives in Dade County. Angel could have been entertaining a girlfriend, but there was the matter of his ugliness. I couldn't picture a woman spending time with him by choice. By process of elimination, that left call girls. Now that I thought of it, the *Herald* would have mentioned it if the woman had been a relative or a fiancée. I didn't know who Angel might have hired, but I certainly knew someone who was plugged into that part of Miami society. It had been a while since I talked to her, but I still could dial her number from memory.

"Suzanne?" I said.

"Lupe!" I heard her familiar, high-pitched little-girl voice. She sounded delighted to hear from me. "*Hola, chica!* How's the P.I. business?"

Sweet Suzanne was like a lifetime friend to me. Although we didn't meet or speak very often, we always instantly picked up where we had left off the last time we saw one other. And from time to time we helped each other out professionally—no questions asked.

Suzanne was originally from a tiny town outside of Minneapolis. She had long ago shed any trace of farm-fresh innocence, but she was smart enough not to let on. She was tall, with cornflower-clear blue eyes, a peaches-and-cream complexion never darkened by the sun, and platinum-blond hair. She stood out in Miami crowds, a fact upon which she never failed to capitalize. She confided to me once that her gynecologist had told her she was the only one of his patients without a tan line. She was savvy and knew the worth of her distinctiveness, working diligently to maintain her pallor.

Sweet Suzanne was also Dade County's premiere madam. She had started out as a call girl, but after making enough money and connections, began managing the most sought-after stable of girls in Miami. Her client list—male and female—read like a who's who of the business, media, and sports figures of South Florida. She was the local equivalent of the infamous Madame Claude of Paris.

"*Hola* yourself," I said to her. I couldn't resist teasing her. "So, how's the sex business? Now that Viagra's on the market, I'll bet your girls don't have to work as hard."

Suzanne gave the throaty laugh that was so loved by her clients. "*Sí,* that's true."

A beat of silence passed between us. Suzanne laughed

again and said, "Lupe, I know you too well. This isn't a social call. I hate to rush you, but I have someone coming over in a couple of minutes. I need time to prepare."

I didn't really want to know what that meant, so I quickly said, "Do you have an Angel Estrada on your client list?"

No sooner had I spoken the words than I felt a chill on the line.

"I should have known you were plugged into that one, Lupe," Suzanne said. She sounded almost melancholy. "Angel was no angel. But you probably know that. My girls hated to be with him. He had to pay extra."

"Suzanne, I barely knew the man," I said hastily. "He helped me out on a couple of cases. I was just going to ask if it was one of your girls who found the body."

"*Gracias a Dios* you didn't know him too well." Suzanne was fluent in Spanish, and she always peppered her speech with unaccented phrases. "He wasn't the kind you want to get too close to."

"How so?" I asked, wincing.

"The man was an animal."

"So it was one of your girls who found him," I said.

"*Sí*, it was Ingrid. She went there for a date and found him dead on the bed."

I said nothing. I hoped Suzanne's appointment was late, because I wanted more details.

"Ingrid found Angel with a pair of panty hose wrapped around his throat," Suzanne added. "He was strangled when she got there. And that's all she knows."

"The paper said he was dressed. Is that true?"

"That's what Ingrid told me," Suzanne said.

"So he didn't die during fun and games?"

"No, not unless he had another call girl over before Ingrid," Suzanne explained. "But that's not likely. Angel was a regular. Ingrid said he could barely perform with her. He was just passive. There's no way he would have been with another girl before he had a date with her."

"So you're saying he was murdered," I offered.

I heard a buzzing in the background. Suzanne's guest had arrived. *Mierda.*

"Hey, Lupe, I have to go," she said. "Call me soon, all right? We'll get together. It's been too long."

Suzanne was speaking in such a rush that I could barely understand her.

"So you think Angel was murdered?" I repeated. "Strangled?"

Suzanne sighed. "I think so," she said. "And it was no great loss, if you ask me. Call me, OK, *chica?* I miss you!"

She hung up. I put the phone down slowly.

Angel Estrada, murdered. Why? He wasn't exactly a fine, upstanding pillar of the community. Had he been killed over a shady deal, or because he knew something that made him dangerous to someone? And was it a coincidence that he'd been killed within hours of meeting with me?

I blinked, wondered whether there was a connection. Whether someone might come looking for me next.

Leonardo was right. We should have a *lavado* to ward off evil spirits. Suddenly, it felt as though they were all around me.

After I hung up with Suzanne, I mulled things over for a minute. Obviously Ingrid had called the police for self-protection after discovering Angel's body, to make sure that the crime wasn't pinned on her by someone who witnessed her going in or out of the condo. In Suzanne's line of work it was far better to cooperate with the authorities than to hide anything from them. Concealing information would eventually backfire, and as a bonus, from time to time the police helped Suzanne out with information—such as the time they warned her that a crusading prosecutor with political ambitions had set his sights on her operation.

I hadn't liked Angel, but I certainly wouldn't have wished his life to end as it had. Now, though, I had to be concerned whether anything connected his murder back to me. I knew I couldn't just sit around and wait.

I picked up the phone and hit a number on my speed dial. Alvaro would have been appalled to know who I was calling.

"Detective Anderson, please," I requested.

Silence on the line, then a couple of grunts that I recognized as two men communicating with each other.

"Anderson here."

"This is Lupe Solano."

"Hey, Lupe. Long time, huh?" In his laconic fashion, Detective Anderson actually seemed pleased to hear from me, although he probably knew that when he did, a dead body was invariably lurking somewhere. "So, is this a social call, you want to talk about old times? Or have you found some more bodies you need me to deal with?"

This was what, for Anderson, passed for humor. I could picture him in his khaki suit—the same one he always wore, the one he probably slept in. He would be slouching at his desk, the phone tucked under his chin, his gray eyes narrowing with suspicion. Very little surprised him. I figured doctors had a hard time finding a pulse on him, although I was sure, if I listened hard enough, I would find his acute and active brain humming away as he processed information. Detective Anderson was a rarity in Miami: he was part of an endangered species, what the census-takers called "non-Hispanic whites."

"Well, I am calling you about a body. But you've already found it." I chose my words very carefully. "It's about Angel Estrada. I read the article in the *Herald*."

I certainly wasn't going to let Anderson know I'd received inside information from Sweet Suzanne.

"Oh, God. That's my case," he groaned. I couldn't blame the poor man for his reaction. I knew he was thinking of the body count on the last case on which we were both involved.

"Don't worry. I wasn't working for the victim, or for anything connected to him," I said.

"OK," Anderson said, noncommittal.

I shook my head silently, unable to believe the chain of coincidences that was following me. What were the chances that, of all the homicide investigators in Dade County, Detective Anderson would have the lead on Angel's death?

"Listen, I knew you'd be reconstructing Angel's final hours," I told him. "So I thought I should tell you I had lunch with him yesterday at the Grand Bay Hotel."

As soon as I said it, I worried that I'd revealed too much. The *Herald* reported only that Angel was dead, not that he'd been murdered. But I had tipped my hand already, just by calling Anderson. Of course, by telling me he was the investigator on the case, he was reconfirming my information. It was a delicate game we tended to play, circling each other.

"Did you know him well?" Detective Anderson asked.

"Not really. It was a business lunch." As always, I wanted to cooperate as much as possible without revealing too much. "Angel Estrada had helped me out on a couple of cases."

"Were you collaborating on anything current?" Anderson asked.

I could see where he was going. He was looking for a motive for Angel's death. As a private eye, I could feasibly help him with that. The fact was, I wanted to know the same thing. For Detective Anderson it was a professional matter; for me, it was an issue of my personal safety.

"No," I said.

I liked and respected Anderson. He'd always been fair to me, and had helped me out more than once. But I didn't feel obliged to tell him anything about Angel's proposal to me. It would be betraying a confidence.

"No?" he asked. "That's it?"

"Mostly we followed up on the old cases," I said. "It was a keeping-in-touch kind of lunch."

"You're not holding out on me, are you, Lupe?" Anderson asked. I had forgotten how well he'd gotten to know me. "Because, if you are, grateful as I am that you got in touch with me, I'll still come down hard on you."

"It was just a lunch. Honestly." Which was, in a sense, true. "I'll tell you if I think of anything that could help your investigation."

"All right. I'm sure you will." Anderson's tone softened.

"I might as well tell you some of the details, seeing as how you knew him and you were one of the last people to see him alive. You're going to tell me if you think of anything new, right?"

He took my silence for a yes.

"Angel Estrada was found lying in his bed, face up, fully clothed, with a pair of panty hose around his neck," Anderson recited.

I made a noncommittal noise. Sweet Suzanne's information, as usual, was dead on.

"It's too soon yet for the medical examiner's report, but I'm assuming he was strangled by the panty hose," Anderson continued. "That's the preliminary finding, anyway. Approximate time of death was nine P.M. We can nail that one down pretty well because the body was still warm when the victim was found."

"What about the scene?" I asked. Might as well push my luck.

"The crime-scene guys didn't see anything that jumped out at them," Anderson replied. "Either the guy was a neat freak, or else he had a hell of a housekeeper. The place was immaculate. Wish my apartment was as clean."

"Maybe you could get a referral for a cleaning service from Angel's address book," I mused.

Anderson paused, unsure whether I was joking. "Anyway, that should make the tech's job a lot easier. They swept for hair, fibers, all that. I'm waiting for their report."

"Any marks or bruises on the body?" I asked. "Or just around the neck?"

I heard a faint rustle of paper as Anderson flipped through his notes. "Well, you know, with this kind of strangulation you get the usual bruises and contusions," he said. "The ones on the victim's neck were consistent with strangulation. But I have to tell you, Lupe, it was hard to see his bruises with the naked eye because his neck and face were so dark with blood. Whoever did this had a strong grip."

That must have been how they ruled out Suzanne's call girl, who I doubted was a bodybuilder capable of such extremely violent strangulation.

"Any chance he was playing games with himself and got carried away?" I asked.

"Autoerotic asphyxiation?" Anderson said. "No chance. None at all. I've seen a few of those cases. This victim's injuries were too severe to have been self-inflicted."

"What about the panty hose?" I asked. "What's with that?"

"I have no explanation," Anderson said. "Unless it was a clumsy attempt to make us think it was an accident, that the victim died during autoerotic asphyxiation."

"Maybe the killer knew something about Angel," I said. "I wouldn't know. But maybe he was into those kinds of games, and the killer used this knowledge to try to make it look like an accident."

I had managed to give Anderson a good idea without tipping the fact that I knew a call girl had found Angel. I didn't want Anderson learning about my sources of information.

Anderson was quiet for a moment, thinking this over. "A good theory," he said. I heard him write something down. "It's still early in the investigation. You know how one thing leads to another. We'll wait and see what comes back from the lab."

"Can you call me when you get the report?" I asked. I didn't know how long Anderson's spirit of cooperation was going to last, but I figured there was no harm trying to prolong it.

"Lupe, are you sure you're not holding back on me?" Anderson snapped back. "You're awfully interested in the case for someone who says she barely knew the victim."

"Put yourself in my situation," I answered. "A man I worked with a couple of times was found murdered just hours after I had lunch with him. Wouldn't you want to know what happened—out of professional curiosity?"

Anderson murmured something to himself. He knew I was an inveterate bullshitter, but he also knew that, overall, I was a stand-up investigator.

"I suppose," he sighed. "But I know how your mind works. I think you know more than you're telling me, and I'm not too proud to say that I could use some help on this. You knew the guy, you saw him right before the murder. And you have a good investigative mind."

I blushed at the compliment. Anderson rarely doled out praise.

"I'd rather have you working with me on this than going off by yourself," he continued. "Which is what I know you're going to do, all your protestations to the contrary."

"Thanks for the kind words," I said, sidestepping the main content of what he'd said to me. "So you'll call me?"

He sighed again, sounding exhausted. "OK. I'll call you when I get results from the lab."

Until then I needed to find out if I had anything to fear.

"One more thing," Anderson said. "The victim had a brother. Did you know about him?"

"Sorry," I replied. "Angel might have mentioned him once. But that's it."

"We're trying to find him," Anderson said. "I thought you might be able to help me."

"I can't help you," I said.

"Lupe, give me something," Anderson replied.

I paused. "I know Angel's brother came over with him on the Mariel," I offered. "He has family in Cuba."

"Now was that so hard?" Anderson asked, then hung up.

I wondered if Angel's mother and sister in Cuba had been

notified yet about the death. Another Cuban family had been separated permanently by the forces of history and politics. What a waste.

"Lupe," Leonardo announced on the intercom, breaking through my suddenly melancholy thoughts. "Tommy's on line one."

I blinked at the light on the phone for a few seconds before I registered what my cousin had told me. It had been quite a while since Tommy McDonald and I had spoken. We used to talk nearly every day. But that was before Alvaro came into the picture.

I picked up the receiver. "*Hola*," I said.

"*Querida!*" Tommy's voice boomed over the wire. As soon as I heard his tone, he had my attention. He wanted something from me. "How have you been?"

"Fine. And you?" I replied warily. I had missed him, though I would have cut my own throat before admitting it.

"How's your schedule?" Tommy asked teasingly. "Keeping busy?" Then he added, in a probing manner, "Or has your Cuban boyfriend been occupying all your time?"

Tommy McDonald, curious about my relationship with Alvaro, sounding jealous? I couldn't believe it. His veins were supposed to be filled with ice water.

"Busy enough," I said without commenting on his question. The events with Alvaro at Tuscan Steak had left unhealed wounds, so I decided to stick to business. "Why? Do you have a case for me?"

"Maybe." Tommy paused, put off balance by my obvious attempt to keep the conversation on a professional footing. I could picture him sitting in his office, chair tipped back as far as it would go, his long legs stretched out over his huge mahogany desk, smoking a Montecristo Number One, looking out at Biscayne Bay outside his window.

"Maybe yes, or maybe no?" I pressed.

"I think you'll be interested in what I have to talk to you about," he countered. "You want to hear?"

I thought for a second. Tommy knew me very well. If he thought I'd be interested, then it would invariably be something that captured my imagination.

"Civil or criminal?" I asked.

"Could be both," Tommy said. "It's just up your alley, since I hear you're now specializing in Cuban art."

My eyes widened. Art again. Tommy knew me too damned well. I had shared my feelings with him when we were working the Wilfredo Lam case for Tia Alicia. Tommy understood that the recovery of appropriated artworks played into my passion for, and fascination with, my homeland.

"I'm pretty busy, Tommy." I knew it was a lame response, but I had mixed feelings. I also knew that once I heard about the case, I would be hooked.

"Tell you what," he said. "Are you busy tonight? We could have dinner. Then I'll spell everything out for you."

I had no plans. Alvaro and I hadn't spoken since the fiasco at Tuscan Steak.

"I don't know," I replied, horrified with myself. Was I becoming a wimp? I knew what dinner with Tommy meant. I would be walking into a personal and professional minefield. When two people had a history together—particularly Tommy and me—nothing was simple or easy.

Alvaro and I had been together for about a year. We had never really discussed our relationship, and it wasn't a formal thing. But it was understood that we were excluding other romantic entanglements. Dinner with Tommy would be an admission to him that the door was still open. Alvaro and I had had a possibly permanent falling out, but meeting Tommy at night could have serious implications.

On a professional level, Tommy knew he could always

convince me to work with him. That's the way it had always been. But I was already swamped with planning the Miranda case and with the consequences of Angel's death. I knew my ego would never let me turn a good case down, even one that I didn't have the time to work. Of course, this wouldn't be the first time I worked several cases simultaneously.

"An early dinner," Tommy said in his most persuasive voice. "I'll pick you up at your office at seven."

He knew I was weakening. My resistance was fading away like a Miami sunset.

"Please, Lupe, even if you don't agree to work the case, at least give me some guidance on it. That's all, really. I need some help, and you know a lot about this Cuban art stuff."

It wasn't every day that the most successful criminal-defense attorney in Dade County came begging for my help. Most of all, I was unwilling to let my doubts take hold— they felt too much like weaknesses. No one ever told me what to do. If I wanted to have dinner, then I would have dinner.

"OK. Seven it is." I hung up before I could get into any more trouble.

I shook my head as I put the phone down. We had both known I was going to accept. The question now: what exactly had I agreed to?

10

I had barely put down the phone after talking to Tommy when it rang again. I picked up, then tried not to shudder when I heard Lucia Miranda's raspy voice on the line. There was a lot of static in the background, but not enough to disguise Lucia's irritatingly grating speech.

"Guadalupe? This is Lucia Miranda. Can you hear me?"

"Not really," I said. "This isn't a very clear connection. Is there a number where I can call you back?"

"No, I'm on a cellular," Lucia replied. "I'll move and see if the reception improves."

I waited while Lucia presumably sought out a better spot. When she came back on the line, much of the static was gone.

"That's better," I said. "How are you?"

I knew this wasn't a social call, but there were proprieties to be observed.

"Not well at all," Lucia snapped. "I'm at Baptist Hospital with Mama. We're at the emergency room. We've been here for more than two hours, and still no one has helped her. She collapsed at the house and I called 911. Now I know it would have been faster to drive her to the doctor's office myself."

"I hope it's not serious," I said. I wasn't sure what sort of comment Lucia was trying to evoke from me, although I knew where Lucia was heading with this.

"Now, listen to me, Lupe." Lucia must have started moving around, because the static hiss reappeared on the line. "I know this is putting pressure on you, but I must have your decision regarding the tapestry. Mama is not well, and I fear that her time is short."

"You know I can't guarantee anything," I began. "What you're asking is very risky—both for me and for the tapestry. If I get caught trying to smuggle it back to Miami, then the Cuban government will throw me in jail."

I paused, hoping Lucia would understand the gravity of what I was saying. I could almost feel Alvaro's presence hovering like an unwelcome guest, breathing on my neck with seething disapproval.

"Also, the government would then confiscate the tapestry," I added. "You'd never see it again. Have you thought about that?"

"Of course I realize that," Lucia said, irritated. "But then we don't have possession of it now either, do we?"

"You do and you don't," I countered. "You don't have physical possession of it, but as far as you know it's still safely hidden in the secret basement in Havana. Maybe one day, when the situation changes, you'll be able to go back and retrieve it legally."

The telephone spit out a haze of noise into my ear. These weren't optimal conditions under which to be having such a crucial conversation.

"Mama will not last that long," Lucia said. "We have heard that Fidel Castro is on the verge of death for years. All those inside sources, saying that he has Parkinson's, cancer, God only knows what else. All that is nothing but *mierda*. Wishful thinking! But, Lupe, Mama's cancer is real!"

Lucia's voice rose and became even more strident. I could tell that the stress was getting to her.

As I thought about Lucia Miranda, I was almost softened up to the point of feeling sorry for her. She was in her fifties, unmarried, and had devoted most of her adult life to her family and, more to the point, her parents. First her father had fallen ill, now her mother. The other five children were all men, with families of their own, so all the responsibility for her parents fell on Lucia. That had been her function in life for as long as anyone could remember. If she'd had a love interest somewhere along the way, then nothing became of it—I surely would have heard otherwise, the way upper-class Cuban-exile gossip traveled.

The more I thought about it, the more it made sense. Lucia's life was devoted to her mother now, and if she were unable to make her mother's dying wish come true, her own life would be a failure. This was a sort of final validation of the choices she had made.

"You have a point," I allowed. "But the risks involved in bringing the tapestry out of Cuba are enormous."

Not the least of which was the prospect of my spending the rest of my life in a Cuban jail—not exactly the Ritz-Carlton or the Four Seasons. I closed my eyes, willed away visions of Alvaro's scowling face.

"Look, Lupe, I cannot discuss this with you any longer," Lucia snapped. "Do you want the job or not?"

"*Sí.*"

The word came out of my mouth much more easily than I thought it would. This undoubtedly meant that Alvaro and I were finished. How could we keep seeing each other when I had gone against something he felt so strongly about? He was progressive and liberal, but he was still a Cuban man. He would never be able to forgive me. And I wasn't sure I could forgive him for bringing Mami into it.

I heard Lucia's sigh of relief, even through the static buzz. "Oh, wonderful. Tell me what you're going to charge. I'll have a check at your office first thing in the morning."

If only all my clients were so forthcoming with their wallets and checkbooks. In spite of my deep hurt and burning disappointment over the way things were left between Alvaro and me, I felt a sense of peace now that I had taken the case. Clearly the repercussions of what I'd agreed to had yet to hit me—although I knew seeing the check would soften the blow.

"I really have no idea what this is going to cost," I said, unwilling to lock myself into a number. Even ordinary cases often ran up fees much higher than I had initially imagined. And I didn't want to have to keep going back to Lucia for more money.

Another thought occurred to me. If I went to Cuba—which I wasn't sure would be necessary—and I was caught trying to smuggle out the tapestry, then I needed to have lots of cash for legal fees and all the bribes I would have to fork out. It wasn't to my advantage to work the case on an hourly basis—I needed a big retainer up front.

"Well, you'll need money to get started," Lucia said. "Just tell me how much."

I paused. "Thirty thousand."

A second of silence. "All right. It will be there in the morning."

"Thank you," I replied. I felt a moment of panic. It was still possible to back out, wasn't it?

No, it wasn't. I was in. I had been hooked from the moment Lucia told me about the eighth tapestry.

Was it because Mami had loved the tapestries so much, was that why I was willing to take this insane risk? Was it to honor my mother, and her belief that the eighth tapestry had existed?

Maybe. I knew one thing, though. I sure as hell wasn't taking the case so that Leonardo could buy more gym equipment to shrink his Cuban ass.

Lucia hung up, giving me no escape.

I reached into my desk drawer and pulled out the manila envelope she'd left. I plopped it in front of me and stared at it, leaving it unopened.

Then I sighed and tipped the envelope. The first thing that fell out was the silver ring with its pair of keys. Keys, I thought. They opened doors, such as that of the secret Miranda basement in Havana. They also locked doors, such as prison cells. I wondered which I would be facing in the next couple of weeks.

Promptly at seven I heard the buzz of our outer door chiming. I hated that noise and, as I got up to answer it, cursed the fact that I had never gotten Leonardo to change it to a nice bell chime or whatever was the fashion nowadays.

I looked through the door. Tommy, right on time. I felt like a schoolgirl when my heart gave a little kick. He looked better than ever, dressed in a Saville Row double-breasted dark gray suit with faint pinstripes. He wore a light pink shirt, with white collar and cuffs, crisp even at this hour after a day of the punishing Miami heat. His red Ferragamo tie depicted animals, perhaps aardvarks, cavorting amid exotic trees. Tommy always looked perfectly groomed, even after a long session in bed. How he managed it was beyond me. I could only attribute it to a gift from whatever Irish saint protected him.

"Lupe, *querida*." Tommy took my hands in his and slowly bent down to kiss my cheek. "You are as beautiful as ever."

Oh, he was smooth. I wished there had been time to shower and change before dinner. I felt grubby and underdressed in my jeans and T-shirt, my usual office attire when not meeting clients.

"Thank you." I smiled. "You look terrific as well."

I picked up my purse from Leonardo's desk and started turning off lights in preparation for locking up the office. Tommy watched me in silence, then, when I was finished, put his hand lightly under my elbow to escort me out. I cursed the espadrilles on my feet; they emphasized the height difference between us of more than a foot. I didn't like to be at any sort of disadvantage with a man, especially Tommy.

"I thought we could go to Le Festival for dinner," Tommy offered. "It's quiet there, and we'll be able to talk in private."

Somehow Tommy managed to make this sound suggestive. Le Festival was a French restaurant on Salzedo Street in the Gables with an unhurried, Old World ambiance that was frequented mostly by locals. It was ideal for a long conversation and, I thought, Alvaro would never go there. The fact that Alvaro and I had a fight didn't mean that I wanted to flaunt my dinner with Tommy in his face.

The restaurant was only a few minutes from my office. I saw the valet's eyes light up when he saw Tommy's Rolls-Royce turn into the driveway. Tommy was known throughout Miami as an extravagant tipper.

We were escorted to a table in the main room. The maitre d' handed us menus, gave Tommy the wine list. Tommy ordered a Gevrey Chambertin, which we had enjoyed together many times in the past. I tried not to think about the fact that it was also what Alvaro and I had been drinking several nights before. The waiter arrived and recited the specials as he opened and poured the wine. We made our choices and sat side by side in comfortable silence. It didn't seem possible that so much time had passed since we had been together.

I figured I'd better start discussing business before other matters interfered. "Tell me about the case," I said.

Behind his glasses, Tommy's light brown eyes shone with intelligence and a certain fire that I recognized.

"I obviously don't have to explain to you the need for secrecy on the matters we're about to discuss," he said. He took a big sip of wine, wiped his mouth. "But I'll mention it anyway."

"Duly noted."

"I told you this had to do with Cuban art," Tommy began. I nodded. "My client, a Cuban, has been accused of buying stolen property. He's being sued by the wronged party—the 'real owner' of the property in question."

"And this 'real owner' is another Cuban, right?" I asked. "And the piece of property is Cuban art that the wronged party used to own in Cuba?"

"Right on both counts." Tommy drained his glass, reached for the bottle to pour another. The waiter appeared from nowhere, intercepted the bottle, and carefully refilled both our glasses.

"Don't torture me," I said. "Tell me more." My curiosity was killing me. I wondered if I knew either of the parties involved.

"Lupe, you know perfectly well that I'm not at liberty to discuss the details of the situation. Unless . . ." He let the thought dangle.

"Unless I'm the investigator of record," I said, finishing his sentence. Tommy looked up as our dinners arrived, sized up his veal chop like a true predator. I could see that he wasn't budging. It was time to fish or cut bait. If I was going to find out more, I was going to have to agree to work on the case.

Oh, what the hell.

"OK, I'm in," I said. "Talk."

Tommy chewed a slice of veal, took a sip of wine. I knew he was trying to conceal a look of triumph.

"My client—" he began, then stopped. "Oh, sorry. *Our* client bought a Tomas Sanchez landscape for a quarter million dollars. The man who claims to be the rightful owner says he can document the fact that the painting was, in fact, his property."

"Where did your client buy the painting?" I lost interest in my veal with Calvados sauce, a rare occasion for me.

"Our client," Tommy corrected me. "He bought it from a gallery in Coral Gables—one that's no longer doing business."

"What about—"

Tommy preempted my question. "The gallery owner? Nowhere to be found. Naturally."

"So your—*our* client is the 'deep pockets'?"

Tommy nodded. We had worked our way through the bottle of wine, with half our main courses left to be finished. There was obviously nothing to be done but order a second bottle, which Tommy did with a discreet gesture.

"Our client claims he thought he had clear title to the painting," Tommy explained. "He says he knew the painting had come out of Cuba, but he thought that it had changed hands legitimately, that the owner had sold it years ago. Apparently it changed hands a few times before it reached the gallery. He even showed me the provenance. I think our guy is on the up-and-up, Lupe. But you never know."

I understood Tommy completely. Clients had sworn to us both on their sainted mothers in Heaven, with the straightest of faces, that what they were saying was the truth, when in fact they were lying through their teeth—their poor sainted mothers could be expelled from Heaven to rot in hell, for all they cared.

"Who are these people, and where do I come in?" I asked. My interest in the veal had returned, and I set about eating it.

Tommy watched me eat with amusement. He had always said that it was a pleasure to take me to a restaurant. No designer lettuce, dressing on the side, for me.

The veal was so delicious that I had to restrain myself from mopping up the remaining Calvados sauce with a piece of bread. I knew Mami was watching from Heaven, and she would be compelled to do penance if she witnessed me acting in such a savage manner. She might even be sent to Purgatory to atone for my sins against propriety.

"The client is Fernando Valdez Correa. He's retained me on other matters in the past, with good results, so he brought this to me. Hopefully it won't turn into a criminal case, but you never know."

"OK." I took a deep breath. "And the 'rightful owner'?"

"Mateo Mora." Tommy chuckled, and I joined him. What else could we do, considering who the players were?

Both names were known to me, as well as most other Cuban exiles. Valdez Correa was a "new Cuban" who had arrived during the Mariel in 1980 and who had made a ton of money. He bought a mom-and-pop grocery store and parlayed it into the largest chain of grocery stores catering to Hispanic tastes in the entire Southeast. Then he acquired a chain of hot-sheets motels and upgraded them very successfully into businessmen's hotels. He had the Midas touch, and he was a renowned workaholic. He was always being profiled in stories about exiles who had succeeded in America against the odds. It was rumored that he had sold his mother-in-law's gold wedding ring to stake his first business.

Mateo Mora, on the other hand, was old-guard Cuban—

of the Moras in the sugar business in Cuba. His patrician photograph appeared regularly in the social pages of the *Neuvo Herald* and *Diario de las Americas*. There wasn't a Hispanic charitable foundation in Miami that didn't have him or his wife, Elisa, on the board of directors.

"*Mierda*. No wonder you wanted me to help you," I said. Tommy was a very successful attorney, but he wasn't plugged into the players of Cuban-exile society—unless they had been charged with a crime. He knew I had been born into Miami Cuban society; if there was something I didn't know, I could always find it out.

"I figured you could cut through the shit and tell me about trafficking in Cuban art," Tommy said. "I mean, you really had to dig into the subject when you were helping out your aunt. Right?"

"*Sí*. But those were isolated cases, Tommy," I replied. "I worked them because I was asked to, almost as favors. That doesn't make me an expert in the field."

Tommy said nothing, staring into his wineglass.

"One question," I said. "Did your client know whether the painting was on consignment to the gallery? Or did the dealer claim to own it outright?"

"Good question," Tommy said. "God, you got me there. I don't really remember if we touched on the subject. We should have. I'll have to refer back to the file."

The waiter arrived to clear away our plates. We waited until we were presented with the dessert menus. I had needed a night out like this, I realized. It allowed me a momentary escape from my agreement with Lucia Miranda, from the pitiable image of Angel lying dead in his bed, and from my mixed feelings over walking away from Alvaro.

"I know one thing." Tommy pushed his glasses higher on his nose. "Before he came to me, Valdez Correa tried to find the dealer who sold him the painting in the first place. He told me the guy had just disappeared. The gallery was closed, the place was empty, no one knew anything. He hired a P.I., but it didn't go far. I have the report at my office. I'll have it sent over to you."

The client had gone to another investigator for help. I was burning with curiosity to know which investigator it had been—I was familiar with most P.I.'s in Miami, as well as the quality of their work. Once I knew who it had been, I would be able to tell—without opening the report—whether I would have to duplicate their investigation or if I could trust their work.

"How do you propose we get started?" I asked, a hint of excitement in my voice. Hearing it, I realized how thrilled I was over the prospect of working with Tommy again.

"Obviously I'm looking into the legal aspects," Tommy said. "Such as the purchaser's responsibility regarding ascertaining ownership of artworks and so on. I think you could start by seeing what you can dig up about black market trafficking in art out of Cuba. That's what this is all going to point back to."

I blinked at Tommy. He had no idea what he was saying. Black market art traffic out of Cuba, for me, was what *everything* was beginning to point back to.

"OK. That's a good place for me to begin," I told him. "I have my notes from the Pelaez and the Lam cases, so there's already a body of information to start from. That'll save time."

"I'll courier over the file from the other P.I. first thing in the morning," Tommy said. He began studying the dessert menu with the same intensity that he displayed when he was preparing for trial. The discussion about the case was now over, which was fine with me. I didn't want to have to keep sidestepping the issue of the Miranda case and the Angel Estrada matter, each of which might intersect with the case Tommy had introduced.

Tommy ordered tiramisu. I had double-chocolate mousse cake, with a scoop of vanilla ice cream on the side. We sipped the rest of the wine. This was my favorite kind of business dinner. You'd never see me ordering chicken Caesar salad washed down with sugarless iced tea.

No more conversation took place while we consumed our desserts. No doubt about it—Tommy and I knew where our priorities lay. When we were finished, the plates were so clean that washing them for the next customer would be a formality. We ordered double espressos and large Courvoisiers, then sat back, sated.

I looked over at Tommy. Like me, he was a creature of excess. And there was a gleam in his eye, different from the all-business persona of a few minutes before.

"What?" I asked.

He smiled, almost shyly. "It's been a while, Lupe." I was surprised by the tentative tone of his voice. "I've missed you."

This side of Tommy was surprising, almost shocking. Usually he kept his humanity hidden from view. His idea of a soft side was letting his opponents limp away with their lives.

The thing was, I missed him as well. We went very far back, both professionally and personally. We were deeply embedded in each other's lives, and there was no making that go away.

The waiter brought out our steaming coffees, followed by big balloon glasses half filled with Courvoisier. We alternated sips of coffee with cognac, slipping into an easy enjoyment of one another's company. I really should have seen it coming.

"Got plans?" Tommy asked, barely meeting my eyes before looking away.

"What do you mean?" I asked.

"You know, plans," he said.

"Oh." Now I understood. He wasn't talking long term. As

it had always been between us, we were talking about the here and now.

"Well?" he asked.

I looked into Tommy's eyes, saw his hand moving toward mine on the table. His fingers grazed mine.

"Well?" he repeated.

"Tommy," I said, feeling tentative. "You know about the Cuban lawyer I've been involved with." He nodded slightly. "Well, we had a falling out a couple of days ago."

"A falling out," Tommy said thoughtfully. "Temporary or permanent?"

I shrugged. I wasn't sure, although I wasn't ready to say that my disagreement with Alvaro was definitely going to lead to a permanent split.

"I don't know," I told Tommy. "I just wanted you to know."

I didn't feel like saying much more. Although Alvaro and I had hurt and angered one another, we had been together for a year. I couldn't dismiss my feelings for him, although at the moment I couldn't imagine going back to him. I respected Tommy, and I felt obligated to be as forthcoming with him as possible. It was difficult, though, when I wasn't sure myself what was going on. All I knew at the moment was that I felt right sitting there with Tommy, and I was glad to have such a close friend in my life who understood me so well.

Finally I couldn't stand it any longer. I wasn't going to think about it, I wasn't going to beat it to death with doubts, gnashing of teeth, lamentations and pulling out of hair. Let the cards fall as they may.

"Just get the check," I said. "Then we can get out of here."

I couldn't believe the size of the tip Tommy left in order to get the Rolls brought around as quickly as possible. As I got into the car I saw the valet tucking bills into his vest. Such were the wages of lust.

11

It was after twelve when I got into the office the next day. I didn't need to see Leonardo's look of disapproval to know how he felt about my behavior. I could feel enough negative vibrations coming my way to figure out his opinion. He had known I was having dinner with Tommy, and he was so angry with me that he didn't even offer me coffee, nor did he volunteer to concoct a special drink to counter the effects of a hard night. I knew my appearance told Leo everything he needed to know about what had happened. I had never been able to hide wear and tear very well.

There were a lot of times in the past when I wandered into the office at such a disreputable hour—nearly all of them involving Tommy. Leonardo suspected that Alvaro and I were having troubles—after all, Alvaro hadn't called the office since our dinner, which was unusual. Leo was very fond of my Cuban boyfriend and thought it was time I settled down with a nice Cuban man. For all his far-out ideas and tendencies, my cousin was really quite conservative and protective where I was concerned.

But there was no hiding it, no denying it for me. Tommy and I had reconnected the night before. I hadn't felt the heavy guilt I'd anticipated over being intimate with Tommy while still involved with Alvaro. Perhaps it was because

Tommy knew me so well, and because he never questioned my judgment. It had felt comfortable and perhaps even over-due, like a smoker having a cigarette after a year of ab-staining.

I wanted Tommy to know everything about my time con-straints in the case he'd asked me to work, so I explained to him about the unicorn tapestry and the situation with Angel Estrada. As I'd expected, Tommy's only demand of me was that I be careful. And, of course, he reminded me that he needed to get his case going as soon as possible.

We were lying in bed together after making love, the moonlight shining through Tommy's high-rise window. We had lazily talked about the Tomas Sanchez painting and the case we were now working. I explained to Tommy what I'd learned about the trafficking of artworks appropriated from their legitimate owners. In the course of tracking down the provenance of the Pelaez and the Lam, I had come across an organization based in London called the Art Loss Register, which maintained databases listing stolen and missing valu-able works of art. The registry, set up in 1991, had proven to be invaluable in the cause of returning items to their rightful owners—with a pretty respectable success rate, given the dif-ficulty of the task. I'd had a conversation with one of their directors a few months before and learned how the registry worked. Now it was time to give her another call regarding Cuban art.

I placed the call myself. No sense even talking with Leo-nardo until he had a chance to cool down. My contact at the Art Loss Registry had already left for the day. I was surprised, until I realized that I'd foolishly forgotten to take into account the time difference between Miami and Lon-don. I left a message on my contact's voice mail, reminding her who I was, saying I would call back in the morning.

I hung up the phone and looked out at my parrots. There

was little activity going on; they just perched on their branches, moving little. Maybe they were taking a midday nap. Or perhaps they felt overwhelmed by the enormity of the architectural construction project they had undertaken and decided to regroup before starting again. This was so uncharacteristic, though, that I got up and went over to the window to make sure everything was all right. A couple of them stirred and squawked, as though telling me not to come any closer.

"Don't mind me," I said in a soothing voice.

I returned to my desk, feeling sympathetic to my aviary friends' plight. I was beginning to wonder whether I should have agreed to Tommy's case on top of the Lucia Miranda matter. I could make it all work, I thought, if I broke each case down into manageable proportions. Anyway, I wasn't truly alive unless I was facing a challenge. And it felt right to be working with Tommy again. I had drastically reduced my professional contact with him since I started seeing Alvaro, which was a loss—Tommy and I were nearly always on the same wavelength. We had worked together so many times that we could anticipate each other's thoughts and reactions to what was going on.

I took a deep breath and rested my chin in my hands. I was swimming in dangerous waters. Bringing the tapestry out of Cuba seemed, for the moment, less daunting than what was going on with my romantic life. My feelings for Tommy didn't negate my feelings for Alvaro. Maybe it was unusual, but it didn't seem strange to me to have a strong attraction and fondness for two men at the same time. Men had been acting that way toward women since the beginning of time, hadn't they? So maybe it was fair turnabout for me to behave the same way.

Or was this yet another example of my virtuoso skill at rationalization? What about my suspicion that it wasn't in

my makeup to keep going this way? Why not eat my cake
and have it, too? But no, it was too callous of me to think
that way. I had strong feelings for both Tommy and Alvaro,
I loved and respected each in different ways. They were both
important in my life, and probably always would be.

I realized that all this self-examination wasn't serving my
clients very well. I tore my attention away from the parrots.
Until I got the P.I.'s file from Tommy, there wasn't much
for me to do on his case. I hadn't heard back from Detective
Anderson, so the Angel Miranda matter could wait. Anyway,
I hadn't been shot at or strangled yet—so far so good.

I would have to do some research on the tapestry and
determine how to best get it out of Cuba. I knew the perfect
place to begin. I gathered my things and walked through the
reception area; fortunately, Leonardo was working out in his
gym, so I didn't have to confront him. The familiar sound
of his grunting and groaning filled my ears as I headed out.

I barely returned Osvaldo and Aida's greetings when I got
home, I was in such a hurry to get to the library and look
through Mami's art books on the *Hunt of the Unicorn* tapestries. As I reached for them, a feeling of sadness came over
me and I felt my eyes mist over. No one had opened the
books since Mami died, and she had surely been the last
person to touch them. Aida dusted the library daily but
rarely pulled a book from the shelves. I was surprised to see
how worn-out the art books were from use, with some of
the pages folded over and little notes tucked between them,
written in Spanish in Mami's handwriting, about the beauty
and grace of the unicorns.

I sensed someone enter the room behind me. It was
Osvaldo.

"Lupe, *buenas tardes*," he said in his gentle way. I saw his
eyes pass over the books I was holding. He knew how much
Mami had loved the unicorn tapestries and how much they

meant to her. "You came in so quickly I didn't have an opportunity to ask if I can get you anything."

"No, nothing for now. *Gracias*, Osvaldo," I said. "I'll be in here for a while."

I didn't offer an explanation for what I was doing there, I just clutched the books to my chest in front of the picture window. Osvaldo had seen my watery eyes, and he nodded and slowly left, his steps creaking on the floorboards. If he was surprised or curious about why I was so interested in Mami's books eight years after her death, he didn't show it. Tears fell on my cheeks as I looked through the glossy pages and carefully read the little notes next to her favorite paintings.

The photographs brought back memories of family trips to New York, and of Mami taking us to the Cloisters. I remembered Papi scolding her in a good-natured way, saying that she was wasting the price of admission to the place, since she really only took us to the gallery where the *Hunt of the Unicorn* tapestries were displayed.

I took out the photo of the eighth tapestry, which Lucia had given me, and put it next to the others in the book. I hated to admit it, since the Mirandas were now my clients, but John D. Rockefeller had been right in trying to acquire the last tapestry—they should have been kept together, as a set. Well, if I brought the eighth one into America, they would at least be in the same country.

I heard a soft knock at the door. Osvaldo came into the library bearing a tray with a glass and the fixings for *mojitos*. The tray also contained a small bowl of *mariquitas* glistening with oil. I suspected Osvaldo had been thinking of Mami when he prepared the tray, which contained her favorites.

"It looks like you're going to be here for a while, Lupe," Osvaldo said. "I thought you would need some refreshment."

Osvaldo winked at me, almost too fast to see, and started pouring from the silver shaker without asking my permission.

"*Muchas gracias,*" I replied. The *mojito* would actually be quite welcome, since the excesses of the night before were beginning to wear off.

"Will you be having dinner at home?" Osvaldo asked. "The whole family will be here tonight."

I knew this was a gentle reprimand for all the meals I'd missed at home. "Aida is making *arroz con pollo,*" he volunteered; then, after a pause, he added in a tempting manner, "*Chorreado.*"

Chicken and yellow rice dripping in sauce—the unofficial Cuban national dish. I could feel my hips spreading as the calories rocketed into the stratosphere.

"I'll be here," I said. *Dios mio.* I'd never be able to fit into my clothes after such a meal. And I knew the calories and fat wouldn't stop there. The one and only vegetable on the plate would be sweet plantains, accompanied by an avocado salad swimming in olive oil. Dessert would comprise heaping scoops of *dulce de leche* creamy caramel ice cream. The notion of the four food groups and the nutritional pyramid were unknown to Cubans—or, at best, a source of derisive humor. As a whole, we were such an arrogant, know-it-all group that we felt exempt from such an American concept as regulating the food we ate. For us, a well-balanced meal meant a huge heap of food distributed evenly over the surface of the plate, so it didn't tip or spill over.

Osvaldo left me alone again. I sipped my *mojito* and started reading the text accompanying the photographs in Mami's book. To begin with, I was interested in the physical dimensions of each of the tapestries. My eyes widened when I read that they were more than twelve feet in height. They hadn't seemed that huge when I saw them hanging on the wall at the Cloisters. I flipped through the catalogue. There was no mention of their weight. How the hell was I going to get something so big out of Cuba? Not in carry-on luggage that I could stash in the overhead bin, that was for sure.

There was another problem if I was going to arrange to transport the tapestry, or do it myself. It had to be packaged correctly, so it wouldn't get damaged. The Miranda tapestry had the advantage of being well taken care of for much longer than the other seven—first it had been stashed in Rogelio Miranda's trunk, then hung safe and dry in the Miranda home. Lucia claimed it was in excellent condition—or at least it had been, when she had last seen it forty years before. There was no way of knowing what had happened since then. Hopefully nothing. I certainly didn't want to risk my neck for a tapestry that had been so damaged it fell to pieces in my hands.

I thought about the reality of the tapestry. It was woven out of textiles. Very old textiles. I realized I would have to pay close attention to the conditions under which I brought it out of Cuba. I was going to have to learn about caring for, storing, and transporting old and delicate textiles.

Easier said than done. The weight of the challenge ahead caused me such momentary consternation that I felt compelled to pour another generous *mojito* from the pitcher Osvaldo had left for me. And, of course, no self-respecting Cuban would dare drink a *mojito* without accompanying it with *mariquitas*. If I continued calming my nerves with such high-calorie sedatives, it was going to be me instead of Leonardo who was contacting Santería priests for *lavados*, and exercise-equipment companies for ass-reducing machines.

What the hell. I would certainly lose weight if I got thrown into a Cuban jail. I figured I might as well enjoy myself while I had the chance.

The four Advils I'd consumed with several glasses of orange juice had done little to stop the pounding in my head caused by all the *mojitos* I ended up drinking that night, not to mention all the red wine I'd had while eating a delicious dinner with my family. I should have restrained myself, but there was no way I could eat a bite of Aida's incredible *arroz con pollo* without washing it down with a few glasses of Sangre de Toro. Besides, who knew when I might have such a lavish dinner again?

Driving into the office, I felt sufficiently contrite to consider phoning Alvaro, trying to make amends for the Tuscan Steak debacle of the other night and to atone for having been with Tommy—although I was still smarting from the comment he'd made about Mami, but I was also unhappy that our relationship had probably ended. I thought we should at least stay in communication, before too much time passed and it became impossible for either of us to pick up the telephone. We were both proud maybe to a fault, and perfectly capable of throwing the baby out with the bathwater.

Besides, the truth was that I missed him. He still meant a lot to me. I wanted to hear his voice. My night with Tommy notwithstanding, I still cared for Alvaro and didn't want things to end on a bitter note. I reached for my car phone to make the call but stopped when I felt the plastic receiver graze my fingertips. It would be a delicate call, and I needed to be in better shape when I made it. I knew it was up to me to make the first approach, but I also knew it had to be done right.

Leonardo was in the kitchen, making a racket, banging pots and pans around, engrossed in some culinary experiment that I would no doubt be enlisted to sample later on. I tried not to speculate on what I might be presented with. The Advils were helping, but my mental state was still a little delicate. The pots clattering sounded like someone playing a snare drum inside my head. It was too much effort to go in and deal with him, so I mumbled a greeting and retired to my office to work until I felt better.

I flipped through a Cloisters Museum catalogue that I had brought from home until I found the page I was looking for. I punched in the phone number for the Education Department and asked to speak to the person in charge of information about the *Hunt of the Unicorn* tapestries. I was in luck. The phone went silent, I was transferred, and the person I needed picked up on the first ring.

"Jan Carrol," said a woman's voice.

"Good morning," I began. "I have a question about the *Hunt of the Unicorn* tapestries."

"Is this for a school group?" Jan asked. She had a high-pitched, tinkly kind of voice. I imagined she had a nice job; low-stress, quiet, surrounded by fine art. I wondered if she wanted to switch places.

"Not exactly," I replied. "I'm interesting in finding out the exact weight of an individual tapestry."

"Now that's an unusual question," Jan said.

"I'm doing research on textiles," I said, hoping that vague explanation was enough.

"Well, as far as I know, there are no exact figures for that," she said. "They're taken down on a semiregular basis for maintenance, but I don't think anyone's ever weighed them."

"Is there anyone else I might ask? Maybe someone who works on maintaining the artworks?"

"I don't think so," Jan replied, in a way that told me she felt I was stepping on her toes. "I'm sorry, but I can't provide that information for you. Is there anything else I can help you with?"

I said no, thanks, and hung up after thanking her for her time. *Mierda.* How the hell was I going to bring the tapestry out of Cuba if I didn't even know how much it weighed?

For all I knew, the tapestry could weight fifty pounds—or three hundred. I'd never tried to pick up such a thing before, and I figured few people had.

What exactly was a tapestry? I asked myself. Basically, it was a big rug. An idea came to me; I opened up the bottom drawer of my desk and took out the yellow pages. I flipped to the listings for carpet dealers. I chose the one with the biggest ad, then punched in the first of the six numbers listed there.

"Can I speak to a salesperson, please?" I asked. I heard a few clicks, then I was subjected to the torture of two Barry Manilow songs on some awful easy-listening station. Finally a human being picked up and asked if he or she could help me—for some reason, I couldn't tell their gender. It might have been a side effect of the Barry Manilow songs.

"I'm interested in buying a couple of rugs for my daughter's apartment," I said. "But I have a couple of questions before I drive all the way out there. I live in Davie, and it's a long drive."

I went on for a few minutes, during which I determined that the person on the line was a woman with a deep voice. I figured that if I had to suffer through Barry Manilow, then she had to listen to my fictional story. She was very nice and patient; maybe it was a slow day at the store and she had to look busy.

"So I need a twelve-by-twelve-foot carpet," I said. "For the living room. How much would that weigh? I mean, would it be very heavy?"

"What do you mean, heavy?" the saleswoman asked. "It doesn't really matter. We offer delivery."

"Oh, that's nice of you," I said. "But we might want to move it to another room. And we'll certainly have to move it if my daughter decides to take another apartment. I mean, she's not likely to stay there forever."

"Rugs that size are heavy," she replied, a little irritated with me now. "It's hard for me to say how heavy, exactly. It depends on the quality of the rug you choose—how tight the knots are, the fiber density of the textiles. There are a few factors that are going to affect the weight."

I got the feeling she didn't want to talk to me much longer. "Let's say an average rug of that size," I offered. "Twelve-by-twelve, average quality. What would that weigh?"

I had no idea about the damned knots in the tapestry, or anything of the kind. There was no such information in any of my books, and I didn't think Jan at the Cloisters wanted to talk to me again.

"Somewhere between one and two hundred pounds," the saleswoman said. "Ma'am, why don't you come on in? Then I can really help you. I can't do much for you over the phone."

I didn't blame her for wanting to get rid of me; we had been talking for almost ten minutes, and I was beginning to sound like a nutcase. She was probably also working on commission, and didn't want to waste any more time on someone who was sounding less and less like a paying customer. I thanked her profusely, gave a fictitious name, promised I would be in the very next day, then hung up.

Well, that hadn't gone as well as it could have. I decided to average out the two weights the carpet saleswoman had given me, and to operate on the assumption that the tapestry weighted 150 pounds. In other words, it weighed more than I did. Picking it up and carrying it out of the Miranda house would be out of the question for me alone.

I was feeling better, and I contemplated phoning Alvaro when Leonardo poked his head in the office. A burning smell wafted in after him. He held a cooking spoon in his hand, and wore a sheepish expression. I put my hand over my mouth to keep from laughing when I spotted his red-checkered apron decorated with cut-out black-and-white cows grazing in a field of yellow daisies. It bore the slogan, "Kiss the cook, please." Over the phrase were two ruby-red lips pursed in the shape of a kiss. I noticed that he was wearing the apron over magenta bicycle shorts. He looked like a cross dresser who couldn't decide definitively what gender he was cross-dressing into.

"I'm really, really sorry, Lupe," he said. "I burned a hole in the bottom of your iron skillet—the one that Aida gave us as an office-warming present eight years ago. I was trying out a new recipe for mango tortillas with hummus filling, and I must have used too much oil or something."

"That's all right," I said. "Don't worry about it."

"The whole skillet caught fire when I poured in the oil," he said. "I'm so sorry. Please forgive me."

Leonardo was so contrite that I didn't have the heart to get angry with him. It was almost a blessing that he'd ruined the skillet, because this meant I wouldn't have to taste the nightmarish concoction he was trying to make.

"You want to go out to lunch?" I asked, suddenly famished.

Leo brightened considerably when he saw I was going to forgive him so easily. I wondered how long his new-found vegetarianism would last. Probably about as long as the no-bread, no-fruit, no-vegetable diet he had tried about a year ago. We agreed to meet in the reception area, after he'd had a stab at cleaning up the mess in the kitchen.

In the meantime I had a call to make. But my moment of reckoning was postponed, at least temporarily, because Alvaro wasn't in his office and wouldn't be back until the end of the day.

As much as I hated to admit it, I was relieved he wasn't there. I left a brief message on his voice mail. I could have tried to reach him on his cellular phone, but I didn't want to go overboard. I wanted to offer an olive branch, but there were limits to how much groveling I was willing to undertake.

12

"**S**o, Miss Solano, you're interested in the care of valuable, museum-quality textiles," said Patricia Wainwright, curator of the Center for the Fine Arts. She peered at me eagerly over her bifocals, the glass magnifying her light gray eyes giving her the appearance of a mad scientist trying to talk me into taking part in an experiment.

I hated to be catty, but it was obvious that Patricia had gotten her job on her own merits; I couldn't imagine her sleeping her way to the top. She looked like a caricature of a museum curator, with her high-necked, long-sleeve, floor-skimming pink dress with a pattern of tiny rosebuds—not to mention the white, doilylike lace that adorned her neck and sleeves. Her mousy brown hair was pulled back so tightly that I could see her scalp. She wore no jewelry, no makeup.

"Antique tapestries," she mused. She gave me a piercing, laserlike look that could have dissected a laboratory full of mice without the assistance of a scalpel. I hoped I was passing her inspection.

I had made my appointment earlier that day using my real name, which I typically tried to avoid. I'd had a feeling after speaking with her on the phone that she might be the sort to ask for identification. If she did, I hoped she didn't look too closely at my old U. of Miami ID card.

"I'm thinking about writing my master's thesis on the care and storage of museum fabrics," I said brightly. "I want to include a chapter on tapestries. I thought it would be more valuable to speak with a real expert such as yourself."

Either the compliment sailed right over her head or else Patricia Wainwright was immune to flattery. She looked me over, a pinched smile on her face. I was dressed in a pair of khakis, a white T-shirt, and a sweatshirt tied around my waist. I had even borrowed a North Face backpack from one of my nieces to complete the look. It was a blessing that I looked younger than my thirty years. If I had explained that I was a private investigator, I would have been opening myself up to a lot of uncomfortable questions. I never liked to lie, but sometimes I saw no choice.

"And what exactly do you want to know?" Patricia asked, glancing at the giant clock on the wall between us. I knew she'd probably only consented to speak with me because it was part of her job description as a county employee.

"I have a particular interest in Flemish tapestries of the late Middle Ages," I said. I had done my homework and looked up similar tapestries so I didn't come off like a mental midget. Although the chance of Patricia Wainwright ever making a connection between me and the unicorn tapestries was next to none, experience had taught me there was no such thing as being too careful. I have a one-inch circumference bullet hole in the bottom of my purse from one occasion when I hadn't practiced caution.

"Flemish tapestries," Patricia said. She stared at me, lost in thought. Then she brightened. She opened the gigantic Rolodex on the corner of her desk and started flipping through the cards.

"I just thought of something. I'm not the right person for you to speak with. Here it is. The person you want to talk

to is Señor Mario de Castellanos. A lovely man. Very charm-
ing."

Patricia began writing furiously on a pad of paper. She
paused and looked up at me, her expression suddenly
friendly and conspiratorial.

"He used to be an ambassador from Spain," she said.
"He's a marvelous collector, and an expert on the period
you're asking about."

She handed over the piece of paper. I thanked her, a little
stunned by her willingness to help. "I'm sure he'd love to
speak with you," Patricia added. "He's very knowledgeable
and very gracious."

Patricia Wainwright stood up from her desk, opened up
the door, and looked at me expectantly. "It's been very nice
to meet you," she said, finished with me now. "Good luck
on your thesis."

Right, I thought. And don't let the door hit you on the
way out. Hospitality and solicitousness were obviously not
her strong points. She ushered me out into the hall and
closed the door. I stood there, the slip of paper in one hand
and my purse in the other. I didn't think I had ever been
escorted out of a room so unceremoniously.

Señor de Castellanos's address was in Coral Gables; it was
in one of the new mixed-use buildings that had been built
in the last ten years. I walked out into the morning heat,
pondering my options. Should I call him on my cell phone
and ask to see him right away? I decided I should. I was
dressed to play the part of the student, and I didn't want to
go through complex negotiations with my niece again to get
her to lend me her backpack. As I walked to the parking lot
I opened up my purse. The museum was on West Flagler,
in downtown Miami, where the cost of parking is measured
by the second. I dug out a twenty, hoping it would cover

the forty-five minutes I'd spent meeting with Patricia. Fortunately I was going to bill the Mirandas for the rip-off.

Cell-phone reception was terrible downtown, so I waited until I was headed south on I-95 before making the call. To my surprise, Señor de Castellanos himself answered the phone, on the second ring. His voice was very deep. I gave him my story about being a grad student, then described my meeting with Patricia Wainwright.

"I see," he said. "Then you are on your way? I will look forward to meeting you."

I pressed the End button to terminate the call, shaking my head. If only everything were so easy. I drove as quickly as the traffic pattern would allow—a snail's-pace ten miles over the speed limit—and arrived at de Castellanos's office building within half an hour.

I pulled up to the heavily arched, balustrade-laden, faux Mediterranean structure. It was painted in an earth tone—one of the seventeen colors permitted by Coral Gables building regulations. I parked in the underground garage, pulled the backpack over my shoulders, and generally tried to make myself seem like a student instead of a somewhat weary private investigator trying to find out how to smuggle a priceless artifact out of Cuba.

Señor de Castellanos's office was on the third floor, at the end of an instant-antique-filled hallway. The decor in the place was so overdone that I started to feel scruffy and underdressed. I was glad that, at least, I was wearing espadrilles; the carpeting was so thick that if I had been wearing heels, I surely would have toppled over. I couldn't even imagine what the rents were like in the building. Obviously de Castellanos had money, if this was the kind of place he kept as a private office. This kind of ostentation didn't come cheap.

I rang the doorbell and, a moment later, it was opened by a distinguished-looking older gentleman with silver hair.

"Señor de Castellanos," I said, stepping inside. "I am Lupe Solano. I really want to thank you for—"

"The ambassador will see you shortly," the man said, giving me a tolerant smile.

"Oh," I said. "Sorry. Thanks."

I sat down on a velvet couch against the wall in the reception area. The room was big and airy. And the antiques were noticeably more valuable and varied than the ones in the hallway outside. There was a signed Sorolla beach scene on the wall facing me. I looked to either side; there were a pair of multicolored foot-high Chinese porcelain foo dogs that had been converted into lamps. They were resting in elegance on a pair of Hepplewhite tables arranged on either side of the sofa.

The gentleman who let me in had disappeared, leaving me alone. I let my eyes wander over the art on the walls, the elaborate antique wallpaper, the discreetly opulent furnishings. This room alone was like a sort of museum. I was glad Mami had educated me on art and decor, so that I could appreciate it. I had just zeroed in on a small impressionistic painting in an ornate frame, hanging over a small desk decorated with inlaid ivory, when the door opened. This time it was the real thing. I jumped up as though I had springs in my knees.

"Thank you for seeing me, Ambassador," I said. "I'm very grateful for your time."

With each step that I took—from the outer hall to the reception room and now the inner sanctum—the art and furnishings became more and more impressive. The antiques and paintings that had captivated me in the reception area were fourth-rate compared to those inside the ambassador's office. Two entire walls were covered with floor-to-ceiling

Aubusson tapestries—lush, dark green forest scenes. His desk was thick mahogany, as big as a dining room table and polished to a mirrorlike sheen. The ambassador gestured to one of two club chairs facing his desk. The cushion on the chair was stuffed with down feathers, I realized as I sank into total luxury and comfort.

"Well, Miss Solano," Ambassador de Castellanos said, sitting behind his desk. He was tall and thin, with an aristocratic face and thinning hair combed straight back. I thought he had probably been very handsome when he was young. "On the telephone you indicated you needed information on tapestries?"

"Yes, for a master's thesis," I said. I went on to tell him the same story I'd given Patricia Wainwright. The ambassador listened intently, nodding as I spoke. I felt terribly guilty to be lying to such a dignified and apparently kindly man, but it was too late to turn back.

"Miss Wainwright flatters me by calling me an expert," he finally said, with a thin smile. "But I do have knowledge of the care of medieval tapestries. The main threat to their well-being is deterioration due to poor handling, as well as drastic changes in climate and lighting. As you must know from your research, tapestries are composed of fabrics and dyes that are very sensitive to extremes."

"Absolutely," I agreed.

"We are talking about very old substances," the ambassador said. "The tapestry itself is an object made of woven strands—each strand grows weaker with time. The very dyes used to color them can undermine their structural integrity. This was before the age of synthetic fibers which, crass as they might be, have the advantage of incredible durability."

I diligently jotted notes in a little pad I produced from my backpack. Ambassador de Castellanos went on to describe the many pitfalls in dealing with antique textiles. As I made

more notes, it seemed to me as though the unicorn tapestry
might be better off in its dark, cool basement, away from
prying hands and the elements. I seriously considered calling
Lucia Miranda and telling her that the tapestry might be
ruined if I were to try to take it out of Cuba. I didn't want
to be responsible for the destruction of such a precious work
of art.

"The tapestries must be very heavy, right?" I ventured.

The Ambassador fixed me with a curious look.

"I find it very fascinating that a young lady such as yourself
has an interest in fourteenth- and fifteenth-century Flemish
tapestries," he said. I was disappointed he had not answered
my question about the weight.

"How did you come to have an interest in this particular period?"

His question caught me by surprise. "My mother loved
tapestries," I said hesitantly. "I suppose I inherited my appreciation of them from her."

"And which are your favorites?" Ambassador de Castellanos asked.

My mind went totally blank. I thought about changing the
subject, asking him about himself, but it would be too obvious a ploy.

I tried to recall the material I'd studied before my meeting
with Patricia Wainwright, but I couldn't remember a single
thing. My anxiety made it impossible to retrieve anything
from my memory. I had to say something, I realized, or he
would know I was a fake.

"The *Hunt of the Unicorn*," I said.

The ambassador clapped his hands with pleasure. "*Sí*, I
agree! A very good choice."

I smiled back at him, disgusted with myself for having
revealed that information, however innocuous it might seem
at the moment. I had tripped myself up, and I hoped it

didn't come back to haunt me. The ambassador was obviously plugged into the art world, and if the Miranda tapestry's existence became public anytime soon, he would probably remember our conversation. Now I cursed the fact that I had given him my real name—although I really hadn't had a choice, since he and Patricia Wainwright might speak later and compare notes.

I closed the notepad and zipped it into the backpack. I had a strong need to leave; it had been a long time since I compromised myself in such a fashion, and I didn't want to compound my error by overstaying my welcome. The ambassador struck me as sharp and observant.

"Thank you so much for your time," I said. "Your help has truly been invaluable to me." And he had, except he had not given me information about their weight, making me think he did not know it.

He rose and walked around his desk. "Please, it was nothing," he said with a warm grin. "It is such a pleasure to meet a beautiful young lady, and one who appreciates the *Hunt of the Unicorn* tapestries. It has been some time since I have thought about them. I think this afternoon I will look through my library and refresh my memory on their many subtle pleasures."

Mierda. Mierda. Mierda.

13

I called Detective Anderson as soon as I got back to the office; I wanted to see if he had the lab reports back yet. It had been two days since Angel's body was found, so I knew there was a good chance that the technicians had finished their job.

Anderson wasn't in his office. I reached him on his cellular. He sounded harried and tired.

"It did come in, but I haven't had a chance to read it," he said. "I'm on my way back to my office. Look, Lupe, I'll give you a call as soon as I've looked at it. That's the best I can do."

He hung up on me before I could ask any more questions. I decided not to hold his lack of manners against him. The life of a Dade County homicide investigator wasn't an easy one. I also knew that although Detective Anderson meant to return my call as soon as he could, he might get caught up in another case, and it might be hours before he got back to me.

I reviewed the notes I'd taken from my interview with Ambassador de Castellanos, trying to concentrate and not fixate on the way I'd tipped my hand to him. I glanced out the window at the parrots, then started to doodle on the pad. Finally I sighed, stood up, stretched.

I still hadn't heard back from Alvaro, which I took to be an ominous sign. He was a busy attorney, but no one was so preoccupied that he couldn't take five minutes to return a phone call. It wasn't like him. Perhaps he didn't know what to say to me, since our last interaction had been strained and harsh. In a way, I was relieved. He would ask me whether I had taken the Lucia Miranda case. What was I going to do then?

The parrots were taking a lunch break, munching on avocados. I wondered if they saw nothing but avocados in their dreams. They ate avocados, they lined their nests with the dried-out skins of the fruit, they spit the pulp at each other when they were angry.

This was making me hungry. I would have invited Leonardo, but he had told me he would be on an important personal errand for the rest of the day. I wasn't surprised; looking at the *Farmer's Almanac* on my cousin's desk, I saw there was going to be a full moon that night. Some of Leonardo's friends were getting involved in a religion based on astrology and planetary movement, and Leonardo was considering devoting more time to it. The moon was of primary importance in this sect—somehow, this necessitated trips to Wal-Mart for supplies, and to the *botanicas* in Little Havana for specialty items. Sometimes I longed for the day when Leo's preoccupation with his Cuban ass was the sole focus of his obsessed mindset, rather than one among many.

I gathered my purse, set the alarm, and stepped out into the afternoon heat and humidity. I didn't really have a destination; instead, I thought I would break with convention and walk until I was drawn to a nearby eatery. There were lots of outdoor cafés in the Grove, so it wouldn't be too difficult. Now that I walked I noticed there was actually a nice breeze in the air, cutting through the stifling moisture that permeates nearly every day in South Florida. I thought I detected a slight salty tang, as well as the aroma of flowers from a bunch of window boxes set nose-high outside a legal office's windows.

I had just turned the corner onto Virginia Street when I sensed someone walking behind me, matching my steps. I felt annoyance rather than an immediate sense of danger.

I quickened my pace, hoping he would fall behind. No, I felt the rhythm of his feet slapping the pavement in time with my own. I clutched my purse a little tighter, wedging it beneath my arm. It would be a real pain to have it snatched in broad daylight—not to mention a major embarrassment.

We had walked nearly two blocks when my irritation reached a head. I decided to confront whoever it was at the next intersection; however, that proved to be unnecessary.

"Lupe," a man's voice whispered from behind. I didn't recognize who it was. "Lupe Solano."

Well, it must not have been a mugger. What street robber uses proper names before committing a crime?

I turned around. "Who are you?" I asked.

"Jesus," my follower replied.

My mind went blank. I wasn't sure whether he was swearing or identifying himself—or whether he was an escaped mental patient with delusions of grandeur.

"Jesus Maria Estrada," he said, looking around nervously. His voice was almost too quiet for me to hear. "Angel's brother."

"Oh." I relaxed my grip on my purse. I'd been clutching it so tight that the Beretta inside had been pushing against my ribs. "I'm sorry about Angel."

"Can I talk to you someplace private?" Jesus whispered. He reached out and grabbed my elbow firmly, not in a threatening manner. I didn't appreciate the bodily contact, but I didn't want to make a scene. There was other foot traffic, as well as a café window across the street, from which I saw diners looking out.

"Let's keep walking," I said. Even though he was named for our Savior, I wasn't about to take him back to my office, especially with Leonardo gone. I saw a building across the street and got an idea.

"Starbucks," I said. I couldn't imagine anything bad happening in such a bland, generically benign place.

Jesus loosened his grip on my elbow. As the tension of our meeting abated a little, I got a good look at him. I didn't think he and Angel had been twins, but it was a fair impersonation. The resemblance between them was strong, verging on the uncanny. If I hadn't known that Angel Estrada was lying cold and dead on a slab in the Dade County morgue, I would have thought I was standing right next to him.

We waited for a break in traffic before darting across. Half of the ten or so tables outside Starbucks were empty, and I chose the one closest to the wall. Neither of us went inside to order; instead we sat on opposite sides of the table, sizing each other up.

"Have you spoken to the police?" I asked.

"No. They came to my place looking for me, but I wasn't home." Jesus picked a piece of invisible lint off his jeans, trying to look casual. I tried to hide my fascination. How could two brothers both turn out so completely repulsive in appearance?

"Are you going to call them?" I asked. Jesus wasn't Angel, I had to remind myself. But still, he wasn't exactly conducting himself like a man who had nothing to hide.

"No, I am not." Jesus shook his head.

OK. I folded my hands under the table. A quiet lunch by myself, that's all I had wanted. Now I was sitting at Starbucks with a man who seemed to have no intention of speaking to the authorities about the issue of his brother's murder.

I made sure I could reach into the purse quickly if I needed to. The Beretta was loaded and ready.

"You're putting me in a difficult position," I told him. We spoke quietly, in even tones. The students and fashion victims at the other tables didn't even notice us. "The police are looking for you."

"I know that," Jesus said quietly.

I fixed him with my most serious look. "As a private investigator in the State of Florida, I'm an officer of the court," I said. "I'm bound by law to go to the police with information like this."

Which wasn't strictly true, but I thought I would lay it on thick. It might provoke Jesus to tell me something he intended to hide.

"Listen, Angel told me about you," Jesus said, glancing around. I could sense his nervousness, as if he were ready to leap up from the table and run away at the slightest provocation.

"What did he say?" I asked.

"He told me how you deal in stolen Cuban art," Jesus whispered, very close to my ear. I didn't enjoy having Jesus so near any more than I reveled in close proximity to Angel. I felt a flash of impatient annoyance.

"Look, I don't *deal* in anything," I said. "I'm a private investigator who's dealt with a few art cases. The art wasn't necessarily stolen. Sometimes people don't know the art they've bought was stolen until they're told the truth."

Jesus looked at me blankly. I took a deep breath. I sounded like a pompous ass even to my own ears.

"Look, Jesus," I finally said, "why don't you tell me why you're running from the cops?"

"Whoever killed Angel is going to come after me, too," Jesus said, his voice flat and cold. "If I start talking to the police, then people are going to know where to find me. I have to hide out until I do what I have to do."

"Jesus, you have to tell me about what you've gotten into," I insisted. "Maybe I can help you in some way."

I was thinking about Jesus's safety, honestly I was. But I was also concerned to see that Jesus was frightened and paranoid about something—and that I might be unwittingly implicated in whatever had gotten Angel killed.

Jesus shook his head. "No," he said. "It's better that you don't know anything more than you have to."

"Well, what did you want to see me about?" There was no way I could make Jesus come clean with me. He was as tight-lipped as Angel. It must have been a family trait, one that I wasn't going to be able to reverse on the patio of my local Starbucks.

"Angel said that he spoke to you about Camila," Jesus said.

"Your sister?" I asked.

"*Sí*. Angel said you agreed to the plan."

"He told you *what*?" I cried out. A couple of heads turned.

"The plan," Jesus said helpfully. "The one he told you about two days ago, when you agreed to everything."

"No way. Hold it." I held up a hand like a cop stopping traffic. "I listened to Angel lay out the proposal. That's it."

Jesus looked puzzled, a little unsure of himself. "Angel and I got together right after your lunch. He said you had agreed to the plan, that you were eager to get started."

"He wasn't telling you the truth," I said. I suspected that Jesus was putting me on, but there was no way to check. Obviously I couldn't go to Angel for verification.

"This isn't right," Jesus said. "Angel told me that you agreed it was a brilliant idea, that you were going to put together a plan to get the paintings out of Cuba."

I was speechless. All of a sudden I was an expert smuggler. Of course, I realized, I *was* thinking about how to get the Miranda tapestry off the island. But this was too much, even by my recent standards.

"No, Jesus," I said softly.

Jesus looked away, his mouth working without words coming out. Finally his eyes met mine; to my surprise, they were misted with tears of frustration.

"We contacted Camila in Havana," he said with a twinge of desperation. "And we told her everything was fine in Little Havana. That was the code we had agreed to, meaning that the plan was going forward. You know, we have to be careful because the government listens to telephone conversations."

I sat there, basically stupefied. I was a trained private investigator. Part of my job was remembering minute details of events and conversation, so I could reconstruct them later. I remembered my lunch with Angel, and I was certain I had not agreed to join forces with Angel's plan to smuggle Camila's paintings out of Cuba. Yet, the more I talked to Jesus, the more I was convinced that he was telling the truth as he understood it. Angel had gone back to his brother and said everything was a "go," that it was time to get started.

Every time someone went into or came out of the door near us, I smelled delicious freshly brewed coffee. I could have used a cup at that moment, but I didn't want to risk having Jesus disappear on me.

"Look, Jesus, Angel never even mentioned you by name," I told him. "He talked about Camila's abilities, and the part he wanted her to play. What was your role supposed to be?"

Just then my cellular phone rang. I was tempted to let the voice mail take a message—until I glanced down at the caller ID and saw that this was one call I had to take. I held up a finger apologetically to Jesus and turned on the phone.

"Lupe? Anderson here." My heart jumped. This meant he had the results back from the lab. "I promised to call when I got the report on the Estrada case. You got a minute?"

I turned my head and covered the mouthpiece with my hand. I certainly didn't want Jesus to know that I was talking to the police's lead investigator into his brother's murder. Nor did I want Detective Anderson to know who was sitting across the table from me.

"Thanks a lot," I muttered. Great timing. There was no way I was going to be able to ask detailed questions, not with Jesus there. Still, some information was better than none.

"The cause of death was suffocation by means of the panty hose wrapped around his neck," Anderson began. "No surprise there. Time of death is listed between nine-thirty and ten. The victim was discovered at eleven and we were called in immediately. The victim kept his air-conditioning at sixty-five degrees, so consequently there was very little deterioration of the body."

Anderson read from the report in a toneless, expression-drained voice. He had gone through too many M.E. reports to invest his feelings in the details of any one individual's death.

"Nothing jumps out at me from the crime-scene techs' report," he mused, "except for one thing. Particles of dried oil-paint chips were found in the apartment. Especially in close proximity to the location of the murder."

I tensed, trying not to let Jesus notice. Paint chips. I had no time to dwell on that piece of information, though, because Anderson continued reading.

"Victim's occupation was art dealer." I heard the sound of shuffling papers and Anderson clearing his throat. "I wonder if he painted as well. Says here the bedsheets had tiny bits of paint on them. Well, he worked around paintings. Still . . ."

I could tell from Anderson's tone that he was fishing for information from me, and that he didn't really expect to get anything. I desperately wanted to ask some questions of my own, but by then Jesus was looking at me with a quizzical frown. I shrugged to apologize, pointed at the phone to indicate that I would hang up as soon as I could.

"We haven't found the brother yet," Anderson went on. "Strange. We found his last known residence. The neighbors say they haven't seen him since the day Angel was killed. If he doesn't turn up pretty soon he's going to be at the top of a very short list of suspects—especially since the visitor's log at Angel's apartment says that Jesus Estrada was a frequent visitor. Interestingly, he didn't visit the day of the murder."

More rustling of pages. Jesus was looking around, as though he expected doom at any moment.

"That's all I have for now," Anderson concluded. "We're checking phone records, home and office. The usual drill. I'll keep you posted."

"Thank you. I really appreciate it." Jesus had both hands on the edge of the table, looking ready to bolt.

"You're awfully quiet, Lupe. It's not like you," the detective commented. "Everything all right?"

I shouldn't have been surprised that he picked up on my discomfiture. For all his gruff ways, Anderson was very perceptive, and sometimes surprisingly sensitive.

"Just tired," I said. "Burning the candle."

"Get some sleep, then," Anderson said, making it sound like an order. He hung up.

"Sorry," I said to Jesus, folding the phone and putting it back in my handbag. "I didn't mean to take so long."

Jesus's eyes narrowed. "That wasn't the police, was it?"

I debated with myself for a moment. It felt as though I had been lying all day, and not with a great deal of success.

"Yes. It was the detective on your brother's case," I said. "He said he was looking for you. And that if he doesn't find you soon, he's going to consider you the main suspect."

Jesus's face dropped. "Me? Kill Angel? He was my own brother! They are crazy!"

I widened my eyes to shush him. He was talking too loud, and his voice was carrying. People at a couple of other tables glanced in our direction. I relaxed a little when I saw that they didn't seem to be tourists. Miamians are used to hearing people talk about crime and mayhem—it's part of daily life here. Still, the last thing I needed was for us to attract attention in such a public place.

"What are they supposed to think, Jesus?" I said in a low voice. "You disappeared the day your brother was killed. It's pretty damned suspicious."

And I hadn't failed to notice that, although he emphatically denied killing his brother, Jesus hadn't thought to ask whether the police had any leads.

"I have been where I always am—day and night," Jesus spat out. "Working at my studio. If the police had any brains, then they would know how to find me."

"Studio?" I asked. Jesus was silent. "What kind of studio. Are you a painter?"

"*Si*, just like Camila," Jesus replied with evident pride. "And just like our mother. Angel was the only one in our family who didn't paint."

I tried to say something, but failed. Paint chips. Jesus's studio.

"Angel never knew if he had talent or not." Jesus laughed, a sound that was more like a snort. His beady eyes narrowed even more. "The skin on Angel's hands used to turn red and break out in bumps whenever he dealt with wet paint. Imagine that. A family of painters, and he was allergic to the stuff."

"But he was an art dealer," I said. "How could he be around paintings all day?"

"I said *wet* paint," Jesus explained. "Dry paint was better. And he had some pills he took, to make it more bearable."

I was starting to piece together a few things. Angel must have become an art dealer because of his allergy. He got as close to the family vocation as he could, by buying and selling artworks. But I'd had enough playing amateur psychologist. I had reached a more important conclusion: I trusted Jesus about as much as I'd trusted his brother.

"You started to tell me your role in the plan when the phone rang," I said.

"That's not right," Jesus said with a snicker. "You started to ask me. I had no intention of telling you."

"Well then, why don't—"

"We don't have much time," Jesus said, looking at his watch. "I don't know when the cops might find me."

"Why did you want to see me, Jesus?" I asked again, frustrated with his evasion and a little frightened of him. "It must be important. You know you're taking a big risk."

"Angel is dead," Jesus said. "But that doesn't mean we can't continue with the plan. The three of us—you, me, and Camila."

"You haven't been listening to me," I said, starting to get up. "I never agreed to anything. I'm leaving, and I don't want you to try to contact me again."

"No, you can't." Jesus reached out to stop me, squeezing my arm hard.

I looked down in disbelief. Here we were at Starbucks, lunchtime, in the middle of Coconut Grove. All I had to do was yell for a cop and he would be arrested. I suddenly realized how desperate he was.

I took his hand and lifted it off my arm. I saw that he had some kind of colored substance under his fingernails. Paint?

I suppressed a shudder. Jesus was a painter, after all. It didn't make him a killer.

"Don't you ever touch me again," I said through clenched teeth. "I guarantee you'll regret it."

I fought off the urge to shove the Beretta in his ribs. I didn't pull a gun for the sake of a hollow threat, not even with a fool like this.

Jesus was nonplused. "We have to go on with the plan," he said calmly.

"Why?" I asked, almost laughing at his doggedness.

"Because the plan was what got Angel killed," Jesus hissed. His already-ugly face contorted into something more unsightly. "You're in this, Lupe. You know that."

"You don't know what the hell you're talking about." I was beyond anger. I tried not to let rage—and fear—take over, but my self-control was reaching its limit. Jesus had confirmed what I'd feared—that Angel died over the plan he had tried to draw me into. My hand itched with the impulse to reach for my gun.

"There are only three of us left now," Jesus whispered. "Don't worry, we can still do it without Angel. Don't be frightened. Camila knows all about you."

"I don't want to—"

Jesus stood up, moved next to me.

"Angel told her all about you," he said softly. "How smart you are. How good you are at what you do. We exchange letters through people traveling in and out of Havana—for money, of course. She was thrilled to hear that you were joining us. This idea makes her so happy."

"Does she know about Angel?"

Jesus looked away. "I'm going to have to tell her," he said. "But I know she'll want to go forward anyway. The plan means too much to her to simply let it drop."

I looked at the traffic moving past, all the people oblivious to what a mess my world had become. How had one lunch at the Grand Bay Hotel led to murder and now this vulture insinuating himself into my life?

"Why was Angel killed?" I asked.

Jesus's lips tightened. "Because of the plan," he said again.

He looked angry. Well, tough shit. He wanted me in, but he didn't want to share the gory details. Some business partner.

In the near distance was the sound of emergency sirens. They seemed to be getting closer to where we were. For a paranoid second I wondered if Anderson, somehow, had figured out where I was when we were on the phone.

Jesus backed away suddenly, bumping into his aluminum chair and creating a racket. No one looked up. Either they had long since lost interest or decided we were a pair of dangerous weirdos who should be avoided at all cost. I was starting to think they might be right.

"I'll be in touch," he said. "We have no time to waste."

With that, he sprinted across the street, almost getting plowed over by a tour bus full of Canadians. The tourists looked out the tinted-glass windows with eager expressions, as though titillated to finally see some of the Miami craziness they had heard so much about.

It took me a couple of minutes to compose myself enough to walk away. I didn't even think to go inside and order some coffee. I was more concerned with what I had gotten involved with—and how I was going to get out of it.

I headed back to my office in a haze, almost getting hit by another tour bus. That would have made their Miami experience complete. Something to tell the folks back home in Edmonton.

14

I smelled the cigar before I saw her. I paused there on the dock next to the boat and breathed in the familiar smoke, the scent of nostalgia.

"*Ay, Dios mio,*" a loud voice called out. "Can it be the great detective has come to visit me?"

I should have known that I couldn't surprise Barbara. She was too perceptive, her powers almost otherworldly.

"Barbara!" I cried with pleasure when my friend came up from belowdecks. Until the instant I laid eyes on her, I hadn't realized just how much I missed her.

She crossed the deck in three steps and took me into her arms, crushing me to her Amazonian body. Normally I shied away from physical contact with other women, but with Barbara I broke all the rules. Barbara Perez was a unique woman, and I loved and respected her in a way that defied easy explanation. She was fierce, brave, loyal, and she had an unmatched knowledge of the sea. She was the one person who could help me.

"Now we celebrate," Barbara boomed out. She took me below, to the cabin. I immediately perceived that she was making the boat her home now: there were dishes and laundry, all the stuff of everyday life.

Barbara credited me with saving her life a few years back,

when she had gotten involved in a baby-selling scheme, but as far as I was concerned the opposite was true. I will go to my grave believing that she saved mine.

Once I was comfortably seated, Barbara opened a hatch under one of the portholes and took out a bottle of Bacardi Añejo. She grabbed two dirty-looking glasses and poured four or five inches of amber liquid in each. We toasted with a clink. It had been a long time since I drank rum neat, and I felt it burn as it went down.

I watched Barbara take a long drag on her cigar, her eyes closed, relishing the moment. I noted with admiration that the years hadn't been hard on her. She looked the same as the last time I'd seen her, when I was invited to christen the *Santa Barbara* almost two years before. Barbara had bought the boat with money she earned while working a case with me.

She leaned forward and refilled my glass. She looked beautiful in her element, with the sun filtering through the glass porthole and the smell of salt in the air. She was a mulatto, born in Cuba of a white mother and a black father, and her skin was a rich cocoa color. Her long black curly hair was worn in a waist-length braid. She was barefoot, dressed in a pair of men's shapeless blue cotton pants and a white shirt that made it abundantly clear that she wasn't wearing any lingerie. I guessed that Barbara was about forty, but she had an ageless quality that made it difficult for me to be precise.

"How is your family?" I asked.

I didn't want to ask about her children by names, because I'd lost track of how many she had. I knew of the last two, a pair of twins, because I'd almost had to serve as midwife to their birth.

"Fine, fine," Barbara said. "The children are all visiting with my sister, Ofelia, at her house. Your twins, Lupe, they're so big now."

Barbara spread out her arms like a fisherman describing the size of her catch. She reached for the bottle, a trail of cigar smoke forming a cloud around her head.

"And don't worry, I can have as much as I like now." She patted her stomach. "No more babies." She then squeezed one of her ample breasts. "And no more milk."

I returned her smile. Barbara obviously remembered me lecturing her about drinking while she was pregnant with the twins and nursing her penultimate baby girl. I hated to interfere in anyone's personal life, but watching her swig rum while pregnant was too much for me. I never even brought up the subject of cigars—I was willing to lose some battles in order to win the war.

I took another drink of Añejo, held out my glass for more as she offered. I knew it would be useless to say no.

"*Gracias,*" I said.

"And how is your family?" she asked.

"Very well," I replied.

Barbara nodded with satisfaction. "OK," she said, the cigar sticking out of the corner of her mouth. "Now, what brings you here?"

I loved Barbara's no-bullshit style, though it could be disconcerting at times. I would have eased into the purpose of my visit, but she could sense that I had business in mind.

"Well . . ." I said, looking for the right words.

"You want to go back to Cuba," Barbara said in a loud voice. "And you need a ride."

I almost dropped my glass. Barbara took a long drink, her eyes sparkling over the rim of the glass.

"Actually, yes," I said.

"When? Where?" she asked, as though we were discussing going to a movie.

"*Ayer,*" I said. "Yesterday. Havana."

Barbara took a long drag on her cigar and nodded thoughtfully. "It's harder now than when we went before," she said. "The Coast Guard is everywhere, looking for smugglers."

"So I've heard."

"And what about a boat?" she asked after another long drink. "The *Santa Barbara* is a sailboat. And I don't have the *Mamita* anymore."

"We'll go in my *papi*'s Hatteras," I replied with as much conviction as I could muster. This was a hell of a sticking point. Papi envisioned daily motoring into Havana harbor on the *Concepcion*, Mami's ashes cradled in the urn under his arm, a proud smile on his face as he celebrated the end of Castro's regime. His youngest daughter taking the boat to Havana to illegally smuggle out a tapestry was nowhere in this dream. I was going to have to figure out something, and quickly.

"I see. We'll go in style." Barbara smiled, visibly impressed.

She didn't ask me the reason for the trip. I knew this wasn't for lack of interest, but because she knew I would tell her everything in good time. The trust between us was unbreakable.

"You'll do it?" I asked.

"We did it before," Barbara said with a laugh. "I think we can sure as shit do it again."

We toasted once more, refilled our glasses with Añejo. I was glad that one of us was so confident about our return to the island. The last time we were there, we left behind a few bodies and were fortunate not to be killed ourselves. Barbara acted as though she had forgotten that fact, but I certainly hadn't.

After the next toast, we paused. There was a silence between us as our eyes met. We dropped our smiles, gave each other a very serious nod of recognition.

I had been wrong. Barbara remembered our last trip to

Cuba very well. She remembered the bodies in the countryside, and the blood in the waters of the Florida Straits. Neither of us could ever possibly forget.

"To success," I said, holding out my glass.

"To success," she repeated, clinking hers to mine. "And
to a long life."

We drank in silence for a while, neither of us feeling the
need to say anything more.

15

I spent a sleepless night populated by dreams of men—and not the kind of dreams I enjoyed. The Estrada brothers were there, with Tommy and Alvaro drifting in and out. I was running, trying to keep something terrible from happening to me. And Barbara and her machete were nowhere in sight.

Finally I sat up. The sun wasn't out yet. I turned off the alarm, put my feet on the floor. There was no use trying to rest. I showered and dressed, then went downstairs. At least I had contacted Barbara and set in motion our trip to Cuba— a big step.

The house was silent. It was so early that even Aida and Osvaldo hadn't gotten up. I was left to my own devices for breakfast; it had been a long time since I tried to cook for myself, and I hoped I could pull it off without getting in too much trouble. Better keep it simple, I advised myself. I didn't want to make too much of a mess, since Aida's kitchen was always spotless and I would never hear the end of it if I turned it into a disaster area before she even got out of bed.

I scrounged around until I found the espresso maker, which I filled to the brim with Café Bustelo and set on the stove. I took out a long, thin loaf of Cuban bread and cut off a big piece. I opened up the heavy refrigerator door and found the butter—cursing when I realized that all the varieties were frozen solid. I took an entire stick of salted butter, put it in a glass bowl, and shoved it into the microwave for a minute. Once it had started to melt and sputter, I took it out and slathered it over the bread, then put the whole thing in the oven to broil. I poured half a quart of whole milk into a pan and set it on the stove next to the coffee. All of this made me feel positively domestic—a situation I normally experienced only about every leap year.

I was on a roll, a regular Cuban Martha Stewart, so I got a wicker tray from the stack in the pantry and lined it with a white linen place mat and a matching napkin. My timing was perfect; by then the coffee was percolating, the milk was frothing, and the bread had reached a perfect golden brown. I loaded up the *café con leche*, cup, saucer, basket of bread, and pot of mango marmalade onto the tray, then set out for the terrace.

The sun was just poking up over the horizon, casting an understated glow on the waters of the bay. Instead of sitting at one of the tables, I put the tray down on the edge of the dock, sat down, let my legs dangle over the side. I sipped my coffee, letting my mind come back to life—and gradually letting the tangled events of the week come into focus.

I laughed softly when a thought occurred to me. I had isolated my problem: somehow, someplace along the line, I had made the transformation from private eye to Cuban art smuggler. My only real experience was locating two paintings for a relative and a family friend, yet word had traveled on the Cuban grapevine—where exaggeration was a matter of course—and now, in some people's eyes, I was the woman to come to if you needed artwork clandestinely removed from the island. And then there was the matter of Tommy's case, on which I had done no work.

I dipped my bread in the *café con leche*. I wished our cardiologist neighbor, Dr. Fernandez, was watching; the sight of my eating habits would have warmed his heart. He would never have to worry about HMO's cutting into his business, not as long as there were Cubans like me with such artery-clogging tendencies.

The pelicans were waking up. They were flying low, just skimming the water's surface, searching for minnows to eat for breakfast. I looked over the canal, hoping to spot a manatee, but it was too early for the big slumbering creatures.

I was well into my second coffee when my thoughts crystallized. I knew I couldn't bear to spend another night like the one I'd just suffered through. Having taken action on the Miranda case, I had to dedicate some time to the Estrada matter. Before anything, I had to confront Jesus Estrada and tell him, once and for all, that I wanted nothing to do with his plan—and no amount of insistence on his part was going to change that. I hated to speak ill of the dead, but he needed to know that his brother had been full of shit, that he was lying when he said I wanted a part of their insane plot to bring their sister's paintings out of Cuba. And I was going to get straight answers from Jesus about who killed his brother, and I was going to make damn sure the murderer—or murderers—knew that I wanted nothing to do with Angel's scheme.

Of course there was a problem. I didn't know how I was going to get hold of Jesus. He had told me he would "be in touch." I wasn't going to wait for that, not when someone might decide to deal with me the way they'd dispensed with Angel. I was a detective. I could find Jesus—and then straighten him out.

I polished off the bread and coffee. The mango marmalade was untouched on the tray. I was feeling fire in my veins, and it had seemed too demure and ladylike to spread it on my bread. I took the tray into the kitchen and left it for Aida, feeling my store of domestic spirit spent for the time being.

Everyone was still asleep as I prepared to leave for the office. I was accustomed to the hustle and bustle of my family, and it was strange to move around in morning silence. I had been absorbed with work lately, and hadn't spent much time with them—the usual story. I knew better, though, than to make a bunch of false promises to be good that I wouldn't be able to keep.

There was a lot of traffic on Main Highway, even at that hour. Although, as I looked at the dashboard clock, I realized it wasn't *that* early. A lot of people had business at seven in the morning, and for them it wasn't the crack of dawn. I thanked my good fortune that I saw seven in the morning only on rare occasions, not as a routine matter of course.

Leonardo wasn't in the office yet, so I switched off the alarm, turned on the lights, and put on the day's first pot of coffee. I went into my office and looked out the window. To my pleasure, I saw that the parrots were still sleeping. Some of my influence regarding recognizing the importance of sleep must have rubbed off on them.

I stood behind my desk for a couple of minutes, thinking about how to find Jesus Estrada. I would have to tread carefully, since he was part of an ongoing homicide investigation. I couldn't have the police knowing that I was looking for him.

I picked up the phone and punched in number 5 on the speed dial. A couple of rings later I heard a familiar grunt by way of an answer, followed by a familiar obscenity describing an intimate act between a man and a woman.

"Lupe, this had better be important."

Well, Nestor was awake enough to have read my name on his caller ID.

"*Buenos dias, amor,*" I said in an obnoxiously cheery voice. It was amazing what a gallon of Cuban coffee did for my disposition. Normally I would have been as comatose and surly as Nestor.

"Do you still have your contact at BellSouth?" I asked. I hadn't waited for a reply to my greeting—probably I would have been waiting for a very long time.

"*Sí*. But he's gone up in price." Nestor's voice suddenly sounded lucid. The prospect of a job tended to have that effect on him. "It's riskier now for him—you know, with all those oversight committees breathing down his ass."

I decided not to parse the literal meaning of what he had just described. Nestor Gomez was one of my contract investigators, and he had the best variety of contacts in Dade County. I could always count on him to find a way to uncover information that seemed impossibly hidden. He was motivated by his quest to bring his entire family from the Dominican Republic to Miami. He had only his youngest sister left to bring over, after having successfully transplanted his eleven other siblings and placed them in good jobs, where they were thriving. Puerto Plata's loss was definitely Miami's gain.

"Can you contact him this morning? And put a rush on it?" I asked.

"If the money's green," Nestor replied.

I gave him Angel Estrada's name, number, and a range of dates. I cringed when Nestor quoted me the price. I tried not to dwell on the fact that I had no client to bill for the expense. Having asked for a rush job added up to a third to the usual outrageous price for insider access to phone-company records.

Now I had to wait—my least favorite thing. I picked up the file I'd started on Tommy's case. Inside, it was nothing but a few scribbled notes and an envelope containing the previous investigator's report. I didn't recognize the name on the cover, and I wasn't in the mood to review someone else's work.

I took out a map, a pad of paper, and switched on the desk lamp. For more than an hour I scribbled down a series of scenarios for bringing the Miranda family tapestry out of Cuba on the Hatteras. I realized each possible option had something in common: they all sounded like plots from half-assed B-movies. I didn't want to get discouraged, so I drove to the Dade County public library and read up on the case of museum-quality textiles. I learned that, if anything, Ambassador de Castellanos had downplayed their fragility and the number of ways they could be damaged. Great, I thought, making photocopies.

It was close to three o'clock when Nestor called. I had just returned to the office.

"What do you have for me?" I asked.

"Hello to you, too," Nestor replied.

"I'm sorry. It's just that—"

"I know, I know," Nestor said, world-weary. "It's important. It's always important. Have to have it yesterday. Who cares how hard it is, who cares how much . . ."

I tuned Nestor out for the moment, figuring he would soon tire of the martyr routine. Making me listen to his complaints was the price he sometimes exacted from me.

"Anyway, I have Angel Estrada's home telephone records," Nestor finally said, "for the three days you requested. I'll have them hand-delivered to your office."

"No, fax them," I insisted, knowing how much Nestor hated to do so—he claimed faxes were always impossible to read, and no amount of evidence to the contrary was enough to convince him otherwise.

"If you say so," he sniffed. "I'll have the hard copies couriered over anyway, in case you have trouble reading the fax."

I groaned quietly, knowing how much that would add to

the cost. But I didn't complain. Nestor was the best, and always worth the price.

"Now it's time for you to give me the truth," he said. "Why didn't you tell me how hot this was?"

"What do you mean?" I asked.

"The tech at BellSouth told me the police requested the same information," Nestor said. "It's going to raise the bill for the service, by the way. But, more importantly, why didn't you tell me this Angel Estrada got killed a few days ago?"

"Sorry, Nestor," I said.

"Pulling phone records isn't something we do on a daily basis," he added. "It's serious business."

"I know, I know," I said. He had a right to be angry. I'd been in such a hurry that I hadn't told him that this was a sensitive matter.

"Are you in some kind of trouble?" he asked, his voice softening just a bit. "What's going on, Lupe?"

"I don't want to get you involved, Nestor," I said. "Thanks, really, for helping. And I'm sorry I wasn't up-front with you. Send your bill with the hard copies, and I'll pay in cash."

With Nestor, cash went a long way. Immigration attorneys were notoriously expensive.

"Take care of yourself," he said, sounding resigned to not knowing the whole story. "And be careful. Call me if you change your mind and want to talk to someone."

"You're the best," I said.

After I hung up I immediately felt guilty for not being truthful with Nestor. We had worked together for a long time and become friends, and I knew his irritation with me was founded as much on concern as anything. A moment later I heard the fax machine ringing in the outer office. Nestor had been true to his word.

There was a soft knock at my door. "Waiting for these?" Leonardo said, poking his head inside.

I flinched when I saw how my cousin was dressed. He had outdone himself, obviously violating his previously firm rule that any office wear had to weigh at least eight ounces. He would have been right at home at the Copacabana beach club in Rio. His entire outfit consisted of nothing more than a few strategically placed swatches of synthetic stretchy fabric.

Maybe we *did* need the ass-reduction machine, I thought. I was seeing more of his ass than anyone should, except maybe after dinner and drinks. I was just about convinced we needed a *lavado*.

"Uh, Leo, aren't you cold?" I asked, trying to be delicate and diplomatic.

His lip curled into a pout. "You don't like my outfit."

I bit my tongue. "Well, I like what there is of it," I said.

"It would cover more of me," he huffed, dropping the fax on my desk, "if there was less of me to cover."

He slammed the door on his way out. I shrugged. I had too many concerns already without worrying about Leonardo's body-image problems.

I looked over Nestor's printout—perfectly legible, of course—and immediately saw a pattern. Angel had been calling the same two numbers again and again. I inhaled sharply when I also saw a two-minute call to Havana, Cuba, placed after our meeting at the Grand Bay. At least that part of Jesus's story checked out.

I pulled out the Bresser's guide, which cross-referenced Dade County phone numbers with their addresses. One of the numbers corresponded to an address in Little Havana, the other to an address in Coral Gables. I took out my phone directory and saw that the latter number was for Angel's art business.

That left the Little Havana extension. Jesus wasn't listed with directory assistance—and when I checked, they would have told me if he had an unlisted number. The second number had to belong to him. Probably his service was in someone else's name. I wondered if the police had been effective enough to have uncovered this by now. Maybe not—this was not a high-priority murder case. Anyway, I was sure I had found him.

I checked my Beretta to make sure it was loaded, then left the Little Havana address on Leo's desk. I didn't want to walk into a potentially deadly situation without anyone knowing where I had gone.

"What's this?" Leo asked, looking at the paper. His indignation of a moment ago had vanished; I could tell he sensed the seriousness of what I was doing.

"Someone I need to see."

"Don't be mysterious with me," Leo said.

"I'll tell you later," I promised. "It's not a big deal. I just have to clear up a misunderstanding before it gets out of hand."

16

Jesus lived in a garage apartment behind a dilapidated ranch-style house in Little Havana, two blocks west of Eighth Street. This was not a warm, friendly neighborhood of barbecues and elderly people lazing away the evenings on their front porches. There were black-and-yellow crime-watch signs posted on every available electrical post, tree, and fence. Competing with these were plastic signs depicting snarling dogs, their fangs bared, saliva dripping. If that wasn't off-putting enough, each house's windows were covered in black wrought iron—although, before a thief could think about somehow penetrating the bars, they would have to negotiate ten-foot-high chain-link fences topped with concertina wire.

I was glad I had the Beretta in my purse, although I was vaguely worried about setting off some hidden weapons detector. I couldn't understand the need for such extreme security, since most of the homes looked as though they could be written up by the health department or condemned by the county engineer.

I had been in crack houses that looked better than the home in front of Jesus's garage. The paint was peeling off the place in strips, which accumulated in the brown grass next to the foundation. The windows were so blackened that

I suspected they were covered with thick sheets instead of curtains. The lone concession to aesthetic pride was a little potted cactus next to the front door.

The street was still and quiet, with no traffic. I walked along a narrow path beside the house until I reached a pad-locked gate in front of Jesus's apartment. On the gate, to my relief, was the name "J. Estrada," written in a large, childlike scrawl.

So I had the right place. Now I just had to hope that Detective Anderson hadn't put the place under surveillance yet. I had to hope he wasn't able to devote too much time to the case. It didn't seem too much to ask. I glanced back at the house. The shades were drawn, no signs of life inside.

I looked past a couple of neighborhood-watch and snarling dog signs until I finally found the doorbell. I pressed it, then almost jumped in the air in shock because of its shrill loud-ness. I heard a dog start barking somewhere a couple of yards over.

I waited a full minute before pressing the bell again. There were only two garage windows on this side, and in each heavy curtains were drawn. I guessed people around here didn't much enjoy the light of day.

Nothing. No response.

I really didn't feel like conducting a neighborhood canvas. I looked like a law-abiding, taxpaying citizen, but in this paranoid environment I would probably be shot as a thief. I was already taking a big chance standing there ringing the bell, I thought, since I had skulked around the side of the house. The last time I'd done something like this, I woke up with a lump on my head and a screaming headache.

Anyway, if I went around the area asking questions about Jesus, one of the neighbors might tell the police about me. That would surely put Detective Anderson on notice that I knew more about the case than I was letting on.

I stood there on a patch of concrete, the sun beating down on my head, considering my options. I certainly couldn't leave a note—it might fall into the wrong hands. The last thing I needed was a trail leading back to me—which was why I'd come in person instead of calling, since I had no way of knowing whether the police had put a tap on the phone. Already Nestor and his tech contact at BellSouth knew that I was somehow involved with Angel Estrada. I wanted to keep the number of people privy to that knowledge to a minimum.

I could wait in my car until Jesus showed up. Not an attractive option, and probably not very safe considering the security concerns of the locals. Also, I reminded myself, I wasn't billing anyone for the time I was spending here. Every minute I spent dealing with Jesus was a minute I should have spent on a paying case—especially since Doña Maria was so ill. Anyway, to conduct a proper surveillance on Jesus I would have to notify the cops and tell them I was working in the neighborhood. Such notice with the police was routine, to avoid being stopped by an officer for suspicious behavior. The last thing I needed was to be on record with the Miami P.D. that I was sitting in front of Jesus Estrada's house for hours.

There was only one thing for me to do. Jesus had told me that he had a studio, and I assumed it was also someplace in Miami. He had said he spent the majority of his time there. If I found the studio, then I found Jesus.

I looked around. No one was watching—at least that I could tell. My heart began to thump in my ears as I walked around to the back of the garage. I headed straight for the three large green trash cans alongside the building's wall. I shook my head when I saw that none of them were labeled. Nothing was ever easy. I would have to look through them all.

The cans were located on the property and not the public walkway, which meant that I was now officially trespassing. If someone were to take a shot at me, they might even be able to claim a legal justification—that they were protecting their property. I hadn't been Dumpster diving for quite a while, and it was every bit as nerve-wracking as I'd remembered.

I lifted the first lid, as quietly as possible. Inside were three neatly bundled brown plastic trash bags. I opened the first one, and almost retched at the strong smell of decay. I could barely bring myself to look inside. As soon as I had a look, I closed it up again. Soiled diapers. I thought I was safe in assuming that Jesus had no wife and kids.

I got lucky on the second can. As soon as I undid the tie holding the bag closed, I saw paper towels streaked and smeared with paint; a second later the strong smell of turpentine assaulted my nostrils. There was only one bag in the bin, and I was able to lift it out without much difficulty.

I looked to see if anyone was approaching with a shotgun. So far, so good. Now for the dangerous part. I had to retrace my steps past the house and to my car, this time while holding a full garbage bag. I could think of no plausible explanation if anyone stopped me and asked what the hell I was doing. One of the first rules of investigation is to always have a story ready to explain a compromising situation; this time I just gritted my teeth and jogged out to the street. I was breathing hard, and clutching onto the bag for dear life.

I jammed the key into the Mercedes, unlocked all four doors, and threw the trash bag into the backseat. I jumped in, revved the engine, and peeled out, my tires squealing on the pavement. For all the threatening signs, not a single resident had come out to investigate what I was doing in their neighborhood.

As I drove out of Little Havana, I debated where I should

go to sift through Jesus's trash. I didn't think it was a good idea to go back to the office. It was unlikely to happen, but I didn't want to be found with it in case Detective Anderson paid me a surprise visit. I decided the best thing was to find a public parking lot, go to a private corner, then move to the backseat and quickly go through the bag's contents. It was a good plan, but it also meant that I was going to inspect a load of garbage without the benefit of a pair of plastic gloves.

I drove east toward the Publix supermarket in Coral Gables, all the while trying to rid myself of the nagging fact that by getting rid of Jesus's trash after I looked through it, which I certainly would have to do, I would be destroying evidence and impeding a criminal investigation. Taking it back and replacing it in the can beside the garage was out of the question, although mailing it anonymously to Detective Anderson was an option I considered for about half a second before thinking better of it.

The lot at Publix was only half full. I was able to park under a tree, out of sight lines from the store. I blasted the air conditioner, set the radio to 102.7—my favorite oldies station—and slid into the backseat where I would have room to spread out.

All right, I thought. I take it back. This was the one time when things went easily.

I also thought there might not be a need for a *lavado* after all.

The first piece of paper I unrolled was a rent receipt marked *pagado*—"paid"—dated a month ago for a unit in a warehouse section of northwest Miami, close to the airport. I knew the area: a lot of artists rented cheap space there for studios.

The only drawback to the area was a lack of amenities, a fact that I knew from painful experience. I'd been to a party there about a year ago for an avant-garde Cuban painter's one-man show; after drinking several *mojitos*, I had to use the ladies' room. As soon as I opened the door, I was greeted by the smell of pipes leaking sewage, and a single cracked-porcelain toilet with no seat under an exposed bulb hanging from the ceiling. I decided I would rather risk a trip to the emergency room with a burst bladder. I wasn't one for lady-like prissiness, but I had my limits.

I copied down the address and continued going through the rest of the trash. There were almost no food scraps, which made the job a lot more pleasant. It was obvious that Jesus never cooked. He had an impressive variety of flyers for pizza, Chinese food, and Cuban delicatessens that served take-out meals. The rest of the trash all lent evidence to Jesus's claim to be a painter: rumpled papers, sketches, used brushes, receipts from art-supply stores.

I was done in less than five minutes. There was very little garbage in the bag, though that wasn't surprising for a single person who didn't cook. The trash in the neighborhood was probably picked up twice a week, as in most of Dade County. So this was only three days' worth, at most. I had gotten very lucky that Jesus had thrown out the receipt in that particular bag.

I slid the trash back in the bag, retied it, opened up the door, and walked to the Dumpster. One heave and the bag went over. It was done.

I looked at my watch. *Shit.* It was almost six already. I was going to get stuck in traffic all the way out to the airport. I considered putting off the trip until the next day, but decided I should forge ahead. Each day I was involved with Jesus Estrada—even if that involvement was primarily a product of his dogged refusal to listen to me when I said I wanted no part of his brother's plan—was another day that I was courting danger.

The fact was, I didn't *like* the Estrada brothers. And it had nothing to do with their ugly looks. Angel had been a lowlife, always angling for another buck no matter who it might hurt—in the instance of his forgery-smuggling plan, he would have been hurting the Cuban government, a fact that had clouded my reason long enough for me to actually take him seriously. As for Jesus, he was obviously unbalanced and untrustworthy. I was worried about who had killed Angel, but now I was also worried about Jesus leaping out from every blind corner, the way he had accosted me earlier in the Grove.

I couldn't shake off the growing sense that I was in deepening trouble the longer the Estradas were in my life. And I couldn't face the prospect of another sleepless night. Raccoon circles under my eyes weren't a look that I pulled off well.

Then there was the matter of the eighth unicorn tapestry. Not exactly a nice, safe, rational case to work.

But at least it gave me billable hours. And a chance to help realize an old woman's dying wish.

17

Oh, no.

I had been to enough crime scenes during my career as a private investigator to recognize instantly the distinct sickly sweet odor emanating from the three-inch gap under the metal door of Jesus's studio. I leaned my head against the corrugated metal and took a couple of deep breaths, cautioning myself not to jump to conclusions. I didn't know who had met an untimely end in there. Just because it was Jesus's studio didn't necessarily mean it was Jesus.

The studio was actually an individual concrete storage area, one of many aligned in a long row next to a warehouse. I looked around the open area outside and saw no one. I half hoped to see a warehouse employee who could help, even though that meant the police would find out I'd been there. It was too late to hide my involvement in the Estrada case, I realized.

The place seemed to be deserted, not surprising considering that it was almost eight in the evening. I saw only rows and rows of concrete sheds, each door painted a vivid orange to counterbalance the awful bland sameness of the place. I waited a few minutes, hoping to see someone, but nothing happened. Whoever worked here, patrolling the grounds and helping people gain access to the sheds, was probably well into their happy hour.

I had three choices. I could leave. I could stand there smelling a body decompose in the oppressive evening heat. Or I could do something.

I reached into my purse for the white linen handkerchief Aida insisted I carry because a lady should have one in her possession at all times. I carefully placed it on the rusted doorknob. With my thumb and forefinger I turned the knob a couple of inches.

To my surprise, it moved easily. I almost wished it hadn't. A moment later I had turned it completely. I cracked open the door a couple of inches.

The hell with the handkerchief. I put it back in my purse and took out the Beretta instead. I double-checked to make sure it was loaded, then pushed the door open a few more inches. I'd begun to sweat from fear, and I had to blink to clear the perspiration from my eyes. I felt a trickle of moisture run down my back. I didn't know what I was going to find inside the unit, but I knew I had to go in.

I told myself that, technically, this wasn't breaking and entering. The door, after all, wasn't locked. And I knew the smell of a dead body, and that there was one inside. I was obligated to check it out. I touched the three medals of the Virgin pinned to my brassiere, which my sister Lourdes had given me to wear at all times for protection, said a brief prayer to Her, then pushed open the door all the way.

The stench stopped me for a second, and I had to fight the impulse to run back out. I fought off a gag reflex and paused inside the doorway, waiting for my eyes to adjust to the gloom. Taking out the handkerchief again, I rolled it into a ball and stuffed it over my nose. I had never been so grateful for the fact that Aida used violet sachets to scent all the linens back home.

I groped along the wall until my hand found a light switch. I turned it on.

"Mierda."

The clutter in the small space was unbelievable. Every inch was full of canvases, paint tubes, cans, brushes, rags, easels. There were stacks of debris concentrated in several locations, apparently where Jesus worked. I saw a few half-finished canvases: a landscape, a colorful abstract, a portrait of a young woman.

I picked my way through the mess toward the back of the room. The smell got worse, and I had to press the handkerchief closer to my nose. I had the barrel of the Beretta pointing up, where I could use it. The place was so cluttered that I had trouble picking out what I was seeing. It struck me that someone could conceivably be hiding somewhere.

I wanted to wipe away the sweat running down my face, but both my hands were occupied. I was breathing hard, blinking to keep myself focused. My finger felt tight on the trigger of the gun, and I knew I would probably fire it at any noise.

Jesus's studio wasn't kept at a comfortable sixty-five degrees, as his brother's apartment had been. That was why his body was in such an advanced state of decomposition when I found it splayed in the back of the place. Flies were buzzing around him in a little swarm.

I couldn't move. I just kept looking at what I saw, unable to believe it. Jesus was on his back, an expression of terror fixed upon his features. What was that sticking out of his chest?

A paintbrush.

I looked harder, to make sure it was real. The steel handle of a big paintbrush had been jammed into the middle of Jesus's chest. His hands were curled into claws on either side of it, as though in his final moment he had been trying to reach it to pull it out.

The fluorescent ceiling lights gave off an eerie brightness, shading everything in a sickly green. I crouched down closer to the body and saw that Jesus had soiled himself as his muscles relaxed in death. It was the ultimate indignity, somehow almost unbearably sad.

Jesus's skin was discolored, but because of the light and the heat it was hard for me to make even a vague guess as to the time of death. It was strange that an artist would have such lousy light in his studio; maybe he worked by lamps that I hadn't noticed amid the mess. The smell closer to his body was almost unbearable, and the clutter of objects all around me felt as though it was retaining the lingering heat from outside.

I forced myself to stop staring at Jesus, instead looking around. Satisfied there was no one else in the studio, I carefully tucked the Beretta inside the waistband of my skirt. I reached into my purse for my cell phone, punched in a few numbers, spoke a few facts, and hung up quickly.

Now that I'd placed the call, my time was limited. I had a narrow window in which to look over the place. As soon as the police arrived, it would become a homicide investigation crime scene, and I would be denied further access.

Any action I took might destroy evidence, so I moved gingerly. The place was in such chaotic disorder that it was hard to tell if there had been a struggle or if the killer had taken anything. There were a few spilled cans of paint thinner near Jesus's body, the only evidence I saw of a physical confrontation. My instinct was to rule out robbery—at least for cash, which I doubted Jesus had much of. No, the killer had been after something else. A painting. Or information. I shuddered as I wondered whether Jesus had died because of Angel's scheme—and whether the killer's attention might next turn to me.

I breathed hard of the violet-scented handkerchief, moving to examine more closely the canvases scattered through the room. There were more than I'd realized at first, maybe fifteen, oils in all shapes and sizes.

Now that I had a better look at the paintings, I realized that I was apparently standing in a mini-museum of fine art. But that was impossible. They had to be fake. It looked as though Camila wasn't the only member of the Estrada family who could copy masterpieces.

Jesus's specialty was Cuban artists. I was no art expert—recent public opinion to the contrary—but even I recognized most of these paintings. They were replicas of works by icons of Cuban art: Wilfredo Lam, Tomas Sanchez, Antonia Eiriz, Amelia Pelaez. If they weren't direct copies, they were at least executed in the various artists' styles.

There were art books, magazines, and auction catalogues scattered on a table in the corner. They all had to do with Cuban art and artists, and most of them were open to pages displaying the works I was seeing all around me.

There wasn't much time left. I had called the police almost ten minutes before. I hated leaving the studio without any answers, but I didn't want to risk staying any longer and being caught in the crime scene. There were a lot of rules about maintaining the integrity of crime scenes, and walking around one unauthorized was a sure way to run afoul of the law. I took one last look around, then went back outside.

It was still hot out there, but it was positively arctic compared to the sweltering stillness inside the studio. I finally took the handkerchief away from my nostrils and breathed in big lungfuls of fresh air.

I tugged at my clothes, which were sticking to my body from sweat, while waiting for Detective Anderson and his techs to arrive. I wished I was a smoker. It would have been a perfect moment for a cigarette. After what I'd seen inside the studio, I was almost tempted to start.

The sound of sirens far away grew rapidly louder, closer.

I vaguely wondered why it was necessary to turn them on and rush to a scene where the crime had been committed, the victim already dead. Of course it was all in the name of connecting evidence, of preserving the crime scene like a snapshot moment in time, an instant that would slowly reveal all the meanings and coincidences of a person's final day.

Detective Anderson was leading the pack in his brown county-issued nondescript car. He got out, frowning, and slowly walked toward me.

"So, Lupe, I should have known," he said. "As soon as you take an interest in a case I'm working, another body shows up."

Anderson didn't say this in an accusatory fashion; it was a statement of fact, and one I couldn't argue with.

"Sorry about that," I said. Wherever I went, as far as Anderson was concerned, dead bodies piled up.

The area around the warehouse and storage units was soon a beehive of activity. More cars arrived, parking haphazardly in the lanes between the units. The cops started to seal off the area with yellow-and-black tape.

Anderson leaned back against the hood of his car, took out his notebook. He gave me the once-over, not in a sexual way but with a detective's dispassionate eye. His eyes paused briefly on the bulge at my waist, where the Beretta was still tucked away. I hadn't wanted to put it away while I was waiting for the cops, in case I ran into trouble, but I'd taken the precaution of untucking my T-shirt and letting it hang down to conceal the weapon. I wasn't about to take it out in front of Anderson, and he seemed content not to bring it up.

"You know the drill," he said, flipping to an empty page in his notebook. "Talk to me."

I chose my words very carefully, telling him what little I knew about Jesus Estrada's short, sad life. I knew I had to

tiptoe carefully and not say anything to make Anderson suspect that I was keeping information from him. I stretched
the truth a bit. I said that Jesus had contacted me (true) and
wanted to talk (true) about his brother's death (partly true),
that he asked me to come to his studio (not true) and that
he was dead when I found him (true). I told Anderson the
door was ajar about a foot when I got there, that I had given
it just a little push (not true). No matter how you tabulated
it, I was giving Anderson more truth than falsehood. It
wasn't so bad, especially when I considered the fact that
many people lie to the police routinely, and that the police
are accustomed to it.

I kept talking, trying to get Anderson to tell me how the
investigation into Angel's murder was going.

"I knew the body was Jesus," I said, "because of his strong
resemblance to Angel."

"Uh-huh," Anderson said, not interested. I couldn't blame
him. He had been forthcoming with me about his investigation, and all he'd gotten in return was another corpse and a
vague explanation.

I figured there was a pretty good chance he might come
back at me later, asking questions to clarify my statement. I
knew I could count on Tommy to keep me out of hot water,
in that case. It wouldn't be the first time and, knowing my
own propensity for finding trouble, wouldn't be the last. Besides, I'd worked with Tommy for a long time, I knew the
caliber of his clients and the sort of things they were trying
to get away with. My situation in comparison was a pecca-
dillo, a lark. Anyway, if Tommy wanted to keep working
cases with me, he'd have to make sure I was still licensed
and practicing, and not crossing off the days on a calendar
as a guest of Dade County taxpayers.

It was about midnight when the crime-scene techs were
finished. Jesus's body was taken away to the medical examin-

er's, where an autopsy would determine the official time and cause of death. My guess was that the steel paintbrush jammed into his chest was the culprit, but then, I wasn't a doctor.

It occurred to me how hard it would be to jam an object like that through bone and muscle. It would take a very strong hand. It seemed as though the person who'd done it was sending a message of some kind.

Of course, I didn't know what that message was.

In my statement to Detective Anderson, I completely avoided all mention of the Estrada family's foray into art fraud and the part they had expected me to play. As I drove away from the scene, exhausted and drained of energy, I thought again about what Jesus's death might mean for me.

Two of the four people who were supposedly involved in the smuggling of Cuban art from the island had met with brutal deaths in the past few days. That left Camila and me.

I wondered if Angel Estrada had talked to anyone besides his brother about how he had my commitment to his scheme—a commitment I'd never made, but that might turn out to be my downfall anyway.

What next? I asked myself. Or maybe the better question to ask was: who next?

I turned on the radio, opened up the car windows and let the warm night air wash over me as I hit the freeway. After the events of the week, I felt grateful to be alive. Now I had to figure out how to stay that way.

18

After the events of the evening, I should have collapsed into heavenly dreamless sleep, but that wasn't the case. I tossed and turned for a couple of hours, only to finally drop off around dawn. My sleep was shallow and fitful, and I was in lousy shape when I finally got to the office at mid-morning. Every inch of my body felt sore, my eyes were burning, I had a low-grade headache. It was going to be a long day, but I was involved in three investigations and couldn't afford to take any time off. Time was passing me by too quickly.

I stepped into the doorway and Leonardo sprang out of his chair to get me a *café con leche*. He usually had to give me a lecture about showing up looking like I'd had a rough night; this time, though, he spared me. That was when I knew I really looked like shit. His reaction wasn't exactly a confidence builder for starting the day.

"Thank you," I muttered, accepting the coffee and heading back to my office. Outside the window the parrots were up to their usual activity level. I took some comfort in the fact that they seemed to be over their one-day spell of lethargy. There was probably hope for me as well.

I looked over my message slips. Alvaro had returned my call earlier that morning. My heart jumped when I read his name written in Leo's ornate, curlicue handwriting. I thought about picking up the phone and calling him back right away, but decided to wait until I'd had some coffee and felt more like myself.

There was a message from the director of the Art Loss Register in London. Tommy had also called. There was a message from Detective Anderson. Finally, the last message was from Lucia Miranda.

All right. Everyone involved in my three cases was trying to reach me at the same time. I looked at the clock on the wall and saw that it was only ten in the morning. Basically each person had called me first thing that morning, with the exception of the call from London.

I unfolded the *Miami Herald* and turned to the local section. I hadn't expected to see anything about Jesus in there, since it had been pretty late when the crime reporter was granted access to the scene, but I was mistaken. There was a two-inch paragraph describing the discovery of the body of a Cuban-born painter in his studio, the victim of apparent foul play. No connection was made to the murder of Angel a few days before. I wondered how long it would be before someone at the *Herald* put together the names and the killings.

I put the newspaper down on the corner of my desk and picked up the stack of messages. I tried to think of who to call first. The truth was, none of them were very appealing at the moment.

I heard a tapping at my door. It opened, and Leo stuck his head in. He was holding a pot of coffee in his hand.

"Here," he said, refilling my glass. He had a slightly frightened expression. I must have really looked terrible. Leonardo wasn't above making coffee, but he had never served it to me in my office before.

"*Gracias*, Leo," I said. I turned my coffee cup around so the Cuban flag on it was facing me, just the way I liked it.

"You saw your messages?" Leonardo asked. I could tell from his tone that he was most concerned about Alvaro's, which he had deliberately placed on top of all the others. "I put them on your desk."

I suppressed a smile. Leo put the messages in the same place he had for the past eight years.

"*Sí,* I saw them. *Gracias* again."

Leonardo stood there awkwardly, shifting his weight from one foot to the other, his worry mounting. We always made it a point not to interfere in each other's romantic affairs, unless we were asked. I believed that was one of the reasons we got along so well.

Finally he couldn't stand it anymore. "Lupe, are you all right?" he blurted out.

"I have a lot on my mind," I replied, a little weakly. I didn't want to tell him about the tapestry hanging in a hidden basement in Havana, and that I'd agreed to somehow fetch it. I also didn't want him to know that I might be next on the list of whoever had killed the Estrada brothers—and, even worse, that I was working the case without compensation. And I didn't want to tell him, although I was sure he'd already guessed, that I had rekindled my relationship with Tommy McDonald over yet another case dealing with stolen Cuban art.

Any one of the three would probably have sent my cousin out the door screaming, into the arms of his Santería priest so we could finally have his *lavado.* If he had known the details of my falling out with Alvaro, he probably would have wanted to keep the priest on permanent retainer, like an "of counsel" at a law firm.

Leonardo gave me a skeptical look, realizing I wasn't telling him anything. He also knew from experience that I might keep information to myself as a way of assuming total responsibility for a case; and, since he knew he would accomplish nothing by pressing me, he started to walk out.

"Well, Lupe," he said in a defeated voice, "you know where to find me if you decide you want to talk about it."

"I appreciate it," I said, meaning it. "But don't worry, Leo. I'm just a little tired. I'll be better after a good night's sleep."

A little tired. Right. And Cuba was just a little island.

I took a big gulp of *café con leche*, scalding my mouth in the process. Oh, well, I was Catholic enough to realize that this was a proper punishment for my recent behavior. Anyway, there was no putting it off any longer. I picked up the phone and dialed.

"Alvaro, *hola*," I said when he answered. I tried to keep my voice light. "How are you?"

"Lupe." Alvaro said my name in such a stern way, with such an absence of affection, that I felt a chill. "I don't know what your plans are regarding what we talked about before. Nor do I really want to."

A pause. The hand that held the phone was shaking. The receiver almost slipped from it. I pulled out a tissue to dry off my sweating palm.

"Write down this name, address, and phone number," Alvaro continued in the same ominous manner.

I grabbed one of the pens lying on my desk and reached for a pad of paper.

"Mabel Magali Montenegro," he said slowly. He went on to dictate an address in Havana, followed by a Cuban phone number.

"Who is—"

"Mabel is a lawyer," Alvaro said. "She's also my friend."

My antenna went up. In spite of the fact that I had split with Alvaro and slept with Tommy, I was consumed with curiosity. Was this Mabel a friend? Or a lover, a girlfriend? I knew that Alvaro had traveled to Cuba several times; he certainly could have developed a relationship with a Cuban woman.

"If you get into trouble, call her," Alvaro continued. "That is, if you're allowed to make a call. You might just disappear. After all, you will be there to commit a crime. But if you have a chance, get in touch with Mabel. Tell her the truth about who you are and about why you're there."

"What if she asks how I got her name?"

A legitimate question, but I was also curious about how Alvaro would react, and what he would want me to say to this woman. Anyway, it was better than dwelling on the "you might just disappear" part.

"Use my name, tell her we grew up together," he replied, neatly sidestepping any attempt at putting a label on our relationship. "Above all, be honest with her. She can't help you if she doesn't have information. Remember, Cuba isn't the United States. None of the laws protecting the rights of the accused apply there."

"I see," I said, sensing the anxiety and worry in his voice.

"Once you're in there, you'll be totally on your own," Alvaro said. "But it's your choice."

"Thank you," I said, trying to keep my voice as emotionless as I could. Almost unconsciously, I'd reached under my T-shirt, found the medals of the Virgin pinned to my brassiere, and undid them one by one. Now, I lined them up in a row on my desk, right next to the Cuban attorney's name and number.

"Alvaro," I said, taking a deep breath. "I've been meaning to talk to you about the other night at Tuscan Steak."

"Lupe, please. I don't want to discuss that night. Not now, not ever."

"Let me explain," I insisted, a pleading note in my voice. I could never understand why we don't see how important someone is to us until we're on the verge of losing him or her. "Please let me—"

"I'm sorry," Alvaro said flatly, cutting me off. "You made your feelings known to me that night. I told you how foolhardy what you plan to do is, but I can tell you're still going to risk it. You know it will affect your family and me, but you have no consideration for anyone else. Tell the truth. You're still planning to go, right?"

Until that moment, I had still held out a strand of hope that I wouldn't have to go, that I could somehow bring the tapestry back while staying in Miami. But I knew that was impossible. The only way I could possibly retrieve it was to go to Cuba and bring it back myself.

"*Sí*," I said. "I have to do it."

"Then we have nothing more to discuss," Alvaro said. The sadness and resignation in his voice was enough to break my heart. "I will pray for your safe return. *Adios*, Guadalupe."

He hung up. The harsh click didn't quite mask the sound of my sharp intake of breath.

I held the phone against my ear for so long that a recorded announcement came on the line, asking me if I wanted to make another call. I hung up the phone, slowly pinned the medals back on my brassiere, and sat up straight, my shoulders squared.

I replayed every word of our conversation. At least Alvaro hadn't said that our relationship was over for good. I held out hope that, after my successful return from Cuba, there was a chance we could figure out where we stood. I set aside the complication of Tommy for the moment.

It took me a couple of minutes before I was ready to step out of my office. I had to convince myself that everything was going to work out for the best.

Leonardo and I took our time dawdling over lunch at the Last Carrot, a health-food place on Grand Avenue. I needed to get out of the office and clear my head, and having resolved to spent more time with my cousin, I invited him to have lunch with me. I felt a pang of guilt when I saw how enthusiastically he accepted my invitation. We walked the couple of blocks to the restaurant, talking about what we were going to order—despite the fact that our orders had never varied in all the time we had been going there, nor had the menu.

During lunch we talked about everything except what was going on with me. Sensing a possible chink in my armor, Leonardo brought up the *lavado* again.

"Maybe," I said, holding up my hand when he started beaming. "Listen, I'm not saying yes. I'm saying I'll think about it."

Leonardo smiled at me over his mango shake. I could no longer dismiss the *lavado*, or any other possible way of improving life. It wasn't as though things were going so well for me that I could rule anything out.

I returned my cousin's smile, feeling glad I'd taken him out. Leonardo was always good at distracting me from my problems and worries, and I had almost forgotten how much fun he and I could have just being together.

We walked slowly back to the office, laughing and talking about old cases. We both turned silent in the same moment when we turned the corner to our cottage. There was a shabbily dressed, slightly built middle-aged man waiting on the top step of the office, right next to the door. I reached into my purse and made sure the Beretta was there.

We walked up the driveway, getting closer to the building. Our visitor looked basically harmless, but still I didn't relax. I didn't want any unpleasant surprises, in light of what had been going on. Two murders were enough to make anyone paranoid.

The man looked up, then jumped to his feet. "Señorita Solano?" he asked.

"*Sí*," I replied. "What can I do for you?"

He reached into his pocket. The instant he made his move, I stuck my hand in my bag, pulled out the Beretta, and aimed it at his chest.

"Wait, wait!" the man cried out.

"Lupe! *Dios mio!*" Leonardo squealed.

I don't know which of them jumped higher at the sight of the gun, Leonardo or our visitor. The man put his hands up in the air, then folded them behind his head. He had obviously been watching too many cop shows on TV.

"Please, please, señorita. Don't kill me," he said. He closed his eyes, apparently expecting me to shoot. I was getting the idea that he wasn't here to harm me after all.

"What do you want?" I asked.

"I just came to talk," he said, his eyes still closed. "I was reaching for a piece of paper in my pocket. Nothing more. You have my word."

I tucked the gun in the waistband of my skirt, for the second time in twenty-four hours. If things kept up, I was going to have to start wearing the leather holster I kept in my desk drawer.

As soon as the gun was gone, Leonardo breathed a big sigh of relief. He leaned against the cottage, shaking his head. The man opened his eyes, carefully dropped his hands to his sides.

"What can I help you with?" I asked him.

The man glanced at Leonardo. "Please," he said, "would it be possible for us to speak in private?"

Leonardo arched one eyebrow at me, looking for a sign of what I wanted him to do.

"It's OK, Leo," I said. "Go on inside. I'll let you know if I need any help."

I tried not to let any sarcasm creep into my voice; from his reaction to the sight of the gun, I didn't think Leo was the person I would be calling for help if I got into a life-and-death struggle.

When we were alone I looked at the man expectantly, feeling my patience starting to wear out.

"I came to talk to you about this," he said. He gingerly reached into his pocket again, taking out a carefully folded piece of newspaper. He handed it to me to read. It was the same article I had read in the *Herald* about Jesus's murder, only it was from the Spanish-language *El Nuevo Herald*.

"I don't read English," he said apologetically.

"I know about Jesus Estrada," I told him. "Who are you?"

"My name is Reinaldo Estrada," he said. "I am Angel and Jesus's cousin."

I scanned Reinaldo's features for a family resemblance. He was very ordinary looking, someone I might walk past on the street without even noticing. He was thin, with brown hair and eyes, a slightly pointed nose—he seemed to have escaped the ugliness genes that had taken hold in his cousins.

"I am sorry to have surprised you," he added. "But I knew no other way to contact you."

A phone call would have been a lot less startling, I thought. But I decided that I should go easy on Reinaldo. I had, after all, scared him half to death a few minutes before. And he had lost two close relatives in the past week.

"I'm supposed to give you this," he told me. He reached into his back pocket and took out a thin piece of paper that looked as though it had been folded and refolded many times. He took a step toward me, tentative, obviously still remembering the sight of the Beretta.

I unfolded the paper. There was the name Camila Maria Estrada, an address in Havana.

"Who told you to give this to me?" I asked Reinaldo. "What am I supposed to do with this?"

Reinaldo turned on his heels and started walking away.

"Camila is waiting for you," he called out over his shoulder. "You must contact her."

"Waiting for . . ." I began, then realized Reinaldo had no intention of answering any of my questions. He turned the corner onto the street, jogging. I took off after him, feeling lucky to be wearing flat-heeled shoes that day.

He was too fast for me. He rounded the corner, ran behind a bus, and was gone by the time it pulled away. I stood in the middle of the street, looking in all directions. He could have gone anywhere.

A second later I heard heavy panting behind me. I turned, a second away from reaching for my gun.

"Don't even think about it!" Leonardo shrieked. "I was watching you from the office window the whole time. What happened? Why were you chasing that guy?"

I looked down at the piece of paper in my hand. Camila Maria Estrada. I hoped the Virgin would protect her better than She had protected Camila's brothers. Camila was named for the Virgin, I realized, and I was named after one of the sites where the Holy Mother appeared in an apparition. Was it a coincidence, or was fate closing in on me?

"Come on," I told Leo, pulling on his arm. "We're going to get hit by a car standing out here."

We walked back to the office together, neither of us speaking. Leonardo was still shaken up by the gun and in no mood for conversation. For my part, a million thoughts occupied my mind. And all of them took me back to Cuba.

19

""Is this enough money for everything we're going to need for the crossing?" I asked Barbara, giving her a stack of hundred dollar bills. It was late at night, under a brilliant sky full of stars. Barbara and I were on the deck of her sailboat, sipping Añejo. Every so often the breeze sent the cloud of smoke from her cigar my way. We were relaxed, talking quietly, enjoying our rum.

"That should do it," she replied in a low voice, tucking the money into her brassiere.

I had planned the timetable that we would follow, but Barbara was the more experienced sailor and I was counting on her to determine which supplies we would need. There was also a special set of items I was going to obtain for myself. I had called for, and received, another check from Lucia Miranda. The expedition was flush with cash.

"So, Lupe, we're doing it the same way." I saw the end of Barbara's cigar flare as she inhaled. "We leave from Key West. Only this time we head toward Havana."

Three years before, we had taken the specially outfitted sailboat *Mamita*, landing at Isabela de Sagua, a fishing village on Cuba's north coast. We had left from the Truman Annex Marina in Key West.

"It makes the most sense," I agreed. "It's the shortest distance from the United States to the island. And we can top off the gas tank without having to answer too many questions about what we're going to do."

Barbara laughed loudly. "I bet that gringo is still there, the dockmaster who liked you."

"Henry. That was his name," I fondly recalled, thinking of the dockmaster's muscular legs. I hoped he was there. If things were to go wrong in Cuba, he might help make my last day of freedom more enjoyable.

"*Ay, chica,* if he's there, that would be a good omen." Barbara's long braid flew as she threw her head back and emptied her glass. She reached for the bottle next to her and refilled her glass with a smooth practiced motion.

Barbara had a healthy appetite for life. She had given birth to about a dozen children, mostly by different men. But she never seemed bitter, or to wish that she'd taken a different path. She loved her children fiercely. And as long as there was food on the table, Añejo in a glass, a good cigar to smoke, and gas in the *Santa Barbara,* she seemed to be satisfied. Whenever she needed money, she went fishing. She kept part of the catch to feed her brood and sold the rest.

I also suspected that Barbara had other sources of income. For instance, there was serious money to be made smuggling Cubans off the island to the United States. Barbara was uniquely qualified for that business—she had a boat, and she was a gifted sailor. Her clients, unlike me, wouldn't require a higher-speed craft like Papi's Hatteras. She had extensive knowledge of both the Cuban and South Florida coasts. Most important, she had the kind of temperament for the high degree of risk involved.

The risk was no joke. I remembered a couple of years ago, when a few men—two islanders and an exile—were arrested by Cuban authorities for smuggling people into the United

States. They had received stiff sentences—one smuggler was sentenced to life in prison.

Barbara feared nothing and no one, as far as I could tell. I had seen her sleep, and it was the deep dreamless slumber of the innocent. I had also seen her kill two men to protect us when we were in mortal danger, with an astonishing efficiency and lack of remorse. Barbara filled my glass, and her expression turned serious.

"I need to know a few things," she said. "I've been on other Hatterases, but never one this big."

I reached into my purse for my notebook. I had figured Barbara would want to know details about the *Concepcion*, and I'd copied the boat's specifications onto a sheet of paper from the manuals that came with the craft.

"The boat is fifty-two feet long," I read to her. "Papi has all the best machinery and equipment on it."

"Tell me about the engines." Barbara's eyes narrowed as she listened and puffed on her cigar. She didn't write anything down; the reason for this, I suspected, was that she couldn't read or write. Barbara came from a small fishing village in Cuba near the infamous Bahia de Cochinos—the Bay of Pigs—where an ill-fated invasion by Cuban exiles had taken place in 1961. The village was so tiny that it appeared on very few maps. It was ignored by the government, for the most part, and some of its children had never gone to a school—this despite a very high literacy rate in Castro's Cuba.

"The engines are Twin Detroit Diesel," I read to her.

"Good. Fancy." Barbara nodded her approval. "And no noise from those. They purr like a cat getting its belly rubbed." A large swallow of Añejo, a puff on the cigar.

"Their range is one hundred eighty to two hundred miles," I told her.

"It's ninety from Key West to Havana," Barbara said. It was a figure we were both very familiar with.

"It would be difficult to make the round trip without refueling, wouldn't it?" I asked her.

Barbara thought for a moment. "We need some of that fuel to run the generators," she said thoughtfully. "We can't count on all of it for the engines. It'll also depend on the wind and the tides."

"And our speed, right?" I asked. "That also affects the gas consumption."

Barbara didn't answer. She stared into my eyes, silent.

"What?" I asked.

"I haven't asked you why we're going to Cuba," she said slowly. She held up the lit cigar end, watching the smoke curl in the dark.

I trusted Barbara with my freedom and my life. I certainly could trust her with the purpose of our trip. After all, she was facing the same risks as me.

"We're going to pick up some art," I said.

"Art. What do you mean?" Barbara poured another glass of Añejo. I held up a hand to stop her, but she poured a healthy amount into my glass as well.

"A tapestry," I said. "We're going into Havana to bring out a very valuable tapestry on behalf of its owners."

Barbara mulled over what I had just told her, then chuckled. "That'll be a different cargo," she said. "What size? What weight?"

"Big," I said. "Measured from floor to ceiling. Twelve feet by twelve feet. I don't know the exact weight, but I'm guessing about 150 pounds. Maybe two hundred." I wished that Ambassador de Castellanos had been able to give me that information when I had asked him.

I took a sip of my drink. The damned tapestry outweighed

me by quite a bit. I wasn't sure whether I was going to be able to carry it, if I found myself on my own with it.

"The *Concepcion*, she has some sort of dinghy?" Barbara asked. I noticed that she had begun to sip her Añejo, instead of knocking it back as though it was oasis water.

"A Boston Whaler. Thirteen feet." I knew the craft well; my sisters, nieces, and I often went out in the boat on Biscayne Bay.

"Good, Lupe," Barbara said. "Because the Hatteras can't go all the way to land. It would draw too much water, and it would show up on radar. You understand that, don't you?"

Barbara was down to about the last inch of her cigar. I liked cigar smoke as much as the next Cuban, but I have to admit that breathing an entire Montecristo Numero Uno—even though it was a fine cigar—was getting to be too much for me.

I looked down at my notebook. "The *Concepcion* would need a minimum of four feet six inches under her to keep from going aground," I said. "The Whaler draws only a foot of water. But if it's traveling at a fast speed, it would need more, because the boat would plane."

Barbara nodded approvingly. "There's also the matter of what's considered international water," she said in the tone of a teacher to an able pupil. "The Cubans, of course, claim the most: twelve miles." She rolled her eyes in exasperation. "Others claim five, others three. Whatever, it means anchoring out on the high seas and motoring to shore in the Whaler."

I understood this, but it was frightening to think about Cuba's claim to territorial waters. That very issue had been at the core of the conflict regarding the shooting down of two Brothers to the Rescue planes by Russian MiGs. The Cuban government claimed the planes were on a spy mission, as evidenced by their flying over Cuba's territorial waters, while Cuban exiles maintained they had been flying over international waters.

The more I listened to Barbara, the more I was convinced that she had been to the island more often than our single trip together. It was actually a heartening thought, to realize that she had more experience than I'd imagined.

We sat together without talking for a while, letting the soft rocking of the boat gently lull us. I didn't think I had been that relaxed since Lucia Miranda first walked into my office, a week before. I realized I had to pull myself together or else I was going to fall asleep on the deck of the boat.

"Barbara?" I said.

"*Si*, Lupe?" replied a sleepy voice.

"Do you think we can do it?"

"*Ay*, Lupe," Barbara said, her voice fading as sleep took over. "Of course we can. Have we ever failed at anything we took on together?"

"No," I whispered in return. "Never."

20

The phone rang as soon as we got back to the office. Leonardo answered it, then put his hand over the mouthpiece.

"It's Lucia Miranda," he said.

I shook my head and gave him my usual signals when I didn't want to speak with someone. Leo just stood there, his eyebrows raised expectantly. He obviously could tell that Lucia wasn't going to accept any misdirection or delays. I shrugged in resignation, went into my office, picked up the phone.

"Lucia, *buenas tardes*," I said. "How is your mother?"

"That's why I'm calling," Lucia said, her voice rife with impatience. "She's still in the hospital. But, thank God, she's in her own room and out of intensive care."

"That's good news," I said.

"For the moment," Lucia replied. "But her doctors tell me she could have a relapse at any time."

Lucia was very effective at making sure I knew the noose around my neck was tightening every day. Although I was making plans for getting into Cuba, I had yet to leave. Maybe subconsciously I had thought something would happen to get me off the hook.

"You've received your retainer, right?" Lucia asked with characteristic bluntness.

She knew I'd gotten the money. After all, I'd had to sign for it.

"I have," I said.

"Mama keeps asking about the tapestry," Lucia said. "That is, when she's lucid and aware of her surroundings. I think the fact that she's going to see it is the only thing keeping her alive."

I just sat there, holding the phone, listening. I had my own reasons for agreeing to bring the tapestry back from Cuba, and I was starting to resent Lucia's guilt trip. She didn't seem to care at all that I was risking my freedom and maybe even my life for her family's possession.

I took a deep breath. There was no point getting angry with Lucia. I agreed to take the job, and it had been my own choice. I was also getting paid for it. And I had been familiar with Lucia's personality long before I'd ever heard about the eighth tapestry.

"I understand the delicacy and the urgency of the situation," I said slowly. Then I gave her a brief overview of the research I'd done on handling the tapestry once I found it in Havana. I knew that clients like Lucia were always placated by the understanding that they were getting their money's worth.

"I see," she finally said. "I can tell that you have everything very much under control, Lupe."

I almost fell out of my chair. The woman had actually praised me.

"One last thing," she said. "When can I tell Mama that she will be reunited with her beloved unicorn?"

I knew it couldn't last.

"I have to finalize some arrangements," I said. "Then I'll have a better idea."

Hell, I still had plenty left to figure out. But I wasn't about to let Lucia even remotely suspect that. I knew not to let her see any chinks in my armor.

"We are counting on you," Lucia said. And then she hung up.

A nice lady, I thought. And one who was used to getting what she wanted.

I opened up the Lucia Miranda case file, which was sitting prominently right next to the phone. I leafed through the documents Lucia had given me: the letter from Columbus to Rogelio Miranda, then the certificate of authenticity written up by Albert O. Manfredi.

Albert O. Manfredi. I wondered who he was, and how he had been persuaded to keep quiet about the tapestry he authenticated. The temptation to reveal one of art history's greatest secrets must have been overwhelming, especially to an art expert.

The Mirandas must have paid him—for his expertise and for his subsequent silence. And it must have been a lot.

I looked over the certificate, wondering how I could find out Manfredi's identity. It was unlikely that he was still kicking around someplace. He inspected the tapestry in 1932, and even if he had been in his thirties at the time—very young for an art expert, I figured—he would be about a hundred today.

I couldn't have said specifically why, but it was important that I find out who Albert Manfredi was. I could have simply asked Lucia, but I decided not to. I paused, realizing my instincts were leading me someplace unprecedented. Then I decided I needed to trust those same instincts.

New York was a logical place to start looking. The other tapestries were located there, so the Mirandas might have wanted an expert who could review the tapestries hanging in the Cloisters and then compare them to the eighth tapestry in their possession.

I made a call to New York directory assistance, then phoned the Metropolitan Museum of Art in New York. I told the young man who answered—to my amazement, a real, live, breathing human instead of a recording—that I was a graduate student at U.C. Berkeley, specializing in Medieval Art. I said I needed some information about an art specialist who had once been affiliated with the museum.

"I'll try to help you," the young man said, sounding pleased to have an unusual request come his way. "What's the name of the person you're trying to locate?"

"Albert O. Manfredi," I replied.

I heard the clicking of computer keys in the background. "Manfredi, Manfredi," the man muttered to himself. "Can you spell that for me?"

I spelled the name, double-checking with the document Lucia had given me. My heart started to sink as I heard more clicking. My helper was having trouble locating the name in his files.

"Wait a minute," he said. "This man is a specialist in Medieval Art?"

"He was," I replied. I paused. "I know that he did some research on tapestries from the Cloisters."

"Ah, the Cloisters!" the young man said in triumph. "That's another database. That explains it."

I listened to some more clicking, then heard a satisfied sound. "Got it," he said.

"Terrific," I replied. "Is there a way that I can contact him?"

"I'm afraid not," the young man said. "Were you under the impression that Albert Manfredi was alive?"

"I wasn't sure," I said. Although I was almost certain Manfredi would be dead by then, I hadn't wanted to sound as though I had too much information on the elusive art expert.

I heard the clacking of keys. "Actually, Albert O. Manfredi

passed away in 1932," the young man said. "It's a pretty unusual name, so I'm sure this is the guy you were looking for."

Nineteen thirty-two. Manfredi had died the very same year he inspected the Miranda tapestry. If it was a coincidence, it was an impressive one—and I didn't believe in coincidences to begin with. Something had happened to the curator.

I gave a little self-deprecating laugh. "I guess my research was a little off," I said. "I had no idea. Can you tell me how old he was when he died?"

The young man paused. "Forty," he said. "Not old at all. Especially for an art expert of that era. He would have been just getting started with his career."

"I see," I replied. And maybe someone had precipitated his demise. I wanted to see if I could get more information, but I didn't want to arouse any suspicions. My experience with the ambassador was still fresh in my mind, when I had aroused his interest and probably made an indelible impression in his memory.

"I can see why you wanted to reach Manfredi, if your specialty is Medieval Art," the young man volunteered. "He has a pretty extensive list of accomplishments in our files, for someone who died so young. You mentioned the tapestries at the Cloisters—Manfredi was one of the advisors who put together the *Hunt of the Unicorn* collection."

"An advisor?" I asked. "What does that mean?"

"Let me see." A pause. "He was seconded from the museum to advise John D. Rockefeller when he was putting together the collection to donate to the Cloisters."

Manfredi worked for Rockefeller. I digested this for a moment. Lucia had told me that one of the reasons her family had hidden the eighth tapestry was so that Rockefeller couldn't get his hands on it. Now it turned out that Manfredi was advising the Robber Baron all along.

"I can't thank you enough for your help," I said. "I hope I didn't take up too much of your time."

"No problem," the young man said. "You'd be surprised how rare it is to get an in-depth request from an old file like this one. A lot of this information sat untouched for decades in hard-copy files before it was digitalized a couple of years ago."

I said good-bye, replaced the receiver, and took in the silence of my office. Manfredi was connected to both the Mirandas and to John D. Rockefeller. It seemed possible that Lucia had lied to me about Rockefeller going after their tapestry, and about his being their adversary.

I wondered if there were any other pertinent lies I was going to uncover before I set off for Havana.

21

The moment I opened up the file that Tommy had sent over from his office, I knew that his case wasn't going to be the wham-bam-thank-you-ma'am slam-dunk that I had hoped for. My wish had been to flip through the file, make a call to Tommy with some recommendations, then get back to the Miranda and Estrada matters. Now I could see it wasn't going to be so easy. I wasn't really surprised.

Tommy's client, Fernando Valdez Correa, had tried to locate the gallery owner when the lawsuit against him was filed. He had also retained a private investigator to help him with this, without success. I opened up the report from the P.I., hoping for some direction.

The private investigator employed to locate the gallery dealer was named Martin Osterman. I closed my eyes for a second, tried to find the name in my memory. Nothing. I had never heard of him, or else I'd forgotten. The letterhead on the report cover indicated that his office was on Northwest Eighth Street and Thirtieth Avenue, a marginal neighborhood not far from the Orange Bowl. Osterman certainly didn't charge his clients for the ambiance and the view. I wondered how a powerful and affluent man such as Valdez had come to employ Osterman for such a delicate job.

I started to read the report, ordering myself to clear professional prejudices from my mind. His office was in a lousy part of town, and from the first paragraph of his report I could see that he didn't know how to use the spell check on his computer. Still, this didn't mean that he couldn't do competent work.

Actually, I saw that Osterman had done all the right things. He had run a thorough background check on the gallery owner, Rafael Santamaria. He'd pulled Santamaria's driver's license, finding two speeding tickets and a failure to yield, for which he'd avoided penalties by going to driving school. Motor vehicle records indicated that Santamaria owned a '96 silver Mercedes; the lien holder was First Union Bank. He owned a boat outright, a twenty-seven-foot Mako. He owned a condo in the Sunset Harbor Apartments in Coconut Grove, only three blocks from my office, which he used as a residence and mailing address. He had bought it in '97, and it had an outstanding mortgage of $167,000, at First Nationwide Bank. Santamaria had established a corporation, subchapter S, in '98—the same year he'd opened up his art gallery on Galiano Street in Coral Gables. He'd taken out a three-year lease on the space, paid in advance; there was still six months left on the lease.

Osterman's report stated that he had canvassed the areas where Santamaria lived and worked, but that no one knew anything about the man. Apparently he was very private and had kept to himself. Most of the people Osterman interviewed were completely unaware that Santamaria had been missing; nor, from the tone of the report, did it seem that they particularly cared. There was only one picture of Santamaria in the file—the dealer's driver's license photograph. It was a duplicate, murky and dark. Santamaria looked extremely average, a little heavy in the face, someone I might have walked past a hundred times without noticing.

And that was the extent of the report. I had no idea

whether Osterman had given up the search or had been ordered to stop looking into Santamaria's disappearance. One thing was certain: Osterman's investigation had just gotten started when it ended.

I pulled out the administrative paperwork on the case, finding the bill. I could estimate how long Osterman's work would have taken him and what his costs would have been. Osterman had charged Valdez Correa close to two thousand dollars. I estimated that the bill was padded by about fifteen hundred, assuming that Osterman billed out his time at a standard rate of fifty dollars an hour.

I had hoped that Osterman's report would be more thorough, that he would have saved me a lot of the grunt work. I realized that I was probably going to have to reinterview a lot of the people he'd spoken with; I hoped Osterman hadn't done or said anything to annoy them on the first go-round. In Dade County, as in most places, a majority of private investigators have some sort of law enforcement experience. This was a great advantage in terms of having contacts with the police and federal agencies, and in knowing how these organizations work. Unfortunately, these same investigators often forget that they are now private citizens, and that they can't force citizens to cooperate on an investigation. I didn't know anything about Osterman, but I hoped he had conducted preliminary interviews in a nonthreatening, noncoercive fashion.

I thought about it for a minute or so. I had totally neglected Tommy's case, and before I worked on the other two, I knew I should at least do *something* so Tommy could tell his client the investigation was under way. I decided the best thing would be to speak with Osterman in person. I debated calling him and asking for an appointment, but I didn't want to give him a chance to say no.

I looked at the address on the letterhead again and

groaned. It would take me about half an hour to get there—
and I had no assurances that Osterman would even be at his
office. Still, I was on billable hours. And even if I failed, I
would be able to give Tommy some substantial information
on how I was initiating the investigation.

I made copies of Osterman's report, put it in a file for my
own use, then checked to make sure the Beretta was in my
purse. I didn't think I was going to have a problem with
Osterman, but I needed the sense of security the gun gave
me. My colleague worked in a rough part of town, and I
wanted to be prepared for every eventuality.

"I'll be back in a couple of hours," I called out to Leonardo as I moved quickly through the reception area. My
cousin was in his gym, practicing his mid-morning medita-
tion. He said it helped with his digestion and intestinal
health. I didn't know why he couldn't take a siesta like a
reasonable person, as opposed to sitting immobile, staring
into space, his mouth hanging open like some kind of sea
monster.

In fact, I was grateful not to have to explain to him where
I was going. I didn't want to receive his disapproval for working with Tommy again; I would wait until the retainer check
arrived to share that news with him, which would certainly
soften the blow.

The drive from the Grove to Osterman's office wasn't bad,
the traffic relatively light. I made it in about fifteen minutes,
and without making a complete mockery of the speed limit.
I took this to be a good omen as I drove slowly down Northwest Eighth Street, looking for the address. Finally I spotted
it. I did a double take when I saw that it was a one-story
building completely covered in tiny sky-blue tiles.

I found an empty parking spot right in front of the building; it took me a half-dozen cuts before I managed to parallel
park the Mercedes. It wasn't that the spot was so small, it

was because I couldn't keep my eyes off the building. The little blue tiles shone like bits of cut glass. The walls featured pink-tile flamingoes interspersed over the outer walls in no discernible pattern. The windows facing Eighth Street were protected by iron grills painted a shade of orange that I could only describe as shocking. The door was painted canary yellow with multicolored swirls.

The outer decoration had obviously been the work of someone who was recovering from an LSD trip. I was willing to bet that Osterman, or whoever was responsible, had been at Woodstock or at least had listened to the album quite a few times while in various states of chemical enhancement. I had trouble imagining someone like Fernando Valdez Correa visiting this office—surely he had never seen it when he hired Osterman for the case.

I got out of the car and walked slowly to the front door, blinking. Osterman's was the only name on the door, so I assumed he was the only tenant. I rang the bell and waited. No response. I rang again, this time more insistently. Still nothing.

I turned to leave, disappointed, when I almost ran smack into someone moving up the drive. It took me a startled second to realize it was a postman delivering the mail on a bicycle.

He started to stuff an assortment of letters and catalogues through the slot in the door. When he was done, he smiled at me.

"Looking for Osterman?" he asked. I nodded. "Try next door. At the bar."

He pointed at the building next door, tipped his safari hat at me, and was on his way. I looked at my watch. It was almost three o'clock. Either Osterman knocked off work early or else he was having a liquid lunch. I put another quarter in the meter, giving me an additional twenty minutes, and walked next door.

The bar was as somber as Osterman's office was outrageous. It was painted a dark shade of blue and looked as though it hadn't seen a face-lift in decades. And for some reason I couldn't fathom, the pink neon lights atop the front awning spelled out the word "BRA" in capital letters, rather than "BAR." Maybe it had been the winds of hurricane Andrew that rearranged the sign, or else someone had a lingerie fetish. Another possibility was that the sign had always been that way—a sobering thought.

I opened the door, stepped inside, and was greeted by an icy blast of freezing cold air. That wasn't the only thing that stopped me in my tracks; the place was so dark that I couldn't see more than a few feet in front of me. I waited for my eyes to adjust.

"Can I help you?" asked a disembodied male voice.

I made out the shape of the bar, then the bartender standing behind it, smoking a cigarette. The voice had come from somewhere else, to my right.

"I'm looking for Martin Osterman," I said.

"Are you a process server?" asked the voice. "Because if you are, then he isn't here."

My eyes had started to adjust. I almost wished they hadn't. What a dive: peeling vinyl booths, a chipped Formica bar, a nimbus of smoke. By then I could make out who was addressing me. It could only have been Osterman. The man was a total sixties throwback, a massive bear with a blond ponytail, scruffy beard, and granny glasses perched on the end of his nose. His beer belly looked to be decades in the making. He wore jeans, a checkered work shirt, and, so help me, Birkenstocks on his feet.

Osterman was nursing a Budweiser. Next to it on the table was a pack of Marlboros and a Harley-Davidson lighter. I seemed to have interrupted Osterman's reading of *USA Today*, although I had no idea how he could read in such a dark place. No doubt it was a talent he'd been cultivating for years.

"I'm not a process server, so relax," I said to him. I glanced around. We seemed to be the only two customers in the place.

"Who are you, little lady?" he asked in a raspy voice.

I couldn't believe he had called me that. I could see, though, that Osterman wasn't a total burnout. His eyes darted behind his glasses, and gleamed with intelligence.

"My name is Lupe Solano." I took a chair across from him. "I'm a private investigator here in town."

"Drink?" he offered. I noticed that he certainly took it in his stride to have a private investigator come looking for him in a bar.

"No, thanks. Not just yet." I took out the Santamaria file and placed it on the table between us. "Would you mind if I asked you a few questions about this?"

"Santamaria." Osterman stretched out the sound of the name, as though he enjoyed saying it. "You trying to find that guy, too?"

Osterman seemed to have only a cursory interest in our conversation. It felt as though I was distracting him from his Bud.

"I am." I tapped the report with my forefinger. "It's all here in your report, right? Everything that you uncovered during your investigation?"

"It's all there," Osterman said, a note of defensive pride in his voice.

Osterman sighed, cracked his knuckles. He looked at me warily, and I could tell he was weighing the pros and cons of freely discussing the case with me. Since I had a copy of the report, he seemed to decide that it was all right to talk.

"I could have done more, but I got pulled off the job," Osterman said. "Hold on a minute."

Osterman got up, in the process draining the last of his beer. Without even glancing at the bartender, he walked around the bar and took a fresh beer from the refrigerator against the wall. If Osterman didn't own the place, he certainly enjoyed the privileges of a very regular customer.

"What do you mean, you got pulled off the job?" I asked him when he returned to the table.

"One day I got a call from the client's secretary," Osterman explained. "Said my services were no longer needed, told me to write up what I'd done and enclose a bill with it. A courier was at my office two hours later to pick everything up."

Osterman took a big swallow of his beer, then lit a Marlboro. He stroked his beard with his cigarette hand, apparently enjoying the exercise for his memory.

"The secretary said I'd get paid that afternoon, after the client had a look at the report." Another long swallow; by then half the beer was gone from the new bottle. "Sure enough, that's how it all played out."

"Didn't you think that was strange?" I asked. I would have, but Osterman seemed to be used to all kinds of strange behavior. Sitting there with him, I almost expected Dennis Hopper and Peter Fonda to show up, take the two empty chairs.

"Sure," Osterman said with a shrug. "But I never ask my clients their motives or reasons behind hiring me. If the money is green, then I'm there."

Osterman took another long drink, then looked at his beer with a slightly sour expression. I could have sworn he felt betrayed by its being almost empty after such a short time.

"How did *you* get the case?" I asked him. He looked up at me, for an instant ready to take offense, as though I had suggested he was too much of a lowlife throwback to be hired on an important matter by someone like Valdez Correa.

Which was exactly what I was suggesting. Osterman pursed his lips and made a clucking sound. But he didn't disagree with my unspoken assessment.

"Got it through family," Osterman said. "My brother, Fred Osterman, is chief of security at the Miami Beach Convention Center. His boss there is friends with Valdez Correa. When the boss asked him the best way to find someone who'd sold him stolen property, Fred said he had a cousin who could handle it."

He cocked his head, looked directly into my eyes. He was sharp, sharper than he let on.

"So what's your deal?" Osterman asked. "You working for Valdez Correa?"

"Indirectly," I said. "I've been retained by his lawyer on the case."

Osterman nodded, as though divining some great truth in what I had just said.

"See, when I tried to find Santamaria, there weren't any lawyers on the case muddying the waters." Osterman finished his beer, looked longingly over at the refrigerator for an instant before turning back to me. "Fred gave me the guy's name and sent me on my way. The truth is, I only met Valdez Correa for about five minutes. Fred was the go-between on the whole thing."

Osterman motioned for me to hold on, then got up for another beer. I guessed talking made him thirsty. I couldn't believe the man was a practicing private eye. He must have had some talents to stay in the business, they just weren't particularly visible at the moment.

But his explanation made sense. The client would have initially thought it would be easy to find Santamaria, so he asked his friend to ask his chief of security to look into the matter for him. Once Valdez Correa realized the seriousness of the situation he was facing, he realized that he needed a top lawyer—and a better investigator than his friend's security chief's alcoholic brother.

"Well, what do you think happened to Santamaria?" I asked Osterman. He might not have been the cream of his profession, but I had a hunch he had a pretty good grasp of human nature. And, in spite of myself, I was starting to like him. There was a sparkle of ironic humor beneath his boozy manner, and I got the sense that, on some level, he at least took his work seriously.

"Well, let's see." Osterman lit another cigarette. The last one had burned down, leaving a long tubular ash in the tray. "He might be at the bottom of Biscayne Bay. He might be in the Everglades providing sustenance for the alligators. He might also be in Curaçao, or Havana for that matter."

Osterman tilted his head back and started blowing perfect smoke rings. I hadn't seen the trick done so well since I was in college; back then, guys from the fraternity house would make rings out of cigar smoke, thinking that girls would topple into their beds in admiration.

"Those are some possibilities," I admitted. Although I was really only interested in one. "Why Havana?"

"Because of all the trafficking in art from there," Osterman said.

I looked at him, trying to hide my surprise.

"What do you mean?" I asked.

"You're Cuban, right?" Osterman said. "Don't you know about all those fakes?"

I must have given a convincingly blank look, because Osterman shook his head pityingly, as though he had just come to an epiphany about how naive and ill-equipped for the job I was.

"My brother Fred worked the Latin American art show this year. He said the place was full of fakes. A big fucking problem, man."

I stayed silent. I don't know which shocked me more, Osterman's sudden swearing or his referring to me as a male.

"First there were faked versions of real paintings," Osterman explained. "Then there were fakes that were done in the style of famous painters. Fred said the whole thing was a real disaster. It almost got in the papers. But, you know . . ."

Osterman grimaced, made a little hand gesture and pulled a face. I don't know what I was supposed to glean from this. I understood that Osterman was paranoid, which probably wasn't what he had been trying to communicate.

"Where does Havana come into this?" I asked.

Osterman swirled his beer bottle. "Sure you don't want one?" he asked.

I shook my head. "No. But thanks."

"Well, Fred said the fakes were coming out of Havana," Osterman said. "If our boy Santamaria was selling stolen Cuban paintings, then I bet he was also involved in selling fakes. They go hand in hand."

Osterman looked like an escapee from *Easy Rider*, he drank like a fish and he puffed Marlboros like a smokestack. None of this meant he didn't have the ability to think.

"It's an interesting thought," I said.

Osterman shrugged. "Fred was talking a lot about the problems he was having at the art show. I open my ears and listen. You never know when information is going to come in handy."

I looked over at the bar, where the bartender stood in shadows, watching a TV show with the sound turned almost all the way down. I wondered how many hours these two men spent in this gloom.

"So everything you did is in the report?" I asked.

"That's right." Osterman frowned, squinted behind his granny glasses. "Hey, listen. You need help, you come to me."

"That's nice of you," I said.

Osterman fished a fresh pack of Marlboros out of his shirt pocket, started unwrapping the cellophane.

"Fred told me there were some tough guys involved," Osterman said. "There's a lot of money involved, that always means trouble. I know you're probably carrying, but that ain't going to do much for you. Hate to see a lady like you get hurt."

It was reassuring to see that chivalry wasn't dead. I could tell that, in his own way, Osterman was being sincere. It was touching.

"Thanks," I said with a smile. I got up and tucked the folder under my arm. I steeled myself for stepping outside into what would feel like blinding sunlight.

"Take care," Osterman said with a beatific grin. "Stay well."

Before I left I turned back to him.

"Say, were you at Woodstock?" I asked.

Osterman belted out the loudest, most raucous laugh I'd ever heard. "Guess it shows, huh?"

22

I sat down to lunch with Teodora Gross, a dealer in Cuban art with whom I'd spoken during the Wilfredo Lam case. My contact with her had been pretty limited until that afternoon, but I was starting to understand why her name kept coming up as an expert.

"Let's see," I said, looking down at my notepad. "What sort of documentation do you require when you agree to sell a painting in your gallery?"

We had just started our main courses—salmon and stir-fried vegetables for her, grouper in mango sauce for me—at Nemo's on Collins Avenue in Miami Beach. It had been an encouraging sign when Teodora agreed that ordering a bottle of white wine to accompany lunch would be a good idea. I still feared that each meal might be among my last, so I savored every bite. Of course, that might have just been an excuse to order whatever struck my fancy at that particular moment.

Teodora carefully chose a slice of bread from the basket, then spread just the right amount of butter on it. I understood the deliberate nature of her actions. Some things cannot be rushed—especially food. I sipped my wine and waited for her reply. We were out on the terrace, seated in the shade under an enormous kaobab tree. It had been a long time since I'd lingered over lunch with a woman; it made me realize how much I missed female companionship. My lifestyle didn't allow me much time for friendships to develop.

"Well, the first thing is to check that the seller of the painting is indeed the owner," Teodora said, "that she or he has title and that the painting is free and clear of any encumbrance." She took a dainty bite, chewing slowly before she spoke again.

"How do you do that?"

"I have the seller issue an affidavit," she explained, "a legal document containing a sworn statement that the painting is the seller's to rightfully sell."

She spoke with a light voice, but I could tell the subject was extremely serious to her. That was probably why she was still in business, while so many other galleries had folded.

I had only spoken on the phone with Teodora before that afternoon, never seen her in person. She was about forty. Although it wasn't immediately obvious that she'd gone under the knife, I could see faint scars on her face and neck where she'd had work done. The results had been worth it; Teodora was very pretty. She was petite, with chin-length shiny black hair, black eyes framed by luxurious lashes, and porcelain white skin. She was dressed in a beautiful, light pink two-piece suit that, judging from its tasteful simplicity, must have cost a fortune. A huge square-cut diamond ring on her fourth finger threatened to blind anyone who lingered too long on the sight of her immaculately manicured hands.

I was glad I'd also dressed for the occasion, in my teal Armani linen suit. I knew that Teodora, as the owner of a tony Coral Gables art gallery, had to dress the part. When we met, she ran an experienced eye over my outfit, looking with satisfaction at my Chanel bag—she had no way of knowing about the Beretta inside. I couldn't help but think of my interview the day before with Osterman at the "BRA." It was a study in contrasts.

"Still, you know that people lie," I said to her. "Some people don't care about truth or falsehood on an affidavit, not if it means money for them."

"You don't miss much, do you?" Teodora asked. She took a sip of wine. "I try to trace the history of a painting as far back as I can. And the more complete the provenance, the higher the price I can ask. If the artist is alive, that makes it all a lot easier."

Teodora was eating her salmon with such gusto that I hated to keep questioning her like this. However, it was an expense-account lunch, and I needed information.

"What are the requirements for becoming an art dealer?" I asked.

Teodora raised her hand and made a circle with her thumb and index finger. I tried not to focus on her megaring, but it wasn't easy.

"Zero," she said. "*Nada.* There are no requirements for becoming an art dealer in Miami. You could announce that you were in the business this afternoon. That's really all it takes."

"No license, no background checks? No nothing?" I was dumbfounded that the field was so completely unregulated. No wonder so many people tried to make a go of it. The commission on the sale of one valuable painting was enough to live off for a year.

"That's why buyers should only go to reputable dealers," Teodora said pointedly. "People who have been in the business for a long time, and have a reputation and expertise. Especially these days. There are so many fakes. And paintings being sold by people who don't have a right to ownership.

The buyer is really taking a big risk by doing business with an unknown dealer.''

She took another slice of bread from the basket and, with a slight air of embarrassment, began mopping up her plate with it. My plate as well was almost empty. A mouse couldn't have subsisted on what we were leaving at the table.

I had told Teodora a little bit about why I wanted to meet with her, and now I shared with her a thumbnail sketch of the litigation around the Tomas Sanchez landscape.

"The gallery owner has disappeared completely," I concluded. "We've looked for him, but so far there's no trace."

"What was his name?" she asked. "Santamaria?"

I nodded.

"Never heard of him," she said dismissively. "But even if you do find him, you're still going to hit a dead end. He's never going to tell you the truth about how he acquired the Sanchez painting."

"That was pretty much what I was worried about," I said.

Teodora perused the dessert menu. "At least Tomas Sanchez authenticates all his work," she added. "He lives here in Miami, so he'll be easy for you to contact. You'll be able to determine, if nothing else, whether the painting is a fake."

I jotted down notes. Now my favorite part of the meal had arrived; I looked over the dessert menu, quickly narrowing down my possible choices from six to four. Teodora's face was serious with concentration. I was starting to think we were kindred spirits.

"Let's order three," she said, looking up. "We'll each have one, and we'll split the third."

"Excellent idea," I said.

After we ordered, I steered the conversation back to my case.

"With this Tomas Sanchez painting, I've been led to understand that fraud isn't an issue," I told her. "Ownership is the real problem."

She nodded. "I see. So it isn't a fake."

"Is that a real problem?" I asked. I remembered my conversation with Osterman; it seemed that the old hippie knew what he was talking about.

"Let me give you an example," Teodora said, leaning closer and lowering her voice. "It's estimated that about fifty percent of all the Wilfredo Lam paintings floating around are fakes."

"But how can that be?" I asked. "Isn't there some kind of central place where all his paintings are documented, or something like that?"

"Lam is the best known—and the most prolific—of the Cuban painters," she replied. "However, the man lived and painted all over the world. All that moving around has made it difficult to document his work."

"And artists aren't known as the most stable and meticulous people," I noted.

Teodora rolled her eyes in agreement.

"His widow lives in Paris," she continued. "She's the authority on her husband's work—she's the caretaker, really, of his legacy. She's in a position to authenticate or declare fraudulent individual works by him. Even so, there are a lot of works attributed to Lam that he never saw, much less painted."

"What about other painters?" I asked. I knew I had a great source here, and I wanted to keep her talking. For her part, she seemed to be enjoying herself.

"Same story, but commanding less money." Teodora paused and looked at me; she seemed to realize that I was playing a bit dumb, in order to get as much information as possible. She gave a little shrug, as though it was all the same to her.

"Here's the situation with Cuban art," she said. "The great majority of individuals who collect the paintings are Cuban exiles. Now, it's been more than forty years since Castro came to power. In the beginning, the exiles' primary preoccupation was survival and making a living. But a lot of time has passed, and many exiles have a lot of disposable income. When they want to collect art, naturally they gravitate to Cuban painters."

"That's what Cubans care about," I said. "All things Cuban."

"Exactly," Teodora agreed with a laugh. "So now you have a lot of money floating around, and a lot of demand. It's the perfect situation for the creation of a thriving black market."

Our desserts arrived. Nemo's had outdone itself. I hated to make Teodora keep talking while she was making love to her mango cheesecake, but I couldn't get away from Tommy's case.

"What about the certification and provenance of all those fakes?" I asked. "I mean, buyers aren't likely to spend thousands of dollars on paintings that might be forgeries, are they?"

"You see, Lupe, you've zeroed in on the problem." Teodora delicately wiped her lips on her napkin. "The Cuban government owns a lot of art—essentially confiscated like they confiscated everything in the country. As the government runs lower and lower on cash, it sells valuable pieces. And each time, it certifies the authenticity of the work."

"The certifications aren't reliable," I said.

"That's right." Teodora leaned even closer, dropped her voice to a whisper. "A bunch of 'official' certification documents were stolen from the Cuban National Museum a couple of years ago. Just think of what that's done to the market."

I shook my head, feeling a bit overwhelmed. I realized how lucky I had been to reunite the owners of the Pelaez and the Lam paintings with their artworks. I was starting to think it had been beginner's luck.

"Who in Cuba is in charge of certifying the fakes?" I asked. "I mean, maybe I'm overlooking something, but I don't get it. Isn't flooding the market with forgeries completely shortsighted? Aren't potential buyers going to be turned off to the market when the practice becomes known—personally, I'd rather buy nothing than risk getting burned."

In a flash, I thought of Camila Estrada. From what I knew, she had at least dabbled in art forgery. And then there were the paintings in Jesus Estrada's studio.

"We're talking about Cuban government agencies—museums and the like—issuing these certifications of authenticity," Teodora told me. "Nothing in Cuba happens without government approval from the highest levels. Draw your own conclusions about who's behind this, Lupe."

With that, Teodora started digging into the unbelievably decadent chocolate dessert the two of us were sharing. She took a big bite, a dreamy expression on her face.

"Sure, new buyers can be discouraged from collecting Cuban art," she said. "But the people responsible for the fakes keep on producing them. Some people are more interested in lining their pockets today than worrying about the future. You know. It's human nature."

"Here, let me have some of that," I said. Teodora pushed the plate across the table to me. As I let the sensuous flavor of dark chocolate caress my taste buds, my thoughts came back to Camila.

"Who are the artists in Cuba producing the forgeries?" I asked.

"Well, look," Teodora said with a gentle laugh. "I don't

have their names and addresses. But you can imagine. They're trained in the fine arts, and they do what they need to do in order to survive. I don't blame them, really. We all know the situation in Cuba, the shortages and the poverty since the Soviet Union disappeared and Castro lost his economic safety net.''

Sounded right to me. And, from what little I knew about her, it sounded like Camila.

Teodora and I drank our espressos, both looking at our watches. It had been a long lunch, and neither of us had much more time to spare. I signed for the check, pleased to at least be working a case with billable hours—in contrast to the Estrada investigation. I felt no guilt when I saw the size of the bill—after all, I'd gotten a lot of valuable information. It wasn't my fault that the facts Tommy's client was paying for also piggybacked onto the Estrada situation.

Teodora and I parted on the sidewalk outside Nemo's.

"I never have lunch like this, just talking," she said fondly. "We should do it again."

"I agree." I made sure she had my card.

"Maybe in a couple of weeks," she suggested.

"Sounds great. But . . ." I paused.

"What is it?" she asked.

"Oh, nothing," I said. "I just remembered that I'm going to be traveling on business. Hopefully I won't be gone long."

She flashed a quizzical look that dissolved into a smile. "Where are you headed?" she asked.

I wished I hadn't said anything. But going to Cuba was clouding my thoughts, filling me with a low-level anxiety. I realized that I hadn't wanted to make plans with Teodora because of a lingering worry: that I might be spending the foreseeable future in a Cuban jail cell.

"To Boston," I improvised.

"Sounds great," she replied. "Give me a call when you get back."

I drove into Miami on the MacArthur Causeway, lost in thought about the lunch and the sudden rush of reality that had ended it. I almost missed the sight of a family of dolphins swimming about in the waters of Biscayne Bay, putting on a show in front of Star Island. They looked happy and free, beautiful in the afternoon sun, their sleek muscular bodies shining like they were made of silver. I hoped Gloria Estefan was watching from her bedroom window on Star Island. From one Cuban to another, I knew she would have enjoyed it.

23

Osvaldo approached me as I pulled into the driveway that afternoon.

"Lupe, you had a call from a gentleman," he said.

I was about to ask for more details, but Osvaldo folded his arms and glared at me.

"You've been parking under the poinciana tree next to your office again," he said. "How many times have I told you—you're going to ruin the pain job. *Ay,* Lupe, it's like talking to a brick wall!"

He shook his head in dismay as he walked away, dejected over my total stubbornness.

"I'm sorry, Osvaldo," I called out after him. "You're right. I'll never do it again. I promise!"

"You're never going to get to Heaven if you make promises that you have no intention of keeping." He wagged his finger at me in admonishment; a moment later I saw a smile begin to form at the corners of his lips. This was a game we had been playing for years.

Laughing, I blew a kiss at him and went inside the house. I stopped at the table in the entrance hallway, where messages were kept for various family members.

I thought I was going to fall over when I saw the name written in Aida's neat spidery handwriting. Señor de Castellanos. The ambassador had phoned me—at home. I hadn't given him my number, and I had no idea how he tracked me down.

Osvaldo came in from the garden and found me there, a stricken look on my face. I hated to make mistakes. I sat down on one of the chairs that flanked the table, trying to figure out what had happened.

"I'll get you a *mojito*," Osvaldo said, noticing my agitation. For him, the drink was like Cuban penicillin. He was back in a minute with it, and I drained it in a single gulp, as though it were water being given to me after a lengthy adventure in the Sahara.

Maybe the *mojito* did have powers. I began to figure out how the ambassador had been able to track me down. I had told him I was a graduate student at the University of Miami, working on my master's thesis. All he would need to do was call the university registrar's office and request my number. The information was supposed to be confidential, but someone of the ambassador's stature might have contacts there. Although it had been eight years since I graduated, my information would probably still be on the computer. Hopefully, the fact that I wasn't registered as a student hadn't come up.

It was the only answer, the more I thought about it. All our phone lines at the house had unlisted numbers. I wished I hadn't given my real name to him and to Patricia Wainwright, but it had been the easiest way of presenting myself to them.

I was so deep in thought that I barely noticed it when Osvaldo placed a second *mojito* on a coaster on the table next to me. I happily accepted it; after all, the first had done wonders for my reasoning abilities. As I sipped it I wondered why the ambassador might need to reach me. I thought we had completed our discussion in his office. Of course, there was also the possibility that he wanted to get together with me for reasons that had nothing to do with medieval tapestries.

Well, the ambassador had my phone number, so there was no reason why I couldn't call from home. I always tried not to, since so many people had caller ID on their phones. I went into the library, shut the door behind me, and made the call.

"Ambassador de Castellanos, please," I requested. "This is Lupe Solano returning his call."

"One moment, please." I recognized the voice of the older gentleman I had mistaken for the ambassador when I visited the office.

"Lupe, hello. This is Mario de Castellanos," he said in his smooth, accentless voice. "How are you this afternoon?"

"Fine, thank you," I replied. "You know, I'd like to thank you again for speaking with me. I know your time is valuable."

"That's why I called," he said warmly. "To see how your paper was progressing, and if you have any additional questions. I must say, it is very encouraging to meet a young person who has an interest in art of the medieval period."

I paused for a moment. He sounded sincere. Should I push it? Of course I should.

"There's one thing, actually," I began. "I've been researching the *Hunt of the Unicorn* tapestries, and I came across some writing referring to work done by a man named Albert O. Manfredi."

I reached down and picked up the Miami telephone directory sitting next to the table, started rustling through the pages loudly enough so the ambassador could hear.

"It's here someplace. Oh, dear, I can't find it. I have so many papers on my desk. But I'm sure that was the name. It's very unusual, and easy to remember."

"I know who Manfredi was," Señor de Castellanos said

confidently. "Manfredi was hired by the Cloisters during the period in which the museum was putting its collection together. Of course you came across his name in reference to the unicorn tapestries—he was the individual who worked on collections of medieval art."

"I see," I replied.

"But if I remember correctly, he died young. Before he finished the job." The ambassador sighed. "Someone else finished the work. Poor Manfredi. He was certainly instrumental in the acquisition of the tapestries, but he never saw the exhibit completed."

"How sad for him to fall ill before he could see the tapestries displayed so beautifully at the Cloisters," I said innocently.

"You know, now that I think about it, I'm not so sure he passed away from an illness." The ambassador paused; I could almost hear the wheels turning as he searched his memory. I sensed that he was treading carefully, not wanting to seem like a doddering old man with a failing memory. From meeting him, I knew he was anything but senile.

"Yes, I remember," he said, sounding pleased. "Manfredi is largely forgotten to art historians now, but he was important in his time. If I'm not mistaken, he was actually presumed dead after a long absence from his work."

"You mean he disappeared?" I tried not to sound too eager to learn the fate of a museum curator seventy years before. "It sounds like he vanished without a trace."

"Well, this is the impression I have," the ambassador said slowly. "But there are many other sources of information on the period. Manfredi was more of a curator than a scholar, in the sense that he didn't leave much of a body of work behind."

"Well, I guess there wasn't time," I said, hoping for more information.

"Indeed," the ambassador agreed. "It was a true shame. Manfredi had a good eye."

A silence fell between us. I was reluctant to let the subject go, but I had pushed far enough. Now there was no doubt that, in his mind, the ambassador would link me to the unicorn tapestries.

"Well, Lupe, I would like to offer my services in any way possible to assist you with your thesis," he said.

Uh-oh, I thought. Here it comes.

"Perhaps we could meet and discuss the subject further." Señor de Castellanos coughed. "I am, as you know, considered an expert on the period in question."

"That would be lovely," I said. I had experience in saying no in a way that wouldn't provoke an unwanted reaction. "But for the moment, I'm so pressed with researching and writing the thesis that I have time for little else."

The ambassador accepted my brush-off with aplomb, especially after I promised to be in touch. No doubt about it now, if the existence of the eighth tapestry became known, he would probably associate me with it. However, that was too far off in the future for me to worry about.

After I hung up the phone, I spent a couple of hours pulling out maps and atlases of Cuba from Papi's collection. I pored over details of the coastline, looking at ports and harbors and the roads that led to Havana. It all seemed so simple, looking at it there on paper—although I knew it was a treacherous journey in all respects. I would leave the final determinations to Barbara, in recognition of her expertise and experience.

At the moment, I had two concerns: avoiding whoever had killed the Estradas, and staying out of a Cuban jail. The first step was talking to a certain unpleasant relative of mine who I thought was keeping information from me.

*   *   *

"Lucia, I have a question about one of the documents you gave me." As I spoke to her I tried not to sound as though I doubted any aspect of her story.

"You're still here asking questions?" she barked at me. "Why aren't you on your way to Havana?"

Obviously Lucia had no idea what the trip entailed. In her mind, she had paid me money, so the tapestry should have arrived in Miami with the speed of a Federal Express delivery. I tried not to let her inconsiderate nature get to me.

Lucia ranked as one of my all-time least sympathetic clients. To repay her for her attitude, I resolved right then to pad her bill. I seriously felt I deserved compensation for putting up with her ill-humor.

I had telephoned Lucia the morning after my conversation with Ambassador de Castellanos. I wanted detailed information about Manfredi and his role in the eighth tapestry. The more I learned, the more I was suspicious about what had become of the curator. I could have spoken with Lucia on the phone, but I wanted to see her reactions in person. Also, I requested a detailed diagram of the Miranda house in Havana—with particular attention paid to the location of the trapdoor that accessed the basement room where the tapestry was stored.

I suggested we meet at my office. In a rude tone, Lucia told me she was spending all her time at Baptist Hospital with her mother. If I wanted to speak with her, it would have to be there. I called her cell phone when I was five minutes away, and she left her mother's room long enough to come down and talk—all the while stealing glances at her watch. Apparently, Lucia's mother had taken a turn for the worse, although she was still in her room and hadn't been moved back to intensive care.

"How is your mother?" I asked.

"Not good," Lucia snapped. She stared straight ahead, not

even looking at me. "She should be in intensive care, but the doctors say there is really no point. We've all agreed that there is no longer a requirement for invasive procedures. We're all just waiting."

I felt a pang of sympathy. I had played the same waiting game when Mami was ill and finally died.

"That's why we're meeting out here," Lucia added, tight-lipped. "I don't want Mama asking a lot of questions about the tapestry, getting excited and worried about the details. I want to surprise her with the tapestry's arrival."

"I understand." It was fine with me. I had spent enough time in Miami hospitals, and preferred to avoid them if possible.

"If you understand, why are you here instead of in Havana?" Lucia asked, her tone bitter and cold.

"It's not so easy, Lucia," I told her, fighting to keep my temper in check. "It's not as though I can just board a commercial flight to Havana and get frequent-flier miles for the trip. I'm risking my life and my freedom for this."

"And being paid very well for doing so," Lucia snapped right back.

That was it. I was going to triple the billable hours.

"What is so important that you had to drag me out of Mama's room?" she asked, apparently feeling she had put me in my place.

"You gave me this, a letter verifying the legitimacy of the tapestry," I said. I showed her a copy of Manfredi's letter.

Lucia arched an eyebrow, making it climb so high that I feared it would disappear under her hairline.

"And?" she asked.

"You told me that John D. Rockefeller had been trying to buy the tapestry, that he sent envoys." I spoke slowly, trying not to set Lucia off. She sat there, listening, stone-faced. "In the course of my investigation, I've found out that Albert

Manfredi, the man who wrote this letter, was employed by the Cloisters and—more importantly—also worked with Rockefeller putting together the collection of seven unicorn tapestries."

"So what?" Lucia countered. "The man was an expert in medieval tapestries. That's why he worked for the Cloisters. That's why he was knowledgeable enough to certify my family's tapestry."

I couldn't believe Lucia was so thick-headed that she couldn't understand the point I was making.

"You told me your family hired Manfredi to certify the tapestry before it was hidden," I said. "And the reason your family hid it was because you didn't want Rockefeller to find it and potentially take it from you."

I watched Lucia closely, to see if she was following me. Her beady black eyes gave away nothing. I got the worst of it, having to stare at her face.

"And now I find out that Manfredi worked with Rockefeller." I paused for effect. "What am I supposed to make of this?"

Lucia simply shrugged, as though what I'd just said was trivial and of no consequence.

"I repeated to you the story that's been told from generation to generation in my family," she said. "And, anyway, what are you doing checking on something like that? You're being paid to get the tapestry out of Cuba, not to investigate the tiny details of how it got there."

I was tempted to give back the money and walk away from the case completely. Pride prevented me from doing so. I had never quit a job after taking it, and I wasn't going to let my dislike for the client drive me away. I'd already paid a high price for taking the case—my alienation from Alvaro—so I had a lot invested in its success. The fact that Mami had loved the tapestries so much was a big part of what kept me going. It wouldn't bring her back, but retrieving the tapestry for the world to enjoy would be something that would please her. I knew she was watching me from Heaven.

"You're paying me to make sure I succeed in bringing back the tapestry," I told her. "Investigating background information is what allows me to formulate a plan that, hopefully, will go smoothly."

She did have a point, wondering why I was tracking down Manfredi, but she wasn't the one who would risk her life going to Cuba. More than anything, I wanted to make damn sure that everything Lucia had told me was the truth. I was almost satisfied with what she'd said so far. The story about Manfredi had been passed down through the generations. It was understandable that a certain amount of distortion or embellishment might have taken place somewhere along the line.

"Here is the information you asked for," Lucia said, taking an envelope from her purse and handing it to me. "You will find a detailed map of my family home. On the next page is a diagram and instructions for getting into the basement where the tapestry is stored."

I took the envelope without a word, put it in my Chanel bag.

"This is what I know," Lucia said. She shifted forward, ready to go back inside. "The tapestry is in the basement, under the house in Vedado. My mother wants to see it one last time before she dies. Is there anything else?"

I realized I was being dismissed. I was trying to help her, and her arrogance seemed to be rising by the second. Given her character, I wasn't surprised—although I expected some spirit of cooperation from her. After all, we ostensibly had the same goal in mind. And even though I was being well-compensated, I was the one taking the risks.

"You're sure the house is still a house?" I asked. "That it hasn't been converted into apartments or subdivided? That would make it a lot harder to find the door to the dug-out room."

"It is still a house," she said. "I'm sure of it. And remember—the door is hidden under green linoleum. If the linoleum is still there, it will make your task much easier."

"What about the basement itself?" I asked. "It's been locked up for a long time. It seems the tapestry might have been damaged."

"Impossible," Lucia said with certainty. "The basement was designed with natural ventilation, creating a flow of fresh air but keeping out rainwater. It's perfectly comfortable, and the tapestry will be intact."

"Please give your mother my regards and best wishes," I said, with as much goodwill as I could manage.

We both got up. I turned and walked away without saying good-bye.

I headed for the parking lot, feeling vaguely dissatisfied. I didn't know for certain she was lying, or what possible reason she might have for doing so, but I had a lingering suspicion that she wasn't telling me everything. For now, I would have to give her the benefit of the doubt. Maybe my dislike for her had inflated the Manfredi-Rockefeller connection out of proportion.

There were innocent explanations, after all. Perhaps Manfredi had come to Havana as an envoy for Rockefeller when the Cloisters collection was being assembled; once there, he might simply have been retained by the Mirandas to use his expertise to authenticate the tapestry. He might have pocketed a fee, and returned to New York to tell Rockefeller that the Miranda clan wasn't going to part with the eighth tapestry—or even that the rumors they owned it weren't true.

It had been 1932, and in the United States the Depression was going full force. A lot of people were fortunate to have any kind of job, even one that paid only subsistence wages. Manfredi might have been poorly paid and was in need of some extra cash. The chances of his being caught moonlighting for the other side were slim, since no one had actually laid eyes on the tapestry. I was speculating, but it was a scenario that made sense.

Let's say Lucia Miranda was lying to me, I thought. What reason would she have? It didn't make sense. She had come to me knowing my reputation, that I was an investigator. She would have to know that I wouldn't take her story at face value.

I prayed my line of reasoning was correct. Because if it wasn't, I was walking blind into the most dangerous situation of my life. I wasn't sure if even Mami in Heaven and the Virgin herself could help me then.

24

After seeing Lucia Miranda, I headed back to the office. Baptist Hospital was in Kendall, about a twenty minute drive—enough time for me to do some thinking. Two things were bothering me, and neither had anything to do with Lucia: the two dead Estrada brothers, and whether anything had happened on the homicide investigations, and the issue of Camila Estrada. Her cousin had told me she was waiting to hear from me. I needed to resolve that situation somehow.

As soon as I walked into my office I picked up the phone and punched in a familiar number.

"Anderson here," the homicide detective said a few seconds later; he sounded calm and cool almost to the point of catatonia.

"Hi, it's Lupe Solano."

I tried not to let my feelings become bruised when Anderson groaned in dismay.

"Please, Lupe," he muttered. "Just tell me you haven't found any more dead bodies for me to deal with."

"No, no bodies this time. I promise." I crossed my fingers. "Just checking in to see if there have been any developments on the Estrada cases."

"Nothing for now," Anderson replied. "I wish there was. Both the murders were pretty nasty. A strangulation, a stabbing. Nasty. How about if you tell me something, Lupe: have you been leveling with me? Have you told me everything you know?''

"I'm not holding out on you," I said. Which was almost true. I certainly had no idea who had killed Angel and Jesus.

"Whoever did this isn't playing games," Anderson warned me. "If you know anything, it's in your best interests to come clean."

Obviously my protestations of innocence hadn't made any inroads with Anderson. To my chagrin, I realized that I had developed a bit of a reputation with him.

"I wish I could help you," I said. "But I really have no idea who killed them."

"Well, look," Anderson sighed. "I'll cooperate with you if you cooperate with me. All right? We both want the same thing: to get these murders solved."

"Exactly," I said. "I'm with you on that."

We hung up. I wondered how much our declarations of cooperation really meant. I pictured Anderson at his desk, putting down the phone, wondering the same thing.

I took out the slip of paper containing Camila's address. She wanted me to contact her. Part of me said, So what? I bore no responsibility for her brothers' deaths. If anything, she and her brothers had placed me in possible danger. All I had done was sit down to lunch with Angel Estrada—out of a sense of professional obligation.

But I couldn't just let it go. Angel, Jesus, and Camila had all apparently been convinced that I was going along with their scheme. I had no doubt that the brothers' murders were connected and that there was a strong possibility a murderer was loose in Miami with my name next on his list.

In my mind all roads led to Camila. Twice in as many days I had heard about the thriving market in art forgeries from Cuba. The Estrada family's plan was a new wrinkle on an old theme, but it also didn't preclude Camila from somehow already being involved in art fakery. If that was the case, she must have been pretty tough. Any criminal enterprise involving lots of cash has a tendency to weed out the weak.

The typical primary victim of art forgery was the buyer. The Estradas' scheme represented an innovative idea, because it would be the Cuban government that would be left with the fakes. The more I thought about it, though the Estradas' idea might have been crazy, it could also turn out to be wildly lucrative. Maybe Camila wanted to contact me to warn me about someone who was trying to muscle into their new business.

I didn't know the woman, I had no idea how her mind worked. The only way I would find out about Camila Estrada was to contact her.

I sat back in my chair and looked out at the parrots. They were weaving a garland of branches around the avocado tree. I stared at it for a minute, thinking this new structure looked familiar. Then it occurred to me: the Great Wall of China. They were making a damned good replica of the Great Wall of China.

I smoothed the piece of paper on my desk. How was I going to contact her? I had no contact with anyone in Cuba. I had no family there, no friends. The only person I could think of who could help me was Alvaro, and asking him was totally out of the question.

I had to find another way to make contact with Camila. Jesus had told me how difficult it was to make calls to her in Havana, how the government tapped the lines and eavesdropped on conversations. I would get Camila into trouble by trying to call her. Anyway, there was no number on this paper, just a name and address. I knew that most ordinary Cubans didn't have phones in their homes. Someone in the neighborhood might have one they could borrow in an emergency, or else they might go to a public calling station. So I couldn't just call Camila and ask her to explain herself.

But I needed to reach her quickly, and I didn't think sending letters air mail would be sufficient. That left me with one option: Camila's cousin. At least, he said he was her cousin. I had no way of knowing if he was telling the truth.

I was willing to bet a thousand dollars there was no Reinaldo Estrada in the Miami phone directory, but as an exercise in futility I got out the book anyway. Nothing. There were three full columns of Estradas, and no Reinaldo.

I could conduct a computer search for him, but that would take time and there would be no guarantee of success. I didn't know how long he'd been in the country, whether he was on any databases yet. If he wasn't a Dade County resident, I could probably search forever and never find him.

I put down the white pages, tapped my finger on the desk. *Wait a minute.*

This time I opened up the yellow pages, listings for I through Z. I began skimming entries until I found "Painters." If the three other Estradas were into painting, why not the fourth? Maybe all that painting was hereditary.

I went through all the headings. Paint stores. Paint cleaning services. Paint manufacturing materials. Paint removal. Paints—wholesale and manufacturers. OK, I thought, these weren't the kind of painters I had in mind. Painters who worked in oil on canvas didn't advertise in the phone book. My hunch had been bogus.

Just before I closed the book, my eyes caught the section headed "Painting Contractors."

"Hello," I whispered.

The listing read: *R. Estrada—El Rey de la Pintura.* The king of painting. He was licensed, bonded, insured, had thirty years experience, and was conveniently located in Hialeah. I smiled at the entry. I had my man. Only a Cuban would be arrogant enough to call himself the king of painting.

I started to write a letter to Camila on a plain sheet of paper. The information I wanted to convey to her was surprisingly simple and easy, so it only took me a few minutes. In an anxious moment I realized how deep I had gone, that it would be impossible to ever go back.

Shaking my head, I willed my apprehension away. I reread what I had written and put the letter in an unmarked envelope, along with enough cash for her to do what I asked. I got my bag, checked my gun, and made for the door.

I had an appointment with royalty in Hialeah.

I hated going to Hialeah with a passion. *La ciudad del progreso*—the city of progress—was in northwestern Miami. It was overwhelmingly Cuban, with a mishmash of street names and numbers that made no sense whatsoever. Some streets had two names, others apparently none, and the numbers often went out of sequence. Some were one-way, some two-, some three-way. Some streets bordered canals, and others ended in them. Zoning and code enforcement, to city officials, were synonyms for licenses to steal. No one left government office in Hialeah poorer than they went in. Brown paper bags full of cash floated around City Hall with as much regularity as the Cuban coffee served in paper cups.

Politics in Hialeah were a textbook model of what happened in a city when there were no controls placed over theft and greed. As far as I could tell, three-quarters of Hialeah's elected officials were, or had been at one time or another, under indictment, in jail, or under the witness-protection program. The mayor had been elected five or more times while under a cloud of corruption and criminal charges. I always said they should put polling stations in Hialeah cemeteries, since more dead than live citizens voted in elections there.

I thought carefully about how I was going to deal with my trip there, because any visit to the city required a well-considered plan. From my map I saw that R. Estrada's workshop was just off the Palmetto Expressway. That was good news if it was true, and maybe I wouldn't have to factor in the usual thirty minutes I typically allotted myself for getting lost in the streets of Hialeah.

The map indicated that I could get off at the 103rd Street exit and head west. The workshop would be about a block, two at the most, from the highway. That's what I was counting on—although I knew theory and practice were often two very different things. On my last trip to Hialeah, the street I was counting on taking had been under construction. I'd had to detour so far away that I ended up in Miami Lakes.

I announced to Leonardo that I was going to Hialeah for a couple of hours. He grabbed the edge of his desk, ashen.

"A couple of hours," he snorted. "No one goes to Hialeah for a couple of hours! Remember the last time you went there? I almost reported you as a missing person."

"Laugh it up," I said, watching him wipe away tears of mirth.

"What are you going there for, anyway?" he asked. "I doubt that they have fancy European tapestries there."

Leonardo's comment jolted me back to reality. I had been close-lipped during the past week. Leo knew I was working the Miranda case—he had deposited the hefty retainer—but only that I was "looking into" a lost tapestry for the family. He knew nothing about my intention to travel to Cuba, nor about the other two cases I was pursuing. It wasn't the way I liked to work, but I didn't want to antagonize my cousin. He would go nuts if he knew I was pursuing the Estrada

case with no billable hours, and that I was working with
Tommy again on his case.

I felt a surge of guilt. I was always pretty open with Leonardo, and now I was keeping heavy secrets from him. My
reasons for doing so were less than noble. I didn't want him
to worry about my safety, true, but I also didn't want to
hassle with him trying to stand in my way—which I was sure
he would do. Also, I didn't care to hear his opinion about
my spending time with Tommy again. He had been with-
ering enough about the dinner I'd had with my old flame,
even without knowing the details of what transpired
afterward.

"Something like that," I replied to his question, deciding
that a sin of omission was far preferable to lying. Before he
could ask me anything else, I waved and left.

I was on the highway in five minutes. I turned on the
radio to make the trip less painful. I was switching back and
forth between stations when I heard a familiar voice.

Alvaro.

I turned up the volume and listened, trying to quiet the
beating of my heart. The topic was the immigration policy
of the United States toward Cubans who had arrived by boat
and were being repatriated to the island by the Coast Guard
without ever setting foot on American soil.

"I suppose this gives you pleasure, given your political
stances of the past few years," the announcer said.

I had heard this before. The radio host was attacking Alvaro as though he alone were responsible for the Cubans' fate.

"It doesn't make me happy at all," Alvaro replied in a
calm, measured voice. "But there is a logic to the policy.
The United States, as a sovereign nation, is taking action to
prevent uncontrolled immigration."

Listening to Alvaro, it was very difficult to tell what his
personal political beliefs were. He detailed the government's

position in a balanced, sane fashion. And that's how it should be, I thought, proud of his performance. Alvaro had been called a traitor, a collaborationist, a communist—all because he advocated moderation and communication with the Cuban government. I didn't always agree with him, but I was glad that he didn't let the right-wing radio host bait him into losing his temper.

If we had still been together, I would have called him right after the show and congratulated him. Sadly, things had changed. I wouldn't be calling him any time soon. Maybe in the future, but for now I would have to content myself with listening to his voice on the radio.

The show was almost finished when I reached my exit off the Palmetto. I prayed I had read the map accurately, because in my frame of mind after listening to Alvaro on the radio, the last thing I wanted was to get lost on the streets of Hialeah.

The fates were merciful; I located the workshop just where I thought it would be. I parked on a grassy easement across the street, locked the car, and got my bearings before venturing over to a row of warehouses lined up side by side. As I came closer I saw that the Virgin was smiling over me. I recognized the man busily painting a large wooden desk in an open warehouse doorway.

"Reinaldo!" I called out to him.

I saw the blood drain from his face the moment he spotted me. "Lupe, what are you doing here?" He held the paintbrush slack in his hand, almost dropping it. "How did you—"

"What kind of a detective would I be if I couldn't find you?" I asked him.

His mouth dropped open. He put the brush down edgeways over an open can of white paint. He was wearing a paint-spattered pair of overalls, in spite of the heat. I reached into the pocket of my jeans and took out the letter I'd composed to Camila.

"You said Camila wanted to communicate with me," I said. I held out the envelope. "I don't know how to do that. But I'm sure you do, so please get this to her as quickly as possible."

Reinaldo looked at the envelope, glanced up and down the street.

"It's important that she get this letter right away," I said. To sweeten the pot, I took out a hundred dollar bill and slipped it to him. He pocketed it with a subtle gesture, as though nothing had happened.

"I'll do it," he said. "But now I want you to go away. I don't want to get involved any more than I already am."

"But you *are* involved, Reinaldo," I said. "You're an Estrada. You came to me on Camila's behalf."

Reinaldo started wiping his hands clean with a rag that smelled strongly of chemicals. He shook his head, looking down as he spoke.

"I've kept my distance from my cousins. I don't want to end up like Angel and Jesus," he said. He picked up a paintbrush and pointed it at me; for an instant I had a flash of Jesus in his studio, the brush handle embedded in his chest.

"Easy there." I backed off a step, put my hand in my purse.

"Just go away," Reinaldo said. "I will help you. But you are crazy—you and Camila. You're going to end up with Jesus and Angel. Dead!"

I backed away from his workshop, and Reinaldo pulled down the metal door with a loud bang. The interview seemed to be over.

I was standing there on the sidewalk, sweat trickling down my back, when I felt a surge of temper. I went to the corrugated metal door and started banging on it.

I wanted to know what Reinaldo was keeping from me about his cousins' deaths. And I wanted to know why he thought Camila and I were next. I also wanted to know where he got off, slamming a door in my face after showing up at my office a couple of days before and dragging me deeper into this mess.

The metal shook and rattled as I banged harder. The heat was getting to me, I realized, and I was on the verge of losing control. When I stopped beating on the door, my knuckles began to throb.

"The hell with it," I muttered. As I walked to the car I saw that a couple of men from the warehouse next door had stepped onto the sidewalk to check out the commotion.

I shrugged and got into the Mercedes. I turned on the air conditioner full blast, pointed the vents at my face and neck. I needed to cool off, I needed to decompress.

But there was one more stop I had to make that day.

25

I had a low-grade stress headache, and I was holed up in the air-conditioned comfort of my office. Leonardo was off on some errand, so I was spared having to tell him why I'd gone to Hialeah. I would have been hard-pressed to come up with a plausible response.

And there was no way I was going to tell him about Barbara. If he'd known I had gone to see her, he would figure out that I was contemplating a second trip across the Florida Straits.

I pulled out the three case files from my desk, none of which I'd allowed Leonardo to see. I had scoffed at Reinaldo Estrada's calling himself the king of painting, chalking it up to Cuban arrogance. But had I started to think of myself as *La Reina de las Investigaciones*—the Queen of Investigations? The three cases I was working were too heavy a load, although I kept sensing that they would somehow intersect, that the underworld of Cuban art would reveal its secrets all at once.

Fat chance, I thought. Not as long as I sat there doing nothing. I recalled that I hadn't phoned my contact at the Art Loss Registry in London since our last round of phone tag. I picked up the receiver and dialed an international extension. I asked for Irene Matheson and, to my amazement, was connected.

"Irene, finally!" I blurted out. "This is Lupe Solano, calling from Miami."

"So you do exist!" Irene said, sounding delighted. "I thought I was going to be chitchatting with your assistant until it was time for both of us to retire. So, tell me. How is Miami?"

"It's great. The weather is terrific, the beaches are wonderful." I let it go at that. I would allow Irene in London to entertain the fantasy that Miamians' greatest concern was working on our suntans.

"I envy you," she sighed. I could almost picture her, enveloped in London fog. "Well, Lupe, what can I do for you?"

"Do you remember the last time we spoke?" I began. "I was working on returning some paintings to their rightful owners."

"Of course," Irene recalled. "Cuban art—a Pelaez and a Lam. And you were successful, right?"

"I was," I said. "And as a result I seem to have developed a reputation for being an expert in the recovery of Cuban art."

"Two paintings and you're an expert." Irene sighed again. "I only wish it was that easy here."

"I don't consider myself an expert of any kind," I explained. "I got lucky, and word got around. But now I have other clients who want to track down their paintings as well."

Which wasn't exactly true, but I couldn't go into details with Irene without breaching Tommy's confidentiality with his client.

"Well, Lupe, remember that I can't give out information about *our* clients any more than you can about yours," Irene warned. "But let's see. What can I help you with?"

"Cuban painters—say Mario Carreño, or Rene Portocarrero, or Tomas Sanchez—are their works registered with you?'' I hoped I had succeeded in sidestepping which artist I was really interested in.

"A few of them are,'' Irene replied. "If we're given descriptions and photographs of their works, their paintings are entered into our databases. Then, if the works are offered for sale by someone not authorized to sell them, we alert the rightful owners.''

"Sales where, in which venues?'' I asked. I didn't think that a small one-man gallery in Coral Gables would appear on the London registry's radar screen. "My guess is we're talking about well-known auction houses and large galleries.''

"Mostly, but we also look into individual situations.'' Irene paused. "We do everything we can to help people who've been the victims of art theft.''

"I don't want to sound naive,'' I told her. "But what are the dimensions of the problem?''

"Oh, Lupe,'' Irene exclaimed. "Our estimate is that one in 4,500 works of art sold at auction are stolen. That's a huge number, considering the overall volume of art that changes hands every year.''

"What about dealers in small galleries?'' I asked. "How does a small gallery owner protect himself from dealing in stolen property? Let's say the owner sells a painting that was apparently authenticated but turns out to be stolen. What liability does the gallery owner have?''

"The gallery owner could check with us, for one thing,'' Irene said, "to find out if the particular work is in our database. That offers some protection, but ultimately the responsibility will fall on the dealer.''

I would have bet anything that Rafael Santamaria hadn't taken any such measures before selling the Tomas Sanchez.

"Do you have a lot of Cuban paintings in your database?'' I asked.

"Yes, and more every day,'' said Irene. "Cuban exiles are

trying to claim their possessions, or at least create public notice that a particular work belongs to them—and that anyone buying or selling it is dealing in stolen property."

"The same thing is happening with real estate—sugar plantations, farms, all kinds of properties," I mused.

"So I've heard." Irene was silent for a moment; I heard muffled voices. "Lupe, I'm afraid I have to go to a meeting."

"That's all right," I said. "I really appreciate the time you've taken. You've been very helpful to me."

"Keep me posted," Irene added. "If you get any information about trafficking in stolen Cuban art, let us know. It's an area we're paying increased attention to."

"I'll do that," I promised.

"Who knows, maybe I'll have to come to Miami to look into it," she said. "I wouldn't mind visiting one of those beaches you mentioned."

"Be sure to look me up if you do," I said with a laugh.

After I hung up, I mulled over what I had learned. If Santamaria had known he was selling stolen goods, then his disappearance fit the profile of a criminal going for one big score then skipping town. That might have been the case, but I couldn't be sure. It was also possible that he didn't know the painting he sold was stolen. He might have been the victim of foul play, either as some sort of revenge or to keep him quiet.

I picked up the phone and dialed Tommy's private office line from a button on my speed dial. He picked up on the first ring.

"Hey, Lupe. What's up?"

"Why did your client pull the first detective off the case?" I asked.

Tommy was used to my propensity for dispensing with pleasantries when I had something on my mind. I was growing more convinced that something about the Santamaria situation smelled. Santamaria had a business, a condo, a car, a boat—all the trappings of an established citizen. He wasn't a fly-by-night rip-off artist, and there was no reason to believe that he would choose to vanish without a trace just because he sold a painting of questionable provenance. He had six months remaining on a gallery lease—prepaid, and at very high rent, knowing Coral Gables—and Osterman's report also indicated there were still paintings sitting in the darkened gallery.

And why wasn't Mateo Mora not suing Santamaria along with Fernando Valdez Correa? I knew that Tommy's client was the "deep pockets," but it would also make sense to include the gallery owner as part of the lawsuit.

"You know, Lupe, I admire your dedication and intensity," Tommy said in a wry tone. "But I also wouldn't mind a little civility now and then."

"Sorry, I should be more polite," I said. I waited a beat. "Now—tell me why your client pulled Osterman off the case."

"That happened before I came into the picture," Tommy told me. "Frankly, I didn't think to ask, not once I knew you were taking over the investigation."

"It's going to be important to find out what happened to Santamaria, the gallery owner," I said. "I went to see Osterman. He didn't know why he got pulled off. He didn't seem to care much, either, but that's beside the point."

"What about Osterman?" Tommy asked. "Is he any good?"

"I don't really know much about him." I hesitated, about to try to describe Osterman to Tommy. I decided it would take too long. "But he was doing all the right things. That is, before he was pulled off."

"Well, there's nothing to do but pick up where he left off," Tommy said. "And keep me informed for a change."

Tommy always thought that I was inconsistent in reporting to him. I only briefed him on what I thought he should know, and when he should know it. It seemed more efficient that way. In any case, he shouldn't have been offended—this was pretty much how I conducted myself in all areas of my life, both professional and personal.

"By the way, Lupe," Tommy said. "What's going on with the Mirandas? Any progress on that?"

"It's coming along." I wasn't going to say anything more. If Tommy knew I'd contacted Barbara about returning to Cuba, he would have fired me from his case, hit me with the Baker Act, and stuck me in Jackson Crisis Center under the twenty-one day rule. "I'm working a few angles on it."

"Well, good luck," he said. He didn't seem particularly keen to delve into the details.

I heard a buzzer in the background. I envisioned Sonia, Tommy's secretary, trying to get his attention. Sonia was a bombshell, a Cuban in her early twenties; it was widely assumed in Miami legal and law enforcement circles that she and Tommy were sleeping together. No one believed the unbelievable truth—that she had gotten the job based on her high-level skills and not because of her looks. Sonia, in fact, lived with her parents in Hialeah. Essentially the only times she left the house were to go to church and to her job.

"Thanks," I said to Tommy. I almost added that I would need all the luck I could get, but I stopped myself in time.

"Sorry to rush you, but I have to run," Tommy said. "Sonia's standing here signaling that I'm late for a deposition. But do you want to have dinner tonight? We could continue our discussion under less rushed circumstances."

"That would be great," I said.

I guess Tommy and I were back to business as usual—that is, until and unless Alvaro surfaced in my life again, I thought with a pang. There was no question that Alvaro had left a void in my life, but at least I had Tommy's companionship. Dinner and a conversation. And then on to another kind of business. It was also widely speculated that Tommy and I were sleeping together. Unlike the mistaken assumption about Sonia, in this case the gossip had been correct for a long time.

After hanging up, I got on my computer and accessed the database that would reveal the record of civil transactions conducted in Dade County—in this case, lawsuits filed by or against a particular individual. There was nothing under Rafael Santamaria's name. I researched back ten years, still finding nothing. The man had never engaged in any litigation in Dade County.

It seemed unusual to me. American society is totally litigious. A businessperson operating in Dade County for any period of time will inevitably encounter some sort of legal trouble—usually suing, or being sued by, a disgruntled former employee, partner, or customer. Santamaria's spotless record stood out as a rare instance of an uneventful business history.

Santamaria was beginning to intrigue me. It was almost as though he didn't exist at all. The footprints he had left on Earth were so few, so shallow, that they were like marks in sand erased by the evening tide.

As much as I disliked it, I had a call to make.

"Detective Anderson?" I said. "This is Lupe Solano. And before you ask, no, I'm not calling to report another dead body."

"Thank Heaven for small favors," he said. He sounded more weary than I had ever heard him before.

"Well, I should qualify that," I said. "I don't *think* there's a dead body."

Anderson sighed deeply. "You don't think so," he repeated. "Lupe, either there's dead body or there isn't. Which is it?"

"It's a case I'm working on. One of the witnesses involved seems to have vanished off the face of the earth." I figured this would please him. A potential body was much better than a real one. "I was hoping you could tell me if a person matching his description has been reported missing or found dead."

Rustling papers in the background. "So you suspect foul play?" I could hear the dread in Anderson's voice. I hated to be associated with bad news all the time, but that was just the way it worked out.

"I don't know. But his disappearance is looking more and more suspicious." I tried to sound as hopeful as possible, not wanting to dash his hopes that the person in question would still be living and breathing—that is, not Anderson's responsibility.

"OK. Give me his stats." Anderson exhaled, a sigh so deep I could almost feel it.

"Thank you so much." I knew he was doing me a big favor. Anderson was a by-the-book kind of cop, so it was a big deal that he was helping me. I opened up Osterman's report. "Rafael Santamaria. Hispanic male. DOB of 7/15/55. Five-foot-ten, approximately two hundred pounds. Black hair and eyes—two moles under the left eye."

Except for the moles, the description I gave the detective fit about fifty percent of Dade County's male population. Unfortunately, it was all I had.

Five minutes later the telephone rang. It was Anderson.

"No," he said by way of introduction. He could have been a professor if I opened up the Lupe Solano College of Phone Manners.

"No?"

"No one fitting your description comes up anywhere," Anderson said. "Not at the morgue, not at missing persons. Lupe, is there something I should know about? I mean, why do I get the feeling that my next call from you is going to mean it's time to contact the crime-scene techs?"

"I hope not," I said. "Right now, all I know is that the man is missing."

"OK. If you say so." Anderson sounded completely unconvinced. "Keep me posted. Try not to bring me another body."

"I'll do my best," I said.

Well, now I knew at least that Santamaria wasn't lying on a slab at the morgue while I was wasting energy trying to find him. I also knew he hadn't been reported as missing. It was close to two weeks since his disappearance, and no one had stepped up to inform the authorities that he was gone. Maybe no one in the world cared whether he was lost or found.

I had to pick up where Osterman left off—without the beers and the Marlboros. I was looking for a person who had turned invisible. Osterman's personal habits might have helped me see things and people that weren't there, but that wasn't what I had in mind.

had dinner with Tommy at the Chart House, a seafood restaurant in the Grove on Biscayne Bay. We talked about business and little else, and at the end of the evening, I rather chastely went home instead of going to his apartment. Tommy offered little protest after his initial attempt at persuasion. Maybe we were both just tired, but it didn't feel right. Maybe thoughts of Alvaro were intruding.

Normally when I got home I would have gone straight up to my bedroom. This night I walked out to the terrace instead and stood on the edge of the dock. I leaned over the railing and looked out over the bay. There was a strange feeling inside me; it was almost as though I was being drawn to the open water.

I had been so caught up in the details of going to Havana for the past couple of days—sending the letter to Camila containing the outline of my plan, making plans with Barbara—that I hadn't devoted much time to thinking about how the upcoming voyage was affecting me emotionally. I had spent my life in Miami, but I felt completely Cuban. The trip to the island would be a sort of homecoming. I had been there once, but only in a rural area and for less than a full day. I'd never set eyes on Havana.

It was good that I hadn't wasted time considering my feel-

ings. What I intended to do was so dangerous, the consequences of failure so severe, that I had to put all my energies
into devising a reasonable plan—which I thought I'd done.
Now I had a quiet moment, and I felt a torrent of conflicting
emotions. For one thing: was Alvaro right? Was I going to
Havana to somehow honor my mother by bringing out the
tapestry that confirmed her fondest wishes and most ardent
speculation? And if so, did that justify my actions?

All the exiles I knew who had been to Cuba were deeply
affected by their visits. They all talked about the breathtaking beauty of the island, which couldn't be hidden by the
decay of the place and the despair of the people. Cubans in
exile and Cubans on the island were separated by geography
and politics, but I felt that our hearts beat as one. For my
family, Cuba was everything. It had been that way since I
was a small child, it would always be that way.

We spoke Spanish at home most of the time—it was
important to us not to lose our vocabulary and fluency in
the language. Miami is a thoroughly bilingual city, but one
side effect was that it was easy to slip into Spanglish—with
the unfortunate result that the speaker can lose a degree of
proficiency in both languages. Aida and Osvaldo spoke only
Spanish, so for them there was no choice. As for the youngest family members, Fatima's twins, it would have been
easier to let them substitute English words for Spanish when
they reached an impasse in expressing themselves—still, they
were encouraged to struggle and complete their thoughts in
our native language.

On a less lofty level, the Solano clan sat down every evening and tasted its heritage. Aida cooked primarily Cuban
food, and I could tell from the look in her eyes when she
was preparing the ingredients that she was being transported
back home. Every bite of *arroz con frijoles*—black beans and
rice—or *ropa vieja*—"old clothes," or skirt meat in tomato

sauce—or yucca, or flan, reinforced our ties to Cuba. Although we also knew that, with the scarcity of food on the island, few people there ate nearly as plentifully as we did.

Cuban symbols were everywhere in our house. There was a print of the Cuban flag by Emilio Sanchez hanging proudly in our entranceway. There was a statue of the *Virgen de la Caridad del Cobre*—Our Lady of Charity, the Cuban Virgin—on the front patio. Osvaldo always made sure that She was adorned with fresh flowers. Mami's ashes were prominently displayed in a silver urn on the mantelpiece, awaiting interment in the Cementerio Colon in Havana—a symbol emphasizing the importance of Cuba even in the afterlife.

Sometimes it was difficult to explain to Americans, but the exiles' intense feelings of love, affection, and pride for Cuba and being Cuban were not in opposition to their feelings for the United States. The two realms were separate from one another, and our feelings for Cuba in no sense diminished or negated our bonds to our adopted home.

I walked back from the edge of the dock and made myself comfortable on one of the lounge chairs that were scattered around the terrace. I watched the moonlight playing over the water, thinking: Soon I'm going to be out there, on that water.

I knew the dangers of the trip were very real. The Coast Guard might intercept the boat and arrest Barbara and me before we even got to Cuba. Then there was the sea itself, the tides and currents, the possibility of a storm. Then there were the dangers of being caught once we were in Cuban territorial waters—not to mention being apprehended in Havana itself.

I might not come back from this trip, I thought. And yet I was still excited, my neck still tingled. Part of me feared for my life. The other part loved the danger. I was reveling in being on the edge and tempting fate. I couldn't recall feeling more alive, my senses more sharp.

The Hatteras was docked to my right. I heard the water slapping against the hull. Sometimes a boat would speed past—ignoring the numerous No Wake signs posted all along the Coral Gables waterways—and the water would slap louder against the *Concepcion*. As I listened to the motors, I thought about all the manatees that had been killed by the propellers of careless people. It was almost enough to make me reconsider my opposition to the death penalty.

The Hatteras looked so serene in the moonlight. It wouldn't stay that way for long. I had to concoct a story that would enable me to borrow her for a few days. Telling the truth was completely out of the question. There was no way Papi would allow me to take his beloved *Concepcion* to Cuba. In fact, he would probably have a stroke on the spot if he had any idea what I had in mind.

Whatever plan I came up with, it had to be solid. Papi hated letting the *Concepcion* out of his sight, even if it was just to go into dry dock for routine maintenance. He feared that Castro would fall the precise moment the Hatteras was out of his hands, and that he would be unable to make his triumphant return to Havana. It had been forty years since Castro took power, but Papi was certain pretty much that entire time that Fidel's downfall was imminent. One of Osvaldo's duties was to keep the *Concepcion* fully gassed and the boat's pantry full at all times. About the only item not stocked constantly was the ice chest—Papi had recognized Osvaldo's complaint that this entailed too many trips to the 7-Eleven, and granted a special exception.

The Hatteras looked so large and imposing tied up to the dock. It was secure and safe as a tank, but I knew that on the open sea she would become just another speck on the horizon. My sisters and I all knew how to drive the *Concep-*

cion, because Papi had insisted that we learn once we were old enough. He believed that, as island people, we needed to have the skills to survive in all sorts of situations, and to be able to pilot all sorts of watercraft. Papi was a great believer in self-reliance, a trait he had passed down to his daughters. Sometimes I felt that it was a lesson I had learned too well.

The more I looked at it, the bigger the Hatteras seemed. It wasn't going to be possible to slip it away for a couple of days without anyone noticing, that was certain. The last thing I needed was to have Papi report the boat stolen, and for me to be caught by the Coast Guard. I could deal with the possibility of landing in a Cuban jail, but I'd seen the inside of the Dade County Women's Detention Center—and I wanted no part of it.

I lay there in the evening, a cool wind blowing over me. For a moment I was able to forget about all the challenges ahead, and the deep layers of meaning that represented in my life. I closed my eyes, pretended for just a few minutes that everything was simple, that it was all going to work out.

"Osvaldo, can I speak with you a second, please?" I called out to the old man early the next morning. He was busy dusting some nonexistent debris off the roof of the Mercedes.

All right. I felt like a real shit for what I was about to do. But I'd been up nearly all night thinking, and this was the best I'd come up with. Time was passing, and my options were narrowing. I told myself that if Osvaldo knew the motivations that were driving me, he would help me. Anything for Mami.

"Lupe, *buenos dias,*" Osvaldo said. His face lit up when he saw me. His look of delight made me feel even worse, in spite of my unspoken rationalization that he would help me take the trip for Mami's sake.

I took hold of his arm and gently led him away from the house. I didn't know what would happen if Papi overheard us.

"Osvaldo, I need your help with something I'm planning," I whispered conspiratorially.

"Lupe, child, you know I'd do anything to help you," Osvaldo replied. "You tell me what it is, and it's done."

"Well, you know how I'm seeing Alvaro Mendoza?" I asked. I hoped I wasn't going to fry in hell for this one.

"A nice boy," Osvaldo said, nodding approvingly. "Too much on the left wing, if you know what I mean. But a nice young man nonetheless."

I knew my family was thrilled that I was finally seeing a Cuban man—and not just any Cuban man, but one whose family had known mine for generations. They thought he was too liberal, but they had become accustomed to him and willing to humor him in regard to his politics because of his social background.

"Well, Osvaldo." I tried to blush, probably without much success. I don't think I had ever blushed in my life. "I invited Alvaro to come out with me on the *Concepcion*."

Osvaldo looked puzzled. He glanced up at the house. "Lupe, I don't understand," he said. "You've taken your friends on the *Concepcion* before. Just ask your *papi* when would be a good time."

"Well, this is different," I explained. "This is for an entire weekend."

Osvaldo's eyes widened; he put his hand over his mouth. He was shocked by the very implication that I would spend two nights alone with a man, even one as socially acceptable and well-known to our family as Alvaro. In Osvaldo's eyes, I knew, I was still a virgin—and would remain one until I married. It didn't matter that I was thirty and carried a gun. I was the baby girl of the Solano family, pure and chaste. I waited a moment for Osvaldo to compose himself before continuing.

"It began when Alvaro and I were talking about boats, and how much we enjoy them," I said. "Alvaro mentioned how sad he was when his parents sold the family boat."

That much of the story was true; Alvaro's parents had simplified their material lives after he and his brother had moved out.

"So I invited Alvaro out on the *Concepcion*," I continued. "I don't know exactly how it happened, but the invitation turned into a weekend."

Osvaldo's brow tightened into a complicated topography of wrinkles. "Your *papi* will never give you the *Concepcion* to go for a weekend with a man, not even Alvaro." He tugged at his rag in agitation.

"But I can't withdraw the invitation, Alvaro," I said. "He'll think I'm a total fool, an idiot. He was so happy when I invited him!"

I must have looked completely miserable—not that much of a reach, considering how I was using the old man—because Osvaldo's face softened. "What do you need my help with?" he asked.

"I need an excuse to take the boat," I said. "A story so that Papi thinks the boat needs servicing or something."

Osvaldo looked completely appalled. "You want me to lie to your father?" he asked.

"It wouldn't really be a lie," I said. I inched closer and took his hand. "You see, I would drop the *Concepcion* off at Merrill Stevens, and it could be serviced then. It would really only be a matter of taking the boat for two extra days."

"What if something happened while you had it?" Osvaldo chewed on his bottom lip. "You might crash it, or go aground. It might be stolen!"

Osvaldo practically shuddered as he thought through the

various scenarios. He had a tendency to consider the worst possible eventuality at all times. Once, he seen a tornado touch down in Oklahoma on TV; he tried to get Papi to build a storm shelter under the house, resisting the logic that it was almost meteorologically impossible for such a tornado to hit South Florida. It wasn't much comfort to me that in this case he didn't know the half of it.

"Nothing is going to happen," I reassured him. "We would just go around the bay, maybe down to Key West, or anchor at Elliot Key. Nothing very far. Alvaro was brought up around boats. His family also had a Hatteras."

"Yes, but smaller. It was only thirty-seven feet, not fifty-two like the *Concepcion*," Osvaldo said gravely. I suppressed a smile. The tide had turned, I could sense it. The old man was going to help me. I hoped Mami would forgive me, knowing I was going to bring back the tapestry that would have brought her so much happiness.

"I know it's a huge favor, Osvaldo," I said. "But maybe you could tell Papi you've noticed something wrong with the Hatteras, that she might need to go in for servicing."

"I don't like this," Osvaldo fretted. "Too many things could go wrong."

"I'll take care of it," I promised.

Osvaldo put his hands on his hips. "You know, you are lucky you came to me," he said sternly. "Going off with a man for two days. I understand that things are different now from when I was a young man. But your *papi*—he would explode if he knew."

"That's why I came to you, Osvaldo," I said truthfully. "Because I know that I can always count on you."

"You can't tell anyone about this," he whispered, glancing up at the house with a frightened expression. I knew he was talking about Aida, who tended to be more stern and strict in all things than her husband. "You promise me on your sainted mother. This is between us alone, and it always will be."

"I promise," I said, taking him in my arms for a tight embrace. "I love you, Osvaldo. *Gracias.*"

When I pulled away, I saw that it was his turn to blush. He reached out and lightly touched my cheek.

"You were so worried," he said tenderly. "You are crying. Don't worry, child. You have a right to enjoy yourself. Take it from an old man—life is for the living."

My relief was overwhelming, and the source of the tears that Osvaldo so lovingly wiped away. I had always felt as close as I could to him, as if he were my own grandfather. I felt an even deeper connection now that we were co-conspirators.

I wished I had told him the truth. I wished the biggest adventure in my life was a romantic weekend with Alvaro. But that wasn't the case. I had made a commitment to go to Cuba and return with a treasure of almost unimaginable worth and value. I hoped the magnitude of my achieve-ment—should I succeed—would be enough to someday as-suage my conscience for having been untruthful with Osvaldo.

Osvaldo walked around the side of the house to get on with his day, turning to put a finger over his lips. *Say nothing more about it,* he seemed to be telling me. I smiled at him, feeling a strong mixture of love and relief.

If Osvaldo hadn't helped me, I don't know what I would have done. I had no backup plan, no other way to take Papi's beloved *Concepcion* for a couple of days without his knowing. I was in deep now, having used Alvaro as a cover story for going to Cuba—the very action that had driven him away from me.

I knew I was shameless, but I had done what I needed to do. I didn't like myself for my actions and the way I'd manipulated Osvaldo, but I wouldn't have done it if I had seen another way. The clock was ticking for Doña Maria Miranda.

I was going to have to live with my conscience for a long time. I burned with remorse, but it was overshadowed by a strong sense of determination and a drive to survive the next few days. I also knew that I would have to protect Papi's Hatteras with my life—because if anything happened to it, I would never be able to look him or Osvaldo in the eye again.

27

"I found this under the door when I opened it this morning," Leonardo announced when I got to the office. He handed me a white envelope.

"Gracias." I looked at the unfamiliar handwriting on the front, where my name had been written in pencil in a distinctly feminine script. There was no return address. My heart beat faster; I was pretty sure this was what I had been waiting for.

I closed my office door behind me and moved quickly to my desk. I reached for my silver letter opener and slowly sliced open the envelope, careful not to damage its contents. The quality of the envelope paper was poor, and I had to stop each time it began to tear.

I reached inside and pulled out a single sheet of lined paper. It was a letter to me, written in Spanish. The handwriting matched that on the envelope. The letters were small and cramped together, but I had no trouble making out the words or their meaning.

It was a letter from Camila Estrada. She began by thanking me for being so receptive to her and her brothers. *Receptiva.* I wondered what she meant by that. Both her brothers had been killed within days of each other, and both after meeting with me. I supposed I should be grateful she didn't somehow blame me for their deaths.

Camila apologized for how difficult it was to communicate with her, but said she had received the letter I sent via her cousin. More important, she said she would do as I asked.

Camila went on to say that, as far as she was concerned, we were in agreement. She would look forward to meeting me in person. She stressed that this letter would be her last before we met, because of the dangers of further communication between us.

I put down the letter. That was it. She agreed to my plan. That meant I was leaving. I could barely believe it. I knew that people passed money, letters, and small goods back and forth between Miami and Cuba all the time, although I had never done it. Camila and I had communicated by letter in about the same amount of time as if we'd had to post envelopes across the state.

I must have read the letter more than a dozen times, searching for some sign of duplicity or deceit in its terse paragraphs. Camila's letter had the ring of truth. I hoped my instincts were correct. If I was wrong, I was going to pay dearly.

For the next two days, while Barbara made final preparations for our trip, I worked Tommy's case full-time.

"Tommy, I've searched for Santamaria in every place I can think of." I was on the phone in my office, looking down at one of the most frustrating case files I'd ever worked. "I've gone into his personal and financial dealings. I've canvassed around his home and the gallery. Two whole days, Tommy, and I'm no better off than when I started."

I discovered it really didn't matter that Osterman had been taken off the case early on. When I first read Osterman's report, I had thought about other avenues of investigation. Now I had exhausted them, and the result was the same. I'd been worried about interviewing Santamaria's neighbors a second time, but I shouldn't have been. To a person, they seemed uninterested.

I was starting to think that Santamaria couldn't be found. It was as though he never existed. I showed his picture to the neighbors, who shrugged and said they might recognize him and then again they might not. I talked to the personnel in the building that housed his gallery: the valet who parked his car, the superintendent, the cleaning crew. They all said he was quiet, that he minded his own business, that he hadn't made much of an impression on anyone. A couple of staff members reported receiving Christmas bonuses from him—in cash.

In other words, he was an ideal tenant. No one around his apartment ever saw him with anyone else, female or otherwise. I gave a couple of cash tips, to see if anyone remembered anything they had kept hidden out of a sense of discretion. I should have known better. No one has a sense of discretion anymore. At least all these people had seen Santamaria, and some had even spoken with the man. It was reassuring that he wasn't just a figment of my imagination.

I wasn't used to failure, and I was getting frustrated. Maybe Santamaria had engineered his own disappearance, even planning it in advance. Or else someone might have engineered his disappearance for him. He might be at the bottom of Biscayne Bay.

So far there was no rational, logical answer to this riddle. So I did what any Cuban would: I thought about the role of Cuba in the dealer's life. In my experience, for a Cuban, all paths eventually lead back to the island.

I began conjuring up possible scenarios. Santamaria might have been a Cuban government agent. Why not? I knew that the Cuban government was interested in selling off appropriated artworks. Maybe Santamaria did this for the Castro regime. He might have been living undercover, sent to Miami to sell paintings and funnel the money back to the cash-starved island. His disappearance might then be explained by the fact that he sold a work of contested ownership; he might have been called back to Cuba in order to avoid discovery.

By thinking this way, I realized, I was buying into the commonly held belief of all exile conspiracy theorists: that the Cuban government was manipulating everything that dealt with Cuban affairs, both on and outside the island itself. Part of me felt ridiculous, but I had to consider every possibility.

I started thinking about what little I knew of Santamaria's life. From my experience as an investigator, I knew that the overwhelming majority of cases boiled down to three factors: money, sex, and pride.

I had information on Santamaria's bank accounts. For all his outward trappings of success, the funds in his personal and business accounts had been limited. Every month he wrote checks to his mortgage company and to the lender for his Mercedes. Someone who dealt in expensive art should have had a much larger operating budget than just a few thousand dollars. It was possible that Santamaria was the kind of person who kept only enough money on hand for his expenses, preferring to have the rest working for him at all times. But I had looked into several investment houses and commercial stock-brokerage accounts and come up with nothing. The same was true when I tried to find investments under his company name.

I knew someone in the IRS who could pull Santamaria's tax returns for me, but that measure was a last resort. It was prohibitively expensive, and if I were caught, the penalties were high. And even if I found something incriminating, there was no way such evidence would ever be allowed in a court proceeding.

For a moment I thought about calling Detective Anderson again, to see if anything had changed in the Estrada investigations. While I was on the line with him, I might persuade him to check into whether anyone fitting Santamaria's description had turned up since we last spoke. But I thought better of it. Anderson was already on the alert from my last call, and I knew my name and Santamaria's were linked in his mind. And each time I spoke with him he sounded more burnt out. I knew by then that the Estrada investigations weren't a very high priority with the homicide unit. After all, the victims had no close relatives in America, and time and resources were limited for the Miami police.

I remembered a time a few years ago when there had been so many murders committed in Dade County, in such a short period of time, that the medical examiner's office had run out of space to store corpses. For a while, extra bodies were stored in a refrigerated truck leased from the Burger King Corporation. I couldn't eat a BK burger for years afterward.

"Well, what's next, Lupe?" Tommy asked, jolting me back to reality. "How about if we get together to discuss our next step? Over dinner?"

"Sounds great," I said.

After hanging up with Tommy, I sat back and perused the Santamaria file. I thought about Rafael Santamaria, the man. What if, as I'd already posited, he was an agent of the Castro government? He had to be dedicated and hardworking; I found no evidence of any family or close friends in his daily life. He had a boat, the twenty-seven-foot Mako. Maybe that was for recreation, and maybe it was used to transport goods to and from Cuba.

Santamaria's lack of money was suspicious. The second motivating factor on my list was sex. I had no way of knowing about his sex life, except there was no evidence that he had one. I was certain of one thing: for a Cuban man, on the island or in Miami, or on the moon for that matter, sex was of paramount importance. Politics and religion broke down under the weight of this irrefutable, ineluctable fact.

I looked through the file. The searches all yielded information from 1997 on. Prior to that, the searches reported no records. So he had been in the U.S. for at least three years. No healthy forty-year-old Cuban man was going to do without sex for three years—no matter how deep his patriotism. The slogan of the Cuban revolution was "Socialism or Death." Celibacy was conspicuously absent from the equation. Not even Fidel, the Maximum Leader, would expect one of his agents to abstain from life's pleasures for three years.

Santamaria was a loner. No one spoke of him having a girlfriend, or even being seen in the company of a woman. Yet he had access to at least a reasonable amount of cash. For the second time in two weeks I decided to call up the prevailing expert on Miami's sexual climate.

"Lupe, *querida!*" Suzanne answered in her baby-doll voice. No wonder she was so successful.

"Very well," I replied. "And you?" I could hear a telephone ringing in the background; I knew that, as usual, my time with Suzanne would be limited.

"I don't mean to rush you, Lupe," Suzanne said delicately. "But I have a convention of dentists coming in from B.A. this weekend, and I have to set them up. Right now I'm searching everywhere for tall blond girls who speak fluent Spanish."

"That's a very specific request," I observed.

"Argentines! They're so demanding!" Suzanne laughed. "I swear they care more about the Spanish than the blonde hair. They've taken their 'pure Spanish' to the point where they're more interested in a girl's diction than her measurements."

I had to laugh. To save time, I refrained from comment. "I'm working a missing-person case," I said. "A Cuban guy named Santamaria, an art dealer. Forty years old, lives in the Grove. Is he one of your clients?"

"Doesn't ring a bell," Suzanne said. "But that doesn't necessarily mean anything. A lot of clients don't use their real names, or meet the girls in their own homes."

I heard the whir of a fax machine printing out in the background.

"You have a picture?" she asked. "I could show it around."

"It's not a very good one," I said. "But I can fax it over, along with a more detailed description."

"Sure, but I can't promise anything," Suzanne replied. "I'm glad you called, Lupe. I was going to give you a ring. I have a problem you can help me with. A guy's been bothering one of my girls. He won't leave her alone."

"Stalking?" I asked. It wasn't unusual. Suzanne had come up against problems like that many times. A client would fall hard for one of the girls and become delusional, thinking he would marry her, be her knight in shining armor and take her away from *la vida*. When she inevitably refused to be "saved," he would hound her and make her life miserable. Funny how creeps always followed the same pattern.

"Is she in immediate danger?" I asked.

"I don't think so. It's just annoying," Suzanne said wearily. It couldn't have been easy, running Suzanne's business. It was at least as demanding as running the human resources department of a Fortune 500 company. "It's starting to cramp her style, I think that's what's bothering her the most."

"I'm up to my neck on a couple of cases," I told her. "But I think things are going to clear up in a week or so. Get me the information. I'll give you a call when I have time to look into it.''

"Thanks, *chica*," Suzanne said. "The girl's name is Samantha. I'll have her get in touch with you."

"OK," I said. "And I'll fax over—"

"Hey, the guy you were asking about," Suzanne interrupted. "You said he was a Cuban art dealer?"

"Right."

"Any connection to the other one? Angel Estrada, the one Ingrid found?"

"I don't know," I told her. "I'm working on it."

"Funny," Suzanne mused. "I never thought being an art dealer was what you'd call a real high-risk profession."

"Tell me about it," I said. "I guess it depends on what kind of art you're dealing in."

Suzanne pondered this bit of wisdom for a moment. "Makes me glad I got into such a safe, predictable line of work," she said.

"Me, too," I replied. We both hung up.

28

"**T**ommy?"

"Hmmm?" The sound came from so deep in his body that I new he was in *the zone*.

I sat up in bed. Tommy was motionless beside me, a beatific smile on his face.

"Remember the case I was working for the Mirandas?" I asked him. "The one with the unicorn tapestry?"

"Hmmm."

This response didn't exactly reassure me that Tommy was alert, aware, and able to concentrate fully on my every word. I took it as a meaningful compliment on my performance earlier that evening. It wasn't often that Tommy was spent to the point of being comatose.

"Seems I'm going to have to go to Havana for a few days," I said, trying to break the news as gently as I could.

About thirty seconds of silence passed before Tommy sat straight up in bed. His hair was disheveled; he blinked to focus his eyes.

"What?" he croaked. "When?"

"Soon." Tommy tensed next to me. "I want you to know that I'm not going to be able to work on your case until at least next week."

"Fuck the case." Tommy fumbled on the bedside table

for his glasses. "Talk to me, Lupe. Tell me what you're planning."

"I told you that night at Le Festival that I was working a case for the Mirandas," I said.

"I don't think you mentioned going to Cuba, Lupe." He turned on the bedside lamp, got out of bed and left the room. Was he going to get a rope to tie me up with? No such luck. He returned with a bottle of Courvoisier and two cut-crystal balloon glasses. It looked like we were going to have a serious discussion. He hopped back into bed and poured a healthy amount of brandy in each glass. He handed one to me, and we touched the rims together.

"*Salud,*" Tommy said. I took a sip; as the amber liquor did its work, I felt as though I was submerged in a bathtub full of hot, fragrant perfumed water. I looked over at Tommy. His eyes were closed, either in rapture or in an attempt to gather his strength—I wasn't sure which. I ran my eyes over his naked body. There was something to be said for the personal aspect of this business relationship.

"Now, Lupe." Tommy seemed fortified by the drink. "Explain to me what you're planning to do."

"I'm going to Havana in the *Concepcion.* I'm going to get the tapestry out of the Miranda family home, then bring it back to Miami." I tried to sound sure of myself, as though it were just a simple plan. "And that's it, really."

"That's it, huh?" Tommy looked over at me as though he had just realized I was certifiably insane. "Didn't you learn anything about the danger of going to Cuba from the last time you went there?"

It was *déjà vu,* lying in Tommy's bed on the eve before a foray into Cuban waters, listening to him lecture me.

"I made it there and back safely," I reminded him.

"It was sheer luck, and you know it." Tommy glared at

me. How did I have such an ability to infuriate the men I was involved with? "You can't count on it happening twice."

I sipped my Courvoisier, allowing the atmosphere in the room to cool a bit. Tommy got up; when he returned a minute later, he was puffing on a cigar. He got into bed with a surly grunt and took another long drink of his brandy.

Sometimes I felt I should give up men entirely, become a nun like my sister Lourdes. But then reason set in again. Celibacy wasn't for me. I had a gorgeous naked man lying next to me, angry or not.

"I have it all planned out," I said.

"That's what you said the last time," Tommy pointed out, and correctly. Suddenly he had a thought. "Lupe, you're not going with that Santera, Barbara, are you?"

I bristled at the derision in his voice. I knew that Santeria, a religion originating in Africa which, in Cuba, became overlaid with Catholic elements and saints, was considered by certain individuals who were unfamiliar with it to be a cult. "She's not a Santera. And she's a terrific sailor. She knows the Florida Straits like the back of her hand."

Tommy shrugged, puffed on his cigar, poured himself another drink. Actually, in some ways I thought he and Barbara would get along fine.

"I can see you're determined to go," he said. He put out the cigar, put down his drink, took mine and laid it carefully on the table. He shifted closer to me. "Might as well give you something to remember on those hot, sultry nights alone in a Cuban jail cell."

Tommy knew me too well. He knew what I liked. And he knew better than to try to change my mind.

Osvaldo was waiting for me in the driveway when I returned early the next morning. He didn't comment on the disgrace of the hour at which I was returning, which he often would. It looked like Osvaldo was making an effort to get with the twentieth century.

He quickly walked over to the Mercedes, a finger over his lips to keep me quiet. "I have to talk to you," he whispered.

"*Buenos dias,*" I said. We walked to the side of the house.

"I spoke to your *papi,*" Osvaldo told me. "About the *Concepcion.*"

"Osvaldo, *gracias.*" I leaned over and kissed his cheek.

He blushed, making his *café con leche* cheeks look as though they were sunburned.

"I told your *papi* I thought the *Concepcion*'s engines made a strange sound when I started them yesterday," he said.

"What happened?" I asked. I was starting to sense Osvaldo's growing excitement about our conspiracy. "What did Papi say?"

"This is what could be the problem." The blush faded from Osvaldo's cheeks. "Your *papi* wants to go fishing at Cat Cay this weekend. He wants the *Concepcion* back by Friday."

"Friday." My heart dropped. This was Wednesday. "That's three days from now."

"Well, Lupe," Osvaldo said, chuckling softly, "you and Alvaro are going to have to take your weekend trip during the week."

It took me a couple of seconds to remember what he was talking about. I was almost caught in my own lie. Not only was there no weekend trip, there was no Alvaro.

"I guess we have to leave today," I said weakly. I tried to brighten up, play the part of a woman about to spend two days on a boat in the company of her lover.

"Unless you wait until next week," Osvaldo offered. "But then I would have to come up with another excuse, since the *Concepcion* will already have been to dry dock."

Osvaldo frowned, seeming to indicate that this was as far

as he was going to go. He had already fibbed to Papi, an action I knew he must have agonized over.

"Today is fine," I said. I leaned over and kissed him again. "*Gracias*, Osvaldo. Thank you so much."

"Remember, not a word to anyone, Lupe. Anyone!" He put his finger to his lips. I knew who he was talking about. Aida would have clubbed him with a rolling pin if she knew about his part in my scheme.

"I promise," I said.

"Aida, she wouldn't understand," Osvaldo said with a sweet smile. "But there is enough suffering in life. There should also be sweetness. I am glad that I could help you, Lupe."

I left him polishing off an imaginary speck from Papi's Jaguar, consumed with bittersweet emotions over Osvaldo's affectionate words. But once I was inside the house, reality kicked in.

Friday. How the hell was I going to make this all happen in two days?

As I walked upstairs to shower and change, I reached up without thinking and touched the three medals pinned to my brassiere. I was going to need all the divine protection I could get between then and the end of the week.

For the moment, I would have to make do with a large mug of *café con leche*, followed by a generous portion of Cuban bread. As Napoleon acutely observed, an army travels on its stomach.

I tried not to dwell on the results of his Russian campaign.

29

On the way to the office I stopped by the *Santa Barbara*. Barbara herself was on the boat's deck, going through the considerable amount of provisions she had bought for our journey.

"Good news," I said. "We don't have to keep waiting. In fact, we have to leave later today."

Barbara showed no reaction. She scratched her belly and yawned. "Fine," she said. "But I need more money. I spent everything you gave me and there's still more to buy."

"I thought that might happen," I said. I gave her an envelope full of cash that I'd withdrawn from the bank on the way over. As I handed it over I wished all problems in life could be solved so easily.

She pocketed the envelope. "So, when can we be ready to leave?" I asked her.

"Two hours, three, it doesn't matter," she said with a laugh. "You come back to pick me up. I'll be ready."

"What about your children?" I asked, thinking that she would have to make some kind of child-care arrangements.

Barbara puffed on her morning cigar; for a fleeting instant I saw a flash of sadness pass over her features.

"They're with my sister Ofelia," she said. "They're better off there. At least that's what the lady from children's services said."

It took me a second to process this. Then I was stunned, realizing that her children had been taken away from her. Granted, Barbara's life was unorthodox, and the children's upbringing untraditional, but she was a loving mother. It was hard to believe that the situation had reached the point at which state officials had been called in. I guessed I should have surmised the situation from the lack of children's things on board the *Santa Barbara*.

"You are feeling sorry for me," Barbara announced, making it seem almost like a threat.

"No, it's just that—" I stopped. "I know how much your children mean to you."

"Ofelia had no children of her own," Barbara said, looking away philosophically. "She and her husband, Humberto, they have a big house in Hialeah. Lots of space, big backyard. Children need that."

"Still—" I began.

"They need a home that doesn't rock," Barbara said adamantly. "I'm lucky Ofelia took the *niños*. If not, they go to strangers. Who knows, if I make a little money on this trip with you, enough to get ahead, I might try to get a little place again. Somewhere they will let me live with the youngest ones."

This was as close to an admission of her suffering that I was going to get from Barbara. I was glad to hear they were with family, and it was also good to know that they would be taken care of if something happened to us on the sea.

I waved good-bye from the top of the dock as I left, saying I would be back soon. I hoped Barbara got her children back, and that I would play a small part in it happening. Her children might have lacked some of the amenities staying with her, but they would learn things no school taught. Such as handling a machete and making illegal crossings across shark-infested waters. As I was starting to realize, these were the kind of skills that came in handy later in life.

The sun was pounding down as it only can on a late afternoon in South Florida. The glare was easily overpowering my sunglasses, making everything in my sight appear as though it was surrounded by wavy transparent lines.

I was standing under a thatched hut. A young, deeply suntanned, impossibly blond and blue-eyed boy—he looked as though he had just stepped out of an Abercrombie & Fitch advertisement—was topping off the Hatteras's fuel tanks at the Texaco dock. We were next to the dockmaster's office at the Oceanside Marina, a public marina in Stock Island, just north of Key West. The marina was full, although the *Concepcion* was the only boat receiving service at the moment.

"That'll be $87.98," the boy said in a completely bored tone of voice.

"All right," I said, handing over a hundred. "Just out of curiosity. I'm probably going to come in with a near-empty tank. How much will it cost to refill it?"

The boy paused for a second, calculating in his head. "Well, a little more than $500. About $525, I'd say."

"What?" I asked, stunned. I tried not to sound too incredulous, so he wouldn't remember me if asked. But still, that was a lot of money.

"A Hatteras this size takes five hundred gallons of fuel," the boy explained. "We charge ninety-eight cents a gallon for diesel. Plus there's tax."

"I understand." I was glad I had brought a lot of cash. I was going to need it.

"Oh, I forgot," the teenager said, actually showing a spark of life. "You're going to need oil, too. About fifty quarts. That's about another hundred bucks."

"I'll remember that," I said.

The *Concepcion* had been in our family for years, but I'd never been responsible for fueling her or checking her oil. I could see now that maintaining the boat was like throwing money into the Black Hole of Calcutta. No wonder people said that the two happiest days of a boat owner's life were the day he bought the boat and the day he sold it.

Barbara was tinkering with the ropes tying us to the fueling dock. I could tell from the reaction of the other boaters around the marina that they had never seen someone quite like Barbara skippering a Hatteras. She was huge, her braid hanging down to her waist. She was dressed in a long red-wine skirt topped by a see-through white cotton shirt. She was conspicuously braless, probably not wearing any underwear as well. Instead of wearing rubber-soled boat shoes, she was barefoot. She looked nothing like the models in *Yachting* magazine.

However unusual her appearance, though, I would have matched her boating skills with anyone at the marina. She was sure-footed as a cat on the deck of the Hatteras, and she had confidently adjusted the bumpers to keep the *Concepcion* from hitting up against the dock while we were refueling. It was bad enough that I had to worry about survival, I also had to fret about the condition in which I returned Papi's prize possession.

We had made good time from Miami to Stock Island, motoring at a semileisurely speed of twenty knots per hour. We didn't want to push the *Concepcion*'s engines too hard yet, since she would be working nonstop over the next couple of days.

I waited for the boy to print out my receipt, my mind reviewing all the hasty preparations I had made after Osvaldo informed me that I would have to push up my timetable for borrowing the boat. I had made a few calls at the office, tied up loose ends. I had my cellular with me; although it wasn't turned on, I would be able to check my voice mail every so often. I'd spent the remaining time in a rush, assembling the final few items I would need to implement my plan in Havana.

I told Leonardo I was taking a couple of days off. He had frowned, asked me if anything was the matter. I said no, and that was that. He knew better than to press me. To pacify him, I told him I'd call to check in. I hoped I wouldn't be calling from a Havana jail to ask for my phone messages.

Osvaldo had arranged to have the *Concepcion* waiting at the public dock behind the Merrill Stevens yard. All I had to do was show up with Barbara, stow our gear, and motor away. I was grateful beyond belief that Osvaldo wasn't there with some last minute worry. I don't know how I would have explained Barbara to him. She certainly bore no resemblance to Alvaro. Osvaldo would have thought than my private life was even more interesting than he'd imagined.

All that was left was to wait for nightfall. That morning, I had called the dockmaster's office and asked for dock space. I nearly passed out when I was told there was almost none left; after a lot of haggling, and a bit of histrionics on my part, I was granted a reserved spot at the daily rate of two dollars a foot.

I scanned the horizon, taking in the gathering colors of the fast-approaching sunset. My eyes kept wandering over the people on the various docks. I realized I was hoping to see Henry, the dockmaster at the now-closed Truman Annex Marina. I guess I'd hoped he had taken a job there at Oceanside, but it didn't seem to be the case. Now my mind was cluttered with the memory of the golden hairs on his fine-muscled legs. Some things never change with me, and a lustful appreciation of the male anatomy was certainly one of them.

We were finished refueling. An attendant from the harbormaster's office came by and told us where to find our assigned slip. Barbara adroitly maneuvered the *Concepcion*, and we were docked in less than fifteen minutes. Once the ropes were secured, we breathed a little easier. We both knew it would be our last chance to relax for quite a while.

Barbara disappeared below. A moment later, true to form, she reappeared with a bottle of Añejo—purchased with Lucia Miranda's money—and Papi's Waterford glasses. She poured two healthy amounts and tipped her glass toward mine.

"To success," she toasted, as serious as I had ever seen her. "And to being in Key West again."

When I had taken a swig I met her eyes. "I'm starting to remember what it was like before, the last time," I said.

"*Ay*, you worry too much." She finished her Añejo and lifted her skirt. My suspicion about her lack of underwear was correct, I saw. And, tucked inside the waistband, I also saw the handle of her machete. I didn't look too closely, but I was certain it was the one she'd used to carve up two men on our last voyage.

This time I was the one who grabbed the bottle, pouring two more stiff ones. I even accepted one of the Montecristo Numero Unos—courtesy of Lucia, of course—that Barbara offered me.

A few hours later we set off for the Cuban coast. I turned one last time and looked back at the shoreline of Florida. A couple of days, I said to myself. A couple of days and I would see it again.

30

There are more than three thousand nautical miles of Cuban coastline; we were aiming for just a few feet, in the pitch-black of night. An hour had passed since we cruised out of Stock Island. We saw running lights off in the distance, to indicating distant traffic on the water, but the lights were far off enough that we couldn't determine the nature of the vessels. We were more than a quarter of the way there, and I reminded myself time and again not to get too confident, not to let down my guard.

Under perfect conditions the trip from Key West to the Marina Hemingway should take about four hours. The seas weren't too choppy, and we were making good time—which was critical because we weren't going to have a chance to refuel until we returned to Key West. We weren't actually going to dock at the Marina Hemingway, of course—we were going to anchor at sea, and I was going to take the Whaler into shore. But I had used the marina as a reference point, because the trip between there and South Florida had been so well documented. The U.S.-Havana Regatta ends at the Marina Hemingway, and it has a seven-beam searchlight that can be seen from a distance of seventeen miles.

My goal was to reach the fishing village of Cojimar, less than ten miles east of Havana itself and granting easy access to the capital on the Via Monumental highway. The tiny Cojimar Bay would serve my needs perfectly. The village was famous as the place where Ernest Hemingway spent the last twenty-two years of his life, and where he had written many of his novels. Cojimar Bay was a much better choice for me than the actual Marina Hemingway, where boats arriving were required to clear Cuban customs and immigration. I didn't plan to tell armed customs officers that my reason for bringing the *Concepcion* into Cuban waters was to smuggle out a priceless art treasure.

As far as American laws were concerned, all individuals traveling to Cuba on U.S.-registered vessels needed government authority and permission to do so—documentation that Barbara and I lacked. Without authorization, travelers couldn't engage in normal commerce such as paying for meals, transportation, and lodging on the island. Even paying dockage and mooring fees at a Cuban marina was considered a violation of the law. In addition, travelers to Cuba were allowed to spend only a hundred dollars a day on merchandise on the island. I was glad to know there were at least a couple of laws I wouldn't be breaking: I wasn't going to dock the *Concepcion*, and I didn't think there would be time for any heavy tourist spending.

The most ominous threat, to me, came from an executive order signed in 1996 declaring that any ship captained with an objective of entering Cuban waters could be seized by the United States government. The law was designed to prevent Cuban exiles from launching an attack on Cuba from the U.S. mainland. I could just imagine Papi's reaction when informed by the government that the *Concepcion* had been impounded near Cuban waters. I might have been the queen of *mierda*, but I would have to shovel it by the ton to explain my way out of that one.

Barbara was at the wheel and I was on the prow, binoculars in hand, serving as lookout. Although I had to lock my elbows at my sides to keep them from shaking, I knew we were more likely to encounter real problems on the way back, when we would have both the Coast Guard and the Cuban navy on the lookout for boats smuggling illegal aliens from the island into the United States.

I listened to the soft purr of the motor, the sound of the boat splitting the waves. I grew up in Miami, but whenever I was asked where in Cuba my family was from, I said I was a *Habanera*. All my life I had envisioned going to my family's home in Miramar, a suburb of Havana. The last information we had about the house's fate was that it had been converted into a boarding school for aspiring ballerinas. I knew that Papi had no real hope of reclaiming ownership of the place, but it was a recurring topic of family conversation.

At least it hadn't been converted into a warren of decaying apartments, which was the fate of so many beautiful old Havana homes. I knew there would be no time on this trip to go see the house. It didn't matter, anyway. I would never be able to tell anyone in my family that I'd visited it.

I looked at my watch face in the moonlight. We were into the second hour of the trip, and nothing had happened. An idle thought flitted through my mind: would we be so safe in an hour? In two?

I had expected to see more traffic on the water, from Coast Guard patrols to fishing vessels, but so far there had been little traffic in our path save for a school of dolphins swimming past. I was glad we had no human company, but also a bit apprehensive—the open sea felt unaccountably lonely and cold, a place where we could vanish without leaving behind a single trace.

Scanning the water with the binoculars was tiring my eyes. I looked up at the fishing tower, where Barbara was comfortably installed, and gave her a wave. I tried not to think about the glass of rum that seemed to be permanently attached to her hand. She had a cigar clamped between her teeth, her white shirt flattened against her big breasts, her skirt billowing and her braid bouncing with the undulations of the boat.

She looked comfortable up there, more at ease than the last time we went to Cuba. I suspected more and more that she had parlayed that experience into a regular practice of smuggling Cubans into Florida. It was a growing business—and hugely profitable for anyone with a boat willing to take the risks.

Again I pulled the binoculars to my eyes. I saw a set of lights far to our port side, moving slowly. They had been there for a half hour, and weren't growing any closer. If I had to guess, I'd have said it was a cruise ship. And there was a dim illumination south-southwest on the horizon that might become more distinct in time. There were boats out there somewhere representing America and Cuba, both certain to arrest us if they found out our intentions. Beneath us, in the depths, were the sharks. But for the moment we were a speck on the sea, safe, moving beneath the notice of the forces that could destroy us.

During the third hour the sea traffic started to pick up. I saw another cruise ship in the distance. Soon after there were more lights. A fishing boat, I was sure of it. That meant we were approaching land. In a while I knew I would be able to see the beam from the searchlight at the entrance to Marina Hemingway.

I had programmed the Global Positioning System, Magellan 300 model, inside the cabin. It was a toy that Papi simply had to own after it went on sale the year before. The GPS enabled the Hatteras to aim for a position exactly thirteen miles off the shore, allowing us to anchor at a point lined up with Marina Hemingway. The technology of the thing was amazing. On its screen was our exact position, in longitude and latitude, at all times. I thought about how the *Concepcion* was approaching Cuba with such advanced technological help, while Columbus had come there five hundred years before with a compass and a star chart.

Barbara, not surprisingly, didn't care for gadgets such as the GPS, preferring to sail by sight. She didn't have a GPS on the *Santa Barbara*, which probably accounted for her near-total lack of interest in the information it provided. I ducked inside to check our position, and when I came back out, gave Barbara a thumbs-up. We were very close to the spot in the sea we were aiming for.

In the interest of conserving fuel, Barbara hadn't been running the engines at full speed. Now I noticed a change in the sound coming from belowdecks; the soft purr of the last couple of hours was turning into a pronounced whine. Barbara was accelerating, sensing we were nearly there. The wind picked up, whipping loose strands of hair into my face. I would have tucked them into my Miami Heat baseball cap, but that would have meant putting down the binoculars for a couple of seconds.

I saw more fishing vessels, distinguishable by the shape of their outriggers. I stared straight ahead, trying to make out the searchlight. Still nothing. I started to wonder if both Barbara and the GPS were wrong. For all I knew, we were heading into open waters on a course for Tierra del Fuego.

"Lupe!" Barbara called out. "I see it! I see the searchlight!"

I stared into the binoculars, my heart pounding faster. I was almost there, almost there. We had been traveling for the better part of four hours. Miami was ninety miles behind us, but it might as well have been another planet. Nothing there could help me now.

Then I saw it. The searchlight. I had Marina Hemingway

in my sights. It was time to adjust our calculations, so we could head east toward Cojimar. We were seventeen miles out, cruising at a speed of twenty knots per hour. At any time we could be inside the twelve miles that Cuba considered its territorial waters. I could have checked the GPS, but I didn't want to leave the deck of the boat for a second. I looked out into the darkness, realizing that what I was seeing was the homeland that had been forbidden to me for my entire life. In that impenetrable darkness, waiting to take outline and form with the light of day, was Cuba.

I took a deep breath, looked up at Barbara and made a slicing motion in the air. She immediately responded, and I heard the engines back off. The sea was calm, but still the Hatteras rocked as Barbara idled the motor. I had to hold onto the handrails as I went below to the cabin to read the depth meter—it was time to determine whether we'd found a suitable place to drop anchor.

Water deeper than a hundred feet meant that the anchor wouldn't touch bottom. It was possible to move the *Concepcion* around until we found a good place to drop anchor, but we were loath to do that because of the fuel we would expend. I crossed my fingers as I looked at the electronic readout.

Seventy-five feet. I thanked the Virgin for our good fortune, then gave the OK sign to Barbara. A moment later I heard the metallic clicking of the anchor's chain as it unrolled from the drum on deck. I waited until almost the entire length of the anchor line was let out, then pulled as hard as I could on the rope to make sure it would hold. We didn't want the *Concepcion* to drift off with the tide.

Barbara joined me on the deck. "We got here," she said, scanning the horizon. "Now for the hard part."

"I'm going to get ready," I said. I went below, to Papi's stateroom, leaving Barbara smoking a cigar on deck. She seemed totally unimpressed and unconcerned that she had just dropped anchor in contested waters, at the mercy of the elements and subject to arrest. I hoped I could match her bravado.

It would take me only a couple of minutes to prepare. I snapped a fanny pack around my waist—although I'd always hated them, it was a necessary evil. It contained the money and papers I was taking with me; I covered it with my long T-shirt, hiding it from casual glances. I made sure I had my handheld GPS, linked to the *Concepcion*'s, so I could find my way back to the Hatteras in case the boat drifted while I was gone.

I looked over my outfit in the mirror. Old, faded jeans, a black cotton hooded sweatshirt zipped up in front, sneakers, Miami Heat cap.

Before I left, I sat cross-legged in bed, holding my leather Chanel bag in my lap as a mother might hold her child. I knew I would have to leave it behind, which was something I could accept. I was going to miss my American Express card more than I was willing to acknowledge. But what I was really going to miss was the Beretta. I took it out and inspected it. I felt naked and vulnerable without it, but if I was stopped by government officials, I sure as hell didn't want to be carrying a weapon. Castro's Cuba was a closed society, and possessing a gun carried serious penalties for Cuban citizens—I couldn't imagine the consequences if an exile was caught with one on Cuban soil. I caressed the Beretta softly before I put it in the bag and stowed it under the night table next to the bed. I might have been overly sentimental, but it had saved my life and I felt indebted to it.

Up on deck, I saw that Barbara hadn't been twiddling her thumbs waiting for me. She had begun readying the Boston Whaler in anticipation of lowering it over the side. She had the cover off and was checking its instruments. I looked over the side and saw, to my relief, that the water wasn't too choppy.

"Ready?" she called out to me. Her hand was on the button that would lower the Whaler from its wooden platform on the deck into the water.

"*Sí,*" I said. I fought to keep my breathing regular, inhaling deeply.

Barbara pressed the button. A familiar metal sound, signaling that the cable holding the boat was tightening to swing the Whaler out and over the water. It was tricky. If the water was too rough, the Whaler might swing wildly and smack into the *Concepcion* or, even worse, collide with one of us and pin us to the boat.

I exhaled with a gasp as the Whaler hit water safely right next to the *Concepcion*. It bobbed there, having escaped harm. Barbara unhooked the cable, and then it was attached to the *Concepcion* by just a rope.

I stood on the deck and looked down at the Whaler. I hadn't anticipated how small it would look next to the fifty-two-foot Hatteras.

It was then that everything sank in. I had planned my actions like a general preparing for a military campaign, poring over maps and reports with cold dispassion. Camila was hopefully on the island waiting, having performed her part of the preparations as outlined in the letter I'd sent her.

But it was one thing to plan, and another entirely to suddenly feel the reality of one's death. It was a heavy feeling. For a second I wanted to go back below, lie down in bed in the master stateroom and pull the covers over my head.

"Now it's time," Barbara said with a thin smile. I looked up; she was staring at me, probably having read my swirl of emotions in my features.

The blood was pounding through my body. I felt hyper, my limbs twitching for action. I smelled the salt in the night air, the coolness of the breeze. It was as though each instant was breaking down into tiny components, time telescoping before me.

There was no going back.

I hugged Barbara, touched the medals pinned to my brassiere, and made the sign of the cross. I stepped off the boat, holding tight to the rope that kept me from tumbling into the waters. Without thinking about it, I lowered myself into the Whaler. Within seconds I was untying the cord that attached me to the *Concepcion*.

I fired up the engines without looking back. I was on my way.

31

I was on the water for about five minutes when the sky began to lighten. I had been awake for almost twenty-four hours, but I knew that the adrenaline coursing through my system would probably keep me up for another twenty-four. The last time I'd stayed up so long was when I went clubbing at South Beach with Tommy; we partied all night at Liquid on Washington Avenue. I hoped this occasion would turn out to be as successful and memorable as the other.

I looked back at the Hatteras from the Whaler. Barbara was busy putting up the outriggers. If anyone questioned why she was out there, she could say she was fishing. Barbara had brought along an ice chest full of fresh fish that she could show as proof of her story. It had been her idea, and it added to my suspicion that she'd made more trips into these dangerous waters than the one we shared. I didn't ask any questions, because I didn't want to know the extent of my traveling companion's extracurricular activities.

As soon as I was a safe distance from the *Concepcion*, I steered the Whaler to the east, toward Cojimar Bay. The Whaler could reach speeds of twenty to twenty-five miles per hour, and I calculated that I would reach my destination in about a half hour. It wasn't a long time, but it felt like an eternity to be out there alone, only the sound of the small craft's engines and the mist of seawater in my face to assure me I wasn't dreaming.

Dawn was breaking, and soon there would be enough light for me to see land approaching. I knew that Cuban officials didn't patrol the waters around Cojimar much; the Cuban navy lacked fuel supplies, and it had to target carefully where it chose to expend its resources. Cojimar wasn't high on the list of the Cuban government's top sites to defend, and its relative proximity to Havana made it a perfect place for me to land.

The air was damp and cool on my face, almost chilling me beneath my thick sweatshirt. As I took in the dusky shapes of the waves and the choppy sound as the Whaler cut through the waters, for a moment I felt completely care-free. I enjoyed the sensation, knowing that as soon as I reached land it would be gone.

I pictured Alvaro's face, heard the sound of his voice in my imagination. I was almost to Cuba. In some secret fantasy, I had imagined that he would be part of my return to the island. It felt strangely lonely to be there without him. In my pocket was the name of the lawyer he had given me. Mabel Magali Montenegro, his friend and colleague—and hopefully nothing more. It was reassuring to know that I had someone to contact in case everything fell through.

Cubans can never escape the influence of the island on their lives, and I was no different. As I began to make out a faint outline of land—little more than a smudge in the distance—I felt that *patria* that was imbedded in my DNA. I could picture the power of Cuba over me as though I lived inside a bubble, sustained and nourished by the amniotic fluid that was the essence of the island.

I steered the Whaler toward the Bay, checking my instruments. I could now see the searchlight of the Marina Hemingway to the west with my naked eye. The boat was quickly moving closer to land, and now I could make out the shapes of buildings along the bay. I saw houses on a hill behind the little village, and when I squinted, I saw the outline of an old church on top of the hill.

The coastline, I had heard, was inhospitable around Cojimar. Unfortunately, that information was quickly proving itself true. As I neared the village, the sea grew more and more filthy, filled with the flotsam and jetsam of a community unequipped to properly dispose of its refuse. Looking down at all the garbage in the water, I prayed I wouldn't have to swim in it. I knew I didn't have the immunities to fight off the infection that would come from swallowing some of the water. I had thought about rotting in a Cuban jail, but landing in a hospital was a scenario I hadn't envisioned.

Conditions on the water were changing. I slowed the engine. The waves were getting higher, with whitecaps surfacing. Dawn had broken, which was both a blessing and a curse. I could see the shore better, but people on the shore would also be able to see me. I hoped the residents of Cojimar were like most Cubans—essentially nocturnal, with natural allergies to the early morning hours. So far I hadn't spotted anyone up and around. Hopefully that would remain the case. This wasn't a city, where inevitably a segment of the population would be awake early tending to the streets and utilities in preparation for a busy urban day. Small-scale fishermen could keep their own hours—preferably working late and sleeping late, for my current purposes.

As I slowed I looked to the entrance of the bay. In the morning light I saw the outline of El Torreon, an eighteenth century fortress that was currently being administered by the Cuban military. It wasn't, I hoped, in a state of high alert. Nonetheless, I planned to avoid it and dock out of open sight. A military reception for my arrival wasn't part of my plan.

The configuration of earth around Cojimar was volcanic, making it rough and rocky. Although the Whaler drew only twelve inches of water, I had to be careful to maintain enough space between its hull and the sea floor. A gash in the Whaler would render it unseaworthy, meaning I would be stranded in Cuba. Barbara would wait for me, allotting perhaps a day after my agreed-upon returning time, and then be forced to take the *Concepcion* back to Miami.

I pointed the Whaler east of the fortress, where there was an old dock. I slowed down to a crawl to cut down on noise. Although still only a tiny speck on the water, I felt incredibly conspicuous.

The dock was partially hidden from sight by flowering bougainvillea trees. Perfect. When I had steered the craft close to one of the half-dozen thin pillars supporting the dock, I cut the engine and pulled alongside. I tied up the boat quickly, looked around, listened. I heard only the rhythmic pulse of the waves and the creaking of the old wooden dock.

I reached into the little cooler at my feet and took out a bottle of water. Eyes closed, face toward the sky, I drank the entire contents in a single swig.

It was when I put down the bottle that I saw my welcoming committee.

My first thought was a question. How could Camila Estrada be so impossibly beautiful, when her two brothers had been ugly enough to frighten little children and make hens stop laying eggs?

"It's me. Camila," she called out, waving from her hiding place next to a thick, gnarled tree. I almost had a stroke from fright in that first moment I was aware of her presence. Then a wave of relief rushed over me. It had worked. The old detailed map of Cuba in my family's library had enabled me to pick an obscure spot where we could meet undetected. Part of me had feared that Camila would never show up, that she would be caught or would back out on me. But no, she was there.

"Come on," she said, looking around. "Hurry up!"

I heaved my black bag onto the dock, grunting from the weight of what it contained. I scrambled up from the Whaler onto the dock—which wasn't difficult, since I had been doing it for years at home. Once on the dock, I grabbed the bag and sprinted toward the tree where Camila was hiding. I would have liked to reflect on the fact that I'd returned to Cuban soil, and to let my emotions flow more freely, but there was no time for reflection.

I leaned against the tree and looked at Camila; I was breathing heavily from exertion and excitement, while she seemed completely calm and at ease. She was dressed casually, in a checked pink short-sleeve shirt and white Capri pants. Her long blond hair was pulled back in a ponytail, and she wore no makeup. But there was no denying it: Camila was stunningly beautiful. Her light green eyes shone in the postdawn light, and her perfect features looked as though they could have come from one of the masterpieces she was supposedly so adept at forging.

"It's getting late," she said. "We have to hurry."

Her eyes lingered on me for a moment. It seemed that neither of us was what the other had expected. I picked up my bag and followed her down a weedy path to a small clearing tucked away amid a copse of trees. Her car was well hidden among the Florida pines.

The automobile upon which we were to rely was a two-toned light blue Chevrolet of fifties vintage that could have come right off the set of a gangster movie. It was a miracle that cars like this one were still on the road, given the difficulty of getting parts. Cuban mechanics who arrived in Miami were sought after, and considered the best in the business, because of their long experience keeping relics like this one on the road.

"This was the only car I could get on such short notice," Camila said, walking around to the back of the vehicle. "It wasn't easy. I had to spend nearly all the money you sent me, Lupe, in order to do what you asked. There's almost nothing left."

"No problem, you did fine," I reassured her; her clouded, worried expression softened a fraction.

Camila reached into her pants pocket and took out a set of keys. She carefully unlocked the trunk and motioned for me to put the bag inside. My mouth dropped open when I saw the size of the Chevrolet's trunk. It looked like it could hold the contents of a walk-in closet, and it was perfect for our needs. No wonder the mob guys in the movies favored these kinds of cars to transport bodies. We could have fit four or five people in there.

I put the bag in the very back of the trunk and covered it as best I could with an old towel I found stuffed in the corner. Camila watched me silently. I closed the lid and walked around to the passenger side. I glanced at my Swatch watch. Less than five minutes had passed since I came ashore. If the rest of the plan worked so efficiently, maybe there was hope that we would succeed.

We got in the car; the front seat was like the living room of an efficiency apartment. Camila adjusted the rearview mirror, started the engine, and put the car in gear. The Chevy responded immediately, with a surprisingly soft purr from the engine as we maneuvered slowly down a dirt road.

I watched Camila out of the corner of my eye. There were a thousand questions I wanted to ask, but I knew I should let her concentrate on her driving. Instead I looked around.

I was, after all, in *mi patria*. The circumstances were less than ideal, but I had returned.

The first thing I noticed was that the light looked different, diffused, soft and hazy. Then it hit me: it reminded me of the tint of sunlight I had encountered in the south of France. I smelled the sea air, mixed with a sweetness, a perfume that was somehow seductive, sensual, almost sexual in its intensity. For a second I almost forgot the reason I was there.

The profusion of colors was astounding, now that the sun was starting to rise. It was unlike anything I had ever seen before. Reds, oranges, greens, blues, sharp and distinctive, a fecund landscape exploding with tropical life. Maybe it was the lack of sleep, maybe it was the relief of finally being on solid ground after so many hours at sea—but none of it mattered. I felt that I had come home, to the place where I was meant to be.

We skirted the village of Cojimar and passed a park next to the fortress—El Torreon—which featured a bust of Ernest Hemingway flanked by white Corinthian columns in the center of its rotunda. I had read once that, upon the writer's death, each of the fishermen in the village had contributed some brass to make the bust commemorating the creator of *The Old Man and the Sea*, which in turn had commemorated their lives and struggles.

A few minutes later we turned onto a highway heading west. As we picked up speed I sensed that we were entering the flow of normal life. I had arrived unnoticed. Now I felt relaxed enough at least to speak.

"I want to tell you how sorry I am about what happened to your brothers," I began. "It was a terrible thing that happened to them."

Camila nodded, staring at the road with a sad smile. "*Gracias*," she said softly. Her fine-fingered hands clutched the wheel tightly. She drove for a full minute before speaking again. "What you asked in your letter is very difficult, Lupe," she said. "I did what you asked. But I don't know if it will work."

We were on the Via Monumental, the road leading into Havana.

"After we visit the Miranda house, you will need to do something for me," she added in a more forceful voice. "You know about the copies I have made of the paintings. I will need for you to deal with them for me. It's your part of the bargain."

"All right," I said. I had never agreed to this, but I really had little choice. Now I couldn't have honestly said which part of our plan frightened me the most. I didn't want to sell the paintings for Camila—I wanted no part of trafficking in priceless stolen art, even if it had been stolen from the Castro regime. Now wasn't the time to confront her, though. I had just arrived, and I didn't yet know how far I would get.

I sat back in the worn red leather seat and looked out at the scenery passing by. There was very little traffic on the road, which was a bit surprising. Havana was a city of two million inhabitants. The early hour might have explained the light traffic, or the lack of serviceable vehicles. There was also a shortage of petrol in the new austere, post-Soviet economy of the island. Whatever the reason, I was accustomed to the bumper-to-bumper chaos of Miami. This sedate ride into the city was enough to unnerve me.

"Ah," I said suddenly, the sound escaping involuntarily as I looked ahead.

It had come up so quickly that I hadn't had time to prepare myself. I saw the Malecon—the seafront boulevard— that had stirred my heart so many times from photographs on postcards and in picture books. The Malecon was a symbol of every exile's dreams, hopes, and aspirations. It also represented an inexhaustible well of desperation, hope-lessness, and despair.

It was so beautiful that tears began falling down my cheek. Camila sensed my rush of emotion and reached over to pat my hand in reassurance.

I was seeing it. Havana. The Malecon. Home.

32

"**P**lease, slow down. Just a bit," I asked Camila. "I don't want to forget this."

Spray was coming over the sea wall by the Malecon; in the near distance I could see the old waterfront buildings, and farther, the light-colored high rises of the city. Ahead of us was another old car, an Oldsmobile, being passed by a Russian Lada that, although newer, looked to be in worse shape. I let my eyes linger on the green water, the mix of old colonial and newer, Communist-monumental architecture unfolding before me.

A knowing look passed over Camila's face; she understood the effect this sight was having on me.

"OK," I said. "I'm ready."

I wasn't here as a tourist. I motioned for Camila to pick up speed again, and we headed for the Vedado—the district of the city where the Miranda home was located. I had one request to make, though, before we reached our destination. I had spent so much time looking over maps of the city that I knew we wouldn't have to make a detour.

"The Cementerio de Colon," I said. "It's on our way. Could you please drive by it?"

Camila nodded and turned from El Malecon onto the Calle 23, a wide avenue in the Vedado. The Cementerio de

Colon housed the mausoleum that belonged to my family. My ancestors were buried there.

We drove past. The cemetery's formal name was the Necropolis Cristobol Colon—named after the explorer who had given the eighth tapestry to Lucia Miranda's ancestor centuries ago. I looked through its enormous gates at the tombs, chapels, and stone crucifixes lining the rows of the venerable burial place. I was saddened as, flashing by in a blur, I saw a sign by the front entrance: tours cost one dollar American. I couldn't help but think that Castro was profiting from my ancestors, stealing from them in their eternal repose. I hoped that at least the money went toward upkeep and not into someone's pocket.

Finally we were on our way to the Calle C, near the Calle 15, where the Miranda home was waiting. Camila slowed the car on the street, pulled over. I was transfixed by the morning activity of the city: people walking to their jobs, shirtless children running and yelling. Suddenly I was amid regular life in Cuba. The sudden shift was jarring.

"That's it," Camila said.

I looked up. I wouldn't be needing the front door key that Lucia had given me. The Miranda house, it was immediately clear, was no longer a house. It had been converted into a series of apartments. The place was crumbling, its plaster facade and balconies worn down and showing the brick underneath. The former sky-blue paint showed only in peeling patches. It was, to be blunt, an eyesore.

I could see straight into the courtyard, to the fountain in its center. It was streaked with sediment, and no water spurted from it. I took from my pocket the floor plan that I had asked Lucia to draw up.

"What is it?" Camila asked. "You look irritated."

"It's nothing," I said, surprised that my feelings were showing. This wasn't what I had expected. Lucia had indicated that her family home hadn't been divided into apartments—she had led me to believe that it was occupied by a high government official. Supposedly she had learned of this from an associate who had come to Havana for an academic conference. I didn't care much who lived there, but the fact that it had been turned into many separate dwellings meant I would have a harder time locating the entrance to the hidden basement.

We sat there quietly. I wondered why Lucia hadn't told me the truth. There were two explanations. Maybe Lucia didn't know the reality of the state of disrepair that had befallen the Miranda ancestral home; she might have been clinging to the fantasy that it had retained its splendor. I hoped that was the case. The second possibility was that she had lied to me because, had I known this added level of difficulty to the job, I might have refused to take the case.

I took a deep breath. I had taken too many risks to let this kink in the works deter me.

"This isn't what you expected," Camila said.

"It isn't," I admitted.

"Well, I suppose you'll have to work something out," she replied.

I had to bite my lip to keep from saying anything. I had written to Camila about how I had intended to get into the home—including the fact that I thought it was still a single dwelling.

"Did you come here, like I asked in the letter?" I said. "To see what condition the place was in?"

"I did," she admitted. "But there was no chance to contact you. It would have been too dangerous."

I looked into her green eyes, searching for evidence that she was lying. Perhaps she, like Lucia, feared I would back off had I known the inner floor plan of the house had changed. Maybe she had kept silent because she needed me to come, to see through her side of the scheme.

Camila glanced away at the street, as though not wanting me to see too deeply into her. I felt a flash of danger that simmered down into lingering caution. Camila had concocted the art-forgery scheme with her brothers. She might have been beautiful and winsome, but she was also capable of cold calculation.

My mind was racing. I felt trapped there on the street, in this city where I could be arrested and thrown in jail at any moment. A man walked by the car, staring at me as he passed. Was he an informer for the police? Was there something about me that stood out?

Closing my eyes, I breathed deeply. This was no time to lose my wits and panic. My survival depended on clear thinking.

I had an idea. I looked down at the map Lucia had given me. The house might have been reconfigured, but the trapdoor wouldn't have moved. I had to hope that the renovation had been superficial enough that the trapdoor hadn't been found—which wasn't out of the question, given the fact that the Miranda home was now essentially a tenement. I doubted that a lot of energy or money had gone into refinishing the floors.

"You're going to help me get inside," I said, looking up at Camila. She blinked, surprised. Originally she was only supposed to wait outside for me, ready to pick me up and quickly get away. Tough, I thought. I wasn't asking for her opinion. We were in Cuba. This was not a participatory democracy.

"What are you saying?" she asked in an unsteady voice.

"Drive us someplace where we can take off our clothes," I ordered her.

"Wait," she said. "No."

"Don't get any ideas," I said. "We're going to trade clothes. I need for you to look like a tourist from Miami. The clothes I'm wearing aren't the greatest, but at least they're from the Gap. People might take you for an American if you say the right things."

Camila shook her head nervously as she put the car in gear. She steered around the corner and parked in an alley between two apartment buildings. I began taking off my clothes and passing them over to her.

"Come on," I said. "Hurry up."

I was angry with her for not having told me about the state of the Miranda house. It might have been unfair, since it *was* dangerous for us to communicate between Havana and Miami, but I was feeling ill-used and a little desperate.

Camila was a few inches taller than me, but our body types were essentially the same. Fortunately the Chevrolet was so roomy that we were able to exchange our outfits quickly, with a minimum of knee banging and elbows to the face. When we were done, I looked at Camila approvingly. In the jeans and sweatshirt she wasn't conspicuous, but the fact that she was wearing American brands wouldn't go unnoticed by the residents of the apartment building.

I reached into my fanny pack, took out five twenties and handed them to Camila.

"What am I going to do with these?" she asked.

"Listen carefully." I put the map of the house between us. "The room I need to get to is in the back of the first story. Here, look closely. We have to make sure we go up to the right apartment."

Camila looked at the map, her mouth tight with anxiety. I could sense her intelligence and a certain steely will in her character, but I had no idea whether I could count on her. I was about to find out.

"Knock on the door and tell them that you're a Cuban

American living in Miami," I said. "If they ask, tell them you're from Coconut Grove. You work for American Airlines."

Camila digested this, nodding. At least she was going along. And she was concentrating, which was essential. She had to know the character she was about to portray, or else she might reveal herself.

"You've come here to visit your family's old home," I continued. "They probably won't think anything strange about that. I've heard it happens all the time, when people come to the island—the first thing they want to see is their family home."

"*Sí,*" Camila agreed quietly.

"Here, take this," I said, handing her my Swatch watch. "Getting in isn't good enough. Tell them that you need time alone in the apartment. You want to sit quietly, communicate with the spirits of your dead ancestors. Tell them you had a dream, that your great-grandmother told you to come visit, but that no one can be around or else she'll remain hidden."

Camila nodded. "People are superstitious," she said. "I think I can make them believe it."

"Promise them you mean no harm, then give them the hundred dollars," I said. "If they won't let you stay, offer them the watch. That should do it."

Camila looked at the watch, then strapped it on her wrist. "All right," she said. "I will do it."

I crouched down on the seat as far as I could while still allowing myself a view of the street. Camila put the car in gear, drove slowly around the block, then parked across the street in the same spot as before. Without another word she got out of the car and crossed the street. It was strange to see her dressed in my clothes. I looked down at myself, at the pink checked shirt and white pants I was wearing. I felt a twinge of sadness. These clothes were clean and pressed, but they had turned shabby from age and so many washings. Camila, like most people on the island, was living in poverty in addition to political oppression.

I stared up at the Miranda home. It was bigger than the other homes on the street, though it was built in the same Neoclassical style, with high porticos held up by marble columns. There were chairs on most of the terraces, where residents no doubt spent the afternoons out of reach of the punishing Cuban sun.

A few minutes passed. I stared at the building's entrance. I tried to look casual as people passed by, some glancing at me, others taking no notice. I would have guessed that about five minutes had passed, though I couldn't be sure, since I had given away my watch.

I had started to think about getting out of the car when Camila came out the front entrance. She was followed by a couple and a small child. Camila was smiling, waving goodbye to them while escorting them out, speaking to them in a grateful manner. The family seemed wary, but walked down the street and turned the corner—preoccupied, no doubt, by what they were going to do with the sudden financial windfall that had just come their way.

I counted to sixty. The family was nowhere to be seen. Probably they were going to a café I had spotted around the corner, where they could while away the time. I got out of the car, opened the trunk and—after a quick look around to make sure no one was watching—took out my black nylon bag. I crossed the street and entered the apartment building.

Just inside the entrance was a spectacular courtyard; the walls were worn and decayed, but all around were potted tropical plants. My eyes were drawn to the fountain. Though it also suffered from neglect, I could see that just underneath a layer of sediment was an intricate bronze statue of a young girl pouring water from a pitcher. The floor beneath my feet was dirty and clouded, but I could tell that beneath the grime was white marble.

I crossed to the back. Camila was standing in front of an open doorway corresponding to the area outlined in Lucia's diagram. I pulled Camila inside and closed the door behind us, moved quickly through a small entryway into a hot, dusty sitting room. There was an aged sofa, a couple of chairs, a metal table. Everything looked old, cheap, worn. My eyes flitted over the paucity of possessions the young family owned, then settled on the floor.

I could have knelt down and kissed the ground. It was there, the dark green linoleum that Lucia Miranda had told me about. Though the place had been divided and converted into a warren of apartments, in this little room the flooring had been left as it was for decades.

A glance down at my map, then I stood with my back to the outer wall. I measured fifteen paces from the wall, a spot covered by a threadbare area rug. I dropped down on all fours and started feeling for a crack in the linoleum. The years had left a layer of embedded grime in the flooring, making it hard to feel any features in its original surface.

"Here it is," I said. "At least I think."

I looked up at Camila, who was watching nervously. I noticed that she was standing close to the door, probably ready to make her escape if things went badly.

"Give me that bag, please," I said, motioning to the black nylon duffel. Camila pushed it across the floor with her foot, and I unzipped its side compartment. I passed over a long, sharp carpet knife, which I'd brought in case I had to cut the tapestry away from the conditions in which it was stored. Next to it I found my Swiss Army knife. I picked out the biggest, sharpest blade, which was capable of slicing through the linoleum.

I sliced through the flooring, careful to keep my cuts clean and precise. I would have to replace the flooring when I was done, hopefully well enough to disguise the damage I had done.

I had sliced away a big enough piece. Carefully, I edged it off the floor and pulled it away. I put it down next to me.

"What are you looking for?" Camila asked.

"I found it," I said.

The floor of the place was concrete under the linoleum, with one significant exception: the little wooden door flush with the floor that I was now looking down upon. There was a single keyhole.

"Damn," I whispered to myself. "Lucia was telling the truth."

I looked up at Camila with triumph. She looked haunted by the sight of the little door appearing so incongruously in this shabby apartment; she leaned back against the wall, one hand raised to her forehead to mop away the sweat collecting there.

From the bag I took out a little pouch. I picked out the key Lucia had given me for the basement door, inserted it in the keyhole. Before I turned it I closed my eyes and said a silent prayer. My free hand reached up to touch my medals. A thousand things could have gone wrong. I could have the wrong key. The lock could have rusted. The family could come back at just that moment.

But no. The key turned as easily as if it had been oiled that morning. I pulled back the door and coughed at the dust that floated up from its hinges.

"Wait for me," I ordered Camila. "I won't be long."

"Don't be," Camila said, gesturing to the torn-up floor, the open door. "I don't think I could explain this."

I pulled a heavy duty flashlight out of the black bag, tossed the bag over my shoulder, and stepped down into the black void.

I aimed the flashlight down as I slowly descended the creaky wooden staircase. One step, two, three. I had expected the air to be stagnant and stale, but Lucia had been right. The air was musty but breathable. I didn't exactly feel like I was taking in the air in a meadow after a spring rain, but I would be able to work without fear of losing consciousness.

Twenty steps, then I reached the basement floor. My flashlight so far revealed a featureless place, with painted plaster walls and no light source. I paused to catch my breath, suddenly realizing that I was in danger of hyperventilating.

It was all right, I told myself. It was just a basement. The Mirandas had been down there countless times. I wanted to glance back upstairs, to see if Camila was still there, but my eyes were successfully adjusting to the darkness and I didn't want to spoil it by looking up at the light.

More deep breaths. I looked across the room and pointed my flashlight. The tapestry was there, just as Lucia had told me it would be. I let out a gasp of surprise.

I stared at the tapestry, entranced. Even illuminated only by a diffused flashlight beam, it was beautiful. The unicorn sprang to freedom in a deep green meadow, the sunlight shining on its fur. It was almost a full minute before I recovered enough to realize that time was running out.

The nylon bag's zipper made a loud ripping noise in the stark silence of the basement. I knelt down and placed the flashlight upright on the floor, using it as a lamp. In the back of the room was a stepladder, which was going to make my job a lot easier. I leaned the ladder against the wall next to the tapestry, then from the bag took out a hammer, a length of rope, and a couple sheets of plastic.

I hung the hammer from the waistband of my pants and climbed the ladder. I felt along the edge of the tapestry until I had located the nails that mounted it to long thin boards, which were in turn affixed to the wall. The tapestry felt dry and cool, rough to the touch. I began chipping away the nails and board from the underlying wall—fortunately, since the room was a secret, I didn't have to worry about harming the plaster and could concentrate instead on not damaging the tapestry. And I wasn't going to have to use the crude carpet knife. I wiped my forehead on my blouse, starting to breathe heavily. The basement was cooled by its ventilation, but it was still hot down there. My neck and back began to ache from the exertion of the work I was performing.

Finally I had taken out about a third of the nails. The next part would be more tricky, I realized, because I was going to have to rest the ladder directly against the tapestry. I was terrified that I would tear it or stretch it, so I worked even more carefully than before.

"Lupe?" came a whisper from the top of the stairs, almost too quiet for me to hear.

As I worked I was lowering the fabric to the ground, where I rested it on a sheet of plastic to avoid it becoming soiled.

"What?" I asked, stopping all movement to listen.

"How much longer?" Camila whispered.

"Not much more," I said. "I'm almost done."

"Hurry. They'll be back soon. I'm sure of it."

I tried not to let Camila's attack of nerves affect me. I dropped another segment of the tapestry to the plastic, surprised by how light it turned out to be. My estimate of 150 pounds was too high; if I had to guess, I'd say the tapestry actually weighed seventy, maybe eighty pounds. Which was a damned good thing, because I was going to have to lift it in a few minutes.

I moved the ladder to detach the final third of the tapestry.

I heard the floor creak above me as Camila paced. I had started working on the last series of nails when I looked down at the wall I had exposed. There was a strange bulge in the plaster, about waist-high from the ground. At first I thought it had simply deteriorated with time, since there were areas in the room that had started to become discolored and rough.

After I released the final segment of the tapestry and let it slide down to the floor, I climbed down the ladder with a heavy sigh. I had managed not to damage the precious textile. I knelt down and began fastidiously rolling and folding the tapestry, still wiping sweat from my eyes, the sound of my breath heavy and loud in the confined space.

I looked up again at the wall that had been hidden behind the tapestry. The strange bulge looked even more pronounced from ground level. I knew there wasn't time to investigate, but I stood up anyway and ran my hand along the plaster.

I knelt down again, this time wrapping the folded tapestry in the plastic sheets. These weren't the ideal conditions for transporting a priceless work of art, but I had done my best. As soon as the tapestry arrived in Miami I was sure it would receive the best treatment money could buy.

A moment later I stuffed the tapestry in my bag. To make room, I was going to have to leave the folding ladder behind. I tugged at the bag to gauge its weight; it was heavy, but I was confident I could drag it up the stairs.

"What is that?" I whispered to myself. I stared again at the strange buckling protrusion in the plaster. I knew it was a bad idea, but I had to check it out—after all, when would I ever be there again?

I let the bag settle to the ground and picked up the hammer. I used the claw end to scrape away the plaster, pulling out big dusty chunks and dropping them to my feet. I was hitting something hard underneath, I realized, something hidden within the wall. My first thought was that it was another art treasure, something so valuable that perhaps even Lucia Miranda didn't know of its existence.

The section of wall gave way with one good rap from the hammer. I closed my eyes from the shower of plaster, hoping that one of the tenants in the nearby apartments couldn't hear the commotion.

"What the hell are you doing down there?" Camila asked from the top of the stairs. "We have to get out."

"One more minute," I promised.

There was a big wooden box buried inside the wall. I had exposed maybe half of it, and I guessed that it was about five feet long.

My arms were burning with exhaustion, and my neck felt like a tightly wound coil. I had sweated entirely through Camila's clothes. I kept digging at the wall around the box until I had exposed it enough to move it back and forth. I tugged hard at it, trying to drag it out of the wall.

With a loud noise it slid off its resting place. The front end of the box tumbled out of the wall while the back end caught in the plaster. The box opened up and dislodged its contents at my feet.

"Oh," I whispered to myself in the gloomy darkness as a skull hit the ground and rolled across the room, out of the range of my flashlight beam. I froze, unable to move, and pointed the flashlight downward. A pile of bones and decayed clothes were resting on my feet.

"Lupe!" Camila called to me, louder than before. "It's been almost half an hour!"

I stared at the bones. Was this Cuba's version of the Catacombs, some kind of burial ground? It might have been some kind of old burial ground, I thought.

But wait. The bones were old. There was no telling how

old, just that the flesh had decayed from them. But the box had been planted in the wall sometime after the basement was constructed. That meant this body was of twentieth century vintage.

I fought off a wave of nausea as I gently allowed the bones to slide off my feet. I knelt down next to them and took out the Swiss Army knife, starting to poke through the bones and cloth to see what I might find.

"Lupe!" whispered Camila. I heard the top step creak.

"Stay there!" I hissed. "One more minute! I promise!"

As I moved the femur aside I realized that my deduction about the body's age had been correct. These were not the bones of Tainos or Ciboneyes, the original inhabitants of Cuba who had been killed by Spanish colonizers. Neither of them would have been likely to own the man's leather wallet that I found in the pile of bones.

I opened up the wallet, shone the light into it.

A moment later I had solved another mystery—the whereabouts of the art expert Albert O. Manfredi. He was right here, a pile of bones on the ground. Using an extra piece of plastic, I began shoving him back into his casket, apologizing under my breath for having disturbed his eternal rest.

33

"**L**upe!" Camila called out from the top of the stairs, frantic now. "I can see the family! They're across the street!"

"Coming!" I yelled up to her. I wrapped Manfredi's wallet in plastic and put it in the nylon bag. I tucked my head under the strap, squared the weight in the middle of my back, and lifted. It was going to be tough, but the bag's straps turned it into a kind of sling, enabling me to carry a lot more weight than usual.

I took a deep breath and started up the stairs. They creaked beneath my feet, and I had to keep a hand on the wall to balance myself. By the time I reached the top, I was panting and light-headed. Camila was standing over the trapdoor, a look of wide-eyed terror on her face.

I dropped the bag, closed the trapdoor behind me, and pulled the piece of linoleum back to its place.

"Here," I told Camila. "I need your help. Smooth that back into place and put the rug where it was."

I headed for the open window next to a beat-up wooden desk, then pulled a chair under the window. This was my best way out—not through the front door, sweaty and dirty, carrying a heavy bag like a burglar. The window was in the back of the house, and led into the narrow alley between the Miranda house and the apartments next door—at least I hoped it did.

One end of the bag's strap in my hand, I hopped onto the chair and slid onto the windowsill. I threw one leg out just as I heard a loud banging on the apartment's front door. Camila was still kneeling on the floor, trying to smooth the linoleum with her hands. She was shaking her head with frustration, whispering to herself, her hands shaking violently.

"Hold them off!" I whispered. "Tell them you need another minute alone with your great-grandmother."

Camila got up and went to the door to do as I said. From her frightened expression, I was sure the family would have no problem believing that she had been communing with the spirit world.

I looked down; the window was about ten feet off the ground. I had been right, at least, about the alley—after my ten-foot drop, I would land on some rough asphalt. But at least there seemed to be no one around who would see me. I pulled the bag up, using my weight as a counterbalance. It wasn't easy, and for a second I thought I was going to lose my grip and tumble out, leaving the tapestry behind.

Camila came running into the room. "It's not working," she said. "I didn't open the door because they sound angry. There's a chain on the door, but they're threatening to break it."

I could hear pounding on the door, louder this time. I motioned for Camila to help, and she hoisted the bag up onto the windowsill. She was very slender, but also much stronger than I would have guessed. I let the bag drop out the window, waved quickly to Camila, and then followed it.

My landing was less than perfect. The fall was longer than it looked, and when I landed my wind was knocked out of me. I lay there on the pavement, gasping, waiting for my respiration to return. It took almost a full minute, and I began to worry that a family member would come to the window of the apartment and see me lying there.

Finally my breaths were coming again, shallow and ragged. I dusted myself off, pulled the bag back onto my back, and walked to the end of the alley. I emerged onto the street and walked slowly and deliberately to the Chevrolet, acting as though nothing were out of the ordinary. I put the bag in the trunk and covered it up again as best I could with the old towel. I opened the passenger-side door and slid in. It was only then that the realization of what I had done began to sink in.

When Camila found me, I was sitting in the car shaking.

"Are you all right?" she asked with a worried expression.

"Yes. I think so." I had never felt so spent, so exhausted, so bone tired. Even thinking about what had happened in the last twenty-four hours was too daunting, too demanding.

I looked at Camila. "Let's get out of here," I said.

She needed little more encouragement to start the engine and step on the accelerator. I lay back in my seat, my eyes closed, feeling the motion as we sped away. I had accomplished what I set out to do. I touched one of the medals on my chest, thanked the Virgin for watching over me.

I fantasized that when I opened my eyes I would be safe and sound in my bedroom in Miami. But that wasn't going to be the case.

I opened them. Havana sped by as Camila picked up speed, heading for the highway again. I remembered there was another facet of the plan remaining to be accomplished: Camila's.

34

By the time I was composed enough again to open my eyes, I saw that we were back on the Malecon, heading east. Only an hour had passed since we were there last, but the boulevard seemed to have taken on a different character. It was late enough in the morning for there to be a lot more pedestrian traffic; I saw the faces mingling in the bustling crowd, the wide range of skin hues that indicated the racially mixed and integrated society that Cuba had become. The sun's light seemed to have changed, lending each of the crashing waves little rainbows in their aqueous spray.

It seemed to me that most of the people on the street were milling about, moving with no real urgency or sense of purpose. Everyone seemed to be waiting—for what, I had no idea. It must have been deeply sad to be a young person in such a stagnant society, waiting for a change of some sort to take place.

"Where are we going now?" I asked Camila, though I suspected I knew. It was time for me to pay her back for her help getting the tapestry out of the Miranda home.

"To my studio," she replied. Her eyes were locked on the road, her thin arms holding tight to the wheel. The anxiety that she had exhibited in the apartment was gone now, replaced by a look of cold determination.

She drove on, saying nothing else. I would have liked to know more, but her tone had suggested that she was in charge, that events would unfold according to her design from now on. I wondered if keeping her intentions tightly secreted away was a trait she had cultivated growing up in Communist Cuba. In turn, she hadn't asked me why I had come up from the basement in such a dirty and disheveled condition. I don't think she had any idea what I'd just been through.

My thoughts moved to Manfredi's wallet, which was still in the bag in the trunk. I wished I had it with me, so I could look through it, but I wasn't sure I trusted Camila enough to risk her seeing whatever I might find.

I looked out at the waters of the Florida Straits smashing against the sea wall of the Malecon, dissolving into a spray that misted against the windshield. I wondered how Barbara was doing on the *Concepcion*, whether Cuban or American authorities had discovered her anchored out there.

I glanced over at Camila again, fighting off a wave of panic. What did I know about this woman, anyway? Only what her brothers and cousin had told me about her, that she had remained in Cuba with her mother when the brothers left during the Mariel boatlift. That she was a painter who was capable of copying works by Cuban masters. That she was involved in the plan to exchange fakes for treasures.

I wished I had a better sense of her. I could tell that she was strong and determined, but I had no idea what motivated her. Sex, greed, and power were the usual determiners of human behavior, and I didn't know enough about Camila Estrada to say which applied to her. I began to fear that I might have made a pact with the devil in order to get the unicorn tapestry out of Cuba. I might have been so single-minded in my pursuit of the case that I threw in my lot with the wrong person.

This was a hell of a time to be having these sorts of doubts. I reminded myself that, when we were in the apartment, she had hung in there with me. She could have run away when I was taking too long, or when there was a knock on the door. Camila had proven herself to me, I decided.

Camila turned to the left and pointed. "Look," she said. "The Hotel Nacional. You've heard of it?"

I nodded, surprised by the way she had broken the silence between us. Of course I knew about the Hotel Nacional. It was Havana's answer to New York's Plaza Hotel or the Waldorf-Astoria, integral to the city's history, built in a Moorish architectural style. It was flamboyant and loud, with a history of catering to both tourists and mobsters.

"Quite a place," she said, betraying a hint of nervousness. For the first time I realized that Camila might be having doubts about whether she could trust me.

At the corner of 64 Street, Camila made a left, drove for two short blocks, then made a sharp right into an alley. We were in a residential district, with apartments rising on either side. My heart started to beat faster as she stopped the Chevrolet in front of an iron gate. Behind it seemed to be a garden apartment.

"Come with me," Camila said, turning off the motor. She hopped out, looking around nervously.

I was still damp with sweat and dirty from my exertions at the Miranda house. But I dispensed with vanity and hopped out of the car. Camila led me along a tiny footpath overgrown with weeds next to a wall. I was glad to be wearing pants, because as I walked I saw that the ground was rife with tropical vines laden with thorns.

"Stay here," Camila said, her voice little louder than a whisper.

I waited while she raised the rusty latch of a gate and went inside. I rubbed my eyes, felt a hint of the fatigue that threatened to overwhelm me the moment I let down my guard. I wanted nothing more than to end my Cuban experience, to go home. Being in Havana was nothing like I'd envisioned. I knew my memories would be of sweat, exhaustion, fear, and doubt.

Camila returned; she pushed at the rusty iron gate and motioned for me to hurry inside. I looked around, making sure we were alone, then stepped into the tiny garden.

"Here. Inside." Camila led the way into a cramped dark room. This was her studio, I realized. The walls were of chipped brick and sagging plaster. Art supplies were arranged neatly in rows atop an old table, the brushes and tubes of paint looking old and fastidiously tended to.

Camila went to the back corner and pulled back an old plastic tarpaulin. Underneath it was a stack of about eight paintings, neatly tied together with string. They were all frameless, although they were stretched taut over skeletons of what I assumed was wood.

She looked up at me with a wry smile. "These are the ones," she said.

I went over to the paintings and started flipping through them. I was no expert, but I recognized what I saw. Two Rene Portocarreros. Two Mario Carreños. One Wilfredo Lam. One Amelia Pelaez. One Emilio Sanchez. One Antonia Eiriz.

I looked up at Camila with what must have been a dumbstruck expression. I couldn't even begin to calculate the value of these paintings. It was a treasure stash of the crème de la crème of Cuban masters.

"These are real, right?" I asked stupidly.

Camila nodded. "The fakes are already hanging in the government residences. I substituted them one by one as I painted them over the last several years."

I nodded appreciatively, trying to comprehend the enormity of what she had done. The planning, the risk, the countless hours spent duplicating works by Cuba's greatest paintings. I had thought she was determined, but now I thought that her activity was nothing less than an obsession.

"What do you want me to do with these?" I asked, tensing.

She looked at me for a long time, seeming to wrestle with the question within herself. From someplace close by I heard a dog begin to bark.

"Here's what I ask from you, in return for helping you in the apartment," she said. "Take these paintings to Miami. Return them to their rightful owners—with my compliments."

"I . . . I don't get it," I blurted out, pointing at the paintings. "You and your brothers were going to get rich from your plan. You worked years to accomplish this."

"My brothers died because of these paintings." She looked away, her eyes clouding with tears. "When I got your letter, I was still thinking about selling these, but what would be the point? There's nothing to spend it on here."

"Who thought of the idea to create the fakes and sell them?" I asked.

"It was me," she said. "Angel loved it."

"He wanted to screw the government, right?"

Camila smiled. "He laughed so much when he talked about it."

I was heartened that Camila hadn't asked me to sell these paintings for her. I probably would have done it—although it was totally illegal and shaky on moral grounds—but at least now I was spared trying to figure out how to handle the situation.

"Why don't you come to Miami?" I asked her, the words coming out before I had time to consider what I was saying.

"After Mami died, I applied for a visa to leave," she said,

wiping her eyes on a clean cloth from the table. "I tried the lottery, but I was denied."

I knew that Camila was referring to the twenty thousand visas granted annually by the United States to prospective Cuban immigrants.

"So this is your payback," I said. "The Cuban government will be stuck with the fakes, while the real artworks will be with their rightful owners in exile."

"Money was never important to me," Camila explained with conviction. "I paint with love. The money was for my brothers. I thought it would help them."

Sure. Several million dollars would have been welcomed by Angel and Jesus, I imagined.

"But what's going to happen to you?" I asked.

She shook her head. "I have no family. My mother is dead, my brothers are dead. I barely know my cousin Reinaldo. I am going to live out the rest of my life here in this hell, with the government telling me what to paint and how to paint it. With no freedom. Here I will be a slave. But the paintings will be free. Do you understand?"

I thought I did. The Cuban government had appropriated everything on the island. In a real and meaningful way, Camila was going to liberate an important part of the country's heritage.

I realized that I had misjudged her, that my suspicions had been misplaced. I had thought Camila was being cryptic and evasive, but I now realized these were traits probably everyone in Cuba shared after living their lives in a police state. Camila had come upon a solution that was, to my mind, honorable and just.

But that still didn't explain why her brothers had died.

"Who killed your brothers, Camila?" I asked. "And why?"

Camila shrugged. "I don't know, Lupe," she said. "I wish I did, but I have no idea what was going on in Miami. My brothers never told me. All I knew was that Angel met you, and that you were going to help."

Great.

"I have to go back," I said. I looked down at the eight canvases. They weren't huge, but the idea of getting them onto the Whaler, along with the tapestry, was daunting.

Camila picked up a pile of burlap bags, dropped them next to the paintings. She counted out four, handed them to me along with a roll of string.

"You do half," she said.

Just touching such valuable treasures made me deeply nervous. I started wrapping one in burlap, careful not to touch the canvas's surface. Camila had no such qualms; she worked quickly and with familiarity. I saw her pause for just a second before she wrapped each one, looking at it one final time.

When we were finished, Camila stacked the paintings neatly and took them to the door by the garden.

"Wait here," she said, opening the door and peering out.

She stepped outside, walked through the small garden, then opened the gate to the alley where the Chevrolet was parked.

"It's safe," she whispered to me, hustling back into the studio and grabbing two paintings. We worked quickly, loading up the trunk in two trips.

I got in the front seat and leaned my head back. Camila locked the gate, got in the front seat and started the engine.

"Ready to go?" she asked.

I looked at her and laughed. "Is the Pope Catholic?" I asked.

A moment later she was laughing, too. We pulled out onto the road, beginning to make our way back to Cojimar. It was a long time before our gales of nervous cackling subsided.

35

We returned the way we had come, first on the Avenida 5, then the Malecon to the Via Monumental. This time I wasn't thinking about the sights of the city, even though I had no idea when I would see it again. My thoughts were instead preoccupied with the trip back to the *Concepcion*, and the millions of dollars worth of art I would be carrying with me.

Camila was still wearing my Swatch watch; I stole a glance at it. It was just past eleven. I could barely comprehend how much we had accomplished in such a short time.

Camila was concentrating intently on her driving, and seemed to be off in her own world. I would have liked to talk with her more, get to know her, but it felt indelicate to impose upon her solitude. It seemed unreal to think that soon we would split up forever—or at least until Castro fell and I was able to return to Cuba legally.

She soon turned off the Via Monumental and took a secondary road that I remembered from earlier that morning—what seemed like a lifetime ago. I could almost smell the seawater as I pictured the Whaler waiting for me, ready to take me home. Within a few minutes she turned onto the dirt road that had been my first impression of the path to Havana. In the distance I saw the flowering bougainvillea trees marking the location of the Whaler. I strained to see the boat but couldn't. In an instant the slight peace I'd achieved was gone, replaced by fear and mounting panic.

What if the Whaler was gone? Camila slowed the car. She tensed next to me, and I realized she was also looking for the boat. We exchanged glances, too anxious to speak.

We took a slight bend in the road, and suddenly the Whaler appeared. It was bobbing serenely in the water, and had been hidden from us by a trick of perspective from the road. Camila and I sighed in unison. There was no Plan B had the Whaler been discovered and taken away by a thief or the Cuban authorities. My only resort would have been to call Mabel, Alvaro's lawyer friend—and then tell her that I was stranded in my attempt to smuggle out a medieval tapestry and eight Cuban national art treasures.

Camila was watching me out of the corner of her eye. She tried to laugh, to recapture the nervous merriment we'd shared earlier, on the road from Havana. The attempt failed, though, sounding forced, revealing that her nerves were every bit as shot as mine.

She parked the Chevrolet under the same Florida pine that had disguised it earlier that morning, turned off the engine and hopped out. She opened up the trunk and started unloading it, not even bothering to look around. Now that we were close to the end, I could tell that she couldn't wait to be rid of me and to return to her normal life. The feeling was very mutual.

I got out and came around to the back of the car. Camila had quickly unloaded the eight canvases; only the tapestry remained. I had leaned deep into the trunk to pull it out when I heard a voice behind us.

"Excellent," the man said. "Thank you both for doing all the heavy lifting. Now I'll take custody of those items."

I froze, my upper body in the Chevrolet's cavernous trunk,

my hand on the bag containing the tapestry. I had no idea who was talking to us, but I was certain it wasn't good news. Carefully, trying not to draw attention to my movements, I took my hand off the bag's handle and unzipped the side pocket where I'd stashed the few tools that fit.

"What is this?" I heard Camila ask. She sounded more angry than frightened.

"What do you think this is?" the man asked with a bitter laugh. "You've been good enough to collect these items, and now you're handing them over to me."

I prayed for Camila to keep him occupied a moment longer, so the man wouldn't notice what I was doing. All I could think of was my determination that I wasn't going to be stopped—not after what I'd been through, and not so close to success.

I stood up slowly, not wanting to startle the man behind me. As I turned around I saw that he was standing directly between me and the Whaler. I didn't place him at first, although I was able to identify the .357 Magnum in his hand, pointed at Camila.

"Miss Solano," the man said, moving the gun to cover us both.

"You know me," I said. "No fair. I don't know—"

I stopped speaking. He was a Hispanic, a little under six feet, about two hundred pounds. No great looker. And he had two moles under his left eye. *Mierda*.

I had finally found Rafael Santamaria.

My mind raced. I had thought he might be a Cuban agent. Did this mean we were under arrest? But he was alone. None of it made sense.

"So I guess you're doing a little art appreciation," I said.

Santamaria laughed, a harsh sound. He pointed the gun at the burlap bags and the tapestry still in the trunk.

"I'll need you to load those onto my boat for me," he

said. "Forgive my lack of chivalry, but I have an old soccer injury that prevents me from performing manual labor."

I took a step toward the water. There it was, hidden until then by the same trick of perspective that had disguised the Whaler from us on the road: his Mako, the same one I'd come across in Osterman's report.

Camila and I looked at each other and shrugged. We had no choice, not with the gun pointed at us. She picked up two of the paintings and started toward the dock. I did the same. We made two trips each, placing the paintings in a pile on the dock next to Santamaria's boat. The art dealer supervised, motivating us by keeping the gun alternating between our chests. Finally only the tapestry was left.

"Hey, you. Detective," Santamaria called out to me. "You carry that. You hauled it out of the basement all by yourself, so I know you can handle it. Your friend here looks a little weak."

I was horrified as I digested what he had said and its implications.

"Have you been watching us today?" I blurted, picturing him, thinking about the valuable works of art he would no doubt be relieving us of. I felt like a fool—why hadn't I considered that I might have been followed?

"Today, sure," Santamaria said with a look that verged on lascivious. He was stocky, with darting eyes and a bulbous nose. "Yesterday, the day before that. Hey, does that Cuban lawyer know you've been two-timing him with the *gringo*?"

I tried not to let on that he had touched a nerve. I cursed my carelessness as I pulled the black canvas bag out of the trunk.

"I guess you put one over on me," I said.

"That's right," Santamaria said, smug and self-satisfied. "You were looking for me when I was right behind your back the whole time. The hunter becomes the game."

He turned to Camila, his eyes wandering over her body. "You, come here," he said, pointing the gun at her.

Camila looked at me, as though asking me what she should do. I cocked my head, indicating that she should do as he ordered. Santamaria took out a coil of rope from his pocket, tucked the gun in the waistband of his pants, and grabbed Camila from behind. He was obviously much stronger than her, and she cried out in pain as he tied her hands behind her back. I watched, waited. I felt badly for her, but there was nothing I could do. A moment later he had pulled out the gun again, releasing Camila with a slight shove that almost toppled her off her feet. She looked up at me, wild-eyed with fear.

"You did it, didn't you?" I said to him. "You killed Angel and Jesus Estrada."

Camila's face turned pale; I thought she might collapse to the ground, but she managed to remain standing halfway between me and Santamaria.

"I might have," Santamaria said in a voice dripping with contempt. "You're the detective. You tell me what happened."

That stung. The man was doing nothing to endear himself to me. "Now come on," he said. his voice turning serious. "Get that fucking tapestry down to my boat before I blow your head off."

I heaved the heavy bag onto my back, using the straps again to make a sling. I took a few steps toward the dock, and Santamaria pointed the gun at Camila again. He had a strange look in his eyes.

"Get in," he said, pointing at the open trunk. Camila's mouth opened in horror, no sound coming out. She blinked as her eyes filled with tears. Santamaria took a step closer to her.

I was still holding the tapestry. I suddenly understood that as soon as the tapestry was in his boat, Santamaria was going to force me into the trunk of the Chevrolet as well. Camila and I would be finished. Our options were growing fewer by the second.

Santamaria stepped closer to Camila, the gun pointed at her face. "Get in!" he yelled, angry.

Camila raised a leg and perched herself on the rim of the trunk. Without the use of her arms, it was almost impossible for her to balance herself. She leaned into the trunk and dropped in, smacking her head hard against the edge of the metal.

I felt paralyzed. I wished the Cuban authorities would show up, arrest us, anything to keep that trunk from being the last place I would ever see. I would rather take my chances in a Cuban jail than with the gun-waving art dealer.

Santamaria turned around. "You, what did I tell you?" he yelled at me. "Get the tapestry in the boat! Now!"

I moved slowly, heading toward the boat. My mind raced with images, possibilities. I realized that my life might end there.

Once I was on the dock, I knew I had to take a chance. I let my knees buckle and fell, the big bag coming down on top of me. I pretended to be pinned down there, right on the edge of the water.

"*Mierda*," Santamaria said impatiently. "Can't you watch what you're doing?"

"It's heavy," I answered weakly. I pretended to struggle to get up, then dropped to my knees.

"Give me that!" Santamaria barked. He pulled hard at the strap across my chest, yanked it roughly over my neck.

The Magnum was pointed at my ribs. But as Santamaria took the bag from me, his hand moved a full foot. He was pointing the gun at nothing.

He realized his mistake too late. By then I had plunged the blade of my carpet knife deep into his chest.

"Ay, Dios mio, Lupe!" Camila called out from the trunk of the car. "You killed him!"

I was standing still as a statue, my hands out in front of me as though fending off an invisible attacker. I balled my hands into fists, shook my head so violently that I felt muscles straining in my neck. I had to pull it together. What happened in the next few minutes could determine the rest of my life.

I was on the dock, Santamaria's body at my feet. A rapidly spreading bloodstain appeared on his shirt, running out onto the wood of the dock itself. His eyes were wide open, his mouth agape in eternal surprise.

I ran back to the car, slid Camila onto her side, and tried to untie her hands. The knot was too tight, though, and all I succeeded in doing was rub my hands and Camila's wrists raw.

"What's the matter?" she asked. Her skin was starting to bleed, and panic infused her voice.

"Can't get it," I muttered, tugging at the knot.

"Cut it," she said. "Can't you cut it?"

I didn't reply, knowing that's what I should have done in the first place. I looked at the knot again. It was too tight for me to deal with.

"I'll be right back," I told her.

Fear flashed over her face, as she thought for an instant that I would leave her there. I jogged back to the dock and knelt over Santamaria's body. I heard Camila gasp as I pulled the carpet knife out of his chest.

The knife came out with such force that I almost tumbled backward off the dock. Along with the knife came a geyser of blood, spraying my face and Camila's clothes. I held my breath, desperately trying not to vomit as I ran back to the car.

Camila saw me approach, her eyes agog, saying nothing. I tried not to think about what I looked like, covered in blood, holding a knife. It took about a dozen strokes of the knife to free her hands. She quickly hopped out of the car, rubbing her wrists.

"Come on," I said, grabbing her wrist. "We have to get out of here."

"Lupe, what are you talking about?" Camila shrieked, trying to pull away from me.

"You can't stay here!" I pushed her in the direction of the dock, almost knocking her off her feet.

"I can't leave Cuba!" she protested, on the verge of turning hysterical. "What are you saying? This is my home!"

"If you stay, they'll say you killed him!" I pointed the knife in Santamaria's direction. "They'll find out about the fakes! They'll put you in jail for the rest of your life!"

I took her in my arms and shook her. "You said this was a hell for you!" I yelled. "You wanted to get your visa! The hell with your visa! Get in the boat!"

She closed her eyes, shaking her head and stammering. "I don't—" she began. "But what if I—if—"

We were making such a commotion that it was a matter of time before we were caught and sent permanently up shit creek. I couldn't afford to stand there debating with Camila—although I was certain she was finished if she stayed behind.

So I did the only logical thing. I pulled back my right fist and punched her square in the jaw. She went down like a sack of potatoes. I slung her over my shoulder, high on adrenaline now, and carried her to the deck of the Whaler. After I made sure she was all right, I loaded the eight paintings, then the bag containing the tapestry, into the boat.

I hopped off onto the deck. Santamaria's body was close to the edge of the dock; it would take nothing to push him in. Before I did that, though, I pulled the spool of rope from his back pocket and cut off two segments. I quickly bound his hands and feet.

I jogged back to the scrubby area around the Chevrolet, selected an armload of rocks, then stuffed them in Santamaria's pants and shirt. It wasn't much, but I hoped it would keep him from rising to the surface immediately. With luck, the crabs would get to him. That would definitely slow the identification process.

After unspooling the rest of the rope, I tied it to his belt. I pushed him into the water with my foot, cringing as I heard the splash below. I lay flat on the dock, rope in hand, and tied him to the posts closest to land. It wasn't great, but it was the best I could do on short notice. I figured someone would show up and steal the Mako soon.

I hopped down into the Whaler, untied the ropes securing her to the dock, fired up the engine. Within a minute I had hit the water, heading north.

With all the extra weight on board, we were riding low in the water. But I thought we would make it. I certainly wasn't going to chuck anything over the side to lighten our load. I gunned the engines and pointed us toward home.

As I steered the boat I screamed at the top of my lungs. Then I did it again. It was the only way I could express the feelings bubbling up from under the surface of my survival instinct. I saw Rafael Santamaria's eyes staring up at me from under each passing wave, and shuddered in the cool spray.

36

"So, Lupe," Osvaldo said. He winked a few times; I started to worry he was going to injure his eye.

"So?" I asked.

"How was your cruise?" he asked in a low voice, smiling.

"My cruise?"

I was on the terrace of the house in Cocoplum having breakfast. It was the Friday morning after my return from Cojimar. The sun was shining down on the waves of Biscayne Bay. I had a big silver pot of steaming *café con leche* in front of me, along with two oversized slices of *pan con mantequilla* awaiting orange marmalade. The *Miami Herald* was neatly folded next to my white linen place mat.

"Oh, my cruise. With Alvaro," I said. "It was good. Very good."

Osvaldo nodded, standing up straight. The conspirators were to keep their code of silence. He walked off, whistling a tune, a little extra spring in his step.

When I motored the Whaler from Cojimar, I was out in the open seas staring at the GPS when I realized that the *Concepcion* wasn't anchored where I'd left it. I got out the binoculars, and before I could begin to panic, I saw it. It was a bit off course, but that didn't matter as I steered the craft toward the Hatteras.

"You found me," Barbara called down when I pulled up alongside. "Sorry I'm not where you left me. The winds and the tides were getting strong, and the boat was starting to drag anchor. I had to turn on the engines and idle. I hated to burn the fuel, but it was my only choice."

Barbara acted as if nothing was out of the ordinary when she saw me return in different clothes than I'd worn when I left. She didn't raise an eyebrow at the bloodstains, nor did she comment when we lifted Camila out of the boat and took her down to the master cabin. I was reminded that Barbara was the ideal companion for an expedition such as this.

We unloaded the Whaler in a couple of trips, moving as fast as we could, stealing glances at the waters around the *Concepcion*. We decided on the spot that there was no time to bring the Whaler back into its cradle on the bow, so we simply tied it to the bow and towed it behind us. A few minutes later we were headed north, back to Miami.

I couldn't remember the last time I had slept. I was filthy. I had the blood of the man I'd murdered caked on my clothes. But still I stood on the deck, binoculars in hand, scanning the water. Thoughts of imprisoned smugglers pre-occupied my mind—we were carrying not only stolen art treasures, but a Cuban citizen on the boat. I estimated that Cuban courts would probably sentence us to life in prison if we were caught and arrested.

The trip back seemed endless. The sound of the waves, which normally lulled and relaxed me, seemed to focus my attention. After we passed the halfway mark without event, I began to relax, thinking it was possible we were going to make it back. We stopped at the Merrill Stevens dockyard in Dinner Key. I looked around at the other boats there, unable to comprehend pleasure sailing or fishing, the benign experiences of the sea. As far as I was concerned, I didn't want to go back onto the water in the foreseeable future.

We took a chance that there was enough fuel to get back to Miami, and there was—barely. Barbara motored the *Concepcion* into the marina at dusk. I checked my watch. The trip from Miami to Cuba and back had taken a little more than twenty-four hours.

Camila had woken just before we caught sight of the Florida coast. She came up the stairs from the stateroom, looked around totally confused. She caught my eye and I gave her an apologetic look. All at once she seemed to remember what had happened. She gave me a weak smile and curled up on the sofa in the main cabin while Barbara and I maneuvered the Hatteras into the correct ship's channels to take us to Merrill Stevens.

It was only when we had docked, then moved the artworks from the *Concepcion* to the Mercedes, that we had time to speak. We stood in the dockyard parking lot, surrounded by boats in dry dock. Barbara left for the *Santa Barbara*, eager to see if she could arrange a visit with her children through her sister Ofelia. We shared a long embrace before she departed.

"I'm really sorry I hit you," I told Camila. Dusk was gathering into night. Camila shrank deep into my sweatshirt, looking pale and frail. "I saw no choice, I hope you understand."

"You saved both our lives," she said. She folded her arms. "I know you did what you felt you had to do."

She looked up at me. In spite of all she'd been through, not to mention the discolored area on her chin where I punched her, she remained extraordinarily beautiful.

"I'm filthy and exhausted," I said. I had a sweatshirt on over Camila's clothes, for warmth and to cover up the bloodstains. "I imagine you feel the same way. We should think about taking hot baths and getting something to eat. Then sleep. How does that sound?"

Camila laughed and nodded. "That sounds good," she said.

"There's something you need to know," I told her. "I'm going to get a lot of money for bringing that artwork out of the basement in Havana. I can use it any way I want."

Camila stared at me with her bright green eyes, expectant, not sure what I was getting at.

"You were vital in helping me," I said. "I'm going to get you a suite in a good hotel, teach you about the wonders of American room service and television. Tomorrow night, after you've had a chance to rest, we'll talk about the future and what needs to be done."

"That sounds great," Camila said. She pointed to herself. "But look at me! How can I go to a hotel this way?"

I laughed. "This is Miami," I said. "No one looks at anyone or cares what anyone looks like. As long as the credit card clears and you're not naked or waving a couple of guns, no one's going to notice. We'll get you some new clothes tomorrow. I want you to know you don't have to worry about anything like that."

Camila smiled gratefully. When we got into the Mercedes, I sighed aloud over the comforting feeling of the steering wheel. I checked Camila into a suite at the Mayfair House Hotel in Coconut Grove, where Solano Investigations had a corporate account. She was so exhausted that she stared out the window of the car on the way over without comment. I didn't disturb her, except to say not to worry if she didn't speak English. Only people who don't speak Spanish in Miami have trouble with communication, I explained.

"Charge whatever you need to your room," I told her. She gave me a look of complete incomprehension. "Pick up the phone and say what you want. They will put it on an account for you that I'll pay."

She nodded, seeming to adapt quickly. I hoped I wasn't creating a monster. Once I took her up to the room, I told her I was leaving for the night.

"Keep the door locked and don't call anyone, not yet," I instructed her. "We have to sort things out, and it's best if no one knows you're here."

I was thinking of her cousin Reinaldo, whom she barely knew but would want to contact anyway. When I left her, she was in the bathroom inspecting all the complimentary products on the shelf. I knew they would be put to good use.

I watched the waters of Biscayne Bay lapping against the dock, more at peace than I had been in weeks. There were still loose ends to be dealt with, but I was home. I was alive. I had made it.

I poured my third *café con leche* of the morning. Soon I would call Camila, check that she was all right. I was glad to be able to provide her with a room and some comforts, but I also knew that she couldn't stay at the Mayfair House Hotel forever. Returning to Cuba in the near future was out of the question for her, although I figured that someone with her artistic skills would be able to land some sort of job in Miami. She was in the United States illegally, but I knew just the person to address that problem: Alvaro. But first I would have to attempt some sort of reconciliation with him.

It was almost eleven in the morning. Time to get going. As I stood up I had a flash in my memory of Santamaria's stunned face frozen in death. I imagined the crabs in the water, starting to work on him. I shook my head and willed it away.

I had to go to the office and make a few calls. I'd been doing some thinking since I got up that morning, and a few pieces of the puzzle were coming together. When it was solved, I would try to restore some order to my personal life—a prospect that, at the moment, made my trip to Cuba seem like the pleasure cruise Osvaldo so innocently thought I had taken.

37

Leonardo was in the kitchen when I got to the office. I tried not to react when I saw how he was dressed, in a gold unitard with matching sequins at the wrists, gold Top-Siders on his feet. He looked like a transvestite yacht captain. In his hand was a blender full of some yellowish liquid.

It was nice that things were back to normal.

"Lupe!" he exclaimed when he saw me come in. "I didn't think you'd be back so soon."

"Leo, I missed you too much to stay away for long," I said, kissing him on the cheek. "What's up?"

"I'm inventing a drink. I think I have the secret for shrinking the Cuban ass." He was positively radiant as he brandished the blender. "It's mango juice mixed with Añejo."

Añejo again. I flashed back to Barbara.

"That doesn't sound effective to me," I said. "It sounds like it contains a lot of calories."

"There's a secret ingredient," Leo said. He leaned close to me and whispered, "A dash of Ex-Lax."

I was appalled. "A laxative? Your secret ingredient is a laxative?"

Leo sniffed, looking very proud of himself. "Anyone who drinks this has to lose weight," he said. "And their asses will shrink as a result. It's foolproof."

"I don't want to hear anything more," I said, walking toward my office. Then I had a terrifying thought. I turned and called out, "Make sure you wash that blender out really well when you're done. Remember, we both have to use it."

I went around my desk and sat down heavily. I looked out the window at the parrots, who were adding to their construction projects. If I wasn't mistaken, they were creating a replica of the Tower of London.

I stayed at my desk for a while, jotting down a few theories to see how they looked on the cold, hard page. I was going to have to check out my suspicions before I went around making accusations. I spent the rest of the afternoon making calls and running down leads. I took a break to telephone Camila at the Mayfair House to see how she was doing.

I needn't have worried about her. After we exchanged greetings, she started enthusiastically reading me the room service menu—the whole thing, breakfast, lunch, and dinner. She asked my opinion about what she should eat for lunch, then ran through the list of pay-per-view movies available in her room, trying to select a couple that would be to her taste.

For someone who had never traveled out of Cuba, Camila seemed eager and willing to adapt to the American way of life. It was a relief. I had been worried that she would grieve unduly for her lost life. The adjustment process had just begun, I knew, but I was convinced that Camila was a survivor.

I called Tommy and told him that I was back, safe and sound. He was the least touchy-feely man in the universe, but I could hear the relief in his voice. He insisted we get together right away, but I said no. There were still a couple of things I needed to check out.

At around four o'clock I was ready to call Lucia Miranda on her cell phone.

"Lucia?" I said when she answered. "This is Lupe Solano speaking."

"Lupe!" she exclaimed. "Do you have it? Did you get it?" Her concern for my well-being was touching.

"Yes, I have it."

"What kind of condition is it in?" she demanded. "Do you have it with you? Can I come get it now?"

The questions were pouring out from the phone in such rapid succession that I didn't have time to answer.

"It's in fine condition," I finally said. "By the way, how is your mother? Is she still in the hospital?"

"Oh, yes, she's the same. She's still at Baptist," Lucia replied. "When can I come get the tapestry? Now?"

"Come to my office in one hour," I told her. "I'll have the tapestry for you, along with my bill."

We hung up. I noted that at no time in our conversation had Lucia asked how I was, or thanked me for what I had done for her. It was going to make getting even with her even sweeter.

I took out a pad of paper and started totaling my bill for expenses and services. I couldn't recall ever having been so eager to present a bill to a client. It was a tidy sum even before I started outrageously padding it.

I made a couple more calls then sat back to wait. Less than an hour passed before Lucia entered the outer office. I heard her exchanging pleasantries with Leonardo, and regretted not being out there to see her reaction to my cousin's attire. I wished he would share some of his ass-reducing, diarrhea-inducing potion with her, but I knew he wouldn't.

This was to be our last meeting, and Lucia didn't disappoint me with her appearance. She looked even more like a predatory bird than ever, dressed all black with darting, greedy eyes.

"Lupe!" Lucia waltzed into my office, arms outstretched,

her cheek offered for a kiss. I closed my eyes and air-kissed her. It was absolutely the most I could do.

"*Hola*, Lucia," I said as pleasantly as I could. I pointed to one of the two client's chairs in front of my desk. Lucia's beady eyes flitted around my office, obviously trying to locate the tapestry.

I smiled at her. "First, if you don't mind, I would appreciate it if we could get the financial aspect of our business over with." I didn't wait for her to agree, but instead just handed her the bill.

She looked at it, unflinching, then took a checkbook out of her purse. She signed the check with a flourish and handed it over. I pocketed it as she deliberately took my bill and ripped it into tiny pieces.

"*Gracias*," I said.

"So. Where is it?" Lucia was straining so hard to keep her composure that I saw veins rippling in her neck.

I stood up and walked over to the closet. I opened it up. It was still wrapped in plastic, and I'd draped it over two chairs.

"Here it is," I said.

A metamorphosis came over her. A softness transformed her features. For a fleeting instant I almost felt sorry for her.

"It's in there?" she asked, reverent.

She got up and came around her chair, headed for the closet. I stopped her by loudly clearing my throat.

"Before you look at it," I said, "there are a few things I need to discuss with you."

Lucia glared at me as though I was a bothersome rodent. "What things? What else is left? I have the tapestry—"

"Please. Sit." I pointed at the chair she had just vacated, then reached into my desk drawer and took out Albert O. Manfredi's wallet. I lay it on the desk between us.

"What's that?" Lucia asked suspiciously.

"First things first," I told her. "I did a little checking

around when I got back from Havana, Lucia. I was happy to find out that I didn't need to worry about your mother's health anymore. In fact, apart from the normal aches and pains of age, she's in fine health. Hasn't seen the inside of a hospital in years."

Lucia's chalk-white face assumed an even more startling pallor. "How dare you check up on the affairs of my family," she hissed. "That is not what I hired you to do!"

I ignored her, inwardly amazed by her arrogance. "That's not the only thing I found out about your mother," I added. "Turns out she's recently made inquiries about registering the unicorn tapestry with the Art Loss Registry in London. She's gone as far as getting the official paperwork."

Lucia stared straight ahead. "We both know what that means," I said. "Once the tapestry is officially registered with the Art Loss Registry, the world will be put on notice that it belongs to her. No one can buy or sell it without her permission, or without making compensation to her."

"You're crazy!" Lucia screamed at me. "You have no proof of what you're saying!"

"Here." I handed Lucia a slip of paper with the phone number for the Art Loss Registry. "Call and find out for yourself."

"I'm leaving!" Lucia said, standing up. "I'm calling the police and having you thrown in jail!"

"I'm not finished," I said, standing up as well. "Once the tapestry is registered, then you wouldn't be able to sell it, would you? Your mother's name would be listed as the owner—not yours. You had to get your hands on the tapestry and sell it anonymously before that happened. Your family would be none the wiser, they would just assume that the Cuban government had found it and sold it off—like it's done with so many pieces of art."

"You're guessing," Lucia said with a trace of a smile. "You can't prove anything."

Lucia was correct. I didn't have proof. I was glad she hadn't called my bluff and phoned up the Art Loss Registry. I might have lacked proof, but I did have a dead body.

It was time for show and tell. I reached for Manfredi's wallet. "I found this in your family basement," I said. "In the wall."

"In the wall?" Lucia asked, confused. "What do you mean?"

"Behind the tapestry was a box, hidden in the wall," I explained slowly. "Inside the box was what remained of a person."

"I don't know anything about that," Lucia said, fear suddenly entering her eyes.

"This is the wallet that was with the body," I said. "It belongs to Albert O. Manfredi."

I opened the wallet and emptied its contents. Lucia watched, spellbound. I took out Manfredi's folded travel papers, his staff identification from the Metropolitan Museum.

It was all very interesting. But what had really grabbed my attention was a draft of a handwritten note that Manfredi had apparently been carrying when he died. It stated his opinion that the letter from Christopher Columbus granting Rogelio Miranda possession of the unicorn tapestry was a fraud—and, therefore, the Miranda family could not sell the tapestry because they did not rightfully own it.

I handed the letter over to Lucia and watched her read it.

"What . . . what does this mean?" she asked, looking up at me.

"It means that, in the opinion of an expert, your family was not—and is not—the legal owners of the eighth tapestry."

"It's ours," Lucia protested weakly. "It has been in our family for generations."

"That doesn't mean you legally own it," I said. "It's obvious that Manfredi was killed because of that letter, because he was heading back to New York to report what he had found. Fortunately, whoever murdered Manfredi left his wallet untouched. I suppose it would be ungentlemanly to go through a man's personal possessions—even after you killed him."

"I—" Lucia paused, shaken. "I don't know anything about a man being killed."

"Maybe not, Lucia," I granted. "But someone in your family knew about it. That's the reason the tapestry was hidden in the basement. Not from fear that John D. Rockefeller would steal it, but because someone in your family understood that it didn't legally belong to you."

Lucia seemed to shrink in her chair, her eyes wide as she tried to comprehend what she was hearing.

"I'm not a lawyer, but if the tapestry wasn't a gift from Columbus to your ancestor, then it must belong to Columbus's descendants—or to the crown of Spain." Lucia blinked, started shaking her head. "You didn't have to worry about the Art Loss Register. You sent me for something that wasn't your mother's *or* yours. You went to all this trouble for nothing."

Lucia was apoplectic, beyond shock. I wasn't certain how much she had known about the seventy-year-old dirty secrets of her family, and I might never know. But she had methodically planned to use me in an attempt to rip off her relatives, at the very least.

She had sent me into Cuba, risking my life. Maybe she had believed her own bullshit story about the tapestry's history, but she lied to me from the beginning about her motivation. I had journeyed into danger on her behalf, and paid

dearly with indelible memories that would plague my conscience for the rest of my life.

That was why I was really going to enjoy the next part. There was nothing I could do for Albert O. Manfredi, but there was something I could do with the tapestry—and I imagined it was along the same lines as he would have recommended. He had been sent to buy the tapestry from the Mirandas, but he planned to leave Cuba with the intention of exposing them.

The doorbell rang in the outer office. Perfect timing. I heard Leonardo open the door and welcome our guest. Lucia stiffened, stared at the doorway. She seemed to realize that the drama hadn't ended.

I went to my office door at Leo's knock. "Please come in," I said to our new visitor. I motioned for him to enter.

Ambassador de Castellanos looked as dapper as the first time I'd seen him in his office. He also looked thoroughly confused about the reason I'd invited him to a private meeting.

"Miss Solano." He took my hand and raised it to his lips. I was pleased to see he didn't make actual contact—genuine aristocrats never do. He looked at Lucia Miranda, who was still seated; she looked equal parts enraged and terrified.

"Ambassador, please let me introduce Miss Lucia Miranda," I said.

Ambassador de Castellanos nodded to her, then turned to me. "Miss Solano, I was pleased to hear from you this afternoon. But I have to tell you—I was very surprised when you told me that you are not a student at the University of Miami."

"Sorry about that," I said.

"And that you are a detective!" Ambassador de Castellanos looked positively thrilled with the fact that I was a pri-

vate investigator. If he was happy then, I thought, he was going to be over the moon in a few minutes.

I smiled at Lucia as though nothing was wrong between us. "Señor de Castellanos is the former Spanish ambassador to Cuba," I explained to her in a cordial voice. "He is also an expert in medieval art, and is very familiar with the unicorn tapestries."

Lucia listened intently, seeming to sense that this was leading someplace she didn't want to go. Ambassador de Castellanos simply looked puzzled.

"I interviewed him in connection with our case," I continued, addressing Lucia. "That's why I've asked him here today."

"It has been a pleasure to assist you, Miss Solano," the ambassador said. He clasped his hands together, revealing his eagerness. "But I have to know. Why have you asked me here today?"

I walked over to the closet, opened the door as wide as it would go, and lugged out the folded-up tapestry. I took out my Swiss Army knife and carefully sliced through the plastic. My two companions watched me in silence.

I swept the plastic aside and spread the tapestry out on the floor of my office. It was a world of deep greens, heavenly whites, earthy browns, with phenomenally observed details of small plants and animals surrounding the just-freed mythical animal. All three of us were momentarily transfixed by its majesty and beauty.

"The eighth tapestry," I announced.

None of us moved. Suddenly, I felt a tingling on the back of my neck. My mother was there, I was certain of it. She was looking at the tapestry, reveling in its richness. And she would be so glad to have been proven right in her belief that the series had to continue to a happier conclusion.

I had been through so much to obtain the tapestry that I

almost felt proprietary toward it. But it wasn't mine. Nor
was it Lucia Miranda's. Which brought us to the point of
the meeting.

"Señor de Castellanos, this tapestry is real and authentic,"
I said. He had his hand over his mouth in shock. "It has
been in the safekeeping of Lucia Miranda's family for five
hundred years. And now they would like to return it to its
rightful owners—the people and the crown of Spain."

I didn't know who was more stunned, Lucia or the ambassador.

"Miss Miranda will tell you about its history," I said. "And
why she is giving it to you, in your capacity as a representative of Spain."

I grabbed my purse and the set of files I would need. I
wasn't done that day. I was on a roll, though, with another
wrong to right.

On my way out of the office I handed over Lucia's check
to Leonardo. "Go to the bank and cash this first thing," I
told him. "She might try to stop payment on it. Then deposit
it in our account."

"Got it," Leo replied, taking the check.

I glanced back through my open office door. Lucia was
talking to the ambassador, a small smile on her face. She had
regained her manners, apparently, and recognized that I had
given her an opportunity to come out of this relatively intact—by playing the part of the selfless benefactor who
wanted to bring a priceless treasure to its rightful home.

Which was better for her than my first impulse, which
was to drag her ass out into the public eye and make sure
the world found out what she had been up to. Lucia should
have thanked me, though I doubted she ever would.

I looked back at Leonardo. He had finally gotten a look at
the check, and was bug-eyed at the amount of money it

represented. I understood. We had never before made so much money on a single case.

"What have you been up to?" he whispered.

"I'll tell you later," I said. "I promise."

Leo tucked the check into a crevice of his skimpy unitard. "Whatever it was, it must have been bad," he said. "Because no one gets paid this kind of money for being an angel."

"Truer words were never spoken," I said in return.

38

I got into the Mercedes and left the office, heading over to Tommy's. I could no longer avoid reporting to him. As independent as I prided myself on being, I needed to talk to someone I trusted about the events of the past few days—someone who, I add, might be able to defend me for my actions should they ever become known.

As I drove I wondered how the scene I'd left back at the office was progressing. I had considered donating the tapestry anonymously to the Cloisters, where it could be displayed with the other seven. In the end I was pleased with myself for resolving the Lucia Miranda situation in a satisfactory fashion—the tapestry was returned to those who had a legitimate claim to owning it, and I had been paid very well in the process. Still, I wasn't without doubt. I knew that, in part, anger at Lucia had clouded my decision.

Any way I looked at it, I was finished with the tapestry. I wasn't finished with Tommy's case—although I had some important developments to share with him, such as the fact that I had killed Rafael Santamaria in self-defense.

When I was on the sea coming back to Miami, Santamaria's blood staining my clothes, I had tried to think through the events that might have led to the art dealer lying in wait for me at Cojimar. At first I thought he might have been tipped off by Lucia, but that was impossible. She had no way of knowing where I was landing in Cuba, and there was no reason for her to betray me.

Santamaria had known times and places. I realized that could mean only one thing—he had intercepted the letter I had given Reinaldo Estrada to have delivered to Camila in Havana. But how had Santamaria known Reinaldo, and how had he gotten access to the letter?

The hunter becomes the game. Santamaria had said that to me in Cojimar. I started to think about that turn of phrase, and a couple of new ideas came to me. A chain of events had led to Santamaria lying on that dock with my carpet knife sticking out of his chest, and an outline was forming in my mind of how that came to pass.

Tommy and I had agreed to meet at the bar of the Hotel Place St. in Coral Gables. It was an intimate place with Old World atmosphere, adjacent to the French restaurant on the other side of the corridor. Tommy arrived before me and, by the time I got there, was well into his Jack Daniel's. We were the only patrons in the place, sharing the quiet of the afternoon with a bartender raptly watching the Weather Channel on a television suspended from the ceiling.

"A glass of Cabernet Sauvignon, please," Tommy called out when he saw me. We knew each other's tastes so well that either of us could order a seven-course meal for the other without making an errant selection.

"*Gracias,*" I said. We adjourned from the bar to a private table in the corner. We waited in silence until the wine arrived, then clinked glasses lightly.

"You want to talk about it?" Tommy asked. He looked very tired, but he still seemed curious about what had happened to me.

I had resolved to keep my stiff upper lip. That lasted about fifteen seconds. Everything that had happened in Cuba came out in a torrent. Tommy listened without comment, stopping me only once to go the bar to refresh our drinks.

When I was done, Tommy sighed, took off his glasses and rubbed his eyes.

"I have to think about this," he said.

"I'm not really worried about myself," I said. "But I'm not sure that Santamaria was the person who killed Angel and Jesus Estrada. It isn't right that those crimes should go unpunished."

Tommy cradled his face in his hands. "This is a tough one, Lupe," he said quietly.

"I know."

I would have been happy to go to Detective Anderson right then and there, to come clean and get the problem solved. I knew Tommy would never let me.

Then another thought occurred to me. If someone was in league with Santamaria, they would know by then that he had disappeared. They would assume the worst. And that might mean they would come looking for me for an explanation.

We finished our drinks without talking about it anymore. Then we left together in Tommy's car. I knew I would find a ream of parking tickets on the Mercedes in the morning, since I had left it parked on the street, but I would deal with it tomorrow.

For the moment, for that night, I needed to feel alive.

Exhausted as I was, I couldn't sleep that night. I whispered in Tommy's ear that I was going home. He was in such a deep slumber that he didn't even register the fact that I had no car to go home in, otherwise, gentleman that he was, he would have offered to drive me to the Mercedes. I was glad he didn't awaken. I didn't begrudge him his rest.

We had renewed our sensual knowledge of one another

that night with a fervor we hadn't shared in quite a while. That went far to explain Tommy's comatose state, but I knew I couldn't take all the credit. As usual, he was over-worked, putting in long hours. Anyway, I wanted him rested because, if things went badly in the next day or so, I needed him alert and ready to defend me.

I called for a taxi and waited downstairs in the lobby until it arrived. It was a strange feeling riding a taxi through Miami in the predawn darkness—especially since it was driven by an American, also known as a "non-Hispanic white" in the demographic jargon of Dade County. The day was coming soon when Caucasian Americans in Miami would have to check the box marked "Other."

It was a miracle, I thought when I reached the Mercedes. I expected to see dozens of those ubiquitous white tickets with orange borders stuck to my windshield, but there were none. I took it as a good omen. I typically accrued parking tickets at such an outlandish rate that I collected them in an "in" tray in my office, paying them off once a month just like the American Express bill. It wasn't something I was particularly proud of, it was just an annoying fact of life.

Once in the Mercedes, I drove to the office. There was almost no one else on the road, so I got there in less than ten minutes—a record for Miami's normally traffic-clogged streets.

After turning off the alarm, I set about doing the chores that Leonardo usually performed: turning on the lights, set-ting the espresso maker, bringing the milk to boil for *café con leche*. I wasn't very hungry, since Tommy and I had or-dered Chinese food and eaten it while watching reruns of *Homicide* and *Law & Order* until he fell asleep.

I took a mug of *café con leche* to the office, where I opened up the closet door. Sure enough, the tapestry was gone. I felt a jolt of sadness, as though I had lost a friend. The only

thing left to do was check messages on the answering machine before sitting down at my desk and running through
my plan for the day. Everything had to go well, or else I
might be spending the next decade or so—at least—as a
round-the-clock guest of Uncle Sam.

From the closet I took out the innocuous-looking burlap
bundles that disguised the eight paintings by Cuban masters
that Camila and I had brought out of Cuba. I knew I would
be able to make discreet inquiries and track down their rightful owners, so that aspect of the case didn't trouble me.
What did bother me was that the Estrada brothers' murders
were still unsolved, a situation I had to remedy.

I looked out the window. It was too early for the parrots
to be up. I knew their habits mirrored my own: they liked
to stay up late at night and sleep until mid-morning. I would
only start to worry if they developed a taste for *café con leche*.

When I turned on the answering machine in the reception
area, the first voice I heard jolted me from the relative peace
of the morning.

"Lupe, this is Alvaro." As though he really had to identify
himself. His tone was cautious and measured. "You know, I
ran into Osvaldo at the gas station on Red Road, and he was
behaving really strangely."

My heart thumped. My hands were sweating, a fact that
had nothing to do with the strength of the *café con leche*.

"He was winking at me, and poking me in the ribs. Then
he asked me if I'd gotten seasick lately."

I was clutching the corner of the desk, positively nauseous,
thinking all was lost.

"The only reason I'm telling you this is because I think you
should keep an eye on the old man," Alvaro said, sounding
genuinely concerned. "I've known him all my life, and I've
never seen him confused like this. Has he had a checkup
lately?"

Thank God. Alvaro took Osvaldo's insinuations for senile rambling. Relief flowed through me like a dam opened up after a long drought. I felt a pang of guilt for deceiving both Osvaldo and Alvaro, but told myself it had been for a greater good.

"I hope you're well, anyway," Alvaro concluded.

I played the message over again, thinking I might have missed something. But no, that was all Alvaro had to say to me. At least he was calling me Lupe, and not the formal and forbidding Guadalupe.

I pressed the button to play the next message, still preoccupied with the sound of Alvaro's voice. I was quickly brought back to reality, however, when I heard who had called.

"Lupe, this is Suzanne."

I turned up the volume on the machine.

"I don't know if this is the kind of thing I should say into an answering machine, but what the hell," Suzanne said with a laugh. "If this is Leo listening, then hi, Leo! Put your hands over your ears. If this is Lupe, I'm calling to follow up on that art dealer, Santamaria. I finally heard something about him—lots. Turns out I was talking to the wrong people . . ."

39

When I went to the Mayfair House Hotel, dawn had yet to break. I made my way up to Camila's room and found her bleary-eyed and yawning. Empty room-service dishes and cups littered the room.

"Leave those in the hall," I told her. "Someone will come and get them."

She started to stack up the dishes, a serious expression on her face.

"Look, I'll help you with that," I said. "But please, sit down for a minute. There's something I want to do today. I want to tell you about it, and see if you'll agree to help me."

Camila sat on the edge of the bed; I took a seat at the antique desk in the corner. As I explained what I had planned, her eyes grew wider and wider. She came awake, folding her hands on her lap and listening intently. It was just past six, and I was worried that I was hitting her with too much information too early in the morning.

"OK," she finally said, showing the determined expression I remembered from Cuba. "If that's what we have to do, then I'll help you. It's the least I can do for Jesus and Angel."

"Thank you," I said. "Now let's get some room service."

Though she'd had just a day's rest, Camila seemed like a different woman. Her features were more relaxed and the dark smudges were gone from her eyes. I could see a trace of a bruise on her chin where I'd hit her, but it seemed to be fading fast.

We sat together drinking *café con leche* and eating a basket of rolls. She asked me questions about my plan for that day, asking for details and for the facts and suppositions that influenced my decision. The longer I spoke to her, the stronger and more determined she seemed. She brushed aside my warnings that things might turn dangerous, saying she was grateful that I was trying to bring to justice the people who had murdered her brothers.

I left her there to shower and get ready, returning to my office to make a couple of calls. I had to hurry because we were on a deadline. We wanted to be in front of Reinaldo Estrada's workshop when he arrived that morning. I have always been a firm believer in the surprise-and-ambush technique of investigations. I warned myself not to become overconfident. Something would go wrong, I knew—there were too may variables for things to proceed perfectly. The trick was to react in a way that saved my skin, and Camila's.

I picked up the phone and made one last call. Leonardo answered, his voice muffled by what sounded like a mouthful of cotton.

"Good morning," I said.

"Lupe?" A pause. "What . . . am I late?"

"No, no." I suppressed a laugh. "I need to borrow your pickup truck this morning. I have the spare set of keys. Mind if I come by and pick it up?"

"My truck?" Another long pause. "OK. Take my truck."

"*Gracias,*" I replied. "I'll leave the Mercedes parked in front of your apartment building. You can drive it today."

I was a little surprised that Leo so readily let me borrow his dirty white pickup, but then he probably hoped I would smash it up and he could drive the Mercedes indefinitely.

I had to take one of the paintings out of the closet. I couldn't decide which one to choose, so I closed my eyes and reached in. I came out with the Antonia Eiriz. It was fitting somehow that I chose a painting by a Cuban woman, since just about everyone involved in this case—on my side, at least—was a woman.

I checked to make sure the Beretta was safely tucked inside my bag, looked around the office one last time to see if I might have forgotten anything, then started out. My hand was on the doorknob when I paused. I didn't consider myself an alarmist, but sometimes it paid to be overprepared. With that in mind, I turned around.

A souvenir painting hung over my office sofa—a souvenir of a case I'd worked in which the client had been unable to pay me for my services. I had accepted in lieu of cash a painting of a beautiful royal palm—the official tree of Cuba—standing majestically alone in the countryside. I took down the painting and laid it carefully on the couch. Beneath it was my wall safe; I quickly twirled the dial and unlocked it.

The box holding my backup Beretta was just where I'd left it, way in the back of the safe. I took it out slowly, almost reverently, checked to make sure the magazine was full. Then I put it in a chamois bag in my purse, next to my everyday Beretta. I closed the safe, replaced the painting, and was finally ready to go.

I made a quick stop to exchange cars, then drove to Camila's hotel. It was still nice and early, and Camila was waiting for me as agreed in the hotel lobby. We sped away to Hialeah, neither saying much. Now it was time for action.

Camila stood outside Reinaldo's workshop, waiting for him to arrive. It was still early, but the morning sun had begun to beat down hard. It was going to be a hot one. I watched her through my binoculars from a hiding place a block and a half away, parked under a tree. Camila kicked at the pavement, looking nervous. I didn't blame her. It was no small thing to try to catch a murderer.

After half an hour Reinaldo came driving up in an old red van. He got out, and Camila approached him. I could tell from his body language that he didn't recognize his cousin. He seemed agitated, distrustful. He shook his head and tried to wave her away.

Camila was insistent. She put her hand over her heart, gesticulating, telling her story. Reinaldo dropped his hands to his sides and looked hard into her face. He shrugged, seeming to relent. He motioned her back to his work space and started unlocking the chained gate in front, glancing up and down the street as he did so. He seemed to have bought her story that they were related. Which was the truth. Now I hoped he bought the second part, which wasn't.

Camila was in there for another half hour. She came out alone. She was supposed to tell him that she didn't want a ride anywhere, that she walked every place in Cuba and intended to do the same in Miami. She headed south. I waited a few minutes, saw that she wasn't being followed, and started up Leo's truck. The aged pickup was good cover for me, since it was possible that Reinaldo had seen my Mercedes the first time I visited him.

I picked up Camila about a half mile away. "How did it go?" I asked.

Camila, to my surprise, looked at me with a sad expression. I could see she'd been crying.

"It was not good," she said. "He didn't believe me for a long time. Then he looked at me like I was some kind of ghost."

"I'm sorry, *querida*," I said. I wanted to comfort her somehow. I had known her only a short time but already considered her a friend.

Neither of us said much during the trip to Jesus's garage apartment. I knew it was still unoccupied, that it was paid until the end of the month by Jesus and was still part of an ongoing police investigation. This fact was central to what I intended to do.

I parked the truck on a side street and walked quickly with Camila to the apartment. There were few people around, just as before, and I was familiar enough with the creepy atmosphere in the neighborhood to pay it no mind. Camila, for her part, stared straight ahead. She looked as though she was ready for anything. Tucked under my arm, I carried one of the paintings Camila had taken from Cuba.

Camila suppressed a gasp when, at the front gate to her brother's garage apartment, I reached into my purse and produced a little pouch containing a set of tools. She was an intelligent woman, and she recognized the fact that I was picking the lock and breaking in. I jiggled the lifter pick and the tension wrench until the lock gave way. It certainly saved the trouble of calling a locksmith. After a quick look to make sure no one was watching, we slipped inside the gate.

Instead of locking it again, I affixed a little bell to the bottom of the latch. It would ring whenever the gate was opened. The simpler the better, when it came to life and death.

The lock on the apartment door gave way in seconds. A fairly dexterous three-year-old could probably have picked it. Call me a snob, but even with my limited knowledge of locks, I knew that the one on Jesus's front door was a loser.

We went into the front room. I yearned to rush around, inspect the place, peek into Jesus's things. I had to remind myself that this was where Camila's brother had lived. My investigative impulses had to give way to simple respect. She walked in slowly, looking around with a meditative expression. She hadn't seen her brother in years, and had probably pictured the place in her mind many times.

"Camila," I said in a quiet voice, getting her attention. I reached inside my purse and took out the chamois bag containing the second Beretta. I took it out of the bag. "Do you know how to use one of these?"

Camila recoiled as though I had showed her a rattlesnake ready to strike. I realized that she probably had little if any experience with firearms. As far as I knew, there was no NRA branch in Cuba.

"All you do is point at what you want to hit, then pull the trigger," I said. "Here's the safety, here's how you take it off. Remember, hold your breath right before you squeeze the trigger and don't move. If you're panting when you pull the trigger, your arm will jerk up and down and your aim will be off."

I held out the Beretta for her to take; she refused it, shaking her head and turning away. I looked into her green eyes, took her hand. This was no time to be squeamish. I placed the gun in the middle of her hand, taking care to point the barrel away from us.

She stood there, frozen, staring at the gun. I realized it wasn't going to work. The gun was freaking her out too much for her to possibly use it. I may be tough, but I'm not cruel. I relented, and took the gun back from her. I looked around the room until I saw what I was searching for.

"I'm going to put the gun right here, on this table," I said, moving a big clock to hide it. "It'll be out of sight, but close by in case you need to use it."

Camila closed her eyes, breathing deeply. I knew she could make it, I knew she could keep it together. She just needed a little coaching.

"Camila," I said, making her snap back into reality. "Did

Reinaldo understand clearly that you were staying in this apartment?"

"Yes," she said, relieved not to be talking about the gun. "That is what I told him, and I think he believed me. I also said I had the paintings with me, that they were stored here."

"Good," I said.

That meant I had limited time. I went to the apartment's front door and looked around. There was a small closet to the side of the foyer area just inside the door. I opened it up. Perfect. Unfortunately, it was stacked top to bottom with art supplies. I dug in, taking out boxes of paint and blank white canvas; I took the stuff and stacked it up in the back of the room, next to a little corridor that led to the bathroom.

Then I plopped down on the floor, away from any windows. There was nothing more to do but wait.

Camila took a seat on the couch, flipping through a spiral-bound notebook that Jesus had used for sketches. She turned each sketch in several directions, looking at them with a trained artist's eye. I stared straight ahead, listening. After a while I got up and drank a glass of water in the kitchen area. I returned to my spot on the floor, trying to keep a balance between staying sharp and getting too anxious.

After an hour had passed we heard the tinkle of the bell on the gate. Camila and I snapped out of our reveries and shot worried glances at each other. I grabbed my purse and crawled quickly to the closet next to the front door. Once inside, I pulled the door closed but left it ajar a couple of inches so I could see a portion of the room.

I made it just in time, because a moment later we heard footsteps and a knock on the door. I prayed Camila was going to be up to this, that she didn't let fear overtake her.

"Reinaldo!" she said, sounding surprised. "What are you doing here?"

"Camila," Reinaldo answered somberly.

I tensed when I heard two more sets of footsteps approaching the door. If the steps belonged to who I suspected, then my hunch was paying off.

"Who are these men?" Camila asked.

I couldn't see who the two other men were; they were blocked from my narrow line of sight. I tried to breathe slow and steady, to make no noise at all. My back had already started to hurt, and my nose itched. I suddenly smelled the familiar odor of a burning cigarette.

I heard the front door creak. "Where are the paintings you brought out of Cuba?" Reinaldo asked. "I need to see them."

"Why do you need to see them now?" Camila asked, a slight tremor in her voice.

"Your brothers are dead. You're going to need help selling them," Reinaldo said gruffly. "You don't know your way around Miami. I'll look out for your interests. I'm your cousin, after all. We're family."

Camila said nothing. I was so desperate to see what was going on that I risked opening the door a couple of centimeters more. I saw Camila crossing the room, picking up the Antonia Eiriz and handing it to Reinaldo.

"*Gracias,*" he said. He opened the burlap wrapping and gave the painting a cursory examination. "Nice, very nice. Now where are the other seven?"

"Not here," Camila replied. "Someplace else."

"Where?" Reinaldo asked, all trace of courtesy gone from his voice. I still couldn't see the other two men, but I sensed the atmosphere in the room suddenly turn tense. Now I did the math: three men against two women. Not a good match, but we would hopefully retain the advantage of surprise.

"I only have one here in the apartment," Camila said without elaborating further.

"Camila, I need to have all the paintings," Reinaldo explained impatiently. I saw him fold his arms, heard the stress in his voice.

There was a silence in the room. I heard the floor creak and strained to look out. I still couldn't see the two men, though I saw Camila steal nervous glances at them.

"There's something I need to know," Camila said. "In Havana I met an art dealer. His name was Rafael Santamaria."

Reinaldo wasn't good at keeping a poker face. I heard his sharp intake of breath, saw him drop his arms to his side.

"Santamaria?" he blurted out. "When? Where?"

"He came to my studio to see me," Camila said.

I held my breath in anticipation. It was vital that Reinaldo believe Camila.

"Your studio?" he repeated. "Why did he come there?"

"He told me you sent him," Camila said in a rising voice, sounding perplexed. Reinaldo looked totally surprised. "He came to get the paintings. Just like you two planned."

Reinaldo staggered back a step; for a second I thought he was going to have a stroke.

"Does . . . does Santamaria have the rest of the paintings?" he asked. Camila didn't reply, allowing her cousin to assume the worst.

"Fuck it," another man said. "Let's stop playing nicey-nice with her."

I felt a chill down my back as I recognized the voice of Martin Osterman. Things were going to accelerate quickly, I was sure of it. I took the cell phone from my pocket and held it in the palm of my hand. Timing would be critical. If I made the call too soon, the moment might collapse. If I waited too long, Camila might get hurt.

"Wait, Martin, take it easy," Reinaldo said, holding up his arm. "Let me talk to her."

Osterman moved into my field of vision. He wore the

same checked shirt and Birkenstocks, he had the same pot-belly and beard. But instead of the easygoing hippie I remembered, he looked menacing and wired.

"We don't have time to fuck around here," Osterman barked. "Do you think that piece of shit Santamaria had the *cojones* to go into Cuba and take the paintings himself? Do you believe this bitch?"

I couldn't believe this was the same mellow product of the sixties I had sat with a week before. Woodstock seemed to be forgotten.

Reinaldo looked back and forth between Osterman and his cousin. "If she's lying, how does she know about Santamaria?" he asked.

Osterman had an answer for that. "Maybe her brothers told her."

"But—" Reinaldo began.

"What I want to know is—where is that piece of shit now?" Osterman took a step toward Camila.

I still couldn't see the third man, who was remaining silent, letting things play out. Osterman moved toward Camila, who backed away with a terrified expression. The room was deadly quiet. My finger was itching to make the call on my cell phone, but I had to wait.

I looked down at the phone for a second when a sickening sound made me peer back out into the room. Camila cried out in surprise and pain, dropping back toward the wall. Things were getting physical. I couldn't wait. I pressed the buttons to make a call, then laid the phone down on a box in the closet.

"Where are the fucking paintings?" Osterman asked, blowing smoke in her face. "I killed your two brothers, you bitch. Nothing's going to stop me from doing you, too."

Camila whimpered. I heard the sound of Osterman breathing hard. They were two of the most dreadful sounds

I had ever heard. Suddenly, Osterman lashed out and hit her again. Even Reinaldo cried out in fear.

That did it. I bolted out of the closet with the Beretta pointed straight ahead, a real pistol-packing mama. The three men in the room looked up with expressions of shock.

I finally saw the third man. He was a real bear, just like Osterman. He had a heavy beard, sunglasses, and a tie-dyed T-shirt.

I moved across the room to help Camila, stopping for a second to grab the second gun I'd left hidden on the table. Now I pointed both of them at the three men, my expression defying them to move.

Martin Osterman seemed more amused than frightened. "Well, what do I see with my little eyes. The lady P.I.!"

I ignored him and motioned for Camila to get off the floor. "*Querida*, are you all right?" I was horrified to see blood pouring from the corner of her mouth. I pressed the second gun into her hand, hoping that fear would make her capable of holding it now. "If they move, you shoot them. Remember what I told you about holding your breath."

I moved to the other side of the room, keeping the gun pointed at the men, creating a cross fire. I wanted answers, and I figured the Beretta would speed along the process.

First I addressed the third man. "Fred Osterman?" I said.

It wasn't difficult to see that the two men were related. They were both total sixties throwbacks, obviously worshiping at the altar of Hendrix and Harley-Davidson. I doubted that the man who was head of security at the Miami Beach Convention Center dressed for work in this attire, but you never knew—Miami being notoriously fashion challenged.

I saw movement out of the corner of my eye. Martin Osterman had reached under his plaid shirt and pulled a gun out of the waistband of his jeans. In that instant I cursed myself for taking my eyes off him for even a second. I raised the gun and started to turn just as Osterman pointed his at me.

There was a loud bang, then another, then another.

Everyone in the room froze. I realized that Camila had been a good student. She had held her breath and hit her target. Martin Osterman crumbled to the floor, the gun in his hand, the chain on his wallet clinking with the impact.

That was how Detective Anderson found us, looking like a tableau in a museum. Nothing was moving, save for the blood flowing from the center of Martin Osterman's chest and the smoke curling from the Marlboro still burning between his lips.

40

"Do you want to give your statement here, or do you want to come to my office?" Detective Anderson asked. We were standing on the street outside Jesus's apartment, waiting for the crime-scene techs to finish their job.

I knew Anderson was extending me a huge courtesy by giving me a choice. Anyone else would have been hauled downtown and grilled for the next few hours.

"Let's do it here, please," I said. I was so exhausted I just wanted it all to be over, so I could go home and sleep for the next few days.

"Well, let's find someplace to sit." Anderson looked around at the iron-gate fences and razor wire. "We'll go to my car."

I nodded. "Fine."

We went to his county-issued brown American sedan and got inside. This was the first time I'd ever been in Detective Anderson's car. I noticed instantly that there wasn't a single personal item anywhere. Somehow this didn't surprise me.

"I ought to be pissed off royal at you, Lupe," Anderson began ominously. "You brought me another body. This is getting really annoying. It's like a bad habit neither of us can break."

"I'm sorry," I replied. "I don't do it on purpose."

Anderson just sighed. He took out a little white notebook, the same one he'd just used for the other witnesses' statements, and flipped to a clean page. "Begin."

"First of all," I said, "should I get a lawyer to represent me here before I start speaking?"

"Do what you think you need to do." Anderson looked disappointed. He started to close the notebook. "It's up to you."

"Oh, *mierda*." I waved my hand. "You're not going to screw me. All right, let's talk."

Anderson flipped back to his clean page. "You're right about that," he said.

I chose my words carefully, beginning with my lunch at the Grand Bay Hotel with Angel Estrada, ending with the shooting at Jesus's apartment. I omitted a few things along the way, including my trip to Cuba and anything related to it. I was an expert at giving a story without revealing what I didn't want revealed.

Anderson jotted notes, his face close to the page. I saw a skeptical look cross his features a couple of times, but he didn't interrupt.

"This is all very interesting," he said when I was done. "But there are holes in your story big enough for a meteor to fall through without touching the sides. First of all, you say you weren't actually retained by anyone in the Estrada case."

I nodded.

"And it was an accident that it converged with the case you were hired for by Tommy McDonald?" he asked.

I nodded again.

"McDonald. I should have known," Anderson whispered under his breath.

"I know it's a big coincidence," I offered. "But remember, the art community is small, the Cuban art community even smaller. It was almost inevitable that the two cases would overlap."

Anderson stared at me with a blank, intense expression. I took a deep breath and plunged on.

"I had a feeling that Angel Estrada might be connected to Rafael Santamaria," I said. "They were two art dealers specializing in Cuban art who both worked out of Coral Gables. They had to know each other—or at least know *of* each other."

"That makes sense," Anderson said, jotting something down in his notebook.

We both looked up. The truck from the medical examiner's office had pulled up, meaning the techs were finished with Martin Osterman's body. I shuddered at the memory of him lying on the floor, bleeding from his gunshot wounds.

"Martin Osterman told me he'd been contacted to investigate Rafael Santamaria's disappearance," I continued. "He said he got the job because his brother Fred was chief of security at the Miami Beach Convention Center."

Anderson kept scribbling.

"There's a huge show of Latin American art every winter, and it's held at the Convention Center," I said. "I made a call and got hold of a program left over from last year's, including the location of different exhibitor's booths."

"Nice work," Anderson said, actually complimenting me. "And let me guess. You found out that Angel Estrada's and Santamaria's booths were placed close together."

"Exactly," I replied. "That's probably when they made contact. Angel must have told him about his plan to sell fake Cuban artworks. Angel's brother Jesus was working on them here in Miami. They must have planned to get hold of some certificates of authenticity, really make it look good."

Two men carried out Osterman's body wrapped in dark

green plastic on a stretcher. It was tied with belts so it wouldn't slide off the gurney. What a way to end up.

"So that's the connection," Anderson said. "But who killed the Estradas. And why?"

"Osterman was brought into the picture when he was hired to find Santamaria," I explained. "He was investigating a fake painting sold out of Santamaria's gallery. He said he couldn't find the dealer, but I think he was lying. He *did* find Santamaria, but instead of reporting it, he decided to go to Santamaria and blackmail him about the fakes. I think he basically forced himself into the deal."

Anderson nodded. "But why kill the goose that lays the golden eggs?" he asked. "If Jesus was the source of the fakes, didn't they need him alive and well?"

"I think the Estradas didn't want to cut Osterman into the deal," I said. "It was Santamaria's fault that he was involved at all. Maybe there were too many people getting involved, the slices of the pie were getting too small. Maybe it was because Osterman was an American, since everyone else involved was Cuban."

I also knew there was a bigger dimension to the scheme than selling art forgeries—the plan to steal invaluable paintings in Havana and replace them with fakes. It must have been a defining moment in their enterprise, the moment when the Estrada brothers decided they wanted to cut out Santamaria and Osterman.

I didn't mention this, though. It would have exposed my part in all this—and Camila's. She was under strict orders from me not to talk to the police until she'd consulted with Tommy. For my part, I was protecting Camila from the police by not mentioning her part in any of this. She was staying at her brother's apartment, and the story was that she had just arrived after being notified of Angel's and Jesus's murders. Her immigration status was a problem, as well as the fact that she'd shot a man. I didn't want to add to it by involving her in the art scheme.

"I think the Estradas also wanted to protect their sister," I said, knowing I had to account for Camila somehow. "She's an artist. Santamaria was probably pressuring them to get her involved somehow."

Anderson wrote something in his notebook.

"Everything was going fine until Osterman appeared," I said, speaking openly to my receptive audience. "And they were right not to trust him. Osterman didn't want partners who didn't want him. And he was willing to kill them over it—but in a way that would leave people thinking Santamaria had done it. Ideally, Osterman and Jesus would be the only two left. That meant much bigger pieces of the pie."

"Wait, wait," Anderson said. "Osterman wanted us to think Santamaria was the killer? How do you figure?"

We had been talking in the car for so long that the windows were beginning to fog up.

"Angel was strangled with panty hose. It looked like it might have been a sex game." I paused. "He left Angel fully clothed, though, which was confusing."

Anderson nodded. "But how does that—"

"I talked to a source," I interrupted.

Anderson chewed at his lip. "A source you're not going to reveal. Right?"

"Right," I said. "That's why people keep talking to me. Sorry."

"I'm used to it," Detective Anderson said, a little deflated.

"My source told me about Santamaria's sexual interests," I said, speaking, of course, of Suzanne and the message she'd left for me at the office. "Santamaria liked guys. And he liked to dress like a girl when he was with guys."

"Who the hell knew this?" Anderson asked, irritated.

"My source," I said. "Osterman must have known it, too,

and figured that eventually it would come out. Then Santamaria and Angel would be linked."

"What about the paint chips?" Anderson asked. "And what about Jesus? I don't—"

"Osterman wasn't a master criminal," I said. "He threw the paint chips around to link the murderer to art. He used the panty hose to connect the murder to cross-dressing. I think he was going to do something else to create a false trail to Santamaria. As for Jesus, I think Osterman must have been in a rage. I think he grabbed whatever was available and used it on Jesus—probably because Jesus refused to continue the scheme with him and cut out Santamaria."

"Well, what about Rafael Santamaria?" Anderson asked, flipping to a fresh page. "He should be able to clear a lot of this up."

"He should be," I agreed. "But I don't know where he is."

I rationalized that I wasn't lying to Detective Anderson. I *didn't* know where Santamaria was. He could be out to sea, he could have become lunch for the fish of the Florida Straits.

"And what about Camila Estrada?" Anderson asked.

I paused. It was going to take some work to protect Camila in the coming weeks.

"She came over from Cuba when she heard about her brothers' deaths," I said. "She asked me to help her find out what happened to them."

Anderson flinched, and I realized what I'd said might sound like I thought the Miami Police Department wasn't doing its job.

"Angel had mentioned me to Camila at some point after we worked together," I hastened to add. "Where she's from, people don't trust the authorities."

"Sounds like she's from Miami," Anderson said wryly.

"I was someone she'd heard of to call, that's all," I said. "You know, one Cuban woman to another."

Anderson sat back in his seat. I watched his face carefully, but he was completely devoid of expression. Finally he closed his notebook.

"It all makes sense," he said. "But do you have any proof of any of this?"

"Not really," I said, trying to smile.

"Well, calling 911 during the altercation in Jesus's apartment was a pretty good idea," Anderson said. "Now we have a recorded account of Osterman confessing to the shootings—and of him striking and threatening Camila Estrada. Her killing him was a clear case of self-defense."

"It was lucky, how it worked out," I said.

Anderson put away his notebook. "What about Reinaldo Estrada?" he asked. "How did he get involved in this mess?"

I thought I knew. "Osterman found out about him through his cousins. He must have thought that Camila was coming from Cuba, and that she had her hands on some of Jesus's paintings."

"And Camila didn't know they were fakes to be sold on the black market?" Anderson asked.

"She might have," I allowed. "She was in over her head. She'd never been to America before. Sure, she recognized the paintings, but I don't think it occurred to her that they were anything more than exercises Jesus had done for practice. Remember, there isn't a capitalist market in Cuba."

And, I thought, I might get away with keeping Camila out of it. Reinaldo had kept his distance all along, getting involved only when he was forced to. I was willing to bet he didn't know anything about switching fakes for real paintings, or Camila's deeper role in any of this. He'd let Santamaria look at the letter I was sending to Camila, but I was sure Santamaria didn't divulge its contents to Reinaldo. And

Reinaldo didn't read English. The police would interrogate him, but I was pretty sure Camila and I would come out all right.

My God. It was getting hard to keep all the double crosses straight. Beginning with Lucia Miranda trying to screw her family out of the tapestry, to the art dealers trying to sell fakes, to the partners turning on each other. There was apparently no honor among thieves.

"All right, that's enough for me." Detective Anderson looked at me and almost smiled. "Just don't leave town. I might have some more questions for you."

I knew this was his idea of a joke. Suspects in murder investigations were always given the same warning.

"*Gracias.*" I turned the door handle, ready to exit. If Anderson really did want to talk to me again, I knew, I had better have Tommy in tow.

"And for God's sake, Lupe, quit bringing me bodies. It's starting to put a strain on our relationship."

I laughed as I waved good-bye, grateful beyond belief that Anderson only knew half the story.

41

The three *café con leches* I'd had that morning had already made my heart race. The task ahead of me called for steady nerves, though, and I tried to keep my hand still as I picked up the phone.

"Alvaro?" I asked when he answered.

"*Hola*, Lupe," he replied, not warm or cold, his voice giving nothing away.

Well, at least the situation between us hadn't deteriorated to the point at which I had to identify myself on the phone. I glanced at the parrots outside the office window and plunged in.

"You remember when you left the message about Osvaldo?" I asked. "That you thought he was going senile because he asked you about being seasick?"

"I hope you had him checked out," Alvaro said. "It could be serious at his age."

It was time to swallow my pride and extend the olive branch. I had a lot of making up to do.

"Well, don't worry about him. There's a good reason for the way he was acting." I swallowed hard. "I'd like to explain it to you."

"I'm listening." He wasn't going to make it easy on me.

I took a deep breath. "I want to explain it to you in person."

Total silence on the line.

"All right," he said, warmer.

I let out a sigh of relief loud enough to be heard in Havana.

"Today?" I asked.

"I suppose I could get away this afternoon," he said guardedly, a hint of the old Alvaro coming through.

"Good," I said. "We're going out on the *Concepcion*. Just the two of us."

It simply seemed fitting.